EVERYMAN,

I WILL GO WITH THEE,

AND BE THY GUIDE,

IN THY MOST NEED

TO GO BY THY SIDE

EVERYMAN'S POCKET CLASSICS

MUSIC
STORIES

EDITED BY WESLEY STACE

EVERYMAN'S POCKET CLASSICS
Alfred A. Knopf New York London Toronto

THIS IS A BORZOI BOOK
PUBLISHED BY ALFRED A. KNOPF

This selection by Wesley Stace first published in
Everyman's Library, 2024
Copyright © 2024 by Everyman's Library

A list of acknowledgments to copyright owners appears at
the back of this volume.

All rights reserved. Published in the United States by Alfred A. Knopf,
a division of Penguin Random House LLC, New York, and in
Canada by Penguin Random House Canada Limited, Toronto.
Distributed by Penguin Random House LLC, New York. Published
in the United Kingdom by Everyman's Library, 50 Albemarle Street,
London W1S 4BD and distributed by Penguin Random House UK,
20 Vauxhall Bridge Road, London SW1V 2SA.

everymanslibrary.com
www.everymanslibrary.co.uk

ISBN 978-1-101-90841-9 (US)
978-1-84159-636-5 (UK)

A CIP catalogue reference for this book is available from the
British Library

Typography by Peter B. Willberg

Typeset in the UK by Input Data Services Ltd, Bridgwater, Somerset
Printed and bound in Germany by GGP Media GmbH, Pössneck

Contents

REHEARSAL

THEORY (& PRACTICE)

PERFORMANCE

THE FOOD OF LOVE

IN CONCERT

ENCORE

FOREWORD

Music is the universal language of mankind (Longfellow said it first, apparently) so the opportunities it affords writers are many, and these opportunities have appealed to almost all writers.

The stories in this collection are told in a multiplicity of voices via narrators variously reliable, unreliable, omniscient and invisible, by writers of the Harlem Renaissance and the Southern Gothic, by Indian, French and Russian realists, Bloomsbury modernists, American sci-fi fantasists and postmodernists, and British satirists.

Music offers the possibility of a wonderful set-piece, a litmus test for character: hearts beat faster as the music swells. A melody may jog the memory, happily or unhappily, and the protagonist may lose himself, or find herself, within it. One listener might be wrecked by a Siren's song, another strangely unmoved. Music also has the intriguing narrative potential of either reinforcing or collapsing social distinctions. What was snobbier than a night at the opera? What is more democratic than a music festival? Whether the protagonist is a reluctant student, an audience member, a resentful fan, a jealous composer, or a seasoned performer, the reader can relate.

As a musician, I have a pragmatic approach to the subject, reflected here. Music can indeed express the inexpressible, but I love its nitty-gritty too. The soundcheck, the backstage drama, the onstage screw-ups, how the money works, the day job: will we sell any tickets? When do we load out? And *how* far do we have to drive tomorrow? The pleasures of the lives of musicians – however well-known, whatever the genre – are inseparable from the daily tedium, the frustrations and the disappointments.

This collection is therefore sequenced to reflect a possible musical development: from childhood to the very first lessons (formal or informal) with which a musical journey is likely to begin (during which the drama might be the student's, the teacher's, or both), via the necessary practice and rehearsal (often sabotaged), the embrace or rejection of musical theory, to (finally, finally) the performance – the musicians' most intense moment of communication, catharsis and apotheosis, when they can love, be loved – and its reception. In the end, the audience must decide. In this book, however, we get an encore, as Philip K. Dick's "The Preserving Machine" speculates on the future of music in the age of Artificial Intelligence. He wrote it seventy years ago.

Many of these writers are (or were) musicians themselves: Carson McCullers originally intended to be a concert pianist. "Wunderkind", written when she was seventeen, is autobiographical: "A foreshortening of that memory . . . The imagination is truer than the reality." Jonathan Coe's intriguingly varied compositions – including an album called *9th & 13th* of which his contribution here is the title track – can be heard on Bandcamp. David Gates's brilliantly observed account of the derailment of a would-be rehearsal has the horrible authenticity of learned experience. Some of the stories were themselves inspired by music: Lisa Bolejaka's "Three Voices", by Morton Feldman's piece of the same name. Others inspired music: both *Madame Bovary* and *Howards End* have been operatized.

But of course, one doesn't have to be musical, or even

to love music, to write a great musical story or to sense its potential for literature. Nabokov famously had no ear: "Music, I regret to say, affects me merely as an arbitrary succession of more or less irritating sounds. Under certain emotional circumstances I can stand the spasms of a rich violin, but the concert piano and all wind instruments bore me in small doses and flay me in larger ones." He might be the only novelist who hasn't thought music more powerful than the written word.

The truth is that writing is often at its least persuasive when it strives to be at its most "musical", attempting to free itself from the page, to become the music itself. It's a fool's errand based on an underestimation of the technique musical composition requires, the precision it demands. All of these stories are written by stylists in complete control of their melodies, their rhythm and their tone. They know their "settings". It is their technique that allows their stories to sing, to tell us about singing and listening, not their abandon. Save the histrionics for the ecstasy of performance.

As Hector Berlioz said: "Passionate subjects must be dealt with in cold blood."

Wesley Stace

OVERTURE

HERMANN HESSE

From

GERTRUDE

(1910)

Translated by Hilda Rosner

CHAPTER 1

WHEN I CONSIDER my life objectively, it does not seem particularly happy. Yet I cannot really call it unhappy, despite all my mistakes. After all, it is quite foolish to talk about happiness and unhappiness, for it seems to me that I would not exchange the unhappiest days of my life for all the happy ones.

When a person has arrived at a stage in life when he accepts the inevitable with equanimity, when he has tasted good and bad to the full, and has carved out for himself alongside his external life, an inner, more real and not fortuitous existence, then it seems my life has not been empty and worthless. Even if my external destiny has unfolded itself as it does with everyone, inevitably and as decreed by the gods, my inner life has been my own work, with its joys and bitterness, and I, alone, hold myself responsible for it.

At times, when I was younger, I wanted to be a poet. If I were, I would not resist the temptation of tracing back my life into the dim shadows of my childhood and to the fondly preserved sources of my earliest memories. But the possession is far too precious and holy for me to spoil in any way. All I will say about my childhood is that it was good and happy. I was given the freedom to discover my own inclinations and talents, to create my inmost pleasures and sorrows myself and to regard the future as the hope and product of my own strength and not as something fashioned by a strange power from above. So I passed unnoticed through the schools as an ordinary, little talented, but quiet scholar who was finally left alone as I did not seem to be subjected to any strong influences.

When I was about six or seven years old, I realised that among all invisible powers, I was destined to be most strongly affected and dominated by music. From that time I had my own world, my sanctuary and my heaven that no-one could take away from me or belittle, and that I did not wish to share with anyone. I was a musician although I did not learn to play any instrument before my twelfth year and did not think that I would later wish to earn my living by music.

That is how matters have been ever since, without anything being essentially changed, and that is why on looking back on my life it does not seem varied and many-sided, but from the beginning it has been tuned to one key-note and directed solely to one star. Whether things went well or badly with me, my inner life remained unchanged. I might sail for long periods across foreign seas, not touching a manuscript-book or an instrument, and yet at every moment there would be a melody in my blood and on my lips, a beat and rhythm in the drawing of breath and life. However eagerly I sought salvation, oblivion and deliverance in many other ways, however much I thirsted for God, understanding and peace, I always found them in music alone. It did not need to be Beethoven or Bach: it has been a continual consolation to me and a justification for all life that there is music in the world, that one can at times be deeply moved by rhythms and pervaded by harmonies. Oh, music! A melody occurs to you; you sing it silently, inwardly only; you steep your being in it; it takes possession of all your strength and emotions, and during the time it lives in you, it effaces all that is fortuitous, evil, coarse and sad in you; it brings the world into harmony with you, it makes burdens light and gives wings to the benumbed!

The melody of a folk-song can do all that. And first of all the harmony! For each pleasing harmony of clearly combined notes, perhaps in one chord, charms and delights the spirit, and the feeling is intensified with each additional note; it can at times fill the heart with joy and make it tremble with bliss as no other sensual pleasure can do.

Of all the conceptions of pure bliss that people and poets have dreamt about, it seemed to me that the one of listening to the harmony of the spheres was the highest and most intense. That is where my dearest and brightest dreams have ranged – to hear for the duration of a heartbeat the universe and the totality of life in its mysterious, innate harmony. Alas! how is it that life can be so confusing and out of tune and false, how can there be lies, evil, envy and hate amongst people, when the shortest song and most simple piece of music preach that heaven is revealed in the purity, harmony and close play of clearly sounded notes! And how can I upbraid people and grow angry when I, myself, with all the good will in the world have not been able to make a song and any sweet music out of my life! Inwardly, I am really aware of an imperative urge, of a thirsting desire for one pure, pleasing, essentially holy sound and its fading away, but my days are full of mischance and discord and wherever I turn and wherever I strike, there is never a true and clear echo.

LESSONS

IAN McEWAN

A DUET
(2022)

BERNERS, LIKE MOST schools, was held together by a hierarchy of privileges, infinitesimally graded and slowly bestowed over the years. It made the older boys conservative guardians of the existing order, jealous of the rights they had earned with such patience. Why bestow new-fashioned favors on the youngest when they themselves had tolerated privations to earn the perks of greater maturity? It was a long, hard course. The youngest, the first- and second-years, were the paupers and had nothing at all. Third formers were allowed long trousers and a tie with diagonal, rather than horizontal, stripes. The fourth-years had their own common room. The fifth exchanged their gray shirts for drip-dry white, which they scrubbed in the showers and draped on plastic hangers. They also had a superior blue tie.

Lights-out time advanced by fifteen minutes each year. To start, there was the dormitory shared by thirty boys. Five years later, that was down to six. The sixth form could wear sports jackets and overcoats of their own choice, though nothing colorful was tolerated. They also had a weekly allowance of a four-pound block of Cheddar cheese to be divided among a dozen boys, and several loaves, a toaster, and instant coffee, so they could entertain themselves between meals. They went to bed when they pleased. At the apex of the hierarchy were the prefects. They were entitled to take shortcuts across the grass and shout at anyone lower down the scale who dared to do the same.

Like any social order, it seemed to all but revolutionary spirits to be at one with the fabric of reality. Roland did not question it at the start of the academic year in September, 1962, when he and ten others in his house took possession of their fourth-form common room. After three years' service, this was their first significant step up the ladder. Roland, like his friends, was becoming naturalized. He had acquired the easy manner the school was noted for, with hints of the nuanced loutishness expected of the fourth-years. His accent was changing from his mother's rural Hampshire. Now there was a touch of Cockney, a smaller touch of BBC, and a third element that was difficult to define. Technocratic, perhaps. Self-sure. He recognized it years later among jazz musicians. Not posh, and neither impressed by nor contemptuous of those who were.

In a dormitory shared with nine others, the expression of difficult feelings – self-doubt, tender hopes, sexual anxiety – was rare. As for sexual longing, that was submerged in boasts and taunts and extremely funny or completely obscure jokes. Whichever, it was obligatory to laugh. Behind this nervous sociability was the boys' awareness of a grand new terrain spread out before them. Prior to puberty, its existence had been hidden and had never troubled them. Now the idea of a sexual encounter rose on the horizon like a mountain range, beautiful, dangerous, irresistible. But still far away. As they talked and laughed in the dark after lights-out, there was a wild impatience in the air, a ridiculous longing for something unknown. Fulfillment lay ahead of them, they were cocksure of that, but they wanted it now. In a rural boarding school for boys, not much chance. How could they know what "it" really was when all their information came from implausible anecdotes and jokes? One night, a boy said into the darkness, during a lull, "What if you died before you had

26

it?" There was silence in the dormitory as they took in this possibility. Then Roland said, "There's always the afterlife." And everybody laughed.

When the dormitory talk trailed away into the beginning of sleep, he retreated into his special place. The piano teacher, who no longer taught him, who had kissed him full on the lips when he was eleven, pinched his thigh once, unbuttoned his shorts to tidy his rumpled shirt, did not know she led a double life. There was the woman, the real one, Miss Miriam Cornell, the one who had invited him to lunch in her cottage when he was twelve. He had been too frightened of her to turn up. He saw her occasionally when he was near the sick bay, the stable block, or the music rooms. She would be alone, walking to or from her little red car, after or before a lesson. He never actually passed by her – he made sure of that. Then there was the woman of his daydreams, who did as he made her do, which was to deprive him of his will and make him do as she wished. He had to accept that she was now embedded in a special region of fantasy and longing, and that was where he wanted her to remain, trapped in his thoughts like the tamed unicorn behind its circular fence – the art master had shown the class a picture of the famous tapestry. The unicorn must never be free of its chain, never leave its tiny enclosure.

After three years of two hours a week with Mr Clare, Roland was a promising pianist. He was working his way up the grades. After scraping through Grade 7, Roland was told by his teacher that he was "almost precocious" for a fourteen-year-old. Twice he had accompanied hymns on Sunday, when Neil Noake, by far the school's best pianist, was down with a cold. Among his peers, Roland's status hovered just above average. Being mediocre in sport and in class held him back. But he sometimes said something witty that was repeated about the place. And he had less acne than most.

The fourth-form common room had one table, eleven wooden chairs, some lockers, and a notice board. A further entitlement the boys had not expected appeared each day after lunch – a newspaper, sometimes the *Daily Express*, sometimes the *Daily Telegraph*. Discards from the staff common room. Roland came into the room one afternoon to see a friend sitting with his legs crossed, holding in front of him an open broadsheet, and he realized that they were grownups at last. Politics bored them, as they liked telling one another. As a group, they went for human interest, which was why they preferred the *Express*. A woman set on fire by her *hair dryer*. A madman with a knife shot dead by a farmer, who ended up in prison, to general disgust. A brothel unearthed not far from the Houses of Parliament. A zookeeper swallowed whole by a python. Adult life. In that time, moral standards were high in public life and so, therefore, was hypocrisy. Delicious outrage was the general tone. Scandals became part of their sex education. The Profumo affair was less than a year away. Even the *Telegraph* carried photographs of smiling girls in the news with bouffant hair and eyelashes as thick and dark as prison bars.

Then, in late October, politics in the fourth-form common room became interesting. Unusually, the two newspapers arrived together on the table after lunch. Both were well thumbed, dog-eared, the newsprint softened by many hands, and both showed the same photograph on their front pages. For boys who had recently visited Lakenheath, the nearby U.S. Air Force base, on open day and had touched the cold steel nose of a missile, the way some might a holy relic, the story was compelling: spies, spy planes, secret cameras, deception, bombs, the two most powerful men on the planet ready to face each other down, and possible war. The photograph could have come from the triple-locked safe of an intelligence mastermind. It showed low hills, square fields, wooded terrain scarred white by tracks and clearings. Narrow rectangular labels had helpful pointers: "20 long cylindrical tanks"; "missile transporters"; "5 missile dollies"; "12 prob guideline missiles." Flying their U2 reconnaissance jets at impossible heights, using cameras with exciting telescopic power, the Americans had revealed to the world Russian nuclear missiles on Cuba, only ninety miles from the Florida coast. Intolerable, everyone agreed. A gun to the head of the West. The sites would have to be bombed before they became operational, then the island invaded.

What might the Russians do? Even as the boys of the fourth-form common room affected genuine grown-up concern at this new state of things, the words "thermonuclear warhead" conjured for them, like towering thunderclouds at sunset, a thrilling reckless disruption, a promise of ultimate liberty by which school, routines, regulations, even parents – everything – was to be blown away, a world wiped clean. A boundless adventure was at hand. They knew they would survive; they discussed rucksacks, water bottles, penknives, maps. Roland was by then a member of the photography club and knew how to develop and print. He had clocked some hours in the darkroom working on multiple versions of a view across the river, with oak trees and ferns, six inches by four, rather fine except for an annoying brown streak across the center that he had failed to eliminate. He was listened to with respect as he examined the fresh U2 photo that appeared on the second day. This one had new labels: "erector/launcher equipment"; "8 missile trailers"; "tent areas." Someone passed him a magnifying glass. He leaned

29

in closer. When he discovered the mouth of a tunnel that the C.I.A. analysts had missed, he was believed. One by one, his classmates looked and saw it, too. Others had important theories of their own of what should be done, and what must happen when it was.

Classes went on as usual. No teacher referred to the crisis, and the boys were not surprised. These were separate realms, school and the real world. James Hern, the stern but privately kind housemaster, did not mention in his evening announcements that the world might soon be ending. The somewhat put-upon matron, Mrs Maldey, did not speak of the Cuban missile crisis when the boys handed in their laundry, and she was usually irritated by any threat to her complex routines. Roland did not write about the situation in his next letter to his mother. President Kennedy had announced a "quarantine" around Cuba; Russian vessels, with a cargo of nuclear warheads, were heading toward a flotilla of American warships. If Khrushchev did not order his ships back they would be sunk, and the Third World War could begin. How could that make sense alongside Roland's account of planting nursery fir trees with the Young Farmers Club on boggy land behind the dormitory? Their letters crossed, and hers were as innocent as his. The boys had no access to TV – that was for the sixth form only on certain days. No one listened to or knew about serious radio news. There were some breezy announcements on Radio Luxembourg, but essentially the Cuban missile affair was a drama confined to the two newspapers.

The first rush of boyish excitement began to fade. The official school silence was making Roland anxious. He was most affected when alone. A moody stroll through the oaks and bracken beyond the ha-ha didn't help. For an hour he sat at the foot of the statue of Diana the Huntress, looking toward the river. He might never see his parents again, or his sister Susan. Or get to know his brother Henry better. One evening, after lights-out, the boys were discussing the crisis as they did every night. The door opened and a prefect came in. It was the Head of House. He didn't tell them to quiet down. Instead, he joined their conversation. They began to ask him questions, which he answered gravely, as if he himself were just back from the Crisis Room in the White House. He claimed insider knowledge, and they believed everything he said and were flattered to have him to themselves. He was already a full member of the adult world, and their bridge to it. Three years ago, he had been one of them. They couldn't see him in the darkness, only hear his low certain tone coming from the direction of the door, that school voice of softened Cockney touched with bookish confidence. He told them something startling, which they should have worked out for themselves. In an all-out nuclear war, he said, one of the important targets in England would be the Lakenheath airbase, less than fifty miles away. That meant that the school would be instantly obliterated, Suffolk would become a desert, and all the people in it would be – and this was the word he used – vaporized. *Vaporized.* Several boys echoed the word from their beds.

The prefect left, and the talk slowed and stumbled into the night as sleep took hold. Roland remained awake. The word would not let him sleep. It made sense. Mr Corner, the biology teacher, had told the class not so long ago that the human body was ninety-three per cent water. Boiled away in a white flash, the remaining seven per cent coiling in the air like cigarette smoke, dispersed on the breeze. Or whipped away by the bomb's blast. There would be no heading north with his best friends, rucksacks loaded with survival rations, fleeing like Daniel Defoe's citizens escaping London in the plague year. Roland had not believed in the survival adventure, anyway. But it had kept him from dwelling on what might really happen.

He had never contemplated his own death. He was certain that the usual associations – dark, cold, silent, decay – were irrelevant. These were all things that could be felt and understood. Death lay on the far side of darkness, beyond even nothing. He was dismissive of the afterlife, like all of his friends. They sat through the compulsory Sunday-evening service in contempt of the earnest visiting vicars and their wheedling and beseeching of a nonexistent God. It was a point of honor with them never to utter the responses or close their eyes, bow heads or say "Amen" or sing the hymns, although they stood and opened the hymnal at a random page out of a residual sense of courtesy. At fourteen, they were newly launched on a splendid truculent revolt. It was liberating to be or feel loutish. Satire, parody, mockery were their modes, ludicrous renderings of authority's voice and stock phrases. They were scathing, merciless with one another, too, even as they were loyal. All of this, all of them, soon to be vaporized. He did not see how the Russians could afford to back down when the whole world was watching. The two sides, protesting that they stood for peace, would, for pride and honor's sake, stumble into war. One small exchange, one ship sunk for another, would become a lunatic conflagration. Schoolboys knew that this was how the First World War had begun. They had written essays on the subject. Each country had said it didn't want war, and then each had joined in with a ferocity the world was still trying to understand. This time there would be no one left to try. Then what of that first sexual encounter, that beautiful dangerous mountain range? Blown away with the rest. As Roland lay waiting for sleep, he remembered his friend's question: What if you died before you had it? *It*.

The next day, Saturday, 27th October, was the beginning of half-term. No Saturday lessons, no games, was the extent of it. School would resume on Monday. Some of the London boys had parents coming down. A sixth former had a copy of the *Guardian* and let Roland look. In the Caribbean, the Americans had allowed a Russian oil tanker bound for Cuba to pass. It was assumed that it contained only oil. The Russian ships carrying missiles brazenly strapped to their decks had slowed or stopped. But Russian submarines were reported in the area and new reconnaissance photos showed that work was continuing on the Cuban sites. The missiles were ready for firing. There was a buildup of American military forces in Florida, at Key West. It looked likely that the plan was to invade Cuba and destroy the sites. A French politician was quoted as saying that the world was "teetering" on the brink of nuclear war. Soon it would be too late to turn back.

Roland's bike was on a raised pavement behind the school kitchens, a rusty old racer with twenty-one gears and a slow leak in the front tire that he could never be bothered to fix. The day was warm and almost cloudless. Clear enough to watch missiles sailing in from the east. He came down the slope toward the church at speed, holding his breath against the smell of warmed pig swill from the sty, and at the Berners School lodge turned left toward Shotley. After a mile, he was looking out for his shortcut, a farm track on his right that would take him across flat fields, past Crouch House, along Warren Lane to the duck pond and Erwarton Hall. Every boy at school knew that Anne Boleyn had been happy there, visiting as a child, and that the future King Henry had come to court her. Before she was beheaded in the Tower

33

of London at his command, she asked for her heart to be entombed in Erwarton church. It was said to be in a little heart-shaped box buried underneath the organ.

At the hall, Roland stopped, propped his bike by the ancient gatehouse, crossed the road, and walked up and down. Her house was only minutes away. He wasn't ready. It was important not to arrive sweaty and out of breath. He had spent so much time thinking about and avoiding Erwarton that he felt as if he, too, had spent his childhood here. Minutes later, he was passing a pub and some scattered houses and soon after he was outside her cottage. He knew it by her red car parked on the grass. There was a white picket gate and a brick path that led with a slight curve to her front door. He leaned his bike against the car, pulled his trousers free of his socks, and hesitated. He felt watched, though there was no movement at the two downstairs windows. Unlike the other cottages around, this one had no net curtains. He would have preferred her to come out to him. Greet him and do all the talking.

After a moment, he pushed open the gate and went slowly toward the door. The borders that ran along the path had the ruined look of a forgotten summer. She hadn't yet dug out the dying plants. He was surprised to see old plastic flowerpots on their side and sweet wrappers trodden into the dead leaves. She had always seemed a neat and organized person, but he knew nothing about her. He was making a mistake and should turn back now, before she saw him. No, he was determined to tie himself to his fate. His hand was already lifting the heavy knocker and letting it fall. And again. He heard rapid muffled thumps as she descended the stairs. There was the sound of a bolt withdrawn. She pulled the door open so fast and wide that he was instantly intimidated and couldn't meet her gaze. The first thing he saw was that she was barefoot and her toenails were painted purple.

"It's you." She said it neutrally, without hesitation or surprise. He lifted his head and they exchanged a glance, and for a confused moment he thought he might have knocked at the wrong house. Sure, she recognized him. But she looked different. Her hair was loose, almost to her shoulders. She wore a pale-green T-shirt under a cardigan, and jeans that ended well above her ankles. Her Saturday clothes. He had prepared something to say, an opening, but he had forgotten it. "Almost two years late. Lunch is cold."

He said it quickly. "I had a long detention."

She smiled, and he blushed with helpless pride in his smart reply. It had come from nowhere.

"Come on, then."

He stepped past her into a cramped hallway, with a steep run of stairs in front of him and doors to the left and right.

"Go left."

He saw the piano first, a baby grand squashed into a corner but still taking up a good part of the room. Piles of music on two chairs, two small sofas facing each other over a low table, stacked with books. Today's newspapers were on the floor. Beyond, a door through to a tiny kitchen that gave onto a walled garden.

"Sit," she said, as if to a dog. A joke, of course. She sat opposite and looked at him intently, seeming vaguely amused by his presence. What did she see?

In later years, he often wondered. A fourteen-year-old boy, average height for his age, slender build but strong enough, dark-brown hair, long for the times thanks to the distant influence of John Mayall and, later, Eric Clapton. During a brief stay with his sister, Roland had been taken by his cousin Barry to the Ricky Tick Club at Guildford bus station to hear the Rolling Stones. It was there that Roland's look had been consolidated, for he was impressed by the black jeans that Brian Jones wore. What other changes might Miss Cornell have noted? Voice newly broken. Long, solemn face, full lips that sometimes trembled, as though he were suppressing certain thoughts, greenish-brown eyes behind National Health Service specs, whose plastic rims he had prised off long before John Lennon thought of doing the same. Gray Harris Tweed jacket with elbow patches over a Hawaiian shirt with palm-tree motif. Drainpipe gray flannel trousers were the closest substitute for tight black jeans that the Berners dress code would permit. His winklepicker shoes had a medieval look. He smelled of a lemony cologne. That day he was free of acne. There was something indefinably unwholesome about him. Something lean and snakelike.

Where he sprawled back uneasily on the sofa, she was upright, and now she leaned forward. Her voice was sweet and tolerant. Perhaps she pitied him. "So, Roland. Tell me about yourself."

It was one of those adult questions, impossible and dull. As he politely pushed himself up into a position more like hers, he could think of nothing to talk about other than his piano lessons with Mr Clare. He explained that he was getting an extra hour and a half a week for free. Lately, he told her, he had been learning—

She interrupted him, and, as she did so, she pulled up her right leg and tucked it under her left knee. "I hear you got your Grade 7."

"Yep."

"Merlin Clare says your sight-reading is good."

"I don't know."

"And you've come all this way on your bike to play duets with me."

He blushed again, this time at what he thought was innuendo. He also experienced the beginnings of an erection. He moved a hand across his lap in case it was visible. But she was on her feet and going toward the piano.

"I've got just the thing. Mozart."

She was already sitting at the piano, and he was still on the sofa in a daze of embarrassment. He was about to fail and be humiliated. And sent away.

"Ready?"

"I don't really feel like it."

"Just the first movement. It'll do you no harm."

He could see no way out. He rose slowly, then squeezed behind her to take the left side. As he passed, he felt the warmth coming off the back of her head. When he was sitting down, he became aware of a ticking clock above the fireplace, as loud as a metronome. Against it, keeping time in a duet would be a challenge. Against both would be his agitated heart. She arranged the music before them. D major. A Mozart four-hander. He had played some of it once with Neil Noake, perhaps six months before. Suddenly, she had a change of mind.

"We'll swap. More fun for you."

She stood and stepped away, and he slid along to his right. As she sat down again, she said in that same kindly voice, "We won't take it too fast."

With a slight tilt of her whole body, and raising both hands above the keyboard and dropping them, she brought them in, and off they went at what seemed to Roland a hopeless pace. Like tobogganing down an icy mountain. He was a fraction behind her on the opening grand declaration, so that the piano, a Steinway, sounded like a barroom honky-tonk. In his nervousness he gave a snort of smothered laughter. He caught up with her, and then, too earnest, he was slightly ahead. He was clinging to a cliff edge. Expression, dynamics were beyond him – he could do no more than play the right notes in the right order as they careened across the page. There were moments when it sounded almost good. As they tossed back and forth a little figure in an extended throbbing crescendo, she called out "Bravo!" What a din they were making in the tiny room. When they reached the end of the movement, she flipped the page over. "Can't stop now!" He managed well enough, picking his way through the lilting melody while she played a gentle Alberti bass that bore him along. She pressed against him, leaning to her right as they lifted into a higher register together. He relaxed a little when she almost fumbled a run of notes, a private game of mischievous Mozart. But the movement seemed to last hours, and at the end the black dots that signalled a repeat were a punishment, a renewed jail sentence. The weight on his attention was becoming unbearable. His eyes were smarting. Finally, the movement sank away into its final chord, which he held for a crotchet too long.

Immediately, she stood. He felt close to tears with relief that they were not going to play the allegro molto. But she hadn't spoken, and he sensed that he had disappointed her. She was close behind him. She put her hands on his shoulders, leaned down, and whispered in his ear, "You're going to be all right."

He wasn't sure what she meant. She crossed the room and went into the kitchen. Seeing her bare white feet, hearing the scuffing sound they produced on the flagstones, made him feel weak. A couple of minutes later, she came back with glasses of orange juice, made from actual crushed oranges, a novel taste. By then, he was standing uncertainly by the low table, wondering if he was now expected to leave. He would not have minded. They drank in silence. Then she put her glass down and did something that almost caused him to faint. He had to steady himself against the arm of a sofa. She went to the front door, knelt, and sank the heavy door bolt into the stone floor. Then she came back and took his hand.

"Come on, then."

She led him to the foot of the stairs, where she paused and looked at him intently.

Her eyes were bright.

"Are you frightened?"

"No," he lied. His voice was thick. He needed to clear his throat, but he didn't dare do it in case it made him sound weak or stupid or unhealthy. In case it woke him from this dream. The staircase was narrow. He held on to her hand as she went before him and towed him up. On the landing, there was a bathroom straight ahead and, as downstairs, doors to the right and left. She pulled him to the right. The room excited him. It was a mess. The bed was unmade. On the floor by a laundry basket was a small heap of her under-wear in various pastels. The sight of it touched him. When he knocked, she must have been folding her washing for the week ahead, the way people did on Saturday mornings.

"Take your shoes and socks off."

He did as he was told. He did not like the way his pointed shoes rose up at the tips. He pushed them under a chair.

She spoke in a sensible voice. "Are you circumcised, Roland?"

"Yes. I mean, no."

"Either way, you'll go in the bathroom and have a good wash."

It seemed reasonable enough and, because of that, his arousal drained away. The bathroom was tiny, with a pink bathmat, a narrow bath, and a glass-fronted shower cubicle at a slight lean, and, on a chrome rack, thick white towels of a kind that reminded him of home. On a shelf above the basin he saw a curvy bottle of her perfume and its name, rosewater. He was thorough in his preparations. Displeasing her in any way was what he dreaded most. As he was getting dressed, he peered out a small leaded window under the gable. He had a view across wide fields to the Stour, nearing low tide, with its mudbanks emerging from the silver water like the humped backs of monsters, and sea grasses and circling flocks of seabirds. A twin-masted sailboat was in mid-channel running out with the flow. Whatever was happening here in this cottage, the world would go on, anyway. Until it didn't. Perhaps within the hour.

When he returned, she had tidied the room and turned back the covers. "That's what you'll do every time."

Her suggestion of a future excited him again. She gestured to him to sit beside her on the bed. Then she put her hand on his knee.

"Are you worried about contraception?"

He did not answer. He hadn't given it a thought and was ignorant of the details.

She said, "I could be the first woman on the Shotley Peninsula to be on the pill."

This, too, was beyond him. His only resource was the truth, what was most obvious at that moment. He turned to face her and said, "I really like being here with you." As the words left him, they sounded childish. But she smiled and drew his face to hers and they kissed. Not for very long or very deeply. He followed her. Lips then, glancingly, tips of tongues, then just lips again. She lay back on the bed against the pillows and said, "Get undressed for me. I want to look at you."

He stood and pulled his Hawaiian shirt over his head. The old oak floorboards creaked under him when he stood on

40

one leg to pull off his trousers. Tapered by his mother to keep him in fashion, they were tight over the heels. He was in good shape, he thought, and not ashamed to stand exposed in front of Miriam Cornell. But she said sharply, "All of it."

So he pulled down his underpants and stepped out of them.

"That's better. Lovely, Roland. And look at you."

She was right. He had never known such anticipation. Even as she frightened him, he trusted her and was ready to do whatever she asked. All the time he had spent with her in his thoughts and, before that, all the intimidating lessons at the piano had been a rehearsal for what was about to happen. It was all one lesson. She would make him ready to face death, happy to be vaporized. He looked at her expectantly. What did he see?

The memory would never leave him. The bed was a double by the standards of the time, less than five feet across. Two sets of two pillows. She sat against one set with her knees drawn up. While he was undressing, she had taken off her cardigan and jeans. Her knickers, like her T-shirt, were green. Cotton, not silk. The T-shirt was a large man's size, and perhaps he should have worried about a rival. The folds of the material, brushed cotton, seemed to him voluptuous in his heightened state. Her eyes were also green. He had once thought there was something cruel about them. Now their color suggested daring. She could do anything she wanted. Her bare legs had traces of a summer tan. Her round face, which once had the quality of a mask, now had a soft and open look. The light through the small bedroom window picked out the strength of her cheekbones. No lipstick this Saturday morning. The hair she had worn in a bun for lessons was very fine and strands of it floated up when she moved her head. She was looking at him in that patient, wry way she had. Something about him amused her. She pulled her T-shirt off and let it fall to the floor.

"Time you learned to take a girl's bra off."

He knelt beside her on the bed. Though his fingers shook, it turned out to be obvious enough, how to lift the hooks from the eyes. She pushed the blankets and sheets away. She was holding his gaze, as if to prevent him from gaping at her breasts.

"Let's get in," she said. "Come here."

She lay on her back with her arm stretched out. She wanted him to lie on it, or within it. With her free hand she pulled up the covers, turned on her side and drew him toward her. He was uneasy. This was more like a mother-and-child embrace. He sensed that he should be in a more commanding position. He felt strongly that he shouldn't let himself be babied. But how strongly? To be enveloped like this was sudden, unexpected bliss. There was no choice. She drew his face toward her breasts and now they filled his view and he took her nipple in his mouth. She shuddered and murmured, "Oh, God." He came up for air. They were face to face and kissing. She guided his fingers between her legs and showed him, then took her hand away. She whispered, "No, gently, slower," and closed her eyes.

Suddenly, she pushed the bed covers away and rolled on top of him, sat up – and it was complete, accomplished. So simple. Like some trick with a vanishing knot in a length of soft rope. He lay back in sensual wonder, reaching for her hands, unable to speak. Probably only minutes passed. It seemed as if he had been shown a hidden fold in space where there was a catch, a fastener, and that as he released it and peeled away the illusory everyday he saw what had always been there. Their roles – teacher, pupil – the order and self-importance of school, timetables, bikes, cars, clothes, even words: all of it a diversion to keep everyone from this. It was either hilarious or it was tragic that people should go about their daily business in the conventional way when they knew there was this. Even the headmaster, who had a son and a daughter, must know. Even the Queen. Every adult knew. What a façade. What pretense.

Later, she opened her eyes and, gazing down at him with a faraway look, said, "There's something missing."

His voice came faintly from beyond the cottage walls, "Yes?"

"You haven't said my name."

"Miriam."

"Say it three times."

He did so.

A pause. She swayed, then she said, "Say something to me. With my name."

He did not hesitate. It was a love letter, and he meant it. "Dear Miriam, I love Miriam. I love you, Miriam." And as he was saying it again she arched her back, gave a shout, a beautiful tapering cry. That was it for him, too. He followed her, just one step behind, barely a crotchet.

He went downstairs ten minutes after her. His head was clear, his tread was light, and he took the steep stairs two at a time. The clocks had not yet been turned back and the sun was still high enough. It was not even one-thirty. It would be a delight now to be on his bike, taking a different route to school, the Harkstead way, at speed, passing close by the pine wood that contained the secret lake. Alone, to prize the treasure that no one could take from him, to taste it, sift it, reconstruct it. To get the measure of the new person he was. He might extend the ride, take the farm tracks to Freston. The prospect was sweet. But, first, a goodbye. When he arrived in the sitting room, she was bending down to gather up the papers from the floor. He was not too young to sense a shift of mood. Her movements were quick and tense. Her hair was tied back tight. She straightened and looked at him and knew.

She said, "Oh, no, you don't."

"What?"

She came toward him. "You absolutely don't."

He started to say, "I don't know what you mean," but she spoke over him. "Got what you came for and heading off. Is that it?"

"No. Honestly. I want to stay."

"Are you telling me the truth?"

"Yes!"

"Yes, Miss."

He looked to see if she was making fun of him. Impossible to tell.

"Yes, Miss."

"Good. Ever peeled a potato?"

He nodded, not daring to say no.

She led him into the kitchen. By the sink, in a tin bowl, were five big dirty potatoes. She gave him a peeler and a colander. "Did you wash your hands?"

He tried to sound curt. "Yes."

"Yes, Miss."

"I thought you wanted me to call you Miriam."

She gave him a look of exaggerated pity and continued. "When they're done and rinsed, chop them into four and put them in that pot."

She stepped into some clogs and went into the back garden, and he started work. He felt trapped, bewildered, and at the same time he thought he owed her a great debt. Of course, it would have been wrong, appalling bad manners, to leave. But even if it had been right he would not have known how to withstand her. She had always frightened him. He had not forgotten how cruel she could be. Now it was more complicated; it was worse, and he had made it worse. He suspected that he had brushed against a fundamental law of the universe: such ecstasy must compromise his freedom. That was its price.

The first potato was slow. Like wood carving, at which he had always been useless. By the fourth, he thought he had the hang of it. The trick was to ignore the detail. He quartered and rinsed his five potatoes and put them in the pot of water. He went to the kitchen's half-glazed door to see what she was up to. The light was golden. She was dragging a cast-iron table across the lawn toward a shed. Pausing, then dragging a few inches at a time. Her movements were frantic, even angry. The terrible thought came to him that there might be something wrong with her. She saw him and waved at him to come out.

When he got to her, she said, "Don't just watch. This thing is bloody heavy."

Together, they stored the table in the shed. Then she put a rake in his hands and told him to sweep up the leaves and put them on the compost heap at the bottom of the garden. While he raked beech leaves from next door's tree, she was busy in the borders with her secateurs. An hour passed. He was dumping the last of the leaves on the compost. Across the open space, he could make out a slice of the river, part of an inlet, tinted orange. It occurred to him to step over the low fence into the field, walk around to the front of the cottage, retrieve his bike, and be off. Never come back. It would hardly matter if the world was ending. He could do all that. But it was simple – he couldn't. His urge to leave surprised him as much as his inability to. It was a matter of courtesy to help out, to stay for lunch. He was hungry; the leg of lamb he had seen in the kitchen would be far superior to anything at school. It helped, or simplified matters, minutes later, when Miriam told him to rake the front garden also. He had no choice. As he turned to obey, she pulled him back by the collar of his shirt and kissed him on the cheek. She went indoors to prepare lunch while he pushed a wheelbarrow with his rake around the house and set to work out front. It was harder here. The leaves were massed between and behind thorny rose shrubs along the borders. The rake's head was too wide. He had to go down on all fours and scoop the leaves out with his hands. He gathered up the empty plastic flowerpots, the sweet wrappers, and other rubbish that had blown in. Just beyond her front gate was her car and his bike leaning against it. He tried not to look at it. Perhaps it was hunger that was making him irritable. That and the fiddly nature of the job.

When he was done at last and had returned the rake and the wheelbarrow to the shed, he went indoors. Miriam was basting the lamb.

"Not ready yet," she said, and then she saw him. "Look at the state of you. Your trousers are filthy." She took his hand. "You're all scratched. You poor darling. Get your shoes off. Into the shower with you!"

He let himself be led upstairs. The backs of his hands were indeed bloody from the rose thorns. He felt cared for and just a little heroic. In her bedroom, he undressed in front of her.

Her tone was warm. "Look at you. Big again." She drew him toward her and fondled him while they kissed.

The shower was not a good experience. The water came out in a dribble, with a hair's-breadth turn of the tap between icy and scalding. When he returned to the bedroom, towel round his waist, his clothes were gone. He heard her coming up the stairs.

Before he could ask, she said, "They're in the washing machine. You can't go back to school covered in mud." She passed him a gray sweater and a pair of her beige slacks. "Don't worry. I'm not lending you my knickers."

Her clothes fit well enough, though the slacks looked girlish around the hips. There was an odd little loop that was supposed to go under his heel. He let it drag. As he followed her down the stairs, the thought that they were both barefoot pleased him. At their very late lunch she had a glass of white wine, which she said she preferred at room temperature. He did not know the rules of wine, but he nodded. She poured him some homemade lemonade. At first, they ate in silence, and he was nervous, for he was beginning to understand how quickly her moods shifted. It was also worrying that he was without his clothes. The washing machine was turning, making little moaning sounds. But soon he did not care, because he had a plate of roast lamb, pink, even bloody in places, which was new to him. And seven large pieces of roast potato and much buttery cauliflower. When it was offered, he accepted another plate of meat and then a third and a total of fifteen potato chunks and most of the cauliflower. He would have liked to pick up the half-full gravy boat and drink it all, because it was surely going to be thrown away. But he knew his manners.

Finally, she raised the subject, the only real topic. Since it had been the cause of his visit, he had automatically assumed the matter buried.

"I don't suppose you read the papers."

"I do," he said quickly. "I know what's happening."

"And what do you think?"

He considered carefully. He was so full of food, and he

was also a new person – a man, in fact – and at that moment he was not really bothered. But he said, "We might all be dead tomorrow. Or tonight."

She pushed her plate aside and folded her arms. "Really? You don't look very scared."

His present indifference was a heavy weight. He forced himself to remember how he had felt the day before, and the night before that. "I'm terrified." And then, suddenly feeling the rich aura of his new maturity, he returned her question, in a manner that would never have occurred to a child. "What do *you* think?"

"I think Kennedy and all of America are behaving like spoiled babies. Stupid and reckless. And the Russians are liars and thugs. You're quite right to be frightened."

Roland was astonished. He had never heard a word against the Americans. The President was a godly figure in everything Roland had read. "But it was the Russians who put their missiles—"

"Yes, yes. And the Americans have theirs right against the Soviet border with Turkey. They've always said that strategic balance was the only way to keep the world safe. They should both pull back. Instead, we have these silly dangerous games at sea. Boys' games!"

Her passion astonished him. Her cheeks were red. His heart was racing. He had never felt so grown-up. "Then what's going to happen?"

"Either some trigger-happy idiot out at sea makes a mistake and it all blows up, just like you fear. Or they do the deal they should have done ten days ago, like proper statesmen, instead of driving us all to the brink."

"So you think a war might really happen?"

"It's just possible, yes."

He stared at her. His own position, that they might all

die tonight, was largely rhetorical. It was what his friends and the sixth formers said at school. There was comfort in having everybody say it. But hearing it now from her was a shock. She seemed wise. The newspapers were saying the same kind of thing, but that mattered less. Those were stories, like entertainments. He began to feel shivery. She placed a hand on his wrist, turned it, and found his fingers and interlocked them with hers. "Listen, Roland. It's very, very unlikely. They might be stupid, but both sides have too much to lose. Do you understand?"

"Yes."

"Do you know what I'd like?" She waited for his answer.

"What?"

"I'd like to take you upstairs with me." She added in a whisper, "Make you feel safe."

So they rose without letting go, and for the third time that day she towed him up the stairs. In the fading light of the late afternoon it happened all over again, and again he wondered at himself, how earlier in the day he had been so eager to get away, to regress and become a kid on a bike. Afterward, he lay on her arm, his face level with her breasts, feeling a growing drowsiness begin to smother him. His attention drifted in and out of what she was quietly saying.

"I always knew that you'd come.... I've been very patient, but I knew ... even though you didn't. Are you listening? Good. Because now that you're here you should know. I've waited a very long time. You're not to speak about this to anyone. Not to your closest friend, no boasting about it, however tempting it is. Is that clear?"

"Yes," he said. "It's clear."

When he woke it was dark outside and she had gone. The bedroom air was cold on his nose and ears. He lay on his back in the comfortable bed. From downstairs he heard the front door open and close and then a familiar ticking sound that he could not place. He lay for half an hour in loosely associated daydreams. If the world did not end, then the school term would, in fifty-four days. He would make the journey to his father's latest Army posting, in Germany, to be with his parents for the Christmas holidays, a prospect of comfort and boredom. What he liked was to think about the stages of the journey, the train from Ipswich to Manningtree, where the River Stour ceased to be tidal, change there for Harwich to get the night boat to the Hook of Holland, walk across the railway lines on the quayside and climb up onto the train to Hanover, at all stages checking the inside pocket of his school blazer to make sure his passport was still there.

He dressed quickly in the clothes she had lent him and went downstairs. The first thing he saw was his bike propped against the piano. She was in the kitchen, finishing the washing-up.

She called to him. "Safer in here. I spoke to Paul Bond. Did you know I teach his daughter? It's fine for you to stay overnight." She came toward him and kissed his forehead.

She was wearing a blue dress of fine corduroy, with darker blue buttons down the front. He liked her familiar perfume. Now it seemed that for the first time he really understood how beautiful she was.

"I told him we're rehearsing a duet. And we are."

He wheeled his bike through the kitchen into the garden and propped it by the shed. It was a night of stars and the first touch of winter. Already the beginning of a frost was forming on the lawn that he had raked. It crunched underfoot as he moved away from the kitchen light in order to see the smudged forked road of the Milky Way. A Third World War would make no difference to the universe. Miriam called to him from the kitchen door. "Roland, you'll freeze to death. Get inside."

He went immediately toward her.

That evening they played the Mozart again, and this time he was more expressive and followed the dynamic markings. In the slow movement, he tried to imitate her smooth and seamless legato touch. He thundered his way through the allegro molto and the cottage seemed to shake. It hardly mattered. They laughed about it. At the end, she hugged him.

The next morning, he slept late. By the time he came downstairs, it was even late for lunch. Miriam was in the kitchen preparing eggs. The pages of the Sunday paper, the *Observer*, were spread across an armchair and the floor. There was no change; the crisis continued. The headline was clear – "KENNEDY: NO DEAL TILL CUBA MISSILES ARE MADE USELESS." She gave him a glass of orange juice and made him play another Mozart duet with her, this time the F major. He sight-read all the way. Afterward, she said, "You play the dotted notes like a jazz musician." It was a rebuke he took as praise.

When, at last, they sat down to eat and she turned on the radio for the news, the story had moved on. The crisis was over. They listened to a deep voice, rich in authority, issue the deliverance. There had been an important exchange of letters between the leaders. The Russian ships were turning back, and Khrushchev would order that the missiles be removed from Cuba. The general view was that President Kennedy had saved the world. The Prime Minister, Harold Macmillan, had phoned his congratulations.

It was another cloudless day. The low afternoon sun, well past the equinox, blazed through the glazed upper half of the kitchen door into the little sitting room and spilled across the table. As Roland ate his omelette, he felt again the insidious desire to be off, hurtling along the route he had in mind. Out of the question. He had already been told that while she ironed his clothes he would be washing the dishes. She had earned the right to tell him what to do. But she'd had it from the beginning.

"What a relief," she kept saying. "Aren't you happy? You don't look it."

"I am, honestly. It's amazing. What a relief."

Thirty years later, he would understand the damage, how derailed his life was by her, how distorted his expectation of love. When he was twelve, she had touched and unwound a little coil in his being and, without having to do more, she had possessed him. Two years later, pursued by fear and childish vanity and incoherent desire, he had run to her. It would take him half a lifetime to frame it in such simple terms. But now, here at the sunlit lunch table, many layers below his outward decorum, and barely available to the ignorant boy, was a mere suspicion that he had been cheated of something. The world would go on, he would remain unvaporized. He needn't have done a thing.

CARSON McCULLERS

WUNDERKIND
(1936)

SHE CAME INTO the living room, her music satchel plopping against her winter-stockinged legs and her other arm weighted down with schoolbooks, and stood for a moment listening to the sounds from the studio. A soft procession of piano chords and the tuning of a violin. Then Mister Bilderbach called out to her in his chunky, guttural tones:

"That you, Bienchen?"

As she jerked off her mittens she saw that her fingers were twitching to the motions of the fugue she had practiced that morning. "Yes," she answered. "It's me."

"I," the voice corrected. "Just a moment."

She could hear Mister Lafkowitz talking – his words spun out in a silky, unintelligible hum. A voice almost like a woman's, she thought, compared to Mister Bilderbach's. Restlessness scattered her attention. She fumbled with her geometry book and *Le Voyage de Monsieur Perrichon* before putting them on the table. She sat down on the sofa and began to take her music from the satchel. Again she saw her hands – the quivering tendons that stretched down from her knuckles, the sore finger tip cupped with curled, dingy tape. The sight sharpened the fear that had begun to torment her for the past few months.

Noiselessly she mumbled a few phrases of encouragement to herself. A good lesson – a good lesson – like it used to be— Her lips closed as she heard the stolid sound of Mister

Bilderbach's footsteps across the floor of the studio and the creaking of the door as it slid open.

For a moment she had the peculiar feeling that during most of the fifteen years of her life she had been looking at the face and shoulders that jutted from behind the door, in a silence disturbed only by the muted, blank plucking of a violin string. Mister Bilderbach. Her teacher, Mister Bilderbach. The quick eyes behind the horn-rimmed glasses; the light, thin hair and the narrow face beneath; the lips full and loose shut and the lower one pink and shining from the bites of his teeth; the forked veins in his temples throbbing plainly enough to be observed across the room.

"Aren't you a little early?" he asked, glancing at the clock on the mantelpiece that had pointed to five minutes of twelve for a month. "Josef's in here. We're running over a little sonatina by someone he knows."

"Good," she said, trying to smile. "I'll listen." She could see her fingers sinking powerless into a blur of piano keys. She felt tired – felt that if he looked at her much longer her hands might tremble.

He stood uncertain, halfway in the room. Sharply his teeth pushed down on his bright, swollen lip. "Hungry, Bienchen?" he asked. "There's some apple cake Anna made, and milk."

"I'll wait till afterward," she said. "Thanks."

"After you finish with a very fine lesson – eh?" His smile seemed to crumble at the corners.

There was a sound from behind him in the studio and Mister Lafkowitz pushed at the other panel of the door and stood beside him.

"Frances?" he said, smiling. "And how is the work coming now?"

Without meaning to, Mister Lafkowitz always made her

feel clumsy and overgrown. He was such a small man himself, with a weary look when he was not holding his violin. His eyebrows curved high above his sallow, Jewish face as though asking a question, but the lids of his eyes drowsed languorous and indifferent. Today he seemed distracted. She watched him come into the room for no apparent purpose, holding his pearl-tipped bow in his still fingers, slowly gliding the white horsehair through a chalky piece of rosin. His eyes were sharp bright slits today and the linen handkerchief that flowed down from his collar darkened the shadows beneath them.

"I gather you're doing a lot now," smiled Mister Lafkowitz, although she had not yet answered the question.

She looked at Mister Bilderbach. He turned away. His heavy shoulders pushed the door open wide so that the late afternoon sun came through the window of the studio and shafted yellow over the dusty living room. Behind her teacher she could see the squat long piano, the window, and the bust of Brahms.

"No," she said to Mister Lafkowitz, "I'm doing terribly." Her thin fingers flipped at the pages of her music. "I don't know what's the matter," she said, looking at Mister Bilderbach's stooped muscular back that stood tense and listening.

Mister Lafkowitz smiled. "There are times, I suppose, when one—"

A harsh chord sounded from the piano. "Don't you think we'd better get on with this?" asked Mister Bilderbach.

"Immediately," said Mister Lafkowitz, giving the bow one more scrape before starting toward the door. She could see him pick up his violin from the top of the piano. He caught her eye and lowered the instrument. "You've seen the picture of Heime?"

Her fingers curled tight over the sharp corner of the satchel. "What picture?"

"One of Heime in the *Musical Courier* there on the table. Inside the top cover."

The sonatina began. Discordant yet somehow simple. Empty but with a sharp-cut style of its own. She reached for the magazine and opened it.

There Heime was – in the left-hand corner. Holding his violin with his fingers hooked down over the strings for a pizzicato. With his dark serge knickers strapped neatly beneath his knees, a sweater and rolled collar. It was a bad picture. Although it was snapped in profile his eyes were cut around toward the photographer and his finger looked as though it would pluck the wrong string. He seemed suffering to turn around toward the picture-taking apparatus. He was thinner – his stomach did not poke out now – but he hadn't changed much in six months.

Heime Israelsky, talented young violinist, snapped while at work in his teacher's studio on Riverside Drive. Young Master Israelsky, who will soon celebrate his fifteenth birthday, has been invited to play the Beethoven Concerto with—

That morning, after she had practiced from six until eight, her dad had made her sit down at the table with the family for breakfast. She hated breakfast; it gave her a sick feeling afterward. She would rather wait and get four chocolate bars with her twenty cents lunch money and munch them during school – bringing up little morsels from her pocket under cover of her handkerchief, stopping dead when the silver paper rattled. But this morning her dad had put a fried egg on her plate and she had known that if it burst – so that the slimy yellow oozed over the white – she would cry. And that had happened. The same feeling was upon her now.

Gingerly she laid the magazine back on the table and closed her eyes.

The music in the studio seemed to be urging violently and clumsily for something that was not to be had. After a moment her thoughts drew back from Heime and the concerto and the picture – and hovered around the lesson once more. She slid over on the sofa until she could see plainly into the studio – the two of them playing, peering at the notations on the piano, lustfully drawing out all that was there.

She could not forget the memory of Mister Bilderbach's face as he had stared at her a moment ago. Her hands, still twitching unconsciously to the motions of the fugue, closed over her bony knees. Tired, she was. And with a circling, sinking away feeling like the one that often came to her just before she dropped off to sleep on the nights when she had over-practiced. Like those weary half-dreams that buzzed and carried her out into their own whirling space.

A *Wunderkind* – a *Wunderkind* – a *Wunderkind*. The syllables would come out rolling in the deep German way, roar against her ears and then fall to a murmur. Along with the faces circling, swelling out in distortion, diminishing to pale blobs – Mister Bilderbach, Mrs Bilderbach, Heime, Mister Lafkowitz. Around and around in a circle revolving to the guttural *Wunderkind*. Mister Bilderbach looming large in the middle of the circle, his face urging – with the others around him.

Phrases of music seesawing crazily. Notes she had been practicing falling over each other like a handful of marbles dropped downstairs. Bach, Debussy, Prokofieff, Brahms – timed grotesquely to the far off throb of her tired body and the buzzing circle.

Sometimes – when she had not worked more than three

hours or had stayed out from high school – the dreams were not so confused. The music soared clearly in her mind and quick, precise little memories would come back – clear as the sissy "Age of Innocence" picture Heime had given her after their joint concert was over.

A *Wunderkind* – a *Wunderkind*. That was what Mister Bilderbach had called her when, at twelve, she first came to him. Older pupils had repeated the word.

Not that he had ever said the word to her. "Bienchen—" (She had a plain American name but he never used it except when her mistakes were enormous.) "Bienchen," he would say, "I know it must be terrible. Carrying around all the time a head that thick. Poor Bienchen—"

Mister Bilderbach's father had been a Dutch violinist. His mother was from Prague. He had been born in this country and had spent his youth in Germany. So many times she wished she had not been born and brought up in just Cincinnati. How do you say *cheese* in German? Mister Bilderbach, what is Dutch for *I don't understand you*?

The first day she came to the studio. After she played the whole Second Hungarian Rhapsody from memory. The room graying with twilight. His face as he leaned over the piano.

"Now we begin all over," he said that first day. "It – playing music – is more than cleverness. If a twelve-year-old girl's fingers cover so many keys to a second – that means nothing."

He tapped his broad chest and his forehead with his stubby hand. "Here and here. You are old enough to understand that." He lighted a cigarette and gently blew the first exhalation above her head. "And work – work – work. We will start now with these Bach Inventions and these little Schumann pieces." His hands moved again – this time to

60

jerk the cord of the lamp behind her and point to the music. "I will show you how I wish this practiced. Listen carefully now."

She had been at the piano for almost three hours and was very tired. His deep voice sounded as though it had been straying inside her for a long time. She wanted to reach out and touch his muscle-flexed finger that pointed out the phrases, wanted to feel the gleaming gold band ring and the strong hairy back of his hand.

She had lessons Tuesday after school and on Saturday afternoons. Often she stayed, when the Saturday lesson was finished, for dinner, and then spent the night and took the streetcar home the next morning. Mrs Bilderbach liked her in her calm, almost dumb way. She was much different from her husband. She was quiet and fat and slow. When she wasn't in the kitchen, cooking the rich dishes that both of them loved, she seemed to spend all her time in their bed upstairs, reading magazines or just looking with a half-smile at nothing. When they had married in Germany she had been a *lieder* singer. She didn't sing any more (she said it was her throat). When he would call her in from the kitchen to listen to a pupil she would always smile and say that it was *gut*, very *gut*.

When Frances was thirteen it came to her one day that the Bilderbachs had no children. It seemed strange. Once she had been back in the kitchen with Mrs Bilderbach when he had come striding in from the studio, tense with anger at some pupil who had annoyed him. His wife stood stirring the thick soup until his hand groped out and rested on her shoulder. Then she turned – stood placid – while he folded his arms about her and buried his sharp face in the white, nerveless flesh of her neck. They stood that way without moving. And then his face jerked back suddenly, the anger diminished to a quiet inexpressiveness, and he had returned to the studio.

After she had started with Mister Bilderbach and didn't have time to see anything of the people at high school, Heime had been the only friend of her own age. He was Mister Lafkowitz's pupil and would come with him to Mister Bilderbach's on evenings when she would be there. They would listen to their teachers' playing. And often they themselves went over chamber music together – Mozart sonatas or Bloch.

A *Wunderkind* – a *Wunderkind*.

Heime was a *Wunderkind*. He and she, then.

Heime had been playing the violin since he was four. He didn't have to go to school; Mister Lafkowitz's brother, who was crippled, used to teach him geometry and European history and French verbs in the afternoon. When he was thirteen he had as fine a technique as any violinist in Cincinnati – everyone said so. But playing the violin must be easier than the piano. She knew it must be.

Heime always seemed to smell of corduroy pants and the food he had eaten and rosin. Half the time, too, his hands were dirty around the knuckles and the cuffs of his shirts peeped out dingily from the sleeves of his sweater. She always watched his hands when he played – thin only at the joints with the hard little blobs of flesh bulging over the short-cut nails and the babyish-looking crease that showed so plainly in his bowing wrist.

In the dreams, as when she was awake, she could remember the concert only in a blur. She had not known it was unsuccessful for her until months after. True, the papers had praised Heime more than her. But he was much shorter than she. When they stood together on the stage he came only to her shoulders. And that made a difference with people, she knew. Also, there was the matter of the sonata they played together. The Bloch.

"No, no – I don't think that would be appropriate," Mister Bilderbach had said when the Bloch was suggested to end the programme. "Now that John Powell thing – the Sonate Virginianesque."

She hadn't understood then; she wanted it to be the Bloch as much as Mister Lafkowitz and Heime.

Mister Bilderbach had given in. Later, after the reviews had said she lacked the temperament for that type of music, after they called her playing thin and lacking in feeling, she felt cheated.

"That oie oie stuff," said Mister Bilderbach, crackling the newspapers at her. "Not for you, Bienchen. Leave all that to the Heimes and vitses and skys."

A *Wunderkind*. No matter what the papers said, that was what he had called her.

Why was it Heime had done so much better at the concert than she? At school sometimes, when she was supposed to be watching someone do a geometry problem on the blackboard, the question would twist knife-like inside her. She would worry about it in bed, and even sometimes when she was supposed to be concentrating at the piano. It wasn't just the Bloch and her not being Jewish – not entirely. It wasn't that Heime didn't have to go to school and had begun his training so early, either. It was—?

Once she thought she knew.

"Play the Fantasia and Fugue," Mister Bilderbach had demanded one evening a year ago – after he and Mister Lafkowitz had finished reading some music together.

The Bach, as she played, seemed to her well done. From the tail of her eye she could see the calm, pleased expression on Mister Bilderbach's face, see his hands rise climactically

63

from the chair arms and then sink down loose and satisfied when the high points of the phrases had been passed successfully. She stood up from the piano when it was over, swallowing to loosen the bands that the music seemed to have drawn around her throat and chest. But—

"Frances—" Mister Lafkowitz had said then, suddenly, looking at her with his thin mouth curved and his eyes almost covered by their delicate lids. "Do you know how many children Bach had?"

She turned to him, puzzled. "A good many. Twenty some odd."

"Well then—" The corners of his smile etched themselves gently in his pale face. "He could not have been so cold – then."

Mister Bilderbach was not pleased; his guttural effulgence of German words had *Kind* in it somewhere. Mister Lafkowitz raised his eyebrows. She had caught the point easily enough, but she felt no deception in keeping her face blank and immature because that was the way Mister Bilderbach wanted her to look.

Yet such things had nothing to do with it. Nothing very much, at least, for she would grow older. Mister Bilderbach understood that, and even Mister Lafkowitz had not meant just what he said.

In the dreams Mister Bilderbach's face loomed out and contracted in the center of the whirling circle. The lip surging softly, the veins in his temples insisting.

But sometimes, before she slept, there were such clear memories; as when she pulled a hole in the heel of her stocking down, so that her shoe would hide it. "Bienchen, Bienchen!" And bringing Mrs Bilderbach's work basket in and showing her how it should be darned and not gathered together in a lumpy heap.

And the time she graduated from Junior High.

"What you wear?" asked Mrs Bilderbach the Sunday morning at breakfast when she told them about how they had practiced to march into the auditorium.

"An evening dress my cousin had last year."

"Ah – Bienchen!" he said, circling his warm coffee cup with his heavy hands, looking up at her with wrinkles around his laughing eyes. "I bet I know what Bienchen wants—"

He insisted. He would not believe her when she explained that she honestly didn't care at all.

"Like this, Anna," he said, pushing his napkin across the table and mincing to the other side of the room, swishing his hips, rolling up his eyes behind his horn-rimmed glasses.

The next Saturday afternoon, after her lessons, he took her to the department stores downtown. His thick fingers smoothed over the filmy nets and crackling taffetas that the saleswomen unwound from their bolts. He held colors to her face, cocking his head to one side, and selected pink. Shoes, he remembered too. He liked best some white kid pumps. They seemed a little like old ladies' shoes to her and the Red Cross label in the instep had a charity look. But it really didn't matter at all. When Mrs Bilderbach began to cut out the dress and fit it to her with pins, he interrupted his lessons to stand by and suggest ruffles around the hips and neck and a fancy rosette on the shoulder. The music was coming along nicely then. Dresses and commencement and such made no difference.

Nothing mattered much except playing the music as it must be played, bringing out the thing that must be in her, practicing, practicing, playing so that Mister Bilderbach's face lost some of its urging look. Putting the thing into her music that Myra Hess had, and Yehudi Menuhin – even Heime!

What had begun to happen to her four months ago? The notes began springing out with a glib, dead intonation. Adolescence, she thought. Some kids played with promise – and worked and worked until, like her, the least little thing would start them crying, and worn out with trying to get the thing across – the longing thing they felt – something queer began to happen— But not she! She was like Heime. She had to be. She—

Once it was there for sure. And you didn't lose things like that. A *Wunderkind*. . . . A *Wunderkind*. . . . Of her he said it, rolling the words in the sure, deep German way. And in the dreams even deeper, more certain than ever. With his face looming out at her, and the longing phrases of music mixed in with the zooming, circling round, round, round— A *Wunderkind*. A *Wunderkind*. . . .

This afternoon Mister Bilderbach did not show Mister Lafkowitz to the front door, as he usually did. He stayed at the piano, softly pressing a solitary note. Listening, Frances watched the violinist wind his scarf about his pale throat.

"A good picture of Heime," she said, picking up her music. "I got a letter from him a couple of months ago – telling about hearing Schnabel and Huberman and about Carnegie Hall and things to eat at the Russian Tea Room."

To put off going into the studio a moment longer she waited until Mister Lafkowitz was ready to leave and then stood behind him as he opened the door. The frosty cold outside cut into the room. It was growing late and the air was seeped with the pale yellow of winter twilight. When the door swung to on its hinges, the house seemed darker and more silent than ever before she had known it to be.

As she went into the studio Mister Bilderbach got up from the piano and silently watched her settle herself at the keyboard.

"Well, Bienchen," he said, "this afternoon we are going to begin all over. Start from scratch. Forget the last few months."

He looked as though he were trying to act a part in a movie. His solid body swayed from toe to heel, he rubbed his hands together, and even smiled in a satisfied, movie way. Then suddenly he thrust this manner brusquely aside. His heavy shoulders slouched and he began to run through the stack of music she had brought in. "The Bach – no, not yet," he murmured. "The Beethoven? Yes. The Variation Sonata. Opus 26."

The keys of the piano hemmed her in – stiff and white and dead-seeming.

"Wait a minute," he said. He stood in the curve of the piano, elbows propped, and looked at her. "Today I expect something from you. Now this sonata – it's the first Beethoven sonata you ever worked on. Every note is under control – technically – you have nothing to cope with but the music. Only music now. That's all you think about."

He rustled through the pages of her volume until he found the place. Then he pulled his teaching chair halfway across the room, turned it around and seated himself, straddling the back with his legs.

For some reason, she knew, this position of his usually had a good effect on her performance. But today she felt that she would notice him from the corner of her eye and be disturbed. His back was stiffly tilted, his legs looked tense. The heavy volume before him seemed to balance dangerously on the chair back. "Now we begin," he said with a peremptory dart of his eyes in her direction.

Her hands rounded over the keys and then sank down. The first notes were too loud, the other phrases followed dryly.

Arrestingly his hand rose up from the score. "Wait! Think a minute what you're playing. How is this beginning marked?"

"*An-andante*."

"All right. Don't drag it into an *adagio* then. And play deeply into the keys. Don't snatch it off shallowly that way. A graceful, deep-toned *andante*—"

She tried again. Her hands seemed separate from the music that was in her.

"Listen," he interrupted. "Which of these variations dominates the whole?"

"The dirge," she answered.

"Then prepare for that. This is an *andante* – but it's not salon stuff as you just played it. Start out softly, *piano*, and make it swell out just before the arpeggio. Make it warm and dramatic. And down here – where it's marked *dolce* make the counter melody sing out. You know all that. We've gone over all that side of it before. Now play it. Feel it as Beethoven wrote it down. Feel that tragedy and restraint."

She could not stop looking at his hands. They seemed to rest tentatively on the music, ready to fly up as a stop signal as soon as she would begin, the gleaming flash of his ring calling her to halt. "Mister Bilderbach – maybe if I – if you let me play on through the first variation without stopping I could do better."

"I won't interrupt," he said.

Her pale face leaned over too close to the keys. She played through the first part, and, obeying a nod from him, began the second. There were no flaws that jarred on her, but the phrases shaped from her fingers before she had put into them the meaning that she felt.

When she had finished he looked up from the music and began to speak with dull bluntness: "I hardly heard those harmonic fillings in the right hand. And incidentally, this part was supposed to take on intensity, develop the foreshadowings that were supposed to be inherent in the first part. Go on with the next one, though."

She wanted to start it with subdued viciousness and progress to a feeling of deep, swollen sorrow. Her mind told her that. But her hands seemed to gum in the keys like limp macaroni and she could not imagine the music as it should be.

When the last note had stopped vibrating, he closed the book and deliberately got up from the chair. He was moving his lower jaw from side to side – and between his open lips she could glimpse the pink healthy lane to his throat and his strong, smoke-yellowed teeth. He laid the Beethoven gingerly on top of the rest of her music and propped his elbows on the smooth, black piano top once more. "No," he said simply, looking at her.

Her mouth began to quiver. "I can't help it. I—"

Suddenly he strained his lips into a smile. "Listen, Bienchen," he began in a new, forced voice. "You still play the Harmonious Blacksmith, don't you? I told you not to drop it from your repertoire."

"Yes," she said. "I practice it now and then."

His voice was the one he used for children. "It was among the first things we worked on together – remember. So strongly you used to play it – like a real blacksmith's daughter. You see, Bienchen, I know you so well – as if you were my own girl. I know what you have – I've heard you play so many things beautifully. You used to—"

He stopped in confusion and inhaled from his pulpy stub of cigarette. The smoke drowsed out from his pink lips and clung in a gray mist around the lank hair and childish forehead.

69

"Make it happy and simple," he said, switching on the lamp behind her and stepping back from the piano.

For a moment he stood just inside the bright circle the light made. Then impulsively he squatted down to the floor. "Vigorous," he said.

She could not stop looking at him, sitting on one heel with the other foot resting squarely before him for balance, the muscles of his strong thighs straining under the cloth of his trousers, his back straight, his elbows staunchly propped on his knees. "Simply now," he repeated with a gesture of his fleshy hands. "Think of the blacksmith – working out in the sunshine all day. Working easily and undisturbed."

She could not look down at the piano. The light brightened the hairs on the backs of his outspread hands, made the lenses of his glasses glitter.

"All of it," he urged. "Now!"

She felt that the marrows of her bones were hollow and there was no blood left in her. Her heart that had been springing against her chest all afternoon felt suddenly dead. She saw it gray and limp and shriveled at the edges like an oyster.

His face seemed to throb out in space before her, come closer with the lurching motion in the veins of his temples. In retreat, she looked down at the piano. Her lips shook like jelly and a surge of noiseless tears made the white keys blur in a watery line. "I can't," she whispered. "I don't know why, but I just can't – can't any more."

His tense body slackened and, holding his hand to his side, he pulled himself up. She clutched her music and hurried past him.

Her coat. The mittens and galoshes. The schoolbooks and the satchel he had given her on her birthday. All from the

70

silent room that was hers. Quickly – before he would have to speak.

As she passed through the vestibule she could not help but see his hands – held out from his body that leaned against the studio door, relaxed and purposeless. The door shut to firmly. Dragging her books and satchel she stumbled down the stone steps, turned in the wrong direction, and hurried down the street that had become confused with noise and bicycles and the games of other children.

KATHERINE MANSFIELD

THE SINGING
LESSON

From

THE GARDEN PARTY

(1922)

WITH DESPAIR – COLD, sharp despair – buried deep in her heart like a wicked knife, Miss Meadows, in cap and gown and carrying a little baton, trod the cold corridors that led to the music hall. Girls of all ages, rosy from the air, and bubbling over with that gleeful excitement that comes from running to school on a fine autumn morning, hurried, skipped, fluttered by; from the hollow classrooms came a quick drumming of voices; a bell rang; a voice like a bird cried, "Muriel." And then there came from the staircase a tremendous knock-knock-knocking. Someone had dropped her dumb-bells.

The Science Mistress stopped Miss Meadows.

"Good mor-ning," she cried, in her sweet, affected drawl. "Isn't it cold? It might be win-ter."

Miss Meadows, hugging the knife, stared in hatred at the Science Mistress. Everything about her was sweet, pale, like honey. You would not have been surprised to see a bee caught in the tangles of that yellow hair.

"It is rather sharp," said Miss Meadows, grimly.

The other smiled her sugary smile.

"You look fro-zen," said she. Her blue eyes opened wide; there came a mocking light in them. (Had she noticed anything?)

"Oh, not quite as bad as that," said Miss Meadows, and she gave the Science Mistress, in exchange for her smile, a quick grimace and passed on . . .

Forms Four, Five, and Six were assembled in the music hall. The noise was deafening. On the platform, by the piano, stood Mary Beazley, Miss Meadows' favourite, who played accompaniments. She was turning the music stool. When she saw Miss Meadows she gave a loud, warning "Sh-sh! girls!" and Miss Meadows, her hands thrust in her sleeves, the baton under her arm, strode down the centre aisle, mounted the steps, turned sharply, seized the brass music stand, planted it in front of her, and gave two sharp taps with her baton for silence.

"Silence, please! Immediately!" and, looking at nobody, her glance swept over that sea of coloured flannel blouses, with bobbing pink faces and hands, quivering butterfly hair-bows, and music-books outspread. She knew perfectly well what they were thinking. "Meady is in a wax." Well, let them think it! Her eyelids quivered; she tossed her head, defying them. What could the thoughts of those creatures matter to someone who stood there bleeding to death, pierced to the heart, to the heart, by such a letter—

... "I feel more and more strongly that our marriage would be a mistake. Not that I do not love you. I love you as much as it is possible for me to love any woman, but, truth to tell, I have come to the conclusion that I am not a marrying man, and the idea of settling down fills me with nothing but—" and the word "disgust" was scratched out lightly and "regret" written over the top.

Basil! Miss Meadows stalked over to the piano. And Mary Beazley, who was waiting for this moment, bent forward; her curls fell over her cheeks while she breathed, "Good morning, Miss Meadows," and she motioned towards rather than handed to her mistress a beautiful yellow chrysanthemum. This little ritual of the flower had been gone through for ages and ages, quite a term and a half. It was as much part of the lesson as opening the piano. But this morning, instead of taking it up, instead of tucking it into her belt while she leant over Mary and said, "Thank you, Mary. How very nice! Turn to page thirty-two," what was Mary's horror when Miss Meadows totally ignored the chrysanthemum, made no reply to her greeting, but said in a voice of ice, "Page fourteen, please, and mark the accents well."

Staggering moment! Mary blushed until the tears stood in her eyes, but Miss Meadows was gone back to the music stand; her voice rang through the music hall.

"Page fourteen. We will begin with page fourteen. 'A Lament'. Now, girls, you ought to know it by this time. We shall take it all together; not in parts, all together. And without expression. Sing it, though, quite simply, beating time with the left hand."

She raised the baton; she tapped the music stand twice. Down came Mary on the opening chord; down came all those left hands, beating the air, and in chimed those young, mournful voices:

> Fast! Ah, too Fast Fade the Ro-o-ses of Pleasure;
> Soon Autumn yields unto Wi-i-nter Drear.
> Fleetly! Ah, Fleetly Mu-u-sic's Gay Measure
> Passes away from the Listening Ear.

Good Heavens, what could be more tragic than that lament! Every note was a sigh, a sob, a groan of awful mournfulness. Miss Meadows lifted her arms in the wide gown and began conducting with both hands. ". . . I feel more and more strongly that our marriage would be a mistake . . ." she beat. And the voices cried: *Fleetly! Ah, Fleetly*. What could have possessed him to write such a letter! What could have led up to it! It came out of nothing. His last letter had been all about a fumed-oak bookcase he had bought for "our" books, and a "natty little hall-stand" he had seen, "a very neat affair with a carved owl on a bracket, holding three hat-brushes in its claws". How she had smiled at that! So like a man to think one needed three hat-brushes! *From the Listening Ear*, sang the voices.

"Once again," said Miss Meadows. "But this time in parts. Still without expression." *Fast! Ah, too Fast.* With the gloom of the contraltos added, one could scarcely help shuddering. *Fade the Roses of Pleasure.* Last time he had come to see her, Basil had worn a rose in his buttonhole. How handsome he had looked in that bright blue suit, with that dark red rose! And he knew it, too. He couldn't help knowing it. First he stroked his hair, then his moustache; his teeth gleamed when he smiled.

"The headmaster's wife keeps on asking me to dinner. It's a perfect nuisance. I never get an evening to myself in that place."

"But can't you refuse?"

"Oh well, it doesn't do for a man in my position to be unpopular."

Music's Gay Measure, wailed the voices. The willow trees, outside the high, narrow windows, waved in the wind. They had lost half their leaves. The tiny ones that clung wriggled like fishes caught on a line. ". . . I am not a marrying man . . ." The voices were silent; the piano waited.

"Quite good," said Miss Meadows, but still in such a strange, stony tone that the younger girls began to feel positively frightened. "But now that we know it, we shall take it with expression. As much expression as you can put into it. Think of the words, girls. Use your imaginations. *Fast! Ah, too Fast*," cried Miss Meadows. "That ought to break out – a loud, strong *forte* – a lament. And then in the second line,

78

Winter Drear, make that *Drear* sound as if a cold wind were blowing through it. *Dre-ear*!" said she so awfully that Mary Beazley, on the music stool, wriggled her spine. "The third line should be one crescendo. *Fleetly! Ah, Fleetly Music's Gay Measure*. Breaking on the first word of the last line, *Passes*." And then on the word, *Away*, you must begin to die . . . to fade . . . until *the Listening Ear* is nothing more than a faint whisper . . . You can slow down as much as you like almost on the last line. Now, please."

Again the two light taps; she lifted her arms again. *Fast! Ah, too Fast*. ". . . and the idea of settling down fills me with nothing but disgust—" Disgust was what he had written. That was as good as to say their engagement was definitely broken off. Broken off! Their engagement! People had been surprised enough that she had got engaged. The Science Mistress would not believe it at first. But nobody had been as surprised as she. She was thirty. Basil was twenty-five. It had been a miracle, simply a miracle, to hear him say, as they walked home from church that very dark night, "You know, somehow or other, I've got fond of you." And he had taken hold of the end of her ostrich feather boa. *Passes away from the Listening Ear*.

"Repeat! Repeat!" said Miss Meadows. "More expression, girls! Once more!"

Fast! Ah, too Fast. The older girls were crimson; some of the younger ones began to cry. Big spots of rain blew against the windows, and one could hear the willows whispering, ". . . not that I do not love you . . ."

"But, my darling, if you love me," thought Miss Meadows, "I don't mind how much it is. Love me as little as you like." But she knew he didn't love her. Not to have cared enough to scratch out that word "disgust", so that she couldn't read it! *Soon Autumn yields unto Winter Drear*. She would have

79

to leave the school, too. She could never face the Science Mistress or the girls after it got known. She would have to disappear somewhere. *Passes away*. The voices began to die, to fade, to whisper . . . to vanish . . .

Suddenly the door opened. A little girl in blue walked fussily up the aisle, hanging her head, biting her lips, and twisting the silver bangle on her red little wrist. She came up the steps and stood before Miss Meadows.

"Well, Monica, what is it?"

"Oh, if you please, Miss Meadows," said the little girl, gasping, "Miss Wyatt wants to see you in the mistress's room."

"Very well," said Miss Meadows. And she called to the girls, "I shall put you on your honour to talk quietly while I am away." But they were too subdued to do anything else. Most of them were blowing their noses.

The corridors were silent and cold; they echoed to Miss Meadows' steps. The head mistress sat at her desk. For a moment she did not look up. She was as usual disentangling her eyeglasses, which had got caught in her lace tie. "Sit down, Miss Meadows," she said very kindly. And then she picked up a pink envelope from the blotting-pad. "I sent for you just now because this telegram has come for you."

"A telegram for me, Miss Wyatt?"

Basil! He had committed suicide, decided Miss Meadows. Her hand flew out, but Miss Wyatt held the telegram back a moment. "I hope it's not bad news," she said, no more than kindly. And Miss Meadows tore it open.

"Pay no attention to letter, must have been mad, bought hat-stand today – Basil," she read. She couldn't take her eyes off the telegram.

"I do hope it's nothing very serious," said Miss Wyatt, leaning forward.

"Oh, no, thank you, Miss Wyatt," blushed Miss Meadows. "It's nothing bad at all. It's" – and she gave an apologetic little laugh – "it's from my fiancé saying that . . . saying that—" There was a pause. "I *see*," said Miss Wyatt. And another pause. Then – "You've fifteen minutes more of your class, Miss Meadows, haven't you?"

"Yes, Miss Wyatt." She got up. She half ran towards the door.

"Oh, just one minute, Miss Meadows," said Miss Wyatt. "I must say I don't approve of my teachers having telegrams sent to them in school hours, unless in case of very bad news, such as death," explained Miss Wyatt, "or a very serious accident, or something to that effect. Good news, Miss Meadows, will always keep, you know."

On the wings of hope, of love, of joy, Miss Meadows sped back to the music hall, up the aisle, up the steps, over to the piano.

"Page thirty-two, Mary," she said, "page thirty-two," and, picking up the yellow chrysanthemum, she held it to her lips to hide her smile. Then she turned to the girls, rapped with her baton: "Page thirty-two, girls. Page thirty-two."

> We come here Today with Flowers o'erladen,
> With Baskets of Fruit and Ribbons to boot,
> To-oo Congratulate . . .

"Stop! Stop!" cried Miss Meadows. "This is awful. This is dreadful." And she beamed at her girls. "What's the matter with you all? Think, girls, think of what you're singing. Use your imaginations. *With Flowers o'erladen. Baskets of Fruit and Ribbons to boot.* And *Congratulate.*" Miss Meadows broke off. "Don't look so doleful, girls. It ought to sound warm, joyful, eager. Congratulate. Once more. Quickly. All together. Now then!"

And this time Miss Meadows' voice sounded over all the other voices – full, deep, glowing with expression.

LANGSTON HUGHES

THE BLUES I'M PLAYING

From

THE WAYS OF WHITE FOLK

(1934)

OCEOLA JONES, PIANIST, studied under Philippe in Paris. Mrs Dora Ellsworth paid her bills. The bills included a little apartment on the Left Bank and a grand piano. Twice a year Mrs Ellsworth came over from New York and spent part of her time with Oceola in the little apartment. The rest of her time abroad she usually spent at Biarritz or Juan les Pins, where she would see the new canvases of Antonio Bas, a young Spanish painter who also enjoyed the patronage of Mrs Ellsworth. Bas and Oceola, the woman thought, both had genius. And whether they had genius or not, she loved them, and took good care of them.

Poor dear lady, she had no children of her own. Her husband was dead. And she had no interest in life now save art, and the young people who created art. She was very rich, and it gave her pleasure to share her richness with beauty. Except that she was sometimes confused as to where beauty lay – in the youngsters or in what they made, in the creators or the creation. Mrs Ellsworth had been known to help charming young people who wrote terrible poems, blue-eyed young men who painted awful pictures. And she once turned down a garlic-smelling soprano-singing girl who, a few years later, had all the critics in New York at her feet. The girl was so sallow. And she really needed a bath, or at least a mouth wash, on the day when Mrs Ellsworth went to hear her sing at an East Side settlement house. Mrs Ellsworth had sent a small check and let it go at that – since, however, living to regret bitterly her lack of musical acumen in the face of garlic.

About Oceola, though, there had been no doubt. The Negro girl had been highly recommended to her by Ormond Hunter, the music critic, who often went to Harlem to hear the church concerts there, and had thus listened twice to Oceola's playing.

"A most amazing tone," he had told Mrs Ellsworth, knowing her interest in the young and unusual. "A flair for the piano such as I have seldom encountered. All she needs is training – finish, polish, a repertoire."

"Where is she?" asked Mrs Ellsworth at once. "I will hear her play."

By the hardest, Oceola was found. By the hardest, an appointment was made for her to come to East 63rd Street and play for Mrs Ellsworth. Oceola had said she was busy every day. It seemed that she had pupils, rehearsed a church choir, and played almost nightly for colored house parties or dances. She made quite a good deal of money. She wasn't tremendously interested, it seemed, in going way downtown to play for some elderly lady she had never heard of, even if the request did come from the white critic, Ormond Hunter, via the pastor of the church whose choir she rehearsed, and to which Mr Hunter's maid belonged.

It was finally arranged, however. And one afternoon, promptly on time, black Miss Oceola Jones rang the door bell of white Mrs Dora Ellsworth's grey stone house just off Madison. A butler who actually wore brass buttons opened the door, and she was shown upstairs to the music room. (The butler had been warned of her coming.) Ormond Hunter was already there, and they shook hands. In a moment, Mrs Ellsworth came in, a tall stately grey-haired lady in black with a scarf that sort of floated behind her.

She was tremendously intrigued at meeting Oceola, never having had before amongst all her artists a black one. And she was greatly impressed that Ormond Hunter should have recommended the girl. She began right away, treating her as a protegee; that is, she began asking her a great many questions she would not dare ask anyone else at first meeting, except a protegee. She asked her how old she was and where her mother and father were and how she made her living and whose music she liked best to play and was she married and would she take one lump or two in her tea, with lemon or cream?

After tea, Oceola played. She played the Rachmaninoff *Prelude in G Sharp Minor*. She played from the Liszt *Études*. She played the *St Louis Blues*. She played Ravel's *Pavane pour une Infante Défunte*. And then she said she had to go. She was playing that night for a dance in Brooklyn for the benefit of the Urban League.

Mrs Ellsworth and Ormond Hunter breathed, "How lovely!"

Mrs Ellsworth said, "I am quite overcome, my dear. You play so beautifully." She went on further to say, "You must let me help you. Who is your teacher?"

"I have none now," Oceola replied. "I teach pupils myself. Don't have time any more to study – nor money either."

"But you must have time," said Mrs Ellsworth, "and money, also. Come back to see me on Tuesday. We will arrange it, my dear."

And when the girl had gone, she turned to Ormond Hunter for advice on piano teachers to instruct those who already had genius, and need only to be developed.

2

THEN BEGAN ONE of the most interesting periods in Mrs Ellsworth's whole experience in aiding the arts. The period of Oceola. For the Negro girl, as time went on, began to occupy a greater and greater place in Mrs Ellsworth's interests, to take up more and more of her time, and to use up more and more of her money. Not that Oceola ever asked for money, but Mrs Ellsworth herself seemed to keep thinking of so much more Oceola needed.

At first it was hard to get Oceola to need anything. Mrs Ellsworth had the feeling that the girl mistrusted her generosity, and Oceola did – for she had never met anybody interested in pure art before. Just to be given things for *art's sake* seemed suspicious to Oceola.

That first Tuesday, when the colored girl came back at Mrs Ellsworth's request, she answered the white woman's questions with a why-look in her eyes.

"Don't think I'm being personal, dear," said Mrs Ellsworth, "but I must know your background in order to help you. Now, tell me . . ."

Oceola wondered why on earth the woman wanted to help her. However, since Mrs Ellsworth seemed interested in her life's history, she brought it forth so as not to hinder the progress of the afternoon, for she wanted to get back to Harlem by six o'clock.

Born in Mobile in 1903. Yes, m'am, she was older than she looked. Papa had a band, that is her step-father. Used to play for all the lodge turn-outs, picnics, dances, barbecues. You could get the best roast pig in the world in Mobile. Her mother used to play the organ in church, and when the deacons bought a piano after the big revival, her mama played that, too. Oceola played by ear for a long while until her mother taught her notes. Oceola played an organ, also, and a cornet.

"My, my," said Mrs Ellsworth.

"Yes, m'am," said Oceola. She had played and practiced on lots of instruments in the South before her step-father died. She always went to band rehearsals with him.

"And where was your father, dear?" asked Mrs Ellsworth.

"My step-father had the band," replied Oceola. Her mother left off playing in the church to go with him traveling in Billy Kersands' Minstrels. He had the biggest mouth in the world, Kersands did, and used to let Oceola put both her hands in it at a time and stretch it. Well, she and her mama and step-papa settled down in Houston. Sometimes her parents had jobs and sometimes they didn't. Often they were hungry, but Oceola went to school and had a regular piano teacher, an old German woman, who gave her what technique she had today.

"A fine old teacher," said Oceola. "She used to teach me half the time for nothing. God bless her."

"Yes," said Mrs Ellsworth. "She gave you an excellent foundation."

"Sure did. But my step-papa died, got cut, and after that Mama didn't have no more use for Houston so we moved to St Louis. Mama got a job playing for the movies in a Market Street theater, and I played for a church choir, and saved some money and went to Wilberforce. Studied piano there, too. Played for all the college dances. Graduated. Came to New York and heard Rachmaninoff and was crazy about him. Then Mama died, so I'm keeping the little flat myself. One room is rented out."

"Is she nice," asked Mrs Ellsworth, "your roomer?"

"It's not a she," said Oceola. "He's a man. I hate women roomers."

"Oh!" said Mrs Ellsworth. "I should think all roomers would be terrible."

"He's right nice," said Oceola. "Name's Pete Williams."

"What does he do?" asked Mrs Ellsworth.

"A Pullman porter," replied Oceola, "but he's saving money to go to Med school. He's a smart fellow."

But it turned out later that he wasn't paying Oceola any rent.

That afternoon, when Mrs Ellsworth announced that she had made her an appointment with one of the best piano teachers in New York, the black girl seemed pleased. She recognized the name. But how, she wondered, would she find time for study, with her pupils and her choir, and all. When Mrs Ellsworth said that she would cover her *entire* living expenses, Oceola's eyes were full of that why-look, as though she didn't believe it.

"I have faith in your art, dear," said Mrs Ellsworth, at parting. But to prove it quickly, she sat down that very evening and sent Oceola the first monthly check so that she would no longer have to take in pupils or drill choirs or play at house parties. And so Oceola would have faith in art, too.

That night Mrs Ellsworth called up Ormond Hunter and told him what she had done. And she asked if Mr Hunter's maid knew Oceola, and if she supposed that that man rooming with her were anything to her. Ormond Hunter said he would inquire.

Before going to bed, Mrs Ellsworth told her housekeeper to order a book called "Nigger Heaven" on the morrow, and also anything else Brentano's had about Harlem. She made a mental note that she must go up there sometime, for she had never yet seen that dark section of New York;

and now that she had a Negro protegee, she really ought to know something about it. Mrs Ellsworth couldn't recall ever having known a single Negro before in her whole life, so she found Oceola fascinating. And just as black as she herself was white.

Mrs Ellsworth began to think in bed about what gowns would look best on Oceola. Her protegee would have to be well-dressed. She wondered, too, what sort of a place the girl lived in. And who that man was who lived with her. She began to think that really Oceola ought to have a place to herself. It didn't seem quite respectable. . . .

When she woke up in the morning, she called her car and went by her dressmaker's. She asked the good woman what kind of colors looked well with black; not black fabrics, but a black skin.

"I have a little friend to fit out," she said.

"A *black* friend?" said the dressmaker.

"A black friend," said Mrs Ellsworth.

3

SOME DAYS LATER Ormond Hunter reported on what his maid knew about Oceola. It seemed that the two belonged to the same church, and although the maid did not know Oceola very well, she knew what everybody said about her in the church. Yes, indeedy! Oceola were a right nice girl, for sure, but it certainly were a shame she were giving all her money to that man what stayed with her and what she was practically putting through college so he could be a doctor.

"Why," gasped Mrs Ellsworth, "the poor child is being preyed upon."

"It seems to me so," said Ormond Hunter.

"I must get her out of Harlem," said Mrs Ellsworth, "at once. I believe it's worse than Chinatown."

"She might be in a more artistic atmosphere," agreed Ormond Hunter. "And with her career launched, she probably won't want that man anyhow."

"She won't need him," said Mrs Ellsworth. "She will have her art."

But Mrs Ellsworth decided that in order to increase the rapprochement between art and Oceola, something should be done now, at once. She asked the girl to come down to see her the next day, and when it was time to go home, the white woman said, "I have a half-hour before dinner. I'll drive you up. You know I've never been to Harlem."

"All right," said Oceola. "That's nice of you."

But she didn't suggest the white lady's coming in, when they drew up before a rather sad-looking apartment house in 134th Street. Mrs Ellsworth had to ask could she come in.

"I live on the fifth floor," said Oceola, "and there isn't any elevator."

"It doesn't matter, dear," said the white woman, for she meant to see the inside of this girl's life, elevator or no elevator.

The apartment was just as she thought it would be. After all, she had read Thomas Burke on Limehouse. And here was just one more of those holes in the wall, even if it was five stories high. The windows looked down on slums. There were only four rooms, small as maids' rooms, all of them. An upright piano almost filled the parlor. Oceola slept in the dining-room. The roomer slept in the bed-chamber beyond the kitchen.

"Where is he, darling?"

"He runs on the road all summer," said the girl. "He's in and out."

"But how do you breathe in here?" asked Mrs Ellsworth. "It's so small. You must have more space for your soul, dear. And for a grand piano. Now, in the Village . . ."

"I do right well here," said Oceola.

"But in the Village where so many nice artists live we can get . . ."

"But I don't want to move yet. I promised my roomer he could stay till fall."

"Why till fall?"

"He's going to Meharry then."

"To marry?"

"Meharry, yes m'am. That's a colored Medicine school in Nashville."

"Colored? Is it good?"

"Well, it's cheap," said Oceola. "After he goes, I don't mind moving."

"But I wanted to see you settled before I go away for the summer."

"When you come back is all right. I can do till then."

"Art is long," reminded Mrs Ellsworth, "and time is fleeting, my dear."

"Yes, m'am," said Oceola, "but I gets nervous if I start worrying about time."

So Mrs Ellsworth went off to Bar Harbor for the season, and left the man with Oceola.

4

THAT WAS SOME years ago. Eventually art and Mrs Ellsworth triumphed. Oceola moved out of Harlem. She lived in Gay Street west of Washington Square where she met Genevieve Taggard, and Ernestine Evans, and two or three sculptors, and a cat-painter who was also a protegee of Mrs Ellsworth. She spent her days practicing, playing for friends of her patron, going to concerts, and reading books about music. She no longer had pupils or rehearsed the choir, but she still loved to play for Harlem house parties – for nothing – now that she no longer needed the money, out of sheer love of jazz. This rather disturbed Mrs Ellsworth, who still believed in art of the old school, portraits that really and truly looked like people, poems about nature, music that had soul in it, not syncopation. And she felt the dignity of art. Was it in keeping with genius, she wondered, for Oceola to have a studio full of white and colored people every Saturday night (some of them actually drinking gin *from bottles*) and dancing to the most tomtom-like music she had ever heard coming out of a grand piano? She wished she could lift Oceola up bodily and take her away from all that, for art's sake.

So in the spring, Mrs Ellsworth organized weekends in the up-state mountains where she had a little lodge and where Oceola could look from the high places at the stars, and fill her soul with the vastness of the eternal, and forget about jazz. Mrs Ellsworth really began to hate jazz – especially on a grand piano.

If there were a lot of guests at the lodge, as there sometimes were, Mrs Ellsworth might share the bed with Oceola. Then she would read aloud Tennyson or Browning before turning out the light, aware all the time of the electric strength of that brown-black body beside her, and of the deep drowsy voice asking what the poems were about. And then Mrs Ellsworth would feel very motherly toward this dark girl whom she had taken under her wing on the wonderful road of art, to nurture and love until she became a great interpreter of the piano. At such times the elderly white woman was glad her late husband's money, so well invested, furnished her with a large surplus to devote to the needs of her protegees, especially to Oceola, the blackest – and most interesting of all.

Why the most interesting?

Mrs Ellsworth didn't know, unless it was that Oceola really was talented, terribly alive, and that she looked like nothing Mrs Ellsworth had ever been near before. Such a rich velvet black, and such a hard young body! The teacher of the piano raved about her strength.

"She can stand a great career," the teacher said. "She has everything for it."

"Yes," agreed Mrs Ellsworth, thinking, however, of the Pullman porter at Meharry, "but she must learn to sublimate her soul."

So for two years then, Oceola lived abroad at Mrs Ellsworth's expense. She studied with Philippe, had the little apartment on the Left Bank, and learned about Debussy's African background. She met many black Algerian and French West Indian students, too, and listened to their interminable arguments ranging from Garvey to Picasso to Spengler to Jean Cocteau, and thought they all must be crazy. Why did they or anybody argue so much about life or art? Oceola merely lived – and loved it. Only the Marxian students seemed sound to her for they, at least, wanted people to have enough to eat. That was important, Oceola thought, remembering, as she did, her own sometimes hungry years. But the rest of the controversies, as far as she could fathom, were based on air.

Oceola hated most artists, too, and the word *art* in French or English. If you wanted to play the piano or paint pictures or write books, go ahead! But why talk so much about it? Montparnasse was worse in that respect than the Village.

And as for the cultured Negroes who were always saying art would break down color lines, art could save the race and prevent lynchings! "Bunk!" said Oceola. "My ma and pa were both artists when it came to making music, and the white folks ran them out of town for being dressed up in Alabama. And look at the Jews! Every other artist in the world's a Jew, and still folks hate them."

She thought of Mrs Ellsworth (dear soul in New York), who never made uncomplimentary remarks about Negroes, but frequently did about Jews. Of little Menuhin she would say, for instance, "He's a *genius* – not a Jew," hating to admit his ancestry.

In Paris, Oceola especially loved the West Indian ball rooms where the black colonials danced the beguine. And she liked the entertainers at Bricktop's. Sometimes late at night there, Oceola would take the piano and beat out a blues for Brick and the assembled guests. In her playing of Negro folk music, Oceola never doctored it up, or filled it full of classical runs, or fancy falsities. In the blues she made the bass notes throb like tomtoms, the trebles cry like little flutes, so deep in the earth and so high in the sky that they understood everything. And when the night club crowd would get up and dance to her blues, and Bricktop would yell, "Hey! Hey!" Oceola felt as happy as if she were performing a Chopin étude for the nicely gloved Oh's and Ah-ers in a Crillon salon.

Music, to Oceola, demanded movement and expression, dancing and living to go with it. She liked to teach, when she had the choir, the singing of those rhythmical Negro spirituals that possessed the power to pull colored folks out of their seats in the amen corner and make them prance and shout in the aisles for Jesus. She never liked those fashionable colored churches where shouting and movement were discouraged and looked down upon, and where New England hymns instead of spirituals were sung. Oceola's background was too well-grounded in Mobile, and Billy Kersands' Minstrels, and the Sanctified churches where religion was a joy, to stare mystically over the top of a grand piano like white folks and imagine that Beethoven had nothing to do with life, or that Schubert's love songs were only sublimations.

Whenever Mrs Ellsworth came to Paris, she and Oceola spent hours listening to symphonies and string quartettes and pianists. Oceola enjoyed concerts, but seldom felt, like her patron, that she was floating on clouds of bliss. Mrs Ellsworth insisted, however, that Oceola's spirit was too moved for words at such times – therefore she understood why the dear child kept quiet. Mrs Ellsworth herself was often too moved for words, but never by pieces like Ravel's *Bolero* (which Oceola played on the phonograph as a dance record) or any of the compositions of *les Six*.

What Oceola really enjoyed most with Mrs Ellsworth was not going to concerts, but going for trips on the little river boats in the Seine; or riding out to old chateaux in her patron's hired Renault; or to Versailles, and listening to the aging white lady talk about the romantic history of France, the wars and uprising, the loves and intrigues of princes and kings and queens, about guillotines and lace handkerchiefs, snuff boxes and daggers. For Mrs Ellsworth had loved France as a girl, and had made a study of its life and lore. Once she used to sing simple little French songs rather well, too. And she always regretted that her husband never understood the lovely words – or even tried to understand them.

Oceola learned the accompaniments for all the songs Mrs Ellsworth knew and sometimes they tried them over together. The middle-aged white woman loved to sing when the colored girl played, and she even tried spirituals. Often, when she stayed at the little Paris apartment, Oceola would go into the kitchen and cook something good for late supper, maybe an oyster soup, or fried apples and bacon. And sometimes Oceola had pigs' feet.

"There's nothing quite so good as a pig's foot," said Oceola, "after playing all day."

"Then you must have pigs' feet," agreed Mrs Ellsworth.

And all this while Oceola's development at the piano blossomed into perfection. Her tone became a singing wonder and her interpretations warm and individual. She gave a concert in Paris, one in Brussels, and another in Berlin. She got the press notices all pianists crave. She had her picture in lots of European papers. And she came home to New York a year after the stock market crashed and nobody had any money – except folks like Mrs Ellsworth who had so much it would be hard to ever lose it all.

Oceola's one time Pullman porter, now a coming doctor, was graduating from Meharry that spring. Mrs Ellsworth saw her dark protegee go South to attend his graduation with tears in her eyes. She thought that by now music would be enough, after all those years under the best teachers, but alas, Oceola was not yet sublimated, even by Philippe. She wanted to see Pete.

Oceola returned North to prepare for her New York concert in the fall. She wrote Mrs Ellsworth at Bar Harbor that her doctor boy-friend was putting in one more summer on the railroad, then in the autumn he would intern at Atlanta. And Oceola said that he had asked her to marry him. Lord, she was happy!

It was a long time before she heard from Mrs Ellsworth. When the letter came, it was full of long paragraphs about the beautiful music Oceola had within her power to give the world. Instead, she wanted to marry and be burdened with children! Oh, my dear, my dear!

Oceola, when she read it, thought she had done pretty well knowing Pete this long and not having children. But she wrote back that she didn't see why children and music couldn't go together. Anyway, during the present depression, it was pretty hard for a beginning artist like herself to book a concert tour – so she might just as well be married awhile. Pete, on his last run in from St Louis, had suggested that they have the wedding at Christmas in the South. "And he's impatient, at that. He needs me."

This time Mrs Ellsworth didn't answer by letter at all. She was back in town in late September. In November, Oceola played at Town Hall. The critics were kind, but they didn't go wild. Mrs Ellsworth swore it was because of Pete's influence on her protegee.

"But he was in Atlanta," Oceola said.

"His spirit was here," Mrs Ellsworth insisted. "All the time you were playing on that stage, he was here, the monster! Taking you out of yourself, taking you away from the piano."

"Why, he wasn't," said Oceola. "He was watching an operation in Atlanta."

But from then on, things didn't go well between her and her patron. The white lady grew distinctly cold when she received Oceola in her beautiful drawing room among the jade vases and amber cups worth thousands of dollars. When Oceola would have to wait there for Mrs Ellsworth, she was afraid to move for fear she might knock something over – that would take ten years of a Harlemite's wages to replace, if broken.

Over the tea cups, the aging Mrs Ellsworth did not talk any longer about the concert tour she had once thought she might finance for Oceola, if no recognized bureau took it up. Instead, she spoke of that something she believed Oceola's fingers had lost since her return from Europe. And she wondered why any one insisted on living in Harlem.

"I've been away from my own people so long," said the girl, "I want to live right in the middle of them again."

Why, Mrs Ellsworth wondered further, did Oceola, at her last concert in a Harlem church, not stick to the classical items listed on the program. Why did she insert one of her own variations on the spirituals, a syncopated variation from the Sanctified Church, that made an old colored lady rise up and cry out from her pew, "Glory to God this evenin'! Yes! Hallelujah! Whooo-oo!" right at the concert? Which seemed most undignified to Mrs Ellsworth, and unworthy of the teachings of Philippe. And furthermore, why was Pete coming up to New York for Thanksgiving? And who had sent him the money to come?

"Me," said Oceola. "He doesn't make anything interning."

"Well," said Mrs Ellsworth, "I don't think much of him." But Oceola didn't seem to care what Mrs Ellsworth thought, for she made no defense.

Thanksgiving evening, in bed, together in a Harlem apartment, Pete and Oceola talked about their wedding to come. They would have a big one in a church with lots of music. And Pete would give her a ring. And she would have on a white dress, light and fluffy, not silk. "I hate silk," she said. "I hate expensive things." (She thought of her mother being buried in a cotton dress, for they were all broke when she died. Mother would have been glad about her marriage.) "Pete," Oceola said, hugging him in the dark, "let's live in Atlanta, where there are lots of colored people, like us."

"What about Mrs Ellsworth?" Pete asked. "She coming down to Atlanta for our wedding?"

"I don't know," said Oceola.

"I hope not, 'cause if she stops at one of them big hotels, I won't have you going to the back door to see her. That's one thing I hate about the South – where there're white people, you have to go to the back door."

"Maybe she can stay with us," said Oceola. "I wouldn't mind."

"I'll be damned," said Pete. "You want to get lynched?"

But it happened that Mrs Ellsworth didn't care to attend the wedding, anyway. When she saw how love had triumphed over art, she decided she could no longer influence Oceola's life. The period of Oceola was over. She would send checks, occasionally, if the girl needed them, besides, of course, something beautiful for the wedding, but that would be all. These things she told her the week after Thanksgiving.

"And Oceola, my dear, I've decided to spend the whole winter in Europe. I sail on December eighteenth. Christmas – while you are marrying – I shall be in Paris with my precious Antonio Bas. In January, he has an exhibition of oils in Madrid. And in the spring, a new young poet is coming over whom I want to visit Florence, to really know Florence. A charming white-haired boy from Omaha whose soul has been crushed in the West. I want to try to help him. He, my dear, is one of the few people who live for their art – and nothing else. . . . Ah, such a beautiful life! . . . You will come and play for me once before I sail?"

"Yes, Mrs Ellsworth," said Oceola, genuinely sorry that the end had come. Why did white folks think you could live on nothing but art? Strange! Too strange! Too strange!

THE PERSIAN VASES in the music room were filled with long-stemmed lilies that night when Oceola Jones came down from Harlem for the last time to play for Mrs Dora Ellsworth. Mrs Ellsworth had on a gown of black velvet, and a collar of pearls about her neck. She was very kind and gentle to Oceola, as one would be to a child who has done a great wrong but doesn't know any better. But to the black girl from Harlem, she looked very cold and white, and her grand piano seemed like the biggest and heaviest in the world – as Oceola sat down to play it with the technique for which Mrs Ellsworth had paid.

As the rich and aging white woman listened to the great roll of Beethoven sonatas and to the sea and moonlight of the Chopin nocturnes, as she watched the swaying dark strong shoulders of Oceola Jones, she began to reproach the girl aloud for running away from art and music, for burying herself in Atlanta and love – love for a man unworthy of lacing up her boot straps, as Mrs Ellsworth put it.

"You could shake the stars with your music, Oceola. Depression or no depression, I could make you great. And yet you propose to dig a grave for yourself. Art is bigger than love."

"I believe you, Mrs Ellsworth," said Oceola, not turning away from the piano. "But being married won't keep me from making tours, or being an artist."

"Yes, it will," said Mrs Ellsworth. "He'll take all the music out of you."

"No, he won't," said Oceola.

"You don't know, child," said Mrs Ellsworth, "what men are like."

"Yes, I do," said Oceola simply. And her fingers began to wander slowly up and down the keyboard, flowing into the soft and lazy syncopation of a Negro blues, a blues that deepened and grew into rollicking jazz, then into an earth-throbbing rhythm that shook the lilies in the Persian vases of Mrs Ellsworth's music room. Louder than the voice of the white woman who cried that Oceola was deserting beauty, deserting her real self, deserting her hope in life, the flood of wild syncopation filled the house, then sank into the slow and singing blues with which it had begun.

The girl at the piano heard the white woman saying, "Is this what I spent thousands of dollars to teach you?"

"No," said Oceola simply. "This is mine. . . . Listen! . . . How sad and gay it is. Blue and happy – laughing and crying. . . . How white like you and black like me. . . . How much like a man. . . . And how like a woman. . . . Warm as Pete's mouth. . . . These are the blues. . . . I'm playing."

Mrs Ellsworth sat very still in her chair looking at the lilies trembling delicately in the priceless Persian vases, while Oceola made the bass notes throb like tomtoms deep in the earth.

O, if I could holler

sang the blues,

Like a mountain jack,
I'd go up on de mountain

sang the blues,

And call my baby back.

"And I," said Mrs Ellsworth rising from her chair, "would stand looking at the stars."

REHEARSAL

VIKRAM SETH

From

AN EQUAL MUSIC
(1999)

From PART ONE

1

THE BRANCHES ARE bare, the sky tonight a milky violet. It is not quiet here, but it is peaceful. The wind ruffles the black water towards me.

There is no one about. The birds are still. The traffic slashes through Hyde Park. It comes to my ears as white noise.

I test the bench but do not sit down. As yesterday, as the day before, I stand until I have lost my thoughts. I look at the water of the Serpentine.

Yesterday as I walked back across the park I paused at a fork in the footpath. I had the sense that someone had paused behind me. I walked on. The sound of footsteps followed along the gravel. They were unhurried; they appeared to keep pace with me. Then they suddenly made up their mind, speeded up, and overtook me. They belonged to a man in a thick black overcoat, quite tall – about my height – a young man from his gait and attitude, though I did not see his face. His sense of hurry was now evident. After a while, unwilling so soon to cross the blinding Bayswater Road, I paused again, this time by the bridle path. Now I heard the faint sound of hooves. This time, however, they were not embodied. I looked to left, to right. There was nothing.

As I approach Archangel Court I am conscious of being watched. I enter the hallway. There are flowers here, a concoction of gerberas and general foliage. A camera surveys the hall. A watched building is a secure building, a secure building a happy one.

A few days ago I was told I was happy by the young woman behind the counter at Etienne's. I ordered seven croissants. As she gave me my change she said: "You are a happy man."

I stared at her with such incredulity that she looked down.

"You're always humming," she said in a much quieter voice, feeling perhaps that she had to explain.

"It's my work," I said, ashamed of my bitterness. Another customer entered the shop, and I left.

As I put my week's croissants – all except one – in the freezer, I noticed I was humming the same half-tuneless tune of one of Schubert's last songs:

> *I see a man who stares upwards*
> *And wrings his hands from the force of his pain.*
> *I shudder when I see his face.*
> *The moon reveals myself to me.*

I put the water on for coffee, and look out of the window. From the eighth floor I can see as far as St Paul's, Croydon, Highgate. I can look across the brown-branched park to spires and towers and chimneys beyond. London unsettles me – even from such a height there is no clear countryside to view.

But it is not Vienna. It is not Venice. It is not, for that matter, my hometown in the North, in clear reach of the moors.

It wasn't my work, though, that made me hum that song. I have not played Schubert for more than a month. My violin misses him more than I do. I tune it, and we enter my soundproof cell. No light, no sound comes in from the world. Electrons along copper, horsehair across acrylic create my impressions of sense.

I will play nothing of what we have played in our quartet, nothing that reminds me of my recent music-making with any human being. I will play his songs.

The Tononi seems to purr at the suggestion. Something happy, something happy, surely:

> *In a clear brook*
> *With joyful haste*
> *The whimsical trout*
> *Shot past me like an arrow.*

I play the line of the song, I play the leaps and plunges of the right hand of the piano, I am the trout, the angler, the brook, the observer. I sing the words, bobbing my constricted chin. The Tononi does not object; it resounds. I play it in B, in A, in E flat. Schubert does not object. I am not transposing his string quartets.

Where a piano note is too low for the violin, it leaps into a higher octave. As it is, it is playing the songline an octave above its script. Now, if it were a viola . . . but it has been years since I played the viola.

The last time was when I was a student in Vienna ten years ago. I return there again and again and think: was I in error? Was I unseeing? Where was the balance of pain between the two of us? What I lost there I have never come near to retrieving.

What happened to me so many years ago? Love or no love, I could not continue in that city. I stumbled, my mind jammed, I felt the pressure of every breath. I told her I was going, and went. For two months I could do nothing, not even write to her. I came to London. The smog dispersed but too late. Where are you now, Julia, and am I not forgiven?

2

VIRGINIE WILL NOT practise, yet demands these lessons. I have worse students – more cavalier, that is – but none so frustrating.

I walk across the park to her flat. It is over-heated and there is a great deal of pink. This used not to unnerve me. Now when I step into the bathroom I recoil.

Pink bath, pink basin, pink toilet, pink bidet, pink tiles, pink wallpaper, pink rug. Brushes, soap, toothbrushes, silk flowers, toilet paper: all pink. Even the little foot-operated waste-bin is pale pink. I know this little waste-bin well. Every time I sleep here I wonder what I am doing with my time and hers. She is sixteen years younger than I am. She is not the woman with whom I want to share my life. But, having begun, what we have continues. She wants it to, and I go along with it, through lust and loneliness, I suppose; and laziness, and lack of focus.

Our lessons are a clear space. Today it is a partita by Bach: the E major. I ask her to play it all the way through, but after the Gavotte I tell her to stop.

"Don't you want to know how it ends?" she asks cheerfully.

"You haven't practised much."

She achieves an expression of guilt.

"Go back to the beginning," I suggest.

"Of the Gavotte?"

"Of the Prelude."

"You mean bar seventeen? I know, I know, I should use always my wrist for the E string."

"I mean bar one."

Virginie looks sulky. She sets her bow down on a pale pink silk cushion.

"Virginie, it's not that you can't do it, it's just that you aren't doing it."

"Doing what?"

"Thinking about the music. Sing the first phrase, just sing it."

She picks up the bow.

"I meant, with your voice."

Virginie sighs. In tune, and with exactitude, she goes: "Me-re-mi si sol si mi-fa-mi-re-mi . . ."

"Can't you ever sing without those nonsense syllables?"

"That's how I was taught." Her eyes flash.

Virginie comes from Nyons, about which I know nothing other than that it is somewhere near Avignon. She asked me twice to go there with her, then stopped asking.

"Virginie, it's not just one damn note after another. That second mi-re-mi should carry some memory of the first. Like this." I pick up my fiddle and demonstrate. "Or like this. Or in some way of your own."

She plays it again, and plays it well, and goes on. I close my eyes. A huge bowl of pot-pourri assails my senses. It is getting dark. Winter is upon us. How young she is, how little she works. She is only twenty-one. My mind wanders to another city, to the memory of another woman, who was as young then.

"Should I go on?"

"Yes."

I tell Virginie to keep her wrist free, to watch her intonation here, to mind her dynamics there, to keep her détaché even – but she knows all this. Next week there will be some progress, very little. She is talented, yet she will not apply herself. Though she is supposedly a full-time student, music for her is only one of many things. She is anxious about the college competition for which she will perform this partita.

She is thinking of selling her Miremont, and getting her father – who supports her unstudentlike standard of living – to buy her something early and Italian. She has a grand circle of acquaintance here, scores of friends from all over France who descend on her in every season, vast linked clans of relatives, and three ex-boyfriends with whom she is on good terms. She and I have been together for more than a year now.

As for the one I remember, I see her with her eyes closed, playing Bach to herself: an English suite. Gently her fingers travel among the keys. Perhaps I move too suddenly. The beloved eyes turn towards me. There are so many beings here, occupied, pre-occupied. Let me believe that she breathes, that she still exists, somewhere on this chance sphere

3

THE MAGGIORE QUARTET is gathering for a rehearsal at our standard venue, Helen's little two-storey mews house.

Helen is preparing coffee. Only she and I are here. The afternoon sunlight slants in. A woman's velvety voice sings Cole Porter. Four dark blue armless chairs are arranged in an arc beneath a minimalist pine bookshelf. A viola case and a couple of music stands rest in the corner of the open-plan kitchen-living-dining room.

"One? Two?" asks Helen. "I keep forgetting. I wonder why. It's not the sort of thing one forgets when one is, well, used to someone's coffee habits. But you don't have a habit with sugar, do you? Sometimes you don't have any at all. Oh, I met someone yesterday who was asking after you. Nicholas Spare. Such an awful man, but the more waspish he gets the more they read him. Get him to review us, Michael. He has a crush on you, I'm sure he does. He frowns whenever I mention you."

"Thanks, Helen. That's all I need."

"So do I, of course."

"No crushes on colleagues."

"You're not all that gorgeous."

"What's new on the gardening front?"

"It's November, Michael," says Helen. "Besides, I'm off gardening. Here's your coffee. What do you think of my hair?"

Helen has red hair, and her hairstyle changes annually. This year it is ringleted with careless care. I nod approval and concentrate on my coffee.

The doorbell rings. It is Piers, her elder brother, our first violinist.

He enters, ducking his head slightly. He kisses his sister – who is only a couple of inches shorter – says hello to me, takes off his elegant-shabby greatcoat, gets out his violin and mutters, "Could you turn that off? I'm trying to tune up."

"Oh, just till the end of this track," says Helen.

Piers turns the player off himself. Helen says nothing. Piers is used to getting his way.

"Where the fuck is Billy?" he asks. "He's always late for rehearsal. Has he called?"

Helen shakes her head. "That's what happens, I suppose, if you live in Loughton or Leyton or wherever."

"Leytonstone," I say.

"Of course," says Helen, feigning enlightenment. London for her means Zone 1. All of us except Billy live quite centrally, in or near Bayswater, within walking distance of Hyde Park and Kensington Gardens, though in very different conditions. Piers is quite often irritable, even resentful, for a few minutes after arriving at Helen's. He lives in a basement studio.

After a while Helen quietly asks him how he enjoyed last night. Piers went to listen to the Steif Quartet, whom he has admired for many years, play an all-Beethoven concert.

"Oh, OK," grumbles Piers. "But you can never tell with the Steif. Last night they were going in heavily for beauty of tone – pretty narcissistic. And I'm beginning to dislike the first violinist's face: it looks more and more pinched every year. And after they finished playing the *Grosse Fuge*, they leapt up as if they had just killed a lion. Of course the audience went mad . . . Has Erica called?"

"No . . . So you didn't like the concert."

"I didn't say that," says Piers. "Where is bloody Billy? We should fine him a chocolate biscuit for every minute he's late." Having tuned up, he plays a rapid figure in pizzicato quartertones.

"What was that?" asks Helen, almost spilling her coffee. "No, no, no, don't play it again."

"An attempt at composition à la Billy."

"That's not fair," says Helen.

Piers smiles a sort of left-handed smile. "Billy's only a fledgling. One day twenty years from now, he'll grow into the full monster, write something gratingly awful for Covent Garden – if it's still there – and wake up as Sir William Cutler."

Helen laughs, then pulls herself up. "Now, now, no talking behind each other's backs," she says.

"I'm a bit worried," continues Piers. "Billy's been talking far too much about what he's working on." He turns to me for a reaction.

"Has he actually suggested we play something he's written?" I ask.

"No. Not actually. Not yet. It's just a pricking of my thumbs."

"Why don't we wait and see if he does?" I suggest.

"I'm not for it," says Helen slowly. "It would be dreadful if we didn't like it – I mean if it really sounded like your effusion."

Piers smiles again, not very pleasantly.

"Well, I don't see the harm in reading it through once," I say.

"What if some of us like it and some don't?" asks Helen. "A quartet is a quartet. This could lead to all sorts of tensions. But surely it would be worse if Billy's grumpy the whole time. So there it is."

"Helenic logic," says Piers.

"But I like Billy—" begins Helen.

"So do we all," Piers interrupts. "We all love each other, that goes without saying. But in this matter, the three of us should think out our position – our joint position – clearly, before Billy presents us with a fourth Razumovsky."

Before we can speak further, Billy arrives. He lugs his cello in exhaustedly, apologises, looks cheerful when he sees the chocolate biscuits that Helen knows are his favourites, gobbles down a few, receives his coffee gratefully, apologises again, and begins tuning.

"Lydia took the car – dentist. Mad rush – almost forgot the music for the Brahms. Central Line – terrible." Sweat shines on his forehead and he is breathing heavily. "I'm sorry. I'm sorry. I'm sorry. I'll never be late again. Never ever."

"Have another biscuit, Billy," says Helen affectionately.

"Get a mobile phone, Billy," says Piers in a lazy-peremptory prefect-like tone.

"Why?" asks Billy. "Why should I? Why should I get a mobile phone? I'm not a pimp or a plumber."

Piers shakes his head and lets it go. Billy is far too fat, and always will be. He will always be distracted by family and money worries, car insurance and composition. For all our frustration and rebuke, he will never be on time. But the moment his bow comes down on the strings he is transfigured. He is a wonderful cellist, light and profound: the base of our harmony, the rock on which we rest.

4

EVERY REHEARSAL OF the Maggiore Quartet begins with a very plain, very slow three-octave scale on all four instruments in unison: sometimes major, as in our name, sometimes minor, depending on the key of the first piece we are to play. No matter how fraught our lives have been over the last couple of days, no matter how abrasive our disputes about people or politics, or how visceral our differences about what we are to play and how we are to play it, it reminds us that we are, when it comes to it, one. We try not to look at each other when we play this scale; no one appears to lead. Even the first upbeat is merely breathed by Piers, not indicated by any movement of his head. When I play this I release myself into the spirit of the quartet. I become the music of the scale. I mute my will, I free myself.

After Alex Foley left five years ago and I was being considered as a possible second violinist by Piers, Helen and Billy, we tried out various bits of music together, rehearsed together, in fact played several concerts together, but never played the scale. I did not even know that for them it existed. Our last concert was in Sheffield. At midnight, two hours after it was over, Piers phoned me in my hotel room to say that they all wanted me to join.

"It was good, Michael," he said. "Helen insists you *belong* to us." Despite this little barb, aimed at his sister, doubtless present at the other end, he sounded almost elated – quite something for Piers. Two days later, back in London, we met for a rehearsal and began, this time, with the scale. As it rose, calm and almost without vibrato, I felt my happiness build. When it paused at the top before descending, I glanced at my new colleagues, to left and to right. Piers had slightly averted his face. It astonished me. Piers is hardly the sort of musician who weeps soundlessly at the beauty of scales. I had no idea at the time what was going through his mind. Perhaps, in playing the scale again, he was in some sense letting Alex go.

Today we are running through a couple of Haydn quartets and a Brahms. The Haydns are glorious; they give us joy. Where there are difficulties, we can understand them – and therefore come to an understanding among ourselves. We love Haydn, and he makes us love each other. Not so Brahms. He has always been a cross for our quartet.

I feel no affinity for Brahms, Piers can't stand him, Helen adores him, Billy finds him "deeply interesting", whatever that means. We were asked to include some Brahms in a programme we are due to perform in Edinburgh, and Piers, as our programmer, accepted the inevitable and chose the first string quartet, the C minor.

We saw valiantly away through the first movement without stopping.

"Good tempo," says Helen tentatively, looking at the music rather than at any of us.

"A bit turgid, I thought. We aren't the Busch Quartet," I say.

"You better not say anything against the Busch," says Helen.

"I'm not. But they were them and we are us."

"Talk of arrogance," says Helen.

"Well, should we go on? Or clean up?" I ask.

"Clean up," snaps Piers. "It's a total mess."

"Precision's the key," says Billy, half to himself. "Like with the Schoenberg."

Helen sighs. We begin playing again. Piers stops us. He looks directly at me.

"It's you, Michael. You're sort of suddenly intense without any reason. You're not supposed to be saying anything special."

"Well, he tells me to express."

"Where?" asks Piers, as if to an idiot-child. "Just precisely where?"

"Bar fifteen."

"I don't have anything there."

"Bad luck," I say shortly. Piers looks over at my part in disbelief.

"Rebecca's getting married to Stuart," says Helen.

"What?" says Piers, jogged out of his concentration. "You're kidding."

"No, I'm not. I heard it from Sally. And Sally heard it directly from Rebecca's mother."

"Stuart!" says Piers. "Oh God. All her babies will be born brain-dead."

Billy and I exchange glances. There is something jerky, abrasive, irrelevant about many of our conversations during rehearsals which sits oddly with the exactitude and expressivity we are seeking to create. Helen, for instance, usually says the first thing that comes into her head. Sometimes her thoughts run ahead of her words; sometimes it's the other way around.

"Let's go on," suggests Billy.

We play for a few minutes. There is a series of false starts, no sense of flow.

"I'm just not coming out," says Billy. "I feel like such a wimp four bars before B."

"And Piers comes in like a gobbling turkey at forty-one," says Helen.

"Don't be nasty, Helen," says her brother.

Finally we come to Piers's high crescendo.

"Oh no, oh no, oh no," cries Billy, taking his hand off the strings and gesticulating.

"We're all a bit loud here," says Helen, aiming for tact.

"It's too hysterical," I say.

"Who's too hysterical?" asks Piers.

"You." The others nod.

Piers's rather large ears go red.

"You've got to cool that vibrato," says Billy. "It's like heavy breathing on the phone."

"OK," says Piers grimly. "And can you be a bit darker at one-oh-eight, Billy?"

It isn't usually like this. Most of our rehearsals are much more convivial. I blame it on what we're playing.

"We're not getting anywhere as a whole," says Billy with a kind of innocent agitation in his eyes. "That was terribly organised."

"As in organised terribly?" I ask.

"Yes. We've got to get it together somehow. It's just a sort of noise."

"It's called Brahms, Billy," says Piers.

"You're just prejudiced," says Helen. "You'll come around to him."

"In my dotage."

"Why don't we plan a structure around the tunes?" Billy suggests.

"Well, it sort of lacks tunes," I say. "Not melody exactly, but melodicity. Do I mean that? What's the right word?"

"Melodiousness," says Helen. "And, incidentally, it doesn't lack tunes."

"But what do you mean by that?" says Piers to me. "It's all tune. I mean, I'm not saying I like it, but . . ."

I point my bow at Piers's music. "Is that tune? I doubt even Brahms would claim that was tune."

"Well, it's not arpeggio, it's not scale, it's not ornament, so . . . oh, I don't know. It's all mad and clogged up. Bloody Edinburgh . . ."

"Stop ranting, Piers," says Helen. "You played that last bit really well. I loved that slide. It was quite a shock, but it's great. You've got to keep it."

Piers is startled by the praise, but soon recovers. "But Billy now sounds completely unvibrato'd," he says.

"That was me trying to get a darker colour," counters Billy.

"Well, it sounds gravelly."

"Shall I get a new cello?" asks Billy. "After I've bought my mobile phone?"

Piers grunts. "Why don't you just go up the C-string?"

"It's too woofy."

"Once more, then? From ninety-two?" I suggest.

"No, from the double bar," says Helen.

"No, from seventy-five," says Billy.

"OK," says Piers.

After a few more minutes we pause again.

"This is just so exhausting to play," says Helen. "To get these notes to work you have to dig each one out. It's not like the violin . . ."

"Poor Helen," I say, smiling at her. "Why don't you swap instruments with me?"

"Cope, Helen," says Piers. "Brahms is your baby."

Helen sighs. "Say something nice, Billy."

But Billy is now concentrating on a little yellow score that he has brought along.

"My deodorant experiment isn't a success," says Helen suddenly, raising one creamy arm.

"We'd better get on with it or we'll never get through it," says Billy.

Finally, after an hour and a half we arrive at the second movement. It is dark outside, and we are exhausted, as much with one another's temperaments as with the music. But ours is an odd quadripartite marriage with six relationships, any of which, at any given time, could be cordial or neutral or strained. The audiences who listen to us cannot imagine how earnest, how petulant, how accommodating, how wilful is our quest for something beyond ourselves that we imagine with our separate spirits but are compelled to embody together. Where is the harmony of spirit in all this, let alone sublimity? How are such mechanics, such stops and starts, such facile irreverence transmuted, in spite of our bickering selves, into musical gold? And yet often enough it is from such trivial beginnings that we arrive at an understanding of a work that seems to us both true and original, and an expression of it which displaces from our minds – and perhaps, at least for a while, from the minds of those who hear us – any versions, however true, however original, played by other hands.

DAVID GATES

From
PRESTON FALLS
(1998)

PART TWO, CHAPTER 4

WHEN WILLIS WAKES up it feels like late afternoon, and the Unnamable's rigid. Sort of tries to polish himself off but can't think what to think of. The temptation: Tina bent over in biker shorts. Some taboo there he can't articulate.

He goes downstairs, pisses, starts coffee. Clock says 3:27. Only *mid*-afternoon. Wednesday? So it's tonight he's supposed to go jam with What's-his-name. An hour to get there, probably, and an hour back. Which is crazy. But to play with actual people again? And if he stayed here he'd do what – lie on the couch reading books where the men say *Damme, Sir!* and the women are named shit like Louisa. Peter somebody – no, Philip. Philip Reed. He'd have to leave around eight. So four and a half hours to kill? Well, cook some oatmeal and take a shower and you're down to four. Play guitar a little to get the feel, maybe take another crack at that ceiling? He ends up reading more of *Dombey and Son*.

It's dark again when he loads the Twin and the Tele into the back of the truck. He sticks the guitar stand behind the seat, then decides he'll look like a dilettante and takes it back to the house. Then he wastes more time dithering over tapes; he ends up with Buddy Guy for the drive there, to make his playing subliminally blues-drenched, and Public Enemy to keep him awake on the way back.

He stops at the cash machine in Preston Falls and gets FAST CASH $40. Pitiful: in Chesterton it's FAST CASH $100. But he's only got about a thousand to last him these two months, and nothing coming in. Then over to Stewart's, where he pours a cup of coffee and pisses away a dollar and a quarter of his forty on a *Want Ad Digest*. Showing up early would be pushy, so he sits in a booth and looks through Musical Instruments, Motorcycles, Personals and Farm Equipment. He'd like to find an affordable 8N with a brush hog, not that he could afford it. The coffee gets him queasy, so he goes back up to the counter and buys a kaiser roll with butter *and* peanut butter, on the theory that it's porous. Then he feels as if something big is swelling inside him, pushing up on his heart. Willis and his body, those ancient enemies.

Halfway to Sandgate, he remembers he forgot Calvin Castleman's fucking hundred and fifty dollars.

Philip Reed's directions turn out to be good. The house either is or is not lime green (too dark to tell), but it sure does have a plastic gila monster on the porch roof. Fucker's the size of a German shepherd and glowing, lit from within; you can see the cord going into its mouth. Party boys. Willis comes jolting up the two-rut driveway past the house, as instructed, to a barn where he recognizes Reed's Z-whatever between a rusted-out Econoline van and an old bulbous Volvo from the days before they made them boxy. When he cuts the engine he can hear electric guitars tuning.

He hauls his guitar and amp through the tall barn door, held open by a cinderblock, and follows the sound up steep, trembling stairs to a hayloft, resting that fucking Fender Twin on every other step. When his head clears the floor of the loft, he can see a few sagging brown haybales and, in the far corner, a giant cube of cloudy plastic sheeting over a frame of two-by-fours, and the blurred, faceless forms of people inside. What might be a billed cap. A red shirt. A guitar neck, probably. Willis lugs his stuff over to where two sheets of plastic overlap, parts them with his guitar case and gets a skunky noseful of reefer.

Reed's kneeling on the shag carpeting that covers the hilly floorboards, plugging cords into a couple of stomp boxes, a black Les Paul slung over his shoulder on a tooled-leather strap. He looks up and says, "Hey, *here's* the man."

"I think I found the right place," Willis says, and sportively sniffs the air. There's a drum set (a fat longhair is tightening a snare), a mixing board set up on a card table, two old-time capsule-shaped mikes on mike stands, two speaker horns on sturdy tripods, two scuffed-up floor monitors. For decor, campy LP covers pushpinned to a beam: Lawrence Welk with lifted baton, Sgt Barry Sadler, Jim Nabors, some goony-looking country singer even Willis doesn't recognize: *This Is Tommy Collins*. A rusty oil-drum stove resting on cinderblocks, with a salvaged piece of corrugated aluminum roofing underneath: the stovepipe sticks right out through a circular hole in the wood siding, without a baffle, or flange, whatever you call it.

"Gentlemen?" says Reed. "Doug Willis."

"Hey."

"Hey."

"Okay, we got Sparky" – leveling a finger at the fat-boy drummer – "and Dan" – finger moving to a tall, lanky guy in a plaid hunting cap with the earflaps down – "and Mitch" – to a short guy with bug-eye sunglasses and a red shirt, wearing a low-slung Strat that looks too big on him.

The little Strat guy nods at Willis's case. "So what have we here?"

"Tele," says Willis. "Nothing special. Early seventies."

"Cool," the little guy says. "Come on, early seventies? They hadn't gone to shit *then*. By *any* means."

"Yeah, me either," says Willis.

"You got *that* right," says the drummer. He cocks his head and hits the snare once with a drumstick. Shakes his head.

"So whip it out," says Reed.

"Yeah yeah, whip it out," says the little guy.

"You fuckin' guitar sharks," the drummer says. "Man just *got* here. Here, man – I forgot your name." He offers Willis a stubby brass pipe from an ashtray sitting on his floor tom.

"Oh right," says the one with the earflaps. "Get the fuckin' guy dusted, good idea. Everybody ain't a fuckin' animal like you, man, that they can play behind *that* shit." He picks up a Fender P-bass with most of the finish worn off.

"Fuck you, man," says the drummer. "Try to hoover up enough of that shit of yours to get off, man, I fuckin' choke to death."

"Gentlemen, gentlemen," says Reed.

"Why don't you plug in over there?" says the bass player. He points to a power strip that's plugged, in turn, into an orange cord snaking outdoors through a knothole.

"Here, I got some weed here that's just weed." Reed takes a half-smoked joint out of his shirt pocket.

Willis holds up a hand. "No, I'm good. I just had a bunch of coffee." He stopped smoking dope years ago: officially because it made it harder to stay off cigarettes, actually because it made people around him seem evil. These people *already* seem evil.

"Well, listen," says the bass player, taking his bass off again. "I'm a do a couple lines here and like whoever wants to join me."

"Ah hell," Reed says.

"*Ho*-yeah," says the little Strat guy. "Yeh-yeh-yeh." He puts his tongue out and pants like a dog, which is all Willis needs to cross *him* off.

"Twist my arm," says the drummer.

"Hey, twist my *dick*," says the bass player. "I thought you said you choke to death."

"Hey, I *like* to choke, man." General laughter. "Like those dudes that hang theirself to get a boner, you know?"

"Hmm," Willis says. "I guess a little of *that* never hurt anybody." Suddenly he feels like he has to shit: the excitement of being bad.

The bass player has taken the pushpins out of *This Is Tommy Collins* and set it on top of his amp. He pours white powder from a Band-Aid box onto Tommy Collins's sincere face, and hands the little guitar guy a box of plastic straws and a pair of orange-handled scissors. "Hey, anybody got anything with some kinda edge?" he says. "Never mind, fuck it." He grabs a cassette, dumps out the tape and the paper insert – Stevie Ray Vaughn and Double Trouble – and uses the plastic box to chop and scrape and push the shit into a pair of parallel lines. The little guitar guy hands him a two-inch length of straw, and he bends down and hoovers them up. Then sinks to sit on the floor, snuffling and flogging his nose with his index finger, saying "Wowser."

Willis scrapes together a pair of lines half as long and half as wide, out of both good manners and caution. He snorts a line into each nostril; it stings his sinuses and begins dripping and burning down the back of his throat. Except that his heart's racing just a teeny bit – which is probably just psychological because he's all of, what, five seconds into this – he actually feels surprisingly great, though he does hope his heart won't start going any faster.

He watches the little Strat guy take his turn. Shit, these aren't bad people. He'd actually really like to get to *know* them. "So," he says, "you guys are all married?"

This gets a big laugh. Willis didn't realize what a really funny thing it was to say at this juncture, but he now feels privileged to have the secret key to cocaine humor: to be completely out there, yet at the same time right *in* there.

"Hey, Counselor," the little guy says, "you better step up to the plate. This shit is so fucking excellent, man. It's definitely Howdy Doody Time."

"You're dating yourself," says Reed, straw poised above two ridges of powder.

"Fuck it," says the drummer. "I'm a fuckin' get ripped." He picks up his pipe and starts slapping at his shirt pockets with his other hand, right side, left side, right side.

"Like you ain't fuckin' ripped already." The bass player's back on his feet. "Here, this what you're after?" He hands the drummer a pink butane lighter.

"So we in tune here approximately?" says Reed. "Whew. Holy shit."

"Yeh-yeh-yeh, let's do it," says the little guy. "Break out that bad-ass Telecaster, man."

"Absolutely," says Willis. He opens his case, *snap snap*, and slings his guitar on. "Anybody got a tuner?"

Reed hisses and makes a vampire-repelling cross with his index fingers. "We're strictly organic here. Fuckin' goat cheese, whatever. Mitch, you're in with yourself, right? Whatta you got for an E?"

So they all stand there stoned as pigs, tuning for about eight hours. Twang twang. De de de de de. With the tuner this would take two seconds. But on the other hand it's great, like lights going down at the movies.

"Dan, you somewhere close?" Reed says.

"Fuck if *I* know." The bass player flips his amp off standby, twaddles strings with the first two fingers of his right hand, and big notes come booming out. "Somebody give me a fuckin' G?"

They all stroke G chords at him.

"Yeah, how about just one a you?" he says. The little guy plays a G chord and the bass player starts hitting harmonics and cranking at his tuning pegs, trying to get one howl up level with another howl. "Golden," he says, though it doesn't sound like he's improved things any. "So what are we doing?"

"Can you play 'Far, Far Away'?" says Reed. "Rimshot – where's the rimshot?" He turns around to the drummer. "Ah fuck." The drummer's lying on the floor; he's taken the round seat cushion off its chrome-plated tripod to pillow his head.

"Hey, what about 'Walk This Way'?" says the little guy. "You do 'Walk This Way,' right?" He plays the riff at Willis.

"You know I actually never have?" says Willis. Aerosmith was always too thug for him. "I mean, I *know* the tune."

"You'll pick it right up. Starts off in E, man, then the verse goes to C, like *yah dah DAHT!* up from B flat, like." He plays it to demonstrate, yelling *yah dah DAHT!* as he moves the bar chord up the three frets.

"Right," says Willis. *Normally* this would be within his scope. "Play the hook again? The E part?"

He plays it at Willis again and, amazingly, Willis plays it back at him. Either cocaine is a miracle drug or this hook is something a retard could play. "Yup," says the little guitar guy. "That'll work. Okay? 'Walk This Way'? Starts with the drum thing?"

"Let me get my shit together just a minute here," the drummer says from down on the floor.

"Oh fuck," says the little guy. "Fuckin' Sparky, man."

"Hmm," says Reed. "Looks like time to bring in Iron Mike."

The little guy winces. "Oh *man*? I *hate* fuckin' playing with a fuckin' drum machine. I mean, what do we have a fuckin' real drummer for?"

"Makes a great conversation piece," Reed says. "You got to give him that."

"No problem, man." The drummer's eyes are closed. "Use the thing for a couple songs, man. I'm gonna be right with you."

"Unbelievable," says the little guy. "*Sparky*, man."

"Fuck him. Forget it," Reed says. "So what are we doing, again?"

" 'Walk This Way,' " says the little guy.

"Okay, cool. You got the tune programmed in there, right?"

"That's not the point, man. You know what I'm saying? Last time we played the Cabin we played half the fuckin' night with the fuckin' *drum* machine."

"I don't know, I sort of dug it," says Reed. "Like with his head inside the bass drum? *Crowd* was into it."

"Hey," the bass player says. "The thing keeps better time than him."

"Hey, fuck you," says the drummer.

"Okay, so 'Walk This Way,' right?" Reed says. "Does it start in E?"

"*Je*sus," says the little guy. "No, it starts in fuckin' W."

"And it goes to what, again?" says the bass player. "In that other part?"

"Come on, man. We *played* the fuckin' song last *week*. Through B flat to C. Right?"

"Right right right. Yeah, no, okay, man, I remember it. It's just weird to me. Comin' off a E to a B flat. It's like out of nowhere."

"Yeah, but then you're in C," says the little guy.

"Yeah, I *know* you're in C, but what I'm sayin', Mitch, that little thing is still weird to me."

"Well, that's how the fuckin' song *goes*, man."

"But it seems like it would make more sense if you went A, B, C."

"Are we gonna play this fuckin' thing or what?" Reed says.

"No, let's fuckin' *talk* about it for another fuckin' hour," Mitch says. He takes off his Strat, goes back to the board, does something, and the drum machine starts up: *Boom boom ba-doom-doom-DOOM. Boom boom ba-doom-doom-DOOM. Boom boom ba-doom—*

"Too slow, too slow," the bass player yells.

"That's exactly where we had it last week," says Mitch.

"Bull*shit*."

"Okay, fine, man. You know so fuckin' much about this tune, man, you fix it how *you* want, okay?"

"Well, it's gotta go faster than *that*, man," says the bass player.

"Okay, so put it up where you *want* it. Put it up your ass, all I care. Can we just play the fuckin' song?"

"I *hate* this fuckin' song, you want to know the truth," the bass player says. "Why don't we just play a blues?"

"I suggest we play *something*," says Reed. "Not a blues, necessarily."

"Okay," says Mitch. "You fuckin' masterminds work it out and you let me know, okay?"

Willis wants to think this is still banter. But he doesn't know these people, and it's too much to process when you're having such a great time being high, which he really is.

"Okay, okay, fine," says Reed. "Mitch, why don't you just put the thing on sort of a shuffle, you know, doot ta-doot ta-doot ta-doot-ta, doot ta-doot ta-doot ta-doot-ta." He sings in embarrassing fake Negro: "Checkin' up own mah *bay-bay*, doot ta-doot ta-doot ta-doot, find out what she been puttin' *daown*, ta-doot ta-doot ta-doot ta-doot." The drum machine is still going *boom boom ba-doom-doom-DOOM*.

"So that's what you want to play now?" Mitch says.

"Well, not *that*, necessarily," says Reed.

"So you want like a medium shuffle."

"Well, yeah. *Sort* of medium."

"Five fuckin' hours later . . .," says the bass player.

"Well? So what do *you* have in mind?" Reed says.

"I don't *give* a shit. Why'n't we just play the fuckin' song, man? That way we'll have it the fuck over with."

"Come on, it's a killer *song*, man," Mitch says. "It sounded fucked-up last week because nobody knew it."

"Like we really know it now," says the bass player.

"Hey, the new guy," calls the drummer, still on the floor. "I forgot your name, man. You do any Stones?"

"We're doing this now," Mitch says.

"I'm just askin' him, man," says the drummer.

The drum machine keeps going *boom boom ba-doom-doom-DOOM*.

"Shit, man," Mitch says. "I feel like I'm starting to crash already."

Boom boom ba-doom-doom-DOOM. Boom boom ba-doom-doom-DOOM.

"Hey, can't have that," says Reed. "You mind turning that thing off? Drive me fuckin' bananas."

"I'm just gonna be a second." Mitch takes his Strat off and sets it on the floor with that ugly clang of an electric guitar in standard tuning.

"Fuck *this*." The bass player takes off his bass and goes over and shuts off the drum machine.

"Sweet relief," says Reed.

The bass player looks over at Mitch, who's already snuffling and pawing at his face. "Shit. Is this going to be one of *those* fuckin' nights?"

"Here, while we're at it." Reed gets the joint out of his

shirt pocket, lights it, takes a hit and passes it to the bass player, who takes a hit and holds it out to Willis.

He puts up a hand. "Some reason, I can't play behind that. I might go for a tad more of the other."

"Uh-oh," says the bass player. "I think we got another Spark-man on our hands. Hey, can you play drums?"

The drummer has rolled onto his side to light his pipe, his sloppy stomach bulging out his t-shirt. He sticks up the middle finger of the hand holding the lighter.

"I like to give him shit," the bass player says.

Willis snorts up a pair of inch-long lines. He wants more, but he can take a hint, if that was a hint.

Reed takes another hit off the joint, holds the smoke in, finally lets it out. "By the way. Since we're taking a break. Griff's got to have a name by tomorrow latest so he can put it in the paper."

"Great. We worry about *this* shit and meanwhile we're not even in *tune*," says the little Strat guy.

"You see?" Reed says to Willis. "Mitch's problem is that he still thinks this is about competence. But in a way that's cool too. Sort of that little edge of desperation. It's like, for him, he's been busted back down to a garage band. Whole different energy from just *being* in a garage band, you know what I'm saying?"

"Bullshit," says the drummer from down on the floor. "It ain't even *that*. Where's the fuckin' garage?"

"Figure of speech," says Reed.

"Fuckin' *cows* used to live here, man," says the drummer. "We're playing for like the ghosts of cows, man. Dig on it."

Reed looks at Willis. "This is what I'm up against. So, names. Who's got one?"

"Hey, what about the Grateful something?" says the bass player. "The Grateful Cowfuckers, man."

"Well, on some level that's perfect," Reed says. "But I don't think that's a level we can realistically be on."

"You should call yourselves the Robert Blys," says Willis.

"Love it," says Reed. "But – ah—" He goes *Ssshewww!* and zips his hand past his eyes. "See, he's too much the one thing and you're too, you know, the *other*. Anybody go for Confucius Say?"

"We already been that," says the bass player.

"We *talked* about it. We never actually used it."

"Neon Madmen," says Mitch.

"Too college," says Reed.

"Fuck it," the bass player says. "You want to call it that Jap thing, I don't give a fuck."

Mitch has put his Strat back on. "What about just Jap Thing?"

"I *don't* think so," says Reed.

"Jap thang," Mitch sings, and strikes some totally other chord. "You make mah heart sing."

"Hey, you want to do that?" Reed says. "We should be doing that – that's a fucking fabulous song."

"What about Air Bag?" the drummer calls.

"What the fuck does *that* mean?" says the bass player. "*Air* Bag? I mean, what is that *about*?"

"I was just thinking, you know, about these cars with air bags," the drummer says.

"Air Bag," says Reed. "Done deal. Objections?" The bass player only shrugs.

"Hey, the new guy," calls the drummer. "What Stones shit you do?"

"You fuckin' burnout," says the bass player. "You can do *my* stones."

"So are we going to play this thing or what?" Mitch says. He checks his low E. "Fuck, I'm out."

"What? What are we doing?" says Reed.

"Well, I can see where *this* shit is heading," the bass player says. "Sparky, man, will you fuckin' get up off the fuckin' floor?"

"Fuck him," says Mitch. He turns on the drum machine. *Boom boom ba-doom-doom-DOOM.*

"I thought we were doing 'Wild Thing,' " Reed says.

"Well, could we fuckin' do *something*?" says the bass player.

"Hey, I know. What about we do a line?" says the drummer, still down on the floor. "Shit, that could be like a saying: 'You want to do something, do a line.' I feel like if I did a couple lines I could really get into some playing."

"So get up off your ass," says the bass player.

"That's the problem, man," the drummer says. "I think I might be too fuckin' ripped."

"Shit," says the bass player, taking off his instrument. "What am I, your fuckin' servant?" He brings the stuff over, and the drummer rolls back onto his side while the rest of them circle around.

After these next two lines, Willis finds he's gotten up to a place where it seems a long way back down. He sits on the carpeting and tries to work out a theory about how the mountain landscape could be encoded in microminiature into the molecules of the coca plant, which would account for this steep lofty feeling. Like what is that thing – ontogeny recapitulating phylogeny? Maybe this is a little specious; he's sure it is. Still, it's cool to have come up with the word *specious*.

"Fuckin' Charlie Watts," the drummer's saying. "I love that mother-fucker. Hey, the new guy. You do any Stones?"

"You know something? We should be doing some real biker shit," says Reed. " 'Born to Be Wild,' shit like that."

"What's your point, man?" says the drummer. "Fuckin' Stones ain't *biker* shit? Man, a biker *stabbed* some son of a bitch to that shit, so you don't know what the fuck you're talkin' about. I seen the movie of it, man, several fuckin' times."

"What are we, onto the sixties now?" says Reed.

"That wasn't the sixties, you dick," the bass player says.

"Altamont," says Reed. "Nineteen sixty-nine."

"Well, that's a fuck of a lot different from the sixties," says the bass player.

"Oh really?" Reed says. "That's an interesting remark. How is it that 1969 isn't the sixties?"

"Shit," says the bass player. "Will somebody tell fuckin' Perry Mason here what the fuck I'm tryin' to get across?"

"Danny," Reed says, "you're stretching my sense of camp to the breaking point."

"Yeah, whatever the fuck *that* means," says Dan.

"Hey, are we gonna play or what?" Mitch says. "I'm really pumped to play, you know?"

"I've been *trying* to mobilize you people to play for two *hours* now," says Reed.

"Hey, I don't think I can make it, man," the drummer says. "I feel like I might be too wasted to play."

"Well, if we ain't gonna play," says the bass player, "let's fuckin' get ripped."

"Listen, speaking of ripped," says Willis. "I'd be glad – I don't know if this is tacky, but if people are like chipping in or something."

"Yeah, I don't think you have to sweat it," Mitch says. "Old Calvin just—"

"Hey, Mitch?" says the bass player. "Why'n't you shut your ass?" To Willis he says, "Don't worry about it, man."

"What the fuck?" Mitch says. "I thought this guy—"

"Mitchell," says Reed. "C'm'ere. Talk to you for a second?" He takes off his Les Paul, walks over and parts the plastic sheeting, holding it open; Mitch takes off his Strat and follows him out. The bass player puts his bass back on and flips his amp off standby.

"They're bringin' in a new drummer, man," the drummer says from down on the floor. "I'm not fuckin' *stupid*. See, I get too fucked up to play."

"That ain't what they're talkin' about," says the bass player.

"Yeah, sure. Then it must be the latest stock quotations, man."

Willis can make out the two blurry forms on the other side of the cloudy plastic. The bass player begins to play what sounds like the hook to "Start Me Up." Willis guesses it would be politic to make some noise too. "Cool, you want to do that?" he says. "What Keith does, he takes off the bottom string and tunes to G. That's how he plays *all* that stuff."

"No shit," says the bass player. Willis absolutely can't tell if he's genuinely surprised, or putting him down for saying something everybody already knows, or just doesn't give a fuck.

"Are we in tune, gentlemen?" Reed's back; he and Mitch are slipping guitar straps over their heads. Willis knows Reed's looking at him. But when he finally can't stand it and looks back, Reed's checking his watch. "Night's still young," he says. "So. Enough of this shit."

THEORY
(& PRACTICE)

DONALD BARTHELME

THE KING OF JAZZ
(1977)

WELL I'M THE king of jazz now, thought Hokie Mokie to himself as he oiled the slide on his trombone. Hasn't been a 'bone man been king of jazz for many years. But now that Spicy MacLammermoor, the old king, is dead, I guess I'm it. Maybe I better play a few notes out of this window here, to reassure myself.

"Wow!" said somebody standing on the sidewalk. "Did you hear that?"

"I did," said his companion.

"Can you distinguish our great homemade American jazz performers, each from the other?"

"Used to could."

"Then who was that playing?"

"Sounds like Hokie Mokie to me. Those few but perfectly selected notes have the real epiphanic glow."

"The what?"

"The real epiphanic glow, such as is obtained only by artists of the caliber of Hokie Mokie, who's from Pass Christian, Mississippi. He's the king of jazz, now that Spicy MacLammermoor is gone."

Hokie Mokie put his trombone in its trombone case and went to a gig. At the gig everyone fell back before him, bowing.

"Hi Bucky! Hi Zoot! Hi Freddie! Hi George! Hi Thad! Hi Roy! Hi Dexter! Hi Jo! Hi Willie! Hi Greens!"

"What we gonna play, Hokie? You the king of jazz now, you gotta decide."

"How 'bout 'Smoke'?"

"Wow!" everybody said. "Did you hear that? Hokie Mokie can just knock a fella out, just the way he pronounces a word. What a intonation on that boy! God Almighty!"

"I don't want to play 'Smoke,'" somebody said.

"Would you repeat that, stranger?"

"I don't want to play 'Smoke.' 'Smoke' is dull. I don't like the changes. I refuse to play 'Smoke.'"

"He refuses to play 'Smoke'! But Hokie Mokie is the king of jazz and he says 'Smoke'!"

"Man, you from outa town or something? What do you mean you refuse to play 'Smoke'? How'd you get on this gig anyhow? Who hired you?"

"I am Hideo Yamaguchi, from Tokyo, Japan."

"Oh, you're one of those Japanese cats, eh?"

"Yes I'm the top trombone man in all of Japan."

"Well you're welcome here until we hear you play. Tell me, is the Tennessee Tea Room still the top jazz place in Tokyo?"

"No, the top jazz place in Tokyo is the Square Box now."

"That's nice. OK, now we gonna play 'Smoke' just like Hokie said. You ready, Hokie? OK, give you four for nothin'. One! Two! Three! Four!"

The two men who had been standing under Hokie's window had followed him into the club. Now they said:

"Good God!"

"Yes, that's Hokie's famous 'English sunrise' way of playing. Playing with lots of rays coming out of it, some red rays, some blue rays, some green rays, some green stemming from a violet center, some olive stemming from a tan center—"

"That young Japanese fellow is pretty good, too."

"Yes, he is pretty good. And he holds his horn in a peculiar way. That's frequently the mark of a superior player."

"Bent over like that with his head between his knees – good God, he's sensational!"

He's sensational, Hokie thought. Maybe I ought to kill him.

But at that moment somebody came in the door pushing in front of him a four-and-one-half-octave marimba. Yes, it was Fat Man Jones, and he began to play even before he was fully in the door.

"What're we playing?"

" 'Billie's Bounce.' "

"That's what I thought it was. What're we in?"

"F."

"That's what I thought we were in. Didn't you use to play with Maynard?"

"Yeah I was on that band for a while until I was in the hospital."

"What for?"

"I was tired."

"What can we add to Hokie's fantastic playing?"

"How 'bout some rain or stars?"

"Maybe that's presumptuous?"

"Ask him if he'd mind."

"You ask him, I'm scared. You don't fool around with the king of jazz. That young Japanese guy's pretty good, too."

"He's sensational."

"You think he's playing in Japanese?"

"Well I don't think it's English."

This trombone's been makin' my neck green for thirty-five years, Hokie thought. How come I got to stand up to yet another challenge, this late in life?

"Well, Hideo—"

"Yes, Mr Mokie?"

"You did well on both 'Smoke' and 'Billie's Bounce.' You're just about as good as me, I regret to say. In fact, I've decided you're *better* than me. It's a hideous thing to contemplate, but there it is. I have only been the king of jazz for twenty-four hours, but the unforgiving logic of this art demands we bow to Truth, when we hear it."

"Maybe you're mistaken?"

"No, I got ears. I'm not mistaken. Hideo Yamaguchi is the new king of jazz."

"You want to be king emeritus?"

"No, I'm just going to fold up my horn and steal away. This gig is yours, Hideo. You can pick the next tune."

"How 'bout 'Cream'?"

"OK, you heard what Hideo said, it's 'Cream.' You ready, Hideo?"

"Hokie, you don't have to leave. You can play too. Just move a little over to the side there—"

"Thank you, Hideo, that's very gracious of you. I guess I will play a little, since I'm still here. Sotto voce, of course."

"Hideo is wonderful on 'Cream'!"

"Yes, I imagine it's his best tune."

"What's that sound coming in from the side there?"

"Which side?"

"The left."

"You mean that sound that sounds like the cutting edge of life? That sounds like polar bears crossing Arctic ice pans? That sounds like a herd of musk ox in full flight? That sounds like male walruses diving to the bottom of the sea? That sounds like fumaroles smoking on the slopes of Mt Katmai? That sounds like the wild turkey walking through the deep, soft forest? That sounds like beavers chewing trees in an Appalachian marsh? That sounds like an oyster fungus growing on an aspen trunk? That sounds like a mule deer wandering a montane of the Sierra Nevada? That sounds like prairie dogs kissing? That sounds like witchgrass tumbling or a river meandering? That sounds like manatees munching seaweed at Cape Sable? That sounds like coatimundis moving in packs across the face of Arkansas? That sounds like—"

"Good God, it's Hokie! Even with a cup mute on, he's blowing Hideo right off the stand!"

"Hideo's playing on his knees now! Good God, he's reaching into his belt for a large steel sword— Stop him!"

"Wow! That was the most exciting 'Cream' ever played! Is Hideo all right?"

"Yes, somebody is getting him a glass of water."

"You're my man, Hokie! That was the dadblangedest thing I ever saw!"

"You're the king of jazz once again!"

"Hokie Mokie is the most happening thing there is!"

"Yes, Mr Hokie sir, I have to admit it, you blew me right off the stand. I see I have many years of work and study before me still."

"That's OK, son. Don't think a thing about it. It happens to the best of us. Or it almost happens to the best of us. Now I want everybody to have a good time because we're gonna play 'Flats.' 'Flats' is next."

"With your permission, sir, I will return to my hotel and pack. I am most grateful for everything I have learned here."

"That's OK, Hideo. Have a nice day. He-he. Now, 'Flats.' "

JONATHAN COE

9TH AND 13TH
(1997)

I LIVE ON the corner of 9th and 13th, and I promise you, it's not a good place to be. It's not a place where you'd want to linger. It's the sort of place you pass through; the sort you move on from. Or at least, that's what it is for most people. For everybody but me.

I can't believe I've been living here for more than eighteen months now. I can't believe that every morning, for the last eighteen months, I've been woken up by the rolling of shutters at the Perky Pig Diner and BBQ just across from my apartment. Shortly after that happens, the noises will start downstairs: furniture being shifted, trucks driving in and out right underneath my bedroom, the throb of their revving engines so insistent that even when I try to block it out by putting on my headphones and turning the keyboard's volume up to Max, even then I can still feel it through my feet. I live above the business premises of the Watson Storage and Removal Company: which makes sense, in a way, because like I said, this is a transient place, a place for people on the move, a place for people who are getting ready to pack up and leave.

9th and 13th. Do you know what that sounds like? You can find out for yourself, if there's a piano anywhere nearby. Start with . . . start with a C, if you like. Way down on the keyboard, two octaves below middle C. Hold it down with your little finger, and now stretch your fingers, really stretch them, more than an octave, until your thumb is on a D.

Now play the two notes, and listen to the interval. You've got your 9th. It's slightly rootless, already: those two bass notes that don't quite agree with one another. There's an audible sense of indecision. And now, with the thumb of your right hand, you play a B flat. This adds a kind of bluesy overtone, turns the ambiguous statement of those two notes into a question. It seems to ask: where are we heading? To which the next note – another D – adds nothing except emphasis. Now the question seems even more urgent, but when the F is introduced, it changes everything. All of a sudden the chord feels hopeful, aspiring. There's the hint of an upward movement, the sense that we might be about to arrive somewhere. And then, finally, we add the A, so that we have our 13th interval at last: and listen to how plangent it makes it sound, how wistful. This chord is aching to resolve, to settle on something: C major would be the most obvious place to go next, but it could be A minor, or F major seven, or . . . well, anything. It's so open. As open as a chord can get. Brimming with potential.

9th and 13th. The sound of possibility.

And how long is it since I played those chords, now? How long since *she* came into the bar and stood over the piano as I improvised, in the half-dark, after even the most hardened drinkers had finished up and gone home? I don't know. I lose track. All I remember is that for a few minutes we talked, swapped a few banalities, as my fingers wandered trance-like over the keyboard, tracing the usual patterns, the easy, familiar harmonies that I'm locked into, these days, like a series of bad habits. She was from Franklin, Indiana, she said, and had only pitched up in New York that afternoon. She said she'd given up her job in the local record store and had come to the city to write. To write books. And that's all

I ever found out about her – not even her name, just that she was from Franklin and that she was going to write and that she had dark hair, pulled severely back from her face into a short ponytail, and tiny freckles on either side of her nose, and brown-green eyes that narrowed to a smile whenever I looked at her. Which wasn't very often, I have to say, hunched as I was over the keyboard, picking my way slowly through those well-worn chords, until my hands finally gave up; faltered, and came to rest; came to rest where they always did. The usual place.

9th and 13th.

At which point – at which precise point – she asked me a question.

"Listen," she said. "Is there anywhere . . . do you know of anywhere that I can stay tonight? I don't have anywhere to stay."

The possibilities raised by that question, like the possibilities raised by that chord, hung in the air for as long as it took the notes to decay.

Infinite possibilities.

To take just one of them, for instance. Supposing I had resolved the chord. Supposing I had resolved it in the most obvious way, with a soft – soft but insistent – C major. Perhaps with an A natural in there somewhere, to make it just a little more eloquent. And suppose I had answered her question, by saying: "Well, it's getting pretty late, and there aren't that many places around here. There's always my couch."

What would have happened?

Where would I be now?

This is what would have happened:

Her eyes would have narrowed again, at first, in that

warm, shy, smiling way she had, and then she would have looked away, gathering her thoughts for a moment or two, before turning back to me, and saying:

"Would that be OK? I mean, that's really nice of you . . ."

And I would have said: "No problem. It's just a couple of blocks from here."

"I don't want to put you to any trouble," she would have said. "It'll only be for one night."

But it wouldn't only have been for one night. We both would have known that, even then.

I would have closed the lid of the piano and said goodnight to Andy at the bar, collecting my fee (a thin wad of dollar bills from the cash register), and then opening the door for her, warning her to mind her step on the narrow, dimly lit staircase that led up to the street. She would have had a bag with her, a black canvas hold-all, and I would have offered to carry it, slinging it over my shoulder as I followed her up the stairs, admiring the sway of her back and the shapeliness of the stockinged ankle I would have glimpsed between the bottom of her jeans and her neat brown shoes.

Once out in the street, she would have pulled her coat tightly around herself, and looked to me for guidance – only her eyes visible above the turned-up collar – and I would have taken her arm gently and led her off down West 4th Street, heading north towards 9th and 13th.

"Are you sure this is all right?" she would have asked. "I hate to think I might be imposing."

And I would have said: "Not at all. It's good of you to trust me, really. I mean, a total stranger . . ."

"Oh, but I'd been listening to you play the piano." She would have glanced at me, now. "I'd been in there for a couple of hours, and . . . Well, anyone who plays the piano like that must be a good person." Then a nervous laugh, before offering up the compliment. "You play very nicely."

I would have smiled at that: a practised, rueful smile. "You should tell that to the guy who runs the bar. He might pay me a little more." After which, almost immediately, I would have been anxious to change the subject. "My name's David, by the way."

"Oh. I'm Rachel." We would have shaken hands, a little awkwardly, a little embarrassed at our own formality, and then hurried on to my apartment, because Rachel would have been looking cold, already: her breath steaming in the frosty air, the hint of a chatter in her teeth.

"You probably want to get straight to bed," I would have said, as soon as we got inside, and I would have helped her off with her coat and hung it up in the hallway. I would have showed her where the bed was, and changed the sheets for her while she was in the bathroom. The old sheets and blankets I would have taken with me, using them to make up some sort of bed for myself on the couch. When she had finished in the bathroom I would have gone to check that she had everything she wanted, and then I would have said goodnight, but afterwards I would have lain on the couch for ten minutes or more, waiting for the light in her bedroom to be turned off. But she wouldn't have turned it off. Instead, her bedroom door would have been pulled slowly open, and I would have felt her looking at me, trying to work out if I had gone to sleep, before she tiptoed through into the hallway, and started searching through the pockets of her coat. A few seconds later she would have found what she was looking for and would have come back; and just as she was returning to the bedroom I would have said:

"Is everything OK?"

She would have started, and paused, before saying: "Yes, I'm fine. I hope I didn't wake you." And then: "I forgot my notebook. I always try to write something in it, every night, before I go to bed. Wherever I am."

"That's very disciplined of you," I would have said. And she would have asked me:

"Don't you practise every night? Surely you must practise."

"In the mornings, sometimes. By the time it gets this late, I'm too tired."

She could have turned, and gone, at this point. The silence would have been long enough to allow it. But that wouldn't have happened. I would have sensed that she wanted to stay, and would have said:

"So what are you going to write now?"

"Just a few . . . thoughts, you know. Just a few thoughts about the day."

"You mean like a diary?"

"I suppose."

"I've never done anything like that. Never kept a diary. Have you always kept one?"

"Yes. Since I was a child. I remember, when I was about seven, or eight . . ." We would have talked, then, for fifteen minutes or more. Or rather, I would have listened (because that's always how it is) while she talked; talked, and came closer – sitting on the arm of the couch, at first, then sitting beside me, after I had shifted over to make room for her, her bare thighs in contact with my hips: only the sheets and blankets intervening.

I know, too, what would have happened at the end of those fifteen minutes. How she would have leaned towards me, leaned over me, the heaviness of her body against mine. How her hair, freed now from its ponytail, would have drifted across my face until she brushed it back, and how her lips would have touched mine: her lips dry with the cold. Dry at first. How I would have followed her into the bedroom.

How there would have been a rapid, almost imperceptible shedding of our last remaining clothes. How I would have learned about her by touch, first of all, and by sight only later, when the bedclothes lay dishevelled, thrust aside, strewn across the floor. How willingly she would have given herself to me. And how beautiful she would have been, by the flashes of neon through the uncurtained window. How very beautiful.

How right for me.

That's what would have happened. And this is what would have happened next:

In the morning, we would have had breakfast together at the Perky Pig, and even that would have tasted good, for once. Over refills of coffee, we would have made plans. First of all, there would have been the question of accommodation: it would have been blindingly obvious that we could afford a bigger and better place if we pooled our resources, and moved in together. But that would have presented another problem: her parents, both Christian fundamentalists, would never have countenanced this arrangement. We would have to get married. The suggestion would have been made jokingly, at first, but it would only have taken a few seconds for our eyes to make contact and to shine with the sudden, instantaneous knowledge that it was what we both wanted. Three days later, man and wife, we would have spotted an advertisement in the *New York Review of Books* for a vacant apartment in the West Village, offered at a derisory rent to suitably Bohemian tenants. It would have been the property of a middle-aged academic couple, about to depart for a five-year sojourn in Europe. Arranged over three floors, it would have included an enormous studio room – at the centre of which would have stood a Steinway baby grand, sheened in winter sunshine from the skylight – and a small but adorable garret study with a view over the treetops of Washington Square. In this study, during the next few weeks, Rachel would have written the final chapters of her almost-completed novel. A novel which, after two regretful but encouraging rejections, would have been accepted for publication by Alfred A Knopf, and would have appeared the next September, becoming the sensation of that fall. Meanwhile, as her book climbed the bestseller lists and scooped up prizes, I would have finished my long-projected piano concerto, an early performance of which (at the Merkin Concert Hall, with myself both playing and conducting) would have caught the attention of Daniel Barenboim, who would have insisted on programming it as the chief item in his recital for the "Great Performers" series at Lincoln Centre.

Our son Thelonius would have been born a few months later. Followed, after another couple of years, by our daughter Emily.

Yes, by our daughter Emily . . .

Wait a minute, though: I can hear her crying. I can hear her crying downstairs.

No, it isn't her. It isn't Emily. It's the squeal of those big garage doors at the Watson Storage and Removal Company. Those rusty hinges. The first of the trucks has just arrived.

Do you want to know what I did say to her, instead? Do you want to know how I actually answered that question?

"Sure," I said. "There's an excellent B & B near here. Just around the corner. Halliwell's, on Bedford Street. It's just five minutes' walk." And I looked away, to avoid glimpsing the disappointment that I knew would flare in her eyes, and I played the same two chords again, over and over, and I heard her thank me, and I kept on playing them, and she left, and I played them again, and two days later I went to Halliwell's to look for her, but they didn't know who I meant, and I said her name was Rachel but of course it wasn't, I made that up, I never knew her name, and I carried on playing those two chords and I'm still playing them now, this very moment, 9th and 13th, 9th and 13th, the sound of endless, infinite, unresolved possibilities. The most tantalising sound in the world.

I don't know what chord I should play next. I can't decide.

DANA SPIOTTA

From

EAT THE DOCUMENT
(2006)

JASON'S JOURNAL

DID YOU EVER wonder what your body would look like by age forty if you never exercised, not even once? Gage, my next-door neighbor, answered any curiosity I had on that score. He has recently moved back in with his parents. Really. Apparently that is all the rage among the loser set these days. Gage, in all his dissipated glory, is someone I would call a pal. I first noticed him huffing his stuff onto his parents' lawn on a sunny summer afternoon. He had retreated to the home front for as yet undiscovered reasons. But the important thing here is that he arrived with crates and crates of long-playing vinyl records. Naturally, these caught my eye.

My friends – what few friends I have – are the types of guys who will argue about whether the rare RCA single version of "Eight Miles High" is superior to the track issued on *Fifth Dimension*, the Byrds' album release. It isn't, but it is cool to ask the question because it proves you know there are two versions and you are conversant with both. It is even cooler to maintain that the album – a common, reissued object – does have the superior version, and not the rare, hard-to-find single. (This is true, despite the fact, perhaps inconsequential, that the LP version *is* actually the superior version.) It is perverse, and very sophisticated, in these circles, to maintain the common, popular object is the better object. Only a neophyte or a real expert would argue such a thing. So are you getting the picture on my pals, here?

I knew instantly that Gage was one of us. Or I should say, given his seniority agewise, we were one of him. We who live for bonus tracks, alternate versions, reissues, demos, bootlegs. Cover versions. Obscure European or Japanese reissues in 180-gram vinyl. Or original issue, original packaging. Authenticity. We like the inside story, the secrets. We constantly feel the best, coolest stuff is being withheld from us. In other words: there is never enough information. There is always more stuff to be had. A new master unearthed, a track unnoticed at the end of a long silence on a master tape. In a safety deposit box, in a basement. Someone didn't notice it!

Gage had thousands of albums in plastic protective sleeves. He had boxes of compact discs and stacks of 45 rpm records. I watched him unload them onto the lawn. He was wearing black jeans and a black T-shirt, which didn't conceal his paunch, despite what they say about the slimming effects of all black. But black, particularly all black, as we all know, is very rock-and-roll, very rebellious. Deeply subversive. So look out, right? I remember watching him as he sat and drank a beer, resting between the minivan he was unloading and his room in his parents' house. Apparently winded after like two trips upstairs. I watched him from our yard, and I saw my future, very possibly. At fifteen I already have an alarming jump start on a future paunch. Although mine is more pudge than paunch at this point, I could still see where I was headed.

As much as that thought filled me with disgust, I so badly needed to look through his collection that I walked over and introduced myself. We had seen each other before when he visited over the last five years, but we didn't officially know each other.

At the very front of his stack of vinyl I could see one of

the all-time great "lost" albums – *Oar* by Skip Spence, the schizophrenic guitarist from Moby Grape. He made *Oar* (an album, by the way, of Orphic longing and aching beauty) at twenty-two and then, naturally, like any rock-and-roll genius worth his title, spent the next thirty years in and out of institutions, never to be heard from again. I could tell instantly this was no reissue but an original pressing. I resisted the urge to comment on it, to hold it in my hands, to fondle it beneath its plastic protective sheath. Was it a gatefold? What did it have on the inner sleeve? Did it have a cryptic message carved in the run-out groove? All that would come in time. I didn't want Gage to get too much credit from me too soon. I played it cool, though I practically had a boner thinking about all the possibilities hidden behind that Skip Spence album. It is wonderful to care deeply about something so tangible and possible. It is wonderful to find such joy in something within your grasp, some specific, described, contained universe. Anyway.

He began to explain his temporary move back to suburbia, the saga of the failed offspring back at Mom and Stepdad's. He mock-shuddered as he said the word *suburbia*; we both sneered together at the idea of suburbia, but who are we kidding? We exist because of suburbia. Suburbia is a freak's dreamworld, a world of extra rooms upstairs and long, lazy afternoons with no interference. A place where you can listen to your LPs for hours on end. You can live in your room, your own rent-free corner of the universe, and create a world of pleasure and interest entirely centered on yourself and your interior aesthetic and logic. Suburbia is where you can pursue your individuality, no matter how rancid or recondite: the big generic-development mansions and three-car garages can harbor endless eccentricities. In your room and out of earshot. Sometimes an entire furnished basement

– sorry, lower level – devoted to TVs and stereos and Ping-Pong tables; video games and computers and digital video discs. You can burn CDs and download music, catalog and repeat, buy and trade, all sitting on your ass in the rec room. The recreation room – in suburbia there are whole rooms dedicated to leisure and play and recreation. There is space and time here, and comfort and ease. Just look at me. Just look at Gage.

After our introduction, our brief paragraphs of biographical detail, we segued effortlessly into our obsessions. We have spent the last few weeks together in an orgy of listening. I was relieved to discover that Gage was no don't-touch-the-record collector. He was passionately into listening and playing things for you to listen to. We sat in his room – which has a black light, I kid you not, and the appropriate psychedelic posters to go with it – and we had listening jags, hours of intensity. Jumping promiscuously from "You have that?" to "Wait until you hear this!" But very shortly the novelty began to wear off. We quickly grew less patient with each other's interests. He was deeply into this '70s thing, particularly a lot of deep listenings of Roxy Music's mid- to late '70s albums. I was cool with that, but I had been through it all two summers ago. Naturally he tried to fly the rather perverse opinion that Roxy's late '70s discoish period was really the best stuff, rather than the avant-pop and math-fizz of their earlier experimental stuff. Something along the lines of the "glorious dance music of 1979" (a hyperbolic assertion, which is just so typical of Gage and his ilk, and so utterly false).

"Dude, listen, check out the percussion on this track. Totally conjured on a Jupiter 8. That is all of '80s dance music in a nutshell," Gage said to me.

"Yeah, *dude*. That's quite a legacy to claim."

"That is it. Nothing like those late '70s thick-as-a-brick analog synths, synthesizers that had no shame!"

It was the trend – unspoken but somehow felt everywhere at once – among some music freaks to be into synthesizers, but only the spaceship-landing, proudly precise and artificial vibrato of early- to middle-period predigital synths. Roland Jupiter 8s. Minimoogs. Yeah, sure.

"I don't know, the production is really flat. Like airless."

That was my bullshit response, to call the production "airless," because it just means this music is not flying my flag right now, and I've got several choice albums on deck, all without synthesizers save perhaps a theremin and with production that could supply enough oxygen to feed an army of asthmatic smokers for life. And of course Gage was being totally fascistic about what we had to hear next. But the thing is the guy was in the thrall, so deep into his obsession, his Roxy freak, that he meant it. He was drowning in the circular mess of relativity, the mindfuck of repeated listening, the loss of perspective that comes with looking at something too closely. I know. I've been there. Don't even get me started on the Beach Boys. As I am writing this, it's there. As I was sitting at Gage's trying to listen to his records, I was fondling an original-issue 45 of "God Only Knows." I was humming, no, vibrating, *Pet Sounds*'s songs, in order. And I couldn't wait to satisfy my jones for it. So I knew exactly where Gage was at, but Gage didn't have much perspective for a guy his age, did he? He didn't have a clue how deep in he was, how tragically without perspective. I know the day will come when I won't feel this way about the Beach Boys. I know, at least intellectually, that day will come. Then perhaps I will be all gooey for the genius of early Little Feat or late Allman Brothers or something. And when I realize this I feel a little sad. I could be reading a great book, couldn't I? Or going for a bike ride or meeting a girl at the pool or hacking into someone's bank account. (Or even bathing more often, for God's sake.)

As I sat at Gage's feet – black light hurting my eyes, listening against my will to the perverse whispers of Bryan Ferry – I wondered if my life was going to be one immersion after another, a great march of shallow, unpopular popular culture infatuations that don't really last and don't really mean anything. Sometimes I even think maybe my deepest obsessions are just random manifestations of my loneliness or isolation. Maybe I infuse ordinary experience with a kind of sacred aura to mitigate the spiritual vapidity of my life. But, then again, maybe not.

As soon as I got home from Gage's, I threw on the record I longed to hear. Listening, I reconsidered my earlier despair – no, it is beautiful to be enraptured. To be enthralled by something, anything. And it isn't random. It speaks to you for a reason. If you wanted to, you could look at it that way, and you might find you aren't wasting your life. You are discovering things about yourself and the world, even if it is just what it is you find beautiful, right now, this second.

I am a person, I think, who feels comfortable in my isolation. Even someone like Gage (who is someone with whom admittedly I have a lot in common, a person with whom you might think I would enjoy keeping company) doesn't alleviate my feelings of loneliness. The effort it required just to be around him and tolerate him made me even more lonely. I am at home only in *my own personal* loneliness. The thing of it is I don't necessarily feel connected to Brian Wilson or any of the Beach Boys. But I do, I guess, feel connected to all the other people, alone in a room somewhere, who listen to *Pet Sounds* on their headphones and who feel the way I feel. I just don't really want to talk to them or hang out with them.

But maybe it is enough to know they exist. We identify ourselves by what moves us. I know that isn't entirely true. I know that's only part of it. But here's what else: Lately I find I wonder about my mother's loneliness. Is it like mine? Does she feel comfortable there? And if I am comfortable with it, sort of, why do I still call it loneliness? Because – and I think somehow she would understand this – you can have and recognize a sadness in your alienation and in other people's alienation and still not long to be around anyone. I think that if you wonder about other people's loneliness, or contemplate it at all, you've got a real leg up on being comfortable in your own.

Anyway, the really relevant part, the whole point of why I am writing about this, came yesterday, maybe a month after Gage and I started spending afternoons together. Gage was at my house, and it started creeping toward dinnertime. Dinnertime normally consists of my mother and me watching TV, or reading magazines, or watching TV while reading magazines. Our living area is of a contemporary "open-plan" style so common in the 1970s split-level vernacular. In other words, our dining room, living room and TV room all seamlessly segue into each other. A house designed – with sliding glass doors, cathedral ceilings, open kitchen counters instead of a wall, all of it transparent and divisionless – for bright Californians, not cloudy gray Northwesterners. Other families, like ours, are more suited to low-ceilinged, small, rabbit-warren-type rooms. We need corners and shadows. We need distinct spaces. The simultaneity of these open, integrated living spaces seems obscene to us. We lurk about, uncomfortable, shamed by our own house.

However, the open plan did afford one advantage. Not only are you able to constantly monitor each other but you can constantly monitor the TV, which is in the most central room. So if we were sitting at the dining room table, all we had to do was look up and we would see the TV. We don't have to actually sit in the TV room: no such commitment required. We just have to leave it on, and it will be visible from any room. There are rules, don't misunderstand, there are standards. We watch the news. Occasionally a movie. We do not watch a situation comedy, or a television drama. Not while we are eating. I mean, I don't care, I just like having it on. I usually have one of my crime novels, generally a serial killer book, on hand as well. I read true crime stories, or literary crime stories. But I prefer the real dark ones, thriller-killer stuff, to the corny kind of running sleuth series, but hey, I'll read any kind really. I read them constantly. Serious-ly, I read like a book a day. I can listen to music, read, and be on the Internet all at the same time. And watch TV. I'm not bragging, I mean I'm aware that this is no sterling accom-plishment. It's pretty standard, isn't it? If I went to the gym, which I don't, I would see people reading, and listening to music while also watching the video monitors of TV shows they can't hear. Their eyes might even flick from their page to more than one monitor while getting their heart rates up into target zones and hydrating themselves from water bottles. All at the same time. So I don't think it makes me a genius or a mutant fuck to do all of these things at once. My point is simply that I am accustomed to a lot of controlled simultaneous stimulation.

So usually we would be sitting there and I would be reading one of my books and eating my dinner, looking up between pages or paragraphs, or during a bite, at Jim Lehrer – which is practically medicinal TV – and Mom might comment, and I would then comment back while still not interrupting my activities.

By the time I've finished my dinner, my mother, if one

were to notice, still would not have eaten very much at all. But she will have managed to refill her glass of wine several times. She then will get out her trusty turquoise-and-silver *Tapestry*-era lighter and her little metal elbow pot pipe. Yeah. She usually gets stoned right at the dinner table. That's no shock, though, is it? During which I take my book to the bathroom, where once again, for the life of me, I cannot just do one thing. I get bored, even if it is just for a three-minute crap. Then I go back to my room, check e-mails, my cell phone voice mail, and finish burning a CD of music I've downloaded or traded with some other music freak I found on one of the fan sites.

But that's all the usual thing. The day Gage was hanging late in my room was unusual for us. I was unveiling my most prized possessions, unleashing the holy grail of my Beach Boys collection. The jaw-dropping stuff. So far, Gage seemed only mildly impressed. We were looking through my comprehensive collection of demos from the Beach Boys' fake lo-fi, unproduced, spontaneous, "non"-studio album, *Party!* when she knocked on the door. I ignored the knocking, figuring she would give up. But she continued to knock.

"Yes?" I said through the door. I am always instantly exasperated with her. She said something muffled. I opened up without lowering the music, which was pretty obnoxious, I mean it even annoyed *me*. Does it make sense to do things that annoy yourself? But I like to get her frustrated. I like to make her speak up. She stood there and tried to look past me into my room.

"What?" I said.

"Do you want me to set a plate for your friend?" She eyed Gage, who was mostly obscured behind my generously cut, mammoth jersey. Gage sat on my bed surrounded by stacks

175

of CDs, LPs and 45s. He waved at my mother. He looked at me and shrugged.

"Sure."

She smiled, her eyes darting from Gage to the stuff piled on the bedspread and then to me, her hands worrying the hem of her sweater throughout, all of which I ignored.

"Ten minutes," she said, but I had already begun to close the door on her, so she really had to shout it, "Ten minutes!"

Gage held up an LP. On the cover was a bearded man in a faded, salt-stained blue-green T-shirt. He stands on a grassy hill with the ocean behind him.

"Wow. Is this?"

"Yes."

"I'd love to hear this. Where did you find it?" It was a bootleg of an unreleased solo album by Dennis Wilson, the drummer for the Beach Boys. This album is significant for two reasons, which I will take a moment to explain since it directly bears on a situation that I will soon recount.

First, lost albums. These are the legendary albums that never saw commercial release, or only had a very small release many years ago. Sometimes the tapes are said to have been destroyed, but the chance that they will resurface is always there. For example the Keith Richards–Gram Parsons heroin sessions in the South of France, 1971. The legend is that the music was a mess and Gram dumped the tapes, but one hopes it will be unearthed someday, however sloppy-slurry the playing may sound. Then there are the label disputes, or someone has died. Or the jam sessions meant for private reference only. These eventually surface in legitimate form after years of being available extralegally as bootlegs. The most famous one is *The Basement Tapes*, the Dylan and the Band bootleg that everyone preferred to what Dylan actually put out (*Nashville Skyline*, which, of course, I like and actually prefer to *The Basement Tapes*). There are also great albums that only saw a brief initial release and are now out of print, or were recorded but never actually released for some tragic reason, usually death: solo demos by Pete Ham, the lead singer of Badfinger (classic hugely popular power pop), recorded weeks before his suicide. The solo album of the obscure member of that famously obscure band Big Star (classic unpopular power pop), Chris Bell. Or the previously mentioned album by Skip Spence, or his British counterparts, Syd Barrett and Nick Drake. Made and then disappeared. There are a million. And if they are truly great, they do often make it aboveground. Eventually in expensive box sets or digipaks with liner notes and extra bonus tracks. But until then they are the holy grails of music freaks – probably all related to the finite nature of a dead artist's output. Couldn't there be one more secret album out there, or one more song?

So this album Gage had in hand actually hit all of the above points: it had one disc of an album out of print coupled with its follow-up – a genuine never-released gem. Naturally it was a find. But what is even more important was that this was by Dennis Wilson.

Dennis Wilson is a man I hold very close to my heart. To most people he is still a tragic joke, a colorful loser, a complete disaster. How could I not love him? Dennis was famous for being not only the only Beach Boy who actually surfed but for being so incredibly derelict for the last ten years of his short life that he actually drowned in a boat slip in Marina del Rey in like six feet of water. He was also the "good-looking" Beach Boy. He was also the Beach Boy who hung around Charles Manson because of all the easy drugs and easy pussy. (As if being a rich, handsome rock star didn't give him enough easy drugs and easy pussy and he needed

Charles Manson's, or maybe there was something particularly potent in unbathed, helter-skelter cult pussy.) But what is hardly known about Wilson is that he recorded these two excellent if maudlin solo albums in the bad years before he drowned. This bootleg had both records in one double gatefold album. The second one is truly a "lost" record, nearly done but never released, and actually wonderful. Wilson was just too out of it to bother putting it out. Admittedly there are a lot of plink-plink sob-type piano songs sung in this almost embarrassingly sad, rusty voice. These real dirgy, messed-up vocals, unashamedly full of self-pity and raw emotion. I found it operatic, a complete expression of a tortured, not-too-bright, not-too-gifted, weary guy. But here is the thing, say what you will about skill, technique, control, brilliance: this stuff is truly moving. To me anyway. I don't know why, but I listen to that album and I start bawling, I really do.

So, anyway, Gage sat on my bed, listening to this priceless artifact. I had it cranked way up. He started to roll his eyes, smirking and laughing a bit.

"It's so swoon-on schmaltzy, isn't it?" he said, giggling and then kind of moaning. After a few seconds I realized he was trying to make a parodic facsimile of Dennis Wilson's vocal track. Then he stopped. "Just pathetic, this drunken guy crying about all his suffering, all his cliché regrets." I flicked the needle handle up, interrupting the song, and snatched the album cover out of his hand.

"Time to eat," I said. We stumbled toward the dining room–TV room–kitchen area. As I said, the usual things were not in effect. For Gage's sake we had the TV off. The table was set with a little more formality than normal. My mother even broke out a bottle of some wine that came in a 750-milliliter bottle instead of the 1.5-liter power jug of oenological glory that she usually poured. She filled our wineglasses. I realized then that Gage was fully an adult and actually not that much younger than my mother. For a millisecond I entertained the horrible thought that they were attracted to each other and they would end up together, but that thought was discarded when she proceeded to ask Gage a series of interrogative-type, as opposed to conversational-type, questions.

Gage couldn't really give any answers, or any normal ones. He was eating heartily, though, and talking through his food, so that in fairly regular, small intervals partially masticated bits would fly from his mouth. Amazing. It wasn't as if Gage was saying anything scintillating or really of any consequence at all – surely we could all bear to wait the three seconds it would take until he swallowed his food and chased the swallow with a large gulp of the gold-hued wine from the 750-milliliter bottle. Which, by the way, we finished in no time.

I didn't like the scotch-and-butter smell of the wine. Or the glistening raw yolk yellow of it, but I did like the buzz.

"Why did you leave Los Angeles?" I heard her say as we began bottle two.

"My recording career didn't really take off," Gage said.

"Did you make a living at it?"

The wine was making me more generous. You know what, it made me less bored. I actually listened to this conversation. I listened to it raptly. It compelled me.

"I did some gigging, but mostly I bartended and wrote some rock criticism, which I rarely got paid for."

"I'd like to read it," I said. I really meant it, too.

"Do you like music as much as your son?" Gage finished his food and pushed his plate back toward the center of the table. After he asked his question, I saw him eyeing the remaining food on my mother's plate. He wanted more, but instead he refilled his empty glass, killing the second bottle.

"I do like music, of course. I mean I used to, quite a bit. I don't listen to much anymore," she said. She got up and started clearing the dishes. She returned to the table with another bottle of the same wine. She smiled slightly and went back to the kitchen. We could hear her washing dishes. Gage opened the bottle.

"So what happened to your dad?" he said to me in a semi-whisper.

"Dead," I said, not whispering at all. He nodded like he expected the story.

"Eight years ago he was driving home one night. It was during a snowstorm – do you remember the year we had that freak blizzard? The roads weren't cleared, so conditions were pretty bad. He drove off the road and crashed in a field. He saw some lights, which I guess he thought were a nearby house, but the lights were on the other side of the field. He got about halfway there and passed out in the snow. He died of hypothermia."

"No shit."

"He was totally drunk. He was also a drug dealer. Neither of which I know, of course. All I know is that he was a contractor who died in a car wreck."

"Really."

"He even did time for drug dealing. As I said, I don't know any of this."

"Actually, I think I heard something about that."

"Of course. It just required the most nominal investigating to verify what happened."

"She seems pretty sad about it still."

"Just look at the newspaper report. Five minutes on Lexis-Nexis. But I never talk to her about it. It is clear she doesn't want to discuss it, so it's not like I have to pretend not to know. It never comes up. It's easy. It's amazing how easy it is to live with not talking about the Big Things. Particularly of the past."

"She must miss him, she seems—"

"She's always been like that."

"Like what?"

"Like when I was a kid, I always had this idea that one day she might go out for a bottle of milk and never come back. She would disappear forever."

Gage looked up. She had appeared again.

"What music were you listening to right before dinner?" she said.

"What did you think of it?" I asked. Gage shook his head.

"I liked it," she said. She pushed back her hair and readied her little pipe as she spoke. "That voice sounded so familiar. Who was it?"

"Dennis Wilson. He was the drummer for the Beach Boys," I said.

"Honestly, Jason, I think I know who Dennis Wilson is. I grew up during those days. You're the one who shouldn't know who Dennis Wilson is," she said, now annoyed. Gage laughed.

"I didn't realize you followed popular music," I said.

"How much do you have to follow to know the Beach Boys?" she said. "It's not like the Beach Boys are obscure. I mean Nancy Reagan liked the Beach Boys, I think that disqualifies them from 'cult' status." Gage really guffawed at that. I was unused to my mother being so sarcastic, but I can't say I didn't completely deserve it.

I began, calmly, patiently. "The Beach Boys' extreme commercial popularity is precisely one of the reasons they are cult figures. Cult objects are one of two things: genuinely undiscovered artists and objects that deserved recognition – often with music that is quite conventional, quite as poppy as what is on the charts, but just unheard – or they are famous mainstream artists with secret counterlives in which they created risky, edgy experimental work. Work that very possibly deconstructs their more commercial work. That's the thing – the perversity of it. The subversive, even courageous, quality. And the price must be paid: sometimes they almost ruin their careers. Usually they get destroyed by their label and the mainstream press. This sort of cult stuff is almost always unconventional, formally radical, hugely ambitious, drug-fueled follies that destroy the artists emotionally and physically. But I don't expect you to understand my appreciation for the Beach Boys."

My mother nodded, smiling. She paused for a moment as if she were about to speak, but I had not finished.

"Dennis Wilson is the double whammy, because even though he is well known as the only good-looking Beach Boy, as a musician he is an obscure member of this very famous band—"

"I met Dennis Wilson once," she said softly.

"—and his solo records are therefore truly cult—" She smiled at me. I stopped for a second. She sucked daintily on her pipe.

"What?"

"I said I met Dennis Wilson once," she said.

"Are you serious? When?" I said.

"I met him in a bar in Venice Beach. In 1979, I think. Or maybe 1980."

Okay. A bar in Venice Beach. Do I ask her what she was doing in a bar in Venice Beach? It was pre-me, my mother to be, how can I really imagine that? She is unformed, she is waiting-to-be in my mind. So she started to tell this tale about some scummy bar called the Blue Cantina.

"It was where the surfer guys hung out. And bikers. Hells Angels too."

I struggled to envision my mother among drunken Hells Angels. But I said nothing. You don't want to remind them of their audience at this point, at least not until you get the goods.

"Living in Southern California was pretty depressing in those days. You know, everything was less than it could have been. Just casualties everywhere, drugs and venereal diseases. All dissolute and sleazy – that's what it felt like in 1980. Anyway, I was by myself and I noticed this very tan guy in his late thirties. He was still handsome despite having uncombed hair, a ratty beard and a bloat around his eyes. He wore, I remember, a white linen shirt, which was unbuttoned and hung open. And white painter's pants. His body was still muscular, his belly was still trim. If you didn't look too closely, he would seem just fine." She put down her pipe and picked up her wineglass.

"He kept staring at me, and it was then that I noticed he was barefoot. He had wide, filthy, beat-up feet, and I remember thinking, Why would they let him in with no shoes and pretty much no shirt? He came over to where I was sitting. I knew this would happen because I did make eye contact with him, which is the equivalent of an open invitation in a bar like that."

I could've been spared, couldn't I, the knowledge that my mother knows the lingua franca of seedy biker bars?

"He said hi. I looked at him up close, and he seemed very familiar. Somewhere behind the beard and the shaggy hair. His neck was kind of short, but he was quite striking. And so familiar.

" 'I'm Dennis,' he said."

"No way," I said to Gage.

"I realized it was Dennis Wilson, the cute drumming-and-surfing Beach Boy. He sat down on the banquette across from me and put his hand on the table between us. I wasn't hiding very well my thrill, and how extremely impressed I was that I was talking to Dennis Wilson, however barefoot and disheveled. And drunk, which I also realized. In fact, he was sort of eyeing my drink.

" 'Would you like another?' he said.

" 'Sure,' I said, draining my glass. 'A grapefruit and vodka with salt on the rim.'

" 'Would you mind covering it? I'm short right now.' I shrugged and bought us two drinks. He retrieved them from the bar but this time sat next to me, on my side of the banquette."

"No way," I said, whispering now. For a moment I entertained the fantasy that she was about to reveal that I was actually the love child of Dennis Wilson – no doubt one of many – thus explaining not only my sense of her caginess but also my fixation on all things pertaining to the brothers Wilson – Brian, Carl and Dennis. But of course I wasn't born until 1983, which means I was conceived in 1982, and this story we were hearing just somehow doesn't feel like the beginning of a three-year love affair, you know? No, it sounded like something other than that. She took another toke on her pipe. As did Gage.

"Anyway, I felt sort of bad for him. I had heard how both Dennis and Brian Wilson would go on benders for days at a time. They would tell people in bars, Hey, I'm a Beach Boy, buy me a drink. And sometimes they would even play piano for free drinks. But he didn't say anything about the Beach Boys."

"Are you sure it was him?" I said.

She sighed.

"Okay, okay, go on. Please."

"There was a jukebox. He went over and put a quarter in. He asked me if I wanted to dance. That old Procol Harum song, 'A Whiter Shade of Pale,' started playing."

"Wait, did he pick it or did you?"

"He did."

"He picked a Procol Harum song. What were the other songs on that jukebox?"

"I really don't know, Jason."

"Then what happened?"

"He said, 'I love this song.'

"I said, 'What does this song mean?'

"He said, 'It doesn't mean anything. It feels something.'"

"Right. Wow. Did he put the moves on you?"

My mother smiled at this question. "No, not really. I mean he was probably more interested in getting drunk than getting laid."

"Yeah, right."

"But it was somehow a sweet moment – the afternoon light, the innocent song and this sad guy swaying with me. The world was going from bad to worse, I had been in L.A. way too long, Ronald Reagan had just become president, but America was still a place where you could dance with a barefoot rock star in a nowhere bar in the middle of a weekday afternoon."

So there my mother was, telling me about her moment with Dennis Wilson. And my mother had no business being in L.A. in 1980 and saying she had been there too long. But what did I actually know? She graduated from college in 1972. And she had me in Washington State in 1983. So there are like eleven years I know nothing about. I recall her once saying she left California after she finished school. That she had a falling-out with her parents, and she didn't keep in contact with them. But I don't remember asking for any specifics. Here was a perfect opening to pin her down on some things, but I said nothing. She smiled her vague, receding smile, half apologetic, half fuzzy with substance, and the conversation was over.

Okay, so here's the thing. You don't question these sorts of details, why would you? But what kind of fight do you get in with your parents where you never talk to them again? And moreover, who is this woman, drinking in bars, alone, on weekday afternoons? I'm no genius about people, but something is definitely up.

MARCEL PROUST

From

SWANN'S WAY
(IN SEARCH OF LOST TIME, vol. 1)
(1913)

Translated by Lydia Davis

From PART TWO, "SWANN IN LOVE"

MEANWHILE M. VERDURIN, after first asking Swann's permission to light his pipe ("No ceremony here, you understand; we're all pals!"), went and begged the young musician to sit down at the piano. "Leave him alone; don't bother him; he hasn't come here to be tormented," cried Mme Verdurin. "I won't have him tormented."

"But why on earth should it bother him?" rejoined M. Verdurin. "I'm sure M. Swann has never heard the sonata in F sharp which we discovered; he is going to play us the pianoforte arrangement."

"No, no, no, not my sonata!" she screamed, "I don't want to be made to cry until I get a cold in the head, and neuralgia all down my face, like last time; thanks very much, I don't intend to repeat that performance; you are all very kind and considerate; it is easy to see that none of you will have to stay in bed, for a week."

This little scene, which was re-enacted as often as the young pianist sat down to play, never failed to delight the audience, as though each of them were witnessing it for the first time, as a proof of the seductive originality of the "Mistress" as she was styled, and of the acute sensitiveness of her musical "ear." Those nearest to her would attract the attention of the rest, who were smoking or playing cards at the other end of the room, by their cries of "Hear, hear!" which, as in Parliamentary debates, shewed that something worth listening to was being said. And next day they would commiserate with those who had been prevented from coming that evening, and would assure them that the "little scene" had never been so amusingly done.

"Well, all right, then," said M. Verdurin, "he can play just the andante."

"Just the andante! How you do go on," cried his wife. "As if it weren't 'just the andante' that breaks every bone in my body. The 'Master' is really too priceless! Just as though, 'in the Ninth,' he said 'we need only have the finale,' or 'just the overture' of the Meistersinger."

The Doctor, however, urged Mme Verdurin to let the pianist play, not because he supposed her to be malingering when she spoke of the distressing effects that music always had upon her, for he recognised the existence of certain neurasthenic states – but from his habit, common to many doctors, of at once relaxing the strict letter of a prescription as soon as it appeared to jeopardise, what seemed to him far more important, the success of some social gathering at which he was present, and of which the patient whom he had urged for once to forget her dyspepsia or headache formed an essential factor.

"You won't be ill this time, you'll find," he told her, seeking at the same time to subdue her mind by the magnetism of his gaze. "And, if you are ill, we will cure you."

"Will you, really?" Mme Verdurin spoke as though, with so great a favour in store for her, there was nothing for it but to capitulate. Perhaps, too, by dint of saying that she was going to be ill, she had worked herself into a state in which she forgot, occasionally, that it was all only a "little scene," and regarded things, quite sincerely, from an invalid's point of view. For it may often be remarked that invalids grow weary of having the frequency of their attacks depend always on their own prudence in avoiding them, and like to let themselves think that they are free to do everything that they most enjoy doing, although they are always ill after doing it, provided only that they place themselves in the hands of a higher authority which, without putting them to the least inconvenience, can and will, by uttering a word or by administering a tabloid, set them once again upon their feet.

Odette had gone to sit on a tapestry-covered sofa near the piano, saying to Mme Verdurin, "I have my own little corner, haven't I?"

And Mme Verdurin, seeing Swann by himself upon a chair, made him get up. "You're not at all comfortable there; go along and sit by Odette; you can make room for M. Swann there, can't you, Odette?"

"What charming Beauvais!" said Swann, stopping to admire the sofa before he sat down on it, and wishing to be polite.

"I am glad you appreciate my sofa," replied Mme Verdurin, "and I warn you that if you expect ever to see another like it you may as well abandon the idea at once. They never made any more like it. And these little chairs, too, are perfect marvels. You can look at them in a moment. The emblems in each of the bronze mouldings correspond to the subject of the tapestry on the chair; you know, you combine amusement with instruction when you look at them; – I can promise you a delightful time, I assure you. Just look at the little border around the edges; here, look, the little vine on a red background in this one, the Bear and the Grapes. Isn't it well drawn? What do you say? I think they knew a thing or two about design! Doesn't it make your mouth water, this vine? My husband makes out that I am not fond of fruit, because I eat less than he does. But not a bit of it, I am greedier than any of you, but I have no need to fill my mouth with them when I can feed on them with my eyes. What are you all laughing at now, pray? Ask the Doctor; he will tell you that those grapes act on me like a regular purge. Some people go to Fontainebleau for cures; I take my own little Beauvais cure here. But, M. Swann, you mustn't run away without feeling the little bronze mouldings on the backs. Isn't it an exquisite surface? No, no, not with your whole hand like that; feel them properly!"

"If Mme Verdurin is going to start playing about with her bronzes," said the painter, "we shan't get any music to-night."

"Be quiet, you wretch! And yet we poor women," she went on, "are forbidden pleasures far less voluptuous than this. There is no flesh in the world as soft as these. None. When M. Verdurin did me the honour of being madly jealous . . . come, you might at least be polite. Don't say that you never have been jealous!"

"But, my dear, I have said absolutely nothing. Look here, Doctor, I call you as a witness; did I utter a word?"

Swann had begun, out of politeness, to finger the bronzes, and did not like to stop.

"Come along; you can caress them later; now it is you that are going to be caressed, caressed in the ear; you'll like that, I think. Here's the young gentleman who will take charge of that."

After the pianist had played, Swann felt and shewed more interest in him than in any of the other guests, for the following reason:

The year before, at an evening party, he had heard a piece of music played on the piano and violin. At first he had appreciated only the material quality of the sounds which those instruments secreted. And it had been a source of keen pleasure when, below the narrow ribbon of the violin-part, delicate, unyielding, substantial and governing the whole, he had suddenly perceived, where it was trying to surge upwards

in a flowing tide of sound, the mass of the piano-part, multiform, coherent, level, and breaking everywhere in melody
like the deep blue tumult of the sea, silvered and charmed
into a minor key by the moonlight. But at a given moment,
without being able to distinguish any clear outline, or to give
a name to what was pleasing him, suddenly enraptured, he
had tried to collect, to treasure in his memory the phrase or
harmony – he knew not which – that had just been played,
and had opened and expanded his soul, just as the fragrance
of certain roses, wafted upon the moist air of evening, has
the power of dilating our nostrils. Perhaps it was owing to
his own ignorance of music that he had been able to receive
so confused an impression, one of those that are, notwith-
standing, our only purely musical impressions, limited in
their extent, entirely original, and irreducible into any other
kind. An impression of this order, vanishing in an instant,
is, so to speak, an impression sine materia. Presumably the
notes which we hear at such moments tend to spread out
before our eyes, over surfaces greater or smaller according to
their pitch and volume; to trace arabesque designs, to give
us the sensation of breath or tenuity, stability or caprice. But
the notes themselves have vanished before these sensations
have developed sufficiently to escape submersion under
those which the following, or even simultaneous notes have
already begun to awaken in us. And this indefinite perception would continue to smother in its molten liquidity the
motifs which now and then emerge, barely discernible,
to plunge again and disappear and drown; recognised
only by the particular kind of pleasure which they instil,
impossible to describe, to recollect, to name; ineffable; – if
our memory, like a labourer who toils at the laying down
of firm foundations beneath the tumult of the waves, did
not, by fashioning for us facsimiles of those fugitive phrases,

enable us to compare and to contrast them with those that follow. And so, hardly had the delicious sensation, which Swann had experienced, died away, before his memory had furnished him with an immediate transcript, summary, it is true, and provisional, but one on which he had kept his eyes fixed while the playing continued, so effectively that, when the same impression suddenly returned, it was no longer uncapturable. He was able to picture to himself its extent, its symmetrical arrangement, its notation, the strength of its expression; he had before him that definite object which was no longer pure music, but rather design, architecture, thought, and which allowed the actual music to be recalled. This time he had distinguished, quite clearly, a phrase which emerged for a few moments from the waves of sound. It had at once held out to him an invitation to partake of intimate pleasures, of whose existence, before hearing it, he had never dreamed, into which he felt that nothing but this phrase could initiate him; and he had been filled with love for it, as with a new and strange desire.

With a slow and rhythmical movement it led him here, there, everywhere, towards a state of happiness noble, unintelligible, yet clearly indicated. And then, suddenly having reached a certain point from which he was prepared to follow it, after pausing for a moment, abruptly it changed its direction, and in a fresh movement, more rapid, multiform, melancholy, incessant, sweet, it bore him off with it towards a vista of joys unknown. Then it vanished. He hoped, with a passionate longing, that he might find it again, a third time. And reappear it did, though without speaking to him more clearly, bringing him, indeed, a pleasure less profound. But when he was once more at home he needed it, he was like a man into whose life a woman, whom he has seen for a moment passing by, has brought a new form of beauty, which strengthens and enlarges his own power of perception, without his knowing even whether he is ever to see her again whom he loves already, although he knows nothing of her, not even her name.

Indeed this passion for a phrase of music seemed, in the first few months, to be bringing into Swann's life the possibility of a sort of rejuvenation. He had so long since ceased to direct his course towards any ideal goal, and had confined himself to the pursuit of ephemeral satisfactions, that he had come to believe, though without ever formally stating his belief even to himself, that he would remain all his life in that condition, which death alone could alter. More than this, since his mind no longer entertained any lofty ideals, he had ceased to believe in (although he could not have expressly denied) their reality. He had grown also into the habit of taking refuge in trivial considerations, which allowed him to set on one side matters of fundamental importance. Just as he had never stopped to ask himself whether he would not have done better by not going into society, knowing very well that if he had accepted an invitation he must put in an appearance, and that afterwards, if he did not actually call, he must at least leave cards upon his hostess; so in his conversation he took care never to express with any warmth a personal opinion about a thing, but instead would supply facts and details which had a value of a sort in themselves, and excused him from shewing how much he really knew. He would be extremely precise about the recipe for a dish, the dates of a painter's birth and death, and the titles of his works. Sometimes, in spite of himself, he would let himself go so far as to utter a criticism of a work of art, or of some one's interpretation of life, but then he would cloak his words in a tone of irony, as though he did not altogether associate himself with what he was saying. But now, like a confirmed invalid whom, all of a sudden, a change of air and surroundings, or a new course of treatment, or, as sometimes happens, an organic change in himself, spontaneous and unaccountable, seems to have so far recovered from his malady that he begins to envisage the possibility, hitherto beyond all hope, of starting to lead – and better late than never – a wholly different life, Swann found in himself, in the memory of the phrase that he had heard, in certain other sonatas which he had made people play over to him, to see whether he might not, perhaps, discover his phrase among them, the presence of one of those invisible realities in which he had ceased to believe, but to which, as though the music had had upon the moral barrenness from which he was suffering a sort of recreative influence, he was conscious once again of a desire, almost, indeed, of the power to consecrate his life. But, never having managed to find out whose work it was that he had heard played that evening, he had been unable to procure a copy, and finally had forgotten the quest. He had indeed, in the course of the next few days, encountered several of the people who had been at the party with him, and had questioned them; but most of them had either arrived after or left before the piece was played; some had indeed been in the house, but had gone into another room to talk, and those who had stayed to listen had no clearer impression than the rest. As for his hosts, they knew that it was a recently published work which the musicians whom they had engaged for the evening had asked to be allowed to play; but, as these last were now on tour somewhere, Swann could learn nothing further. He had, of course, a number of musical friends, but, vividly as he could recall the exquisite and inexpressible pleasure which the little phrase had given him, and could see, still, before his eyes the forms that it had traced in outline, he was quite incapable of humming over to them the air. And so, at last, he ceased to think of it.

But to-night, at Mme Verdurin's, scarcely had the little pianist begun to play when, suddenly, after a high note held on through two whole bars, Swann saw it approaching, stealing forth from underneath that resonance, which was prolonged and stretched out over it, like a curtain of sound, to veil the mystery of its birth – and recognised, secret, whispering, articulate, the airy and fragrant phrase that he had loved. And it was so peculiarly itself, it had so personal a charm, which nothing else could have replaced, that Swann felt as though he had met, in a friend's drawing-room, a woman whom he had seen and admired, once, in the street, and had despaired of ever seeing her again. Finally the phrase withdrew and vanished, pointing, directing, diligent among the wandering currents of its fragrance, leaving upon Swann's features a reflection of its smile. But now, at last, he could ask the name of his fair unknown (and was told that it was the andante movement of Vinteuil's sonata for the piano and violin), he held it safe, could have it again to himself, at home, as often as he would, could study its language and acquire its secret.

And so, when the pianist had finished, Swann crossed the room and thanked him with a vivacity which delighted Mme Verdurin.

"Isn't he charming?" she asked Swann, "doesn't he just understand it, his sonata, the little wretch? You never dreamed, did you, that a piano could be made to express all that? Upon my word, there's everything in it except the piano! I'm caught out every time I hear it; I think I'm listening to an orchestra. Though it's better, really, than an orchestra, more complete."

The young pianist bent over her as he answered, smiling

and underlining each of his words as though he were making an epigram: "You are most generous to me."

And while Mme Verdurin was saying to her husband, "Run and fetch him a glass of orangeade; it's well earned!" Swann began to tell Odette how he had fallen in love with that little phrase. When their hostess, who was a little way off, called out, "Well! It looks to me as though some one was saying nice things to you, Odette!" she replied, "Yes, very nice," and he found her simplicity delightful. Then he asked for some information about this Vinteuil; what else he had done, and at what period in his life he had composed the sonata; – what meaning the little phrase could have had for him, that was what Swann wanted most to know.

But none of these people who professed to admire this musician (when Swann had said that the sonata was really charming Mme Verdurin had exclaimed, "I quite believe it! Charming, indeed! But you don't dare to confess that you don't know Vinteuil's sonata; you have no right not to know it!" – and the painter had gone on with, "Ah, yes, it's a very fine bit of work, isn't it? Not, of course, if you want something 'obvious,' something 'popular,' but, I mean to say, it makes a very great impression on us artists"), none of them seemed ever to have asked himself these questions, for none of them was able to reply. Even to one or two particular remarks made by Swann on his favourite phrase, "D'you know, that's a funny thing; I had never noticed it; I may as well tell you that I don't much care about peering at things through a microscope, and pricking myself on pin-points of difference; no; we don't waste time splitting hairs in this house; why not? well, it's not a habit of ours, that's all," Mme Verdurin replied, while Dr Cottard gazed at her with open-mouthed admiration, and yearned to be able to follow her as she skipped lightly from one stepping-stone to another of her stock of ready-made phrases. Both he, however, and Mme Cottard, with a kind of common sense which is shared by many people of humble origin, would always take care not to express an opinion, or to pretend to admire a piece of music which they would confess to each other, once they were safely at home, that they no more understood than they could understand the art of "Master" Biche. Inasmuch as the public cannot recognise the charm, the beauty, even the outlines of nature save in the stereotyped impressions of an art which they have gradually assimilated, while an original artist starts by rejecting those impressions, so M. and Mme Cottard, typical, in this respect, of the public, were incapable of finding, either in Vinteuil's sonata or in Biche's portraits, what constituted harmony, for them, in music or beauty in painting. It appeared to them, when the pianist played his sonata, as though he were striking haphazard from the piano a medley of notes which bore no relation to the musical forms to which they themselves were accustomed, and that the painter simply flung the colours haphazard upon his canvas. When, on one of these, they were able to distinguish a human form, they always found it coarsened and vulgarised (that is to say lacking all the elegance of the school of painting through whose spectacles they themselves were in the habit of seeing the people – real, living people, who passed them in the streets) and devoid of truth, as though M. Biche had not known how the human shoulder was constructed, or that a woman's hair was not, ordinarily, purple.

And yet, when the "faithful" were scattered out of earshot, the Doctor felt that the opportunity was too good to be missed, and so (while Mme Verdurin was adding a final word of commendation of Vinteuil's sonata) like a would-be swimmer who jumps into the water, so as to learn, but chooses a moment when there are not too many people looking on: "Yes, indeed; he's what they call a musician di primo cartello!" he exclaimed, with a sudden determination.

Swann discovered no more than that the recent publication of Vinteuil's sonata had caused a great stir among the most advanced school of musicians, but that it was still unknown to the general public.

"I know some one, quite well, called Vinteuil," said Swann, thinking of the old music-master at Combray who had taught my grandmother's sisters.

"Perhaps that's the man!" cried Mme Verdurin.

"Oh, no!" Swann burst out laughing. "If you had ever seen him for a moment you wouldn't put the question."

PERFORMANCE

JAMES JOYCE

A MOTHER

From

DUBLINERS

(1914)

MR HOLOHAN, ASSISTANT secretary of the *Eire Abu* Society, had been walking up and down Dublin for nearly a month, with his hands and pockets full of dirty pieces of paper, arranging about the series of concerts. He had a game leg and for this his friends called him Hoppy Holohan. He walked up and down constantly, stood by the hour at street corners arguing the point and made notes; but in the end it was Mrs Kearney who arranged everything.

Miss Devlin had become Mrs Kearney out of spite. She had been educated in a high-class convent where she had learned French and music. As she was naturally pale and unbending in manner she made few friends at school. When she came to the age of marriage she was sent out to many houses where her playing and ivory manners were much admired. She sat amid the chilly circle of her accomplishments, waiting for some suitor to brave it and offer her a brilliant life. But the young men whom she met were ordinary and she gave them no encouragement, trying to console her romantic desires by eating a great deal of Turkish Delight in secret. However, when she drew near the limit and her friends began to loosen their tongues about her she silenced them by marrying Mr Kearney, who was a bootmaker on Ormond Quay.

He was much older than she. His conversation, which was serious, took place at intervals in his great brown beard. After the first year of married life Mrs Kearney perceived that such a man would wear better than a romantic person but she never put her own romantic ideas away. He was sober, thrifty and pious; he went to the altar every first Friday, sometimes with her, oftener by himself. But she never weakened in her religion and was a good wife to him. At some party in a strange house when she lifted her eyebrow ever so slightly he stood up to take his leave and, when his cough troubled him, she put the eider-down quilt over his feet and made a strong rum punch. For his part he was a model father. By paying a small sum every week into a society he ensured for both his daughters a dowry of one hundred pounds each when they came to the age of twenty-four. He sent the elder daughter, Kathleen, to a good convent, where she learned French and music and afterwards paid her fees at the Academy. Every year in the month of July Mrs Kearney found occasion to say to some friend:

–My good man is packing us off to Skerries for a few weeks.

If it was not Skerries it was Howth or Greystones.

When the Irish Revival began to be appreciable Mrs Kearney determined to take advantage of her daughter's name and brought an Irish teacher to the house. Kathleen and her sister sent Irish picture postcards to their friends and these friends sent back other Irish picture postcards. On special Sundays when Mr Kearney went with his family to the pro-cathedral a little crowd of people would assemble after mass at the corner of Cathedral Street. They were all friends of the Kearneys – musical friends or Nationalist friends; and, when they had played every little counter of gossip, they shook hands with one another all together, laughing at the crossing of so many hands and said goodbye to one another in Irish. Soon the name of Miss Kathleen Kearney began to be heard often on people's lips. People said that she was very clever at music and a very nice girl and, moreover, that she was a believer in the language movement. Mrs Kearney was well content at this. Therefore she was not surprised when one day Mr Holohan came to her and proposed that her daughter should be the accompanist at a series of four grand concerts which his Society was going to give in the Ancient Concert Rooms. She brought him into the drawing-room, made him sit down and brought out the decanter and the silver biscuit-barrel. She entered heart and soul into the details of the enterprise, advised and dissuaded; and finally a contract was drawn up by which Kathleen was to receive eight guineas for her services as accompanist at the four grand concerts.

As Mr Holohan was a novice in such delicate matters as the wording of bills and the disposing of items for a pro-gramme Mrs Kearney helped him. She had tact. She knew what *artistes* should go into capitals and what *artistes* should go into small type. She knew that the first tenor would not like to come on after Mr Meade's comic turn. To keep the audience continually diverted she slipped the doubtful items in between the old favourites. Mr Holohan called to see her every day to have her advice on some point. She was invari-ably friendly and advising – homely, in fact. She pushed the decanter towards him, saying:

–Now, help yourself, Mr Holohan!

And while he was helping himself she said:

–Don't be afraid! Don't be afraid of it!

Everything went on smoothly. Mrs Kearney bought some lovely blush-pink charmeuse in Brown Thomas's to let into the front of Kathleen's dress. It cost a pretty penny; but there are occasions when a little expense is justifiable. She took a dozen of two-shilling tickets for the final concert and sent them to those friends who could not be trusted to come otherwise. She forgot nothing and, thanks to her, everything that was to be done was done.

The concerts were to be on Wednesday, Thursday, Friday and Saturday. When Mrs Kearney arrived with her daughter at the Antient Concert Rooms on Wednesday night she did not like the look of things. A few young men, wearing bright blue badges in their coats, stood idle in the vestibule; none of them wore evening dress. She passed by with her daughter and a quick glance through the open door of the hall showed her the cause of the stewards' idleness. At first she wondered had she mistaken the hour. No, it was twenty minutes to eight.

In the dressing-room behind the stage she was introduced to the secretary of the Society, Mr Fitzpatrick. She smiled and shook his hand. He was a little man with a white vacant face. She noticed that he wore his soft brown hat carelessly on the side of his head and that his accent was flat. He held a programme in his hand and, while he was talking to her, he chewed one end of it into a moist pulp. He seemed to bear disappointments lightly. Mr Holohan came into the dressing-room every few minutes with reports from the box-office. The *artistes* talked among themselves nervously, glanced from time to time at the mirror and rolled and unrolled their music. When it was nearly half-past eight the few people in the hall began to express their desire to be entertained. Mr Fitzpatrick came in, smiled vacantly at the room, and said:

–Well now, ladies and gentlemen, I suppose we'd better open the ball.

Mrs Kearney rewarded his very flat final syllable with a quick stare of contempt and then said to her daughter encouragingly:

–Are you ready, dear?

When she had an opportunity she called Mr Holohan aside and asked him to tell her what it meant. Mr Holohan did not know what it meant. He said that the committee had made a mistake in arranging for four concerts: four was too many.

–And the *artistes*! said Mrs Kearney. Of course they are doing their best, but really they are not good.

Mr Holohan admitted that the *artistes* were no good but the committee, he said, had decided to let the first three concerts go as they pleased and reserve all the talent for Saturday night. Mrs Kearney said nothing but, as the mediocre items followed one another on the platform and the few people in the hall grew fewer and fewer, she began to regret that she had put herself to any expense for such a concert. There was something she didn't like in the look of things and Mr Fitzpatrick's vacant smile irritated her very much. However, she said nothing and waited to see how it would end. The concert expired shortly before ten and every one went home quickly.

The concert on Thursday night was better attended but Mrs Kearney saw at once that the house was filled with paper. The audience behaved indecorously as if the concert were an informal dress rehearsal. Mr Fitzpatrick seemed to enjoy himself; he was quite unconscious that Mrs Kearney was taking angry note of his conduct. He stood at the edge of the screen, from time to time jutting out his head and exchanging a laugh with two friends in the corner of the balcony. In the course of the evening Mrs Kearney learned that the Friday concert was to be abandoned and that the committee was going to move heaven and earth to secure a bumper house on Saturday night. When she heard this she sought out Mr Holohan. She buttonholed him as he was limping out quickly with a glass of lemonade for a young lady and asked him was it true. Yes, it was true.

–But, of course, that doesn't alter the contract, she said. The contract was for four concerts.

Mr Holohan seemed to be in a hurry; he advised her to speak to Mr Fitzpatrick. Mrs Kearney was now beginning to be alarmed. She called Mr Fitzpatrick away from his screen and told him that her daughter had signed for four concerts and that, of course, according to the terms of the contract, she should receive the sum originally stipulated for whether the society gave the four concerts or not. Mr Fitzpatrick, who did not catch the point at issue very quickly, seemed unable to resolve the difficulty and said that he would bring the matter before the committee. Mrs Kearney's anger began to flutter in her cheek and she had all she could do to keep from asking:

–And who is the *Cometty*, pray?

But she knew that it would not be ladylike to do that: so she was silent.

Little boys were sent out into the principal streets of Dublin early on Friday morning with bundles of handbills. Special puffs appeared in all the evening papers reminding the music-loving public of the treat which was in store for it on the following evening. Mrs Kearney was somewhat reassured but she thought well to tell her husband part of her suspicions. He listened carefully and said that perhaps it would be better if he went with her on Saturday night. She agreed. She respected her husband in the same way as she respected the General Post Office, as something large, secure and fixed; and though she knew the small number of his talents she appreciated his abstract value as a male. She was glad that he had suggested coming with her. She thought her plans over.

The night of the grand concert came. Mrs Kearney, with

her husband and daughter, arrived at the Antient Concert Rooms three-quarters of an hour before the time at which the concert was to begin. By ill luck it was a rainy evening. Mrs Kearney placed her daughter's clothes and music in charge of her husband and went all over the building looking for Mr Holohan or Mr Fitzpatrick. She could find neither. She asked the stewards was any member of the committee in the hall and, after a great deal of trouble, a steward brought out a little woman named Miss Beirne to whom Mrs Kearney explained that she wanted to see one of the secretaries. Miss Beirne expected them any minute and asked could she do anything. Mrs Kearney looked searchingly at the oldish face which was screwed into an expression of trustfulness and enthusiasm and answered:

–No, thank you!

The little woman hoped they would have a good house. She looked out at the rain until the melancholy of the wet street effaced all the trustfulness and enthusiasm from her twisted features. Then she gave a little sigh and said:

–Ah, well! We did our best, the dear knows.

Mrs Kearney had to go back to the dressing-room.

The *artistes* were arriving. The bass and the second tenor had already come. The bass, Mr Duggan, was a slender young man with a scattered black moustache. He was the son of a hall porter in an office in the city and, as a boy, he had sung prolonged bass notes in the resounding hall. From this humble state he had raised himself until he had become a first-rate *artiste*. He had appeared in grand opera. One night, when an operatic *artiste* had fallen ill, he had undertaken the part of the king in the opera of *Maritana* at the Queen's Theatre. He sang his music with great feeling and volume and was warmly welcomed by the gallery; but, unfortunately, he marred the good impression by wiping his nose in his gloved hand once or twice out of thoughtlessness. He was unassuming and spoke little. He said *yous* so softly that it passed unnoticed and he never drank anything stronger than milk for his voice's sake. Mr Bell, the second tenor, was a fair-haired little man who competed every year for prizes at the Feis Ceoil. On his fourth trial he had been awarded a bronze medal. He was extremely nervous and extremely jealous of other tenors and he covered his nervous jealousy with an ebullient friendliness. It was his humour to have people know what an ordeal a concert was to him. Therefore when he saw Mr Duggan he went over to him and asked:

–Are you in it too?

–Yes, said Mr Duggan.

Mr Bell laughed at his fellow-sufferer, held out his hand and said:

–Shake!

Mrs Kearney passed by these two young men and went to the edge of the screen to view the house. The seats were being filled up rapidly and a pleasant noise circulated in the auditorium. She came back and spoke to her husband privately. Their conversation was evidently about Kathleen for they both glanced at her often as she stood chatting to one of her Nationalist friends, Miss Healy, the contralto. An unknown solitary woman with a pale face walked through the room. The women followed with keen eyes the faded blue dress which was stretched upon a meagre body. Some one said that she was Madame Glynn, the soprano.

–I wonder where did they dig her up, said Kathleen to Miss Healy. I'm sure I never heard of her.

Miss Healy had to smile. Mr Holohan limped into the dressing-room at that moment and the two young ladies asked him who was the unknown woman. Mr Holohan said that she was Madam Glynn from London. Madam Glynn took her stand in a corner of the room, holding a roll of music stiffly before her and from time to time changing the direction of her startled gaze. The shadow took her faded dress into shelter but fell revengefully into the little cup behind her collar-bone. The noise of the hall became more audible. The first tenor and the baritone arrived together. They were both well dressed, stout and complacent and they brought a breath of opulence among the company.

Mrs Kearney brought her daughter over to them, and talked to them amiably. She wanted to be on good terms with them but, while she strove to be polite, her eyes followed Mr Holohan in his limping and devious courses. As soon as she could she excused herself and went out after him.

–Mr Holohan, I want to speak to you for a moment, she said.

They went down to a discreet part of the corridor. Mrs Kearney asked him when was her daughter going to be paid. Mr Holohan said that Mr Fitzpatrick had charge of that. Mrs Kearney said that she didn't know anything about Mr Fitzpatrick. Her daughter had signed a contract for eight guineas and she would have to be paid. Mr Holohan said that it wasn't his business.

–Why isn't it your business? asked Mrs Kearney. Didn't you yourself bring her the contract? Anyway, if it's not your business it's my business and I mean to see to it.

–You'd better speak to Mr Fitzpatrick, said Mr Holohan distantly.

–I don't know anything about Mr Fitzpatrick, repeated Mrs Kearney. I have my contract, and I intend to see that it is carried out.

When she came back to the dressing-room her cheeks were slightly suffused. The room was lively. Two men in outdoor dress had taken possession of the fireplace and were chatting familiarly with Miss Healy and the baritone. They were the *Freeman* man and Mr O'Madden Burke. The *Freeman* man had come in to say that he could not wait for the concert as he had to report the lecture which an American priest was giving in the Mansion House. He said they were to leave the report for him at the *Freeman* office and he would see that it went in. He was a grey-haired man, with a plausible voice and careful manners. He held an extinguished cigar in his hand and the aroma of cigar smoke floated near him. He had not intended to stay a moment because concerts and *artistes* bored him considerably but he remained leaning against the mantelpiece. Miss Healy stood in front of him, talking and laughing. He was old enough to suspect one reason for her politeness but young enough in spirit to turn the moment to account. The warmth, fragrance and colour of her body appealed to his senses. He was pleasantly conscious that the bosom which he saw rise and fall slowly beneath him rose and fell at that moment for him, that the laughter and fragrance and wilful glances were his tribute. When he could stay no longer he took leave of her regretfully.

–O'Madden Burke will write the notice, he explained to Mr Holohan, and I'll see it in.

–Thank you very much, Mr Hendrick, said Mr Holohan. You'll see it in, I know. Now, won't you have a little something before you go?

–I don't mind, said Mr Hendrick.

The two men went along some tortuous passages and up a dark staircase and came to a secluded room where one of the stewards was uncorking bottles for a few gentlemen. One of these gentlemen was Mr O'Madden Burke, who had found out the room by instinct. He was a suave elderly man who balanced his imposing body, when at rest, upon a large silk umbrella. His magniloquent western name was the moral umbrella upon which he balanced the fine problem of his finances. He was widely respected.

While Mr Holohan was entertaining the *Freeman* man Mrs Kearney was speaking so animatedly to her husband that he had to ask her to lower her voice. The conversation of the others in the dressing-room had become strained. Mr Bell, the first item, stood ready with his music but the accompanist made no sign. Evidently something was wrong. Mr Kearney looked straight before him, stroking his beard, while Mrs Kearney spoke into Kathleen's ear with subdued emphasis. From the hall came sounds of encouragement, clapping and stamping of feet. The first tenor and the baritone and Miss Healy stood together, waiting tranquilly, but Mr Bell's nerves were greatly agitated because he was afraid the audience would think that he had come late.

Mr Holohan and Mr O'Madden Burke came into the room. In a moment Mr Holohan perceived the hush. He went over to Mrs Kearney and spoke with her earnestly. While they were speaking the noise in the hall grew louder. Mr Holohan became very red and excited. He spoke volubly, but Mrs Kearney said curtly at intervals:

–She won't go on. She must get her eight guineas.

Mr Holohan pointed desperately towards the hall where the audience was clapping and stamping. He appealed to Mr Kearney and to Kathleen. But Mr Kearney continued to stroke his beard and Kathleen looked down, moving the point of her new shoe: it was not her fault. Mrs Kearney repeated:

–She won't go on without her money.

After a swift struggle of tongues Mr Holohan hobbled out in haste. The room was silent. When the strain of the silence had become somewhat painful Miss Healy said to the baritone:

–Have you seen Mrs Pat Campbell this week?

The baritone had not seen her but he had been told that she was very fine. The conversation went no further. The first tenor bent his head and began to count the links of the gold chain which was extended across his waist, smiling and humming random notes to observe the effect on the frontal sinus. From time to time every one glanced at Mrs Kearney.

The noise in the auditorium had risen to a clamour when Mr Fitzpatrick burst into the room, followed by Mr Holohan, who was panting. The clapping and stamping in the hall was punctuated by whistling. Mr Fitzpatrick held a few bank-notes in his hand. He counted out four into Mrs Kearney's hand and said she would get the other half at the interval. Mrs Kearney said:

–This is four shillings short.

But Kathleen gathered in her skirt and said: *Now, Mr Bell*, to the first item, who was shaking like an aspen. The singer and the accompanist went out together. The noise in the hall died away. There was a pause of a few seconds: and then the piano was heard.

The first part of the concert was very successful except for Madam Glynn's item. The poor lady sang *Killarney* in a bodiless gasping voice, with all the old-fashioned mannerisms of intonation and pronunciation which she believed lent elegance to her singing. She looked as if she had been resurrected from an old stage-wardrobe and the cheaper parts of the hall made fun of her high wailing notes. The first tenor and the contralto, however, brought down the house. Kathleen played a selection of Irish airs which was generously applauded. The first part closed with a stirring patriotic recitation delivered by a young lady who arranged amateur theatricals. It was deservedly applauded; and, when it was ended, the men went out for the interval, content.

All this time the dressing-room was a hive of excitement. In one corner were Mr Holohan, Mr Fitzpatrick, Miss Beirne, two of the stewards, the baritone, the bass, and Mr O'Madden Burke. Mr O'Madden Burke said it was the most scandalous exhibition he had ever witnessed. Miss Kathleen Kearney's musical career was ended in Dublin after that, he said. The baritone was asked what did he think of Mrs Kearney's conduct. He did not like to say anything. He had been paid his money and wished to be at peace with men. However, he said that Mrs Kearney might have taken the *artistes* into consideration. The stewards and the secretaries debated hotly as to what should be done when the interval came.

–I agree with Miss Beirne, said Mr O'Madden Burke. Pay her nothing.

In another corner of the room were Mrs Kearney and her husband, Mr Bell, Miss Healy and the young lady who had to recite the patriotic piece. Mrs Kearney said that the committee had treated her scandalously. She had spared neither trouble nor expense and this was how she was repaid.

They thought they had only a girl to deal with and that, therefore, they could ride roughshod over her. But she would show them their mistake. They wouldn't have dared to have treated her like that if she had been a man. But she would see that her daughter got her rights: she wouldn't be fooled. If they didn't pay her to the last farthing she would make Dublin ring. Of course she was sorry for the sake of the *artistes*. But what else could she do? She appealed to the second tenor who said he thought she had not been well treated. Then she appealed to Miss Healy. Miss Healy wanted to join the other group but she did not like to do so because she was a great friend of Kathleen's and the Kearneys had often invited her to their house.

As soon as the first part was ended Mr Fitzpatrick and Mr Holohan went over to Mrs Kearney and told her that the other four guineas would be paid after the committee meeting on the following Tuesday and that, in case her daughter did not play for the second part, the committee would consider the contract broken and would pay nothing.

–I haven't seen any committee, said Mrs Kearney angrily. My daughter has her contract. She will get four pounds eight into her hand or a foot she won't put on that platform.

–I'm surprised at you, Mrs Kearney, said Mr Holohan. I never thought you would treat us this way.

–And what way did you treat me? asked Mrs Kearney.

Her face was inundated with an angry colour and she looked as if she would attack some one with her hands.

–I'm asking for my rights, she said.

–You might have some sense of decency, said Mr Holohan.

–Might I, indeed? . . . And when I ask when my daughter is going to be paid I can't get a civil answer.

She tossed her head and assumed a haughty voice:

–You must speak to the secretary. It's not my business. I'm a great fellow fol-the-diddle-I-do.

–I thought you were a lady, said Mr Holohan, walking away from her abruptly.

After that Mrs Kearney's conduct was condemned on all hands: everyone approved of what the committee had done. She stood at the door, haggard with rage, arguing with her husband and daughter, gesticulating with them. She waited until it was time for the second part to begin in the hope that the secretaries would approach her. But Miss Healy had kindly consented to play one or two accompaniments. Mrs Kearney had to stand aside to allow the baritone and his accompanist to pass up to the platform. She stood still for an instant like an angry stone image and, when the first notes of the song struck her ear, she caught up her daughter's cloak and said to her husband:

–Get a cab!

He went out at once. Mrs Kearney wrapped the cloak round her daughter and followed him. As she passed through the doorway she stopped and glared into Mr Holohan's face.

–I'm not done with you yet, she said.

–But I'm done with you, said Mr Holohan.

Kathleen followed her mother meekly. Mr Holohan began to pace up and down the room, in order to cool himself for he felt his skin on fire.

–That's a nice lady! he said. O, she's a nice lady!

–You did the proper thing, Holohan, said Mr O'Madden Burke, poised upon his umbrella in approval.

VIRGINIA WOOLF

THE STRING
QUARTET
(1921)

WELL, HERE WE are, and if you cast your eye over the room you will see that Tubes and trams and omnibuses, private carriages not a few, even, I venture to believe, landaus with bays in them, have been busy at it, weaving threads from one end of London to the other. Yet I begin to have my doubts—

If indeed it's true, as they're saying, that Regent Street is up, and the Treaty signed, and the weather not cold for the time of year, and even at that rent not a flat to be had, and the worst of influenza its after effects; if I bethink me of having forgotten to write about the leak in the larder, and left my glove in the train; if the ties of blood require me, leaning forward, to accept cordially the hand which is perhaps offered hesitatingly—

"Seven years since we met!"

"The last time in Venice."

"And where are you living now?"

"Well, the late afternoon suits me the best, though, if it weren't asking too much—"

"But I knew you at once!"

"Still, the war made a break—"

If the mind's shot through by such little arrows, and – for human society compels it – no sooner is one launched than another presses forward; if this engenders heat and in addition they've turned on the electric light; if saying one thing does, in so many cases, leave behind it a need to improve and revise, stirring besides regrets, pleasures, vanities, and desires – if it's all the facts I mean, and the hats, the fur boas, the gentlemen's swallow-tail coats, and pearl tie-pins that come to the surface – what chance is there?

Of what? It becomes every minute more difficult to say why, in spite of everything, I sit here believing I can't now say what, or even remember the last time it happened.

"Did you see the procession?"

"The King looked cold."

"No, no, no. But what was it?"

"She's bought a house at Malmesbury."

"How lucky to find one!"

On the contrary, it seems to me pretty sure that she, who-ever she may be, is damned, since it's all a matter of flats and hats and sea gulls, or so it seems to be for a hundred people sitting here well dressed, walled in, furred, replete. Not that I can boast, since I too sit passive on a gilt chair, only turning the earth above a buried memory, as we all do, for there are signs, if I'm not mistaken, that we're all recalling something, furtively seeking something. Why fidget? Why so anxious about the sit of cloaks; and gloves – whether to button or unbutton? Then watch that elderly face against the dark canvas, a moment ago urbane and flushed; now taciturn and sad, as if in shadow. Was it the sound of the second violin tuning in the ante-room? Here they come; four black figures, carrying instruments, and seat themselves facing the white squares under the downpour of light; rest the tips of their bows on the music stand; with a simultaneous movement lift them; lightly poise them, and, looking across at the player opposite, the first violin counts one, two, three—

Flourish, spring, burgeon, burst! The pear tree on the top of the mountain. Fountains jet; drops descend. But the waters of the Rhone flow swift and deep, race under the arches, and sweep the trailing water leaves, washing shadows over the silver fish, the spotted fish rushed down by the swift waters, now swept into an eddy where – it's difficult this – conglomeration of fish all in a pool; leaping, splashing, scraping sharp fins; and such a boil of current that the yellow pebbles are churned round and round, round and round – free now, rushing downwards, or even somehow ascending in exquisite spirals into the air; curled like thin shavings from under a plane; up and up. . . . How lovely goodness is in those who, stepping lightly, go smiling through the world! Also in jolly old fishwives, squatted under arches, obscene old women, how deeply they laugh and shake and rollick, when they walk, from side to side, hum, hah!

"That's an early Mozart, of course—"

"But the tune, like all his tunes, makes one despair – I mean hope. What do I mean? That's the worst of music! I want to dance, laugh, eat pink cakes, yellow cakes, drink thin, sharp wine. Or an indecent story, now – I could relish that. The older one grows the more one likes indecency. Hah, hah! I'm laughing. What at? You said nothing, nor did the old gentleman opposite. . . . But suppose – suppose – Hush!"

The melancholy river bears us on. When the moon comes through the trailing willow boughs, I see your face, I hear your voice and the bird singing as we pass the osier bed. What are you whispering? Sorrow, sorrow. Joy, joy. Woven together, inextricably commingled, bound in pain and strewn in sorrow – crash!

The boat sinks. Rising, the figures ascend, but now leaf thin, tapering to a dusky wraith, which, fiery tipped, draws its twofold passion from my heart. For me it sings, unseals my sorrow, thaws compassion, floods with love the sunless world, nor, ceasing, abates its tenderness, but deftly, subtly, weaves in and out until in this pattern, this consummation, the cleft ones unify; soar, sob, sink to rest, sorrow and joy.

Why then grieve? Ask what? Remain unsatisfied? I say all's been settled; yes; laid to rest under a coverlet of rose leaves, falling. Falling. Ah, but they cease. One rose leaf, falling from an enormous height, like a little parachute dropped from an invisible balloon, turns, flutters waveringly. It won't reach us.

"No, no. I noticed nothing. That's the worst of music – these silly dreams. The second violin was late, you say?"

"There's old Mrs Munro, feeling her way out – blinder each year, poor woman – on this slippery floor."

Eyeless old age, grey-headed Sphinx. . . . There she stands on the pavement, beckoning, so sternly, to the red omnibus.

"How lovely! How well they play! How – how – how!"

The tongue is but a clapper. Simplicity itself. The feathers in the hat next me are bright and pleasing as a child's rattle. The leaf on the plane-tree flashes green through the chink in the curtain. Very strange, very exciting.

"How – how – how!" Hush!

These are the lovers on the grass.

"If, madam, you will take my hand—"

"Sir, I would trust you with my heart. Moreover, we have left our bodies in the banqueting hall. Those on the turf are the shadows of our souls."

"Then these are the embraces of our souls." The lemons nod assent. The swan pushes from the bank and floats dreaming into mid-stream.

"But to return. He followed me down the corridor, and, as we turned the corner, trod on the lace of my petticoat. What could I do but cry 'Ah!' and stop to finger it? At which he drew his sword, made passes as if he were stabbing something to death, and cried, 'Mad! Mad! Mad!' Whereupon I screamed, and the Prince, who was writing in the large vellum book in the oriel window, came out in his velvet skull-cap and furred slippers, snatched a rapier from the wall – the King of Spain's gift, you know – on which I escaped, flinging on this cloak to hide the ravages to my skirt – to hide . . . But listen! the horns!"

The gentleman replies so fast to the lady, and she runs up the scale with such witty exchange of compliment now culminating in a sob of passion, that the words are indistinguishable though the meaning is plain enough – love, laughter, flight, pursuit, celestial bliss – all floated out on the gayest ripple of tender endearment – until the sound of the silver horns, at first far distant, gradually sounds more and more distinctly, as if seneschals were saluting the dawn or proclaiming ominously the escape of the lovers . . . The green garden, moonlit pool, lemons, lovers, and fish are all dissolved in the opal sky, across which, as the horns are joined by trumpets and supported by clarions there rise white arches firmly planted on marble pillars. . . . Tramp and trumpeting. Clang and clangour. Firm establishment. Fast foundations. March of myriads. Confusion and chaos trod to earth. But this city to which we travel has neither stone nor marble; hangs enduring; stands unshakable; nor does a face, nor does a flag greet or welcome. Leave then to perish your hope; droop in the desert my joy; naked advance. Bare are the pillars; auspicious to none; casting no shade; resplendent; severe. Back then I fall, eager no more, desiring only to go, find the street, mark the buildings, greet the applewoman, say to the maid who opens the door: A starry night.

"Good night, good night. You go this way?"
"Alas. I go that."

MAYA ANGELOU

THE REUNION
(1983)

NOBODY COULD HAVE told me that she'd be out with a black man; out, like going out. But there she was, in 1958, sitting up in the Blue Palm Cafe, when I played the Sunday matinee with Cal Callen's band.

Here's how it was. After we got on the stage, the place was packed, first Cal led us into "D. B. Blues." Of course I know just like everybody else that Cal's got a thing for Lester Young. Maybe because Cal plays the tenor sax, or maybe because he's about as red as Lester Young, or maybe just 'cause Lester is the Prez. Anybody that's played with Cal knows that the kickoff tune is gotta be "D. B. Blues." So I was ready. We romped.

I'd played with some of those guys, but never all together, but we took off on that tune like we were headed for Bird-land in New York City. The audience liked it. Applauded as much as black audiences ever applaud. Black folks act like they are sure that with a little bit of study they could do whatever you're doing on the stage as well as you do it. If not better. So they clap for your luck. Lucky for you that they're not up there to show you where it's really at.

Anyway, after the applause, Cal started to introduce the band. That's his style. Everybody knows that too. After he's through introducing everybody, he's not going to say anything else till the next set, it doesn't matter how many times we play. So he's got a little comedy worked into the introduction patter. He started with Olly, the trumpet man. . . . "And here we have a real Chicagoan . . . by way of Atlanta, Georgia . . . bringing soul to Soulville . . . Mr Olly Martin."

He went on. I looked out into the audience. People sitting, not listening, or better, listening with one side of their ears and talking with both sides of their mouths. Some couples were making a little love . . . and some whites were there trying hard to act natural . . . like they come to the South Side of Chicago every day or maybe like they live there . . . then I saw her. Saw Miss Beth Ann Baker, sitting up with her blond self with a big black man . . . pretty black man. What? White girls, when they look alike, can look so much alike, I thought maybe it wasn't Beth. I looked again. It was her. I remember too well the turn of her cheek. The sliding way her jaw goes up to her hair. That was her. I might have missed a few notes, I might have in fact missed the whole interlude music.

What was she doing in Chicago? On the South Side. And with a black man? Beth Ann Baker of the Baker Cotton Gin. Miss Cotton Queen Baker of Georgia . . .

Then I heard Cal get round to me. He saved me for the last. Mainly cause I'm female and he can get a little rise out of the audience if he says, as he did say, "And our piano man is a lady. And what a lady. A cooker and a looker. Ladies and Gentlemen, I'd like to introduce to you Miss Philomena Jenkins. Folks call her Meanie." I noticed some applause, but mainly I was watching Beth. She heard my name and she looked right into my eyes. Her blue ones got as big as my black ones. She recognized me, in fact in a second we tipped eyelids at each other. Not winking. Just squinting, to see better. There was something that I couldn't recognize. Something I'd never seen in all those years in Baker, Georgia. Not panic, and it wasn't fear. Whatever was in that face seemed familiar, but before I could really read it, Cal announced our next number. "Round 'bout Midnight."

That used to be my song, for so many reasons. In Baker, the only time I could practice jazz, in the church, was round 'bout midnight. When the best chord changes came to me it was generally round 'bout midnight. When my first lover held me in his arms, it was round 'bout midnight. Usually when it's time to play that tune I dig right in it. But this time, I was too busy thinking about Beth and her family . . . and what she was doing in Chicago, on the South Side, escorted by the grooviest looking cat I'd seen in a long time. I was really trying to figure it out, then Cal's saxophone pushed its way into my figurings. Forced me to remember "Round 'bout Midnight." Reminded me of the years of loneliness, the doing-without days, the C.M.E. church, and the old ladies with hands like men and the round 'bout midnight dreams of crossing over Jordan. Then I took thirty-two bars. My fingers found the places between the keys where the blues and the truth lay hiding. I dug out the story of a woman without a man, and a man without hope. I tried to wedge myself in and lay down in the groove between B-flat and B-natural. I must of gotten close to it, because the audience brought me out with their clapping. Even Cal said, "Yeah baby, that's it." I nodded to him then to the audience and looked around for Beth.

How did she like them apples? What did she think of little Philomena that used to shake the farts out of her sheets, wash her dirty drawers, pick up after her slovenly mama? What did she think now? Did she know that I was still aching from the hurt Georgia put on me? But Beth was gone. So was her boyfriend.

I had lived with my parents until I was thirteen, in the servants' quarters. A house behind the Baker main house.

Daddy was the butler, my mother was the cook, and I went to a segregated school on the other side of town where the other kids called me the Baker Nigger. Momma's nimble fingers were never able to sew away the truth of Beth's hand-me-down and thrown away clothing. I had a lot to say to Beth, and she was gone.

That was a bring-down. I guess what I wanted was to rub her face in "See now, you thought all I would ever be was you and your mama's flunky." And "See now, how folks, even you, pay to listen to me" and "See now, I'm saying something nobody else can say. Not the way I say it, anyway." But her table was empty.

We did the rest of the set. Some of my favorite tunes, "Sophisticated Lady," "Misty," and "Cool Blues." I admit that I never got back into the groove until we did "When Your Lover Has Gone."

After the closing tune, "Lester Leaps In," which Cal set at a tempo like he was trying to catch the last train to Mobile, was over, the audience gave us their usual thank-you, and we were off for a twenty-minute intermission.

Some of the guys went out to turn on and a couple went to tables where they had ladies waiting for them. But I went to the back of the dark smoky bar where even the occasional sunlight from the front door made no difference. My blood was still fluttering in my fingertips, throbbing. If she was listed in the phone directory I would call her. Hello Miss Beth . . . this is Philomena . . . who was your maid, whose whole family worked for you. Or could I say, Hello Beth. Is this Beth? Well, this is Miss Jenkins. I saw you yesterday at the Blue Palm Cafe. I used to know your parents. In fact your mother said my mother was a gem, and my father was a treasure. I used to laugh 'cause your mother drank so much whiskey, but my Momma said, "Judge not, that ye be not judged." Then I found out that your father had three children down in our part of town and they all looked just like you, only prettier. Oh Beth, now . . . now . . . shouldn't have a chip . . . mustn't be bitter . . . She of course would hang up.

Just imagining what I would have said to her cheered me up. I ordered a drink from the bartender and settled back into my reverie. . . . Hello Beth . . . this is a friend from Baker. What were you doing with that black man Sunday? . . .

"Philomena? Remember me?" She stood before me absorbing the light. The drawl was still there. The soft accent rich white girls practice in Georgia to show that they had breeding. I couldn't think of anything to say. Did I remember her? There was no way I could answer the question.

"I asked Willard to wait for me in the car. I wanted to talk to you."

I sipped my drink and looked in the mirror over the bar and wondered what she really wanted. Her reflection wasn't threatening at all.

"I told him that we grew up . . . in the same town."

I was relieved that she hadn't said we grew up together. By the time I was ten, I knew growing up meant going to work. She smiled and I held my drink.

"I'm engaged to Willard and very happy."

I'm proud of my face. It didn't jump up and walk the bar.

She gave a practiced nod to the bartender and ordered a drink. "He teaches high school here on the South Side." Her drink came and she lifted the glass and our eyes met in the mirror. "I met him two years ago in Canada. We are very happy."

Why the hell was she telling me her fairy story? We weren't kin. So she had a black man. Did she think like most whites in mixed marriages that she had done the whole race a favor?

"My parents . . ." her voice became small, whispery. "My

parents don't understand. They think I'm with Willard just to spite them. They . . . When's the last time you went home, Mena?" She didn't wait for my answer.

"They hate him. So much, they say they will disown me." Disbelief made her voice strong again. "They said I could never set foot in Baker again." She tried to catch my eyes in the mirror but I looked down at my drink. "I know there's a lot wrong with Baker, but it's my home." The drawl was turning into a whine. "Mother said, now mind you, she has never laid eyes on Willard, she said, if she had dreamed when I was a baby that I would grow up to marry a nig . . . a black man, she'd have choked me to death on her breast. That's a cruel thing for a mother to say. I told her so."

She bent forward and I shifted to see her expression, but her profile was hidden by the blond hair. "He doesn't understand, and me either. He didn't grow up in the South." I thought, no matter where he grew up, he wasn't white and rich and spoiled. "I just wanted to talk to somebody who knew me. Knew Baker. You know, a person can get lonely. . . . I don't see any of my friends, anymore. Do you understand, Mena? My parents gave me everything."

Well, they owned everything.

"Willard is the first thing I ever got for myself. And I'm not going to give him up."

We faced each other for the first time. She sounded like her mother and looked like a ten-year-old just before a tantrum.

"He's mine. He belongs to me."

The musicians were tuning up on the bandstand. I drained my glass and stood.

"Mena, I really enjoyed seeing you again, and talking about old times. I live in New York, but I come to Chicago every other weekend. Say, will you come to our wedding? We haven't set the date yet. Please come. It's going to be here . . . in a black church . . . somewhere."

"Good-bye Beth. Tell your parents I said go to hell and take you with them, just for company."

I sat down at the piano. She still had everything. Her mother would understand the stubbornness and send her off to Paris or the Moon. Her father couldn't deny that black skin was beautiful. She had money and a wonderful-looking man to play with. If she stopped wanting him she could always walk away. She'd still be white.

The band was halfway into the "D. B. Blues" release before I thought, she had the money, but I had the music. She and her parents had had the power to hurt me when I was young, but look, the stuff in me lifted me up high above them. No matter how bad times became, I would always be the song struggling to be heard.

The piano keys were slippery with tears. I know, I sure as hell wasn't crying for myself.

GUSTAVE FLAUBERT

From

MADAME BOVARY
(1856)

Translated by Francis Steegmuller

PART TWO, CHAPTER 15

THERE WAS A crowd waiting outside, lined up behind railings on both sides of the entrance. At the adjoining street corners huge posters in fancy lettering announced: "*Lucie de Lammermoor... Lagardy... Opéra...* etc." It was a fine evening; everyone was hot: many a set of curls was drenched in sweat, and handkerchiefs were out, mopping red brows; now and again a soft breeze blowing from the river gently stirred the edges of the canvas awning over café doors. But just a short distance away there was a coolness, provided by an icy draft smelling of tallow, leather and oil – the effluvia of the Rue des Charettes, with its great, gloomy, barrel-filled warehouses.

Fearing lest they appear ridiculous, Emma insisted that they stroll a bit along the river front before going in; and Bovary, by way of precaution, kept the tickets in his hand and his hand in his trousers pocket, pressed reassuringly against his stomach.

Her heart began to pound as they entered the foyer. A smile of satisfaction rose involuntarily to her lips at seeing the crowd hurry off to the right down the corridor, while she climbed the stairs leading to the first tier. She took pleasure, like a child, in pushing open the wide upholstered doors with one finger; she filled her lungs with the dusty smell of the corridors; and seated in her box she drew herself up with all the airs of a duchess.

The theatre began to fill; opera glasses came out of cases;

and subscribers exchanged greetings as they glimpsed one another across the house. The arts, for them, were a relaxation from the worries of buying and selling; that was why they had come; but it was quite impossible for them to forget business even here, and their conversation was about cotton, spirits and indigo. The old men looked blank and placid: with their gray-white hair and gray-white skin they were like silver medals that had been tarnished by lead fumes. The young beaux strutted in the orchestra: the openings of their waistcoats were bright with pink or apple-green cravats; and Madame Bovary looked admiringly down at them as they leaned with tightly yellow-gloved hands on their gold-knobbed walking sticks.

Meanwhile the candles were lighted on the music stands and the chandelier came down from the ceiling, the sparkle of its crystals filling the house with sudden gaiety; then the musicians filed in and there was a long cacophony of booming cellos, scraping violins, blaring horns, and piping flutes and flageolets. Then three heavy blows came from the stage; there was a roll of kettledrums and a series of chords from the brasses; and the curtain rose on an outdoor scene.

It was a crossroad in a forest, on the right a spring shaded by an oak. A group of country folk and nobles, all with tartans over their shoulders, sang a hunting chorus; then a captain strode in and inveighed against an evil spirit, raising both arms to heaven; another character joined him; they both walked off, and the huntsmen repeated their chorus.

She was back in the books she had read as a girl – deep in Walter Scott. She imagined she could hear the sound of Scottish pipes echoing through the mist across the heather. Her recollection of the novel made it easy for her to grasp the libretto; and she followed the plot line by line, elusive, half-forgotten memories drifting into her thoughts only to

242

be dispelled by the onrush of the music. She let herself be lulled by the melodies, feeling herself vibrate to the very fiber of her being, as though the bows of the violins were playing on her nerve-strings. She couldn't take in enough of the costumes, the sets, the characters, the painted trees that shook at the slightest footstep, the velvet bonnets, the cloaks, the swords – all those fanciful things that fluttered on waves of music as though in another world. Then a young woman came forward, tossing a purse to a squire in green. She was left alone on the stage, and there came the sound of a flute, like the ripple of a spring or the warbling of a bird. Lucie, looking solemn, began her cavatina in G major: she uttered love laments, begged for wings. And at that moment Emma, too, longed that she might leave life behind and take wing in an embrace. Suddenly Edgar Lagardy came on stage.

He was pale to the point of splendor, with that marmoreal majesty sometimes found among the passionate races of the south. His stalwart figure was clad in a tight brown doublet; a small chased dagger swung at his left hip; and he rolled his eyes about him languorously and flashed his white teeth. People said that a Polish princess had heard him sing one night on the beach at Biarritz, where he was a boat-boy, and had fallen in love with him; she had beggared herself for him, and he had left her for other women. This reputation as a ladies' man had done no disservice to his professional career. Shrewd ham actor that he was, he always saw to it that his publicity should include a poetic phrase or two about the charm of his personality and the sensibility of his soul. A fine voice, utter self-possession, more temperament than intelligence, more bombast than feeling – such were the principal attributes of this magnificent charlatan. There was a touch of the hairdresser about him, and a touch of the toreador.

He had the audience in transports from the first. He

clasped Lucie in his arms, left her, returned to her, seemed in despair: he would shout with rage, then let his voice expire, plaintive and infinitely sweet; and the notes that poured from his bare throat were full of sobs and kisses. Emma strained forward to watch him, her fingernails scratching the plush of her box. Her heart drank its fill of the melodious laments that hung suspended in the air against the sound of the double-basses like the cries of shipwrecked sailors against the tumult of a storm. Here was the same ecstasy, the same anguish that had brought her to the brink of death. The soprano's voice seemed but the echo of her own soul, and this illusion that held her under its spell a part of her own life. But no one on earth had ever loved her with so great a love. That last moonlight night, when they had told each other, "Till tomorrow! Till tomorrow!" *he* had not wept as Edgar was weeping now. The house was bursting with applause. The whole stretto was repeated: the lovers sang about the flowers on their graves, about vows and exile and fate and hope; and when their voices rose in the final farewell, Emma herself uttered a sharp cry that was drowned in the blast of the final chords.

"What's that lord doing, mistreating her like that?" Charles asked.

"No, no," she answered. "That's her lover."

"But he's swearing vengeance on her family, whereas the other one – the one that came on a while ago – said 'I love Lucie and I think she loves me!' Besides, he walked off arm in arm with her father. That is her father, isn't it, the ugly little one with the cock-feather in his hat?"

Despite Emma's explanations, Charles got everything mixed up, beginning with the duet in recitative in which Gilbert explains his abominable machinations to his master Ashton. The false engagement ring serving to trick Lucie he took to be a love token sent by Edgar. In fact he couldn't follow the story at all, he said, because of the music: it interfered so with the words.

"What difference does it make?" said Emma. "Be quiet!"

"But I like to know what's going on," he persisted, leaning over her shoulder. "You know I do."

"Be quiet! Be quiet!" she whispered impatiently.

Lucie came on, half borne up by her women; there was a wreath of orange blossoms in her hair, and she was paler than the white satin of her gown. Emma thought of her own wedding day: she saw herself walking toward the church along the little path amid the wheatfields. Why in heaven's name hadn't she resisted and entreated, like Lucie? But no – she had been light-hearted, unaware of the abyss she was rushing toward. Ah! If only in the freshness of her beauty, before defiling herself in marriage, before the disillusionments of adultery, she could have found some great and noble heart to be her life's foundation! Then virtue and affection, sensual joys and duty would all have been one; and she would never have fallen from her high felicity. But that kind of happiness was doubtless a lie, invented to make one despair of any love. Now she well knew the true paltriness of the passions that art painted so large. So she did her best to think of the opera in a different light: she resolved to regard this image of her own griefs as a vivid fantasy, an enjoyable spectacle and nothing more; and she was actually smiling to herself in scornful pity when from behind the velvet curtains at the back of the stage there appeared a man in a black cloak.

A single gesture sent his broad-brimmed Spanish hat to the ground; and the orchestra and the singers abruptly broke into the sextet. Edgar, flashing fury, dominated all the others with his high, clear voice. Ashton flung him his homicidal challenge in solemn tones; Lucie uttered her shrill lament;

Arthur sang his asides in middle register; and the chaplain's baritone boomed like an organ while the women, echoing his words, repeated them in delicious chorus. All the characters now formed a single line across the stage; all were gesticulating at once; and rage, vengeance, jealousy, terror, pity and amazement poured simultaneously from their open mouths. The outraged lover brandished his naked sword; his lace collar rose and fell with the heaving of his chest; and he strode up and down, clanking the silver-gilt spurs on his soft, flaring boots. His love, she thought, must be inexhaustible, since he could pour it out in such great quantities on the crowd. Her resolution not to be taken in by the display of false sentiment was swept away by the impact of the singer's eloquence; the fiction that he was embodying drew her to his real life, and she tried to imagine what it was like – that glamorous, fabulous, marvelous life that she, too, might have lived had chance so willed it. They might have met! They might have loved! With him she might have traveled over all the kingdoms of Europe, from capital to capital, sharing his hardships and his triumphs, gathering up the flowers his admirers threw, embroidering his costumes with her own hands; and every night behind the gilded lattice of her box she might have sat open-mouthed, breathing in the outpourings of that divine creature who would be singing for her alone: he would have gazed at her from the stage as he played his role. A mad idea seized her: he was gazing at her now! She was sure of it! She longed to rush into his arms and seek refuge in his strength as in the very incarnation of love; she longed to cry: "Ravish me! Carry me off! Away from here! All my passion and all my dreams are yours – yours alone!"

The curtain fell.

The smell of gas mingled with human exhalations, and

the air seemed the more stifling for being stirred up by fans. Emma tried to get out, but there was a crush in the corridors, and she sank back onto a chair, oppressed by palpitations. Charles, fearful lest she fall into a faint, hurried to the bar for a glass of orgeat.

He had a hard time getting back to the box: he held the glass in both hands because his elbows were being jarred at every other step, but even so he spilled three-quarters of it over the shoulders of a Rouen lady in short sleeves, who began to scream like a peacock, as though she were being murdered, when she felt the cold liquid trickling down her spine. While she took her handkerchief to the spots on her beautiful cerise taffeta gown, her mill-owner husband gave poor clumsy Charles a piece of his mind, angrily muttering the words "damages," "cost," and "replacement." Finally Charles made his way to his wife.

"I thought I'd never get out of there," he gasped. "Such a crowd! Such a crowd!"

And he added:

"Guess who I ran into: Monsieur Léon!"

"Léon?"

"Absolutely. He'll be coming along to pay you his respects."

As he uttered the words the former Yonville clerk entered the box.

He held out his hand with aristocratic casualness; and Madame Bovary automatically extended hers – yielding, no doubt, to the attraction of a stronger will. She hadn't touched it since that spring evening when the rain was falling on the new green leaves – the evening they had said farewell as they stood beside the window. But quickly reminding herself of the social requirements of the situation, she roused herself with an effort from her memories and began to stammer hurried phrases:

"Ah, good evening! You here? How amazing . . .!"

"Quiet!" cried a voice from the orchestra, for the third act was beginning.

"So you're living in Rouen?"

"Yes."

"Since when?"

"*Sh! Sh!*"

People were turning around at them indignantly, and they fell silent.

But from that moment on Emma no longer listened to the music. The chorus of guests, the scene between Ashton and his attendant, the great duet in D major – for her it all took place at a distance, as though the instruments had lost their sound and the characters had moved away. She recalled the card games at the pharmacist's and the walk to the wet-nurse's, their readings under the arbor, the tête-à-têtes beside the fire – the whole poor story of their love, so quiet and so long, so discreet, so tender, and yet discarded from her memory. Why was he returning like this? What combination of events was bringing him back into her life? He sat behind her, leaning a shoulder against the wall of the box; and from time to time she quivered as she felt his warm breath on her hair.

"Are you enjoying this?" he asked, leaning over so close that the tip of his mustache brushed against her cheek.

"Heavens no," she said carelessly, "not particularly."

And he suggested that they leave the theatre and go somewhere for an ice.

"Oh, not yet! Let's stay!" said Bovary. "Her hair's down: it looks as though it's going to be tragic."

But the mad scene interested Emma not at all: the soprano, she felt, was overdoing her role.

"She's shrieking too loud," she said, turning toward Charles, who was drinking it in.

"Yes ... perhaps ... a little," he replied, torn between the fullness of his enjoyment and the respect he had for his wife's opinions.

"It's so hot ..." sighed Léon.

"It is ... Unbearable."

"Are you uncomfortable?" asked Bovary.

"Yes, I'm stifling; let's go."

Monsieur Léon carefully laid her long lace shawl over her shoulders, and the three of them walked to the river front and sat down on the outdoor terrace of a café. First they spoke of her sickness, Emma interrupting Charles now and then lest, as she said, he bore Monsieur Léon; and Monsieur Léon told them he had just come to Rouen to spend two years in a large office to familiarize himself with the kind of business carried on in Normandy, which was different from anything he had learned about in Paris. Then he asked about Berthe, the Homais', and Madame Lefrançois; and since they had no more to say to each other in front of Charles the conversation soon died.

People coming from the theatre strolled by on the sidewalk, humming or bawling at the top of their voices: "*O bel ange, ma Lucie!*" Léon began to show off his musical knowledge. He had heard Tamburini, Rubini, Persiani, Grisi; and in comparison with them, Lagardy, for all the noise he made, was nothing.

"Still," interrupted Charles, who was eating his rum sherbet a tiny bit at a time, "they say he's wonderful in the last act. I was sorry to leave before the end: I was beginning to like it."

"Don't worry," said the clerk, "he'll be giving another performance soon."

But Charles said they were leaving the next day.

"Unless," he said, turning to his wife, "you'd like to stay on by yourself, sweetheart?"

And changing his tune to suit this unexpected opportunity, the young man sang the praises of Lagardy in the final scenes. He was superb, sublime! Charles insisted:

"You can come home Sunday. Yes, make up your mind to do it. You'd be wrong not to, if you think there's the slightest chance it might do you some good."

Meanwhile the tables around them were emptying; a waiter came and stood discreetly nearby; Charles took the hint and drew out his purse; the clerk put a restraining hand on his arm, paid the bill, and noisily threw down a couple of silver coins for the waiter.

"I'm really embarrassed," murmured Bovary, "at the money that you . . ."

The younger man shrugged him off in a friendly way and took up his hat:

"So it's agreed?" he said. "Tomorrow at six?"

Charles repeated that he couldn't stay away that much longer, but that there was nothing to prevent Emma . . .

"Oh," she murmured, smiling a peculiar smile, "I really don't know whether . . ."

"Well, think it over," said Charles. "Sleep on it and we'll decide in the morning."

Then, to Léon, who was walking with them:

"Now that you're back in our part of the world I hope you'll drop in now and then and let us give you dinner?"

The clerk said that he certainly would, especially since he'd soon be going to Yonville anyway on a business matter. They said good night at the corner of the Passage Saint-Herbland as the cathedral clock was striking half past eleven.

LISA BOLEKAJA

THREE VOICES
(2015)

ANDRE IRVING WAS pissed off about going to the Adams Ave Street Fair. Bethanny tricked him by saying they were only having espresso at Lestat's Coffee Shop to talk. He wanted to discuss their off-again-on-again-now-off-again relationship. He was trying to turn it back on. Bethanny wasn't trying to hear him on it. Once they turned the corner of 30th and Adams into a maze of police vehicles blocking the main street from oncoming traffic, Andre knew he had been duped. They had to park five blocks away and walk.

"I'm sorry I lied to you, but you have to hear this singer. She is phenomenal. She used to sing back-up for Zap Mama and Angélique Kidjo."

Andre maneuvered himself among San Diego's uptown denizens of hipsters, skater punks, and street vendors.

"So why is she singing with a garage band, coming from such lofty heights and all?"

"I told you, she took time off to study under Susan Aszodi in the music department. I can't believe you haven't heard of Chocolate Tye. You haven't been a good composer-in-residence if you haven't talked to Susan about her yet."

"What does she sing again?"

"Soprano. She has perfect pitch and can hit six octaves."

"Damn. Six?"

"There's the stage, c'mon."

Bethanny grabbed Andre's arm and dragged him through the throng of people and hustled him towards a mid-sized stage set up on the cross street of Lestat's. An R&B band with numerous members was crowded on the stage: a horn section, drums, bass, two rhythm guitars, two keyboard players, a violinist and three back-up singers. They were serious.

"There she is," Bethanny yelled.

A light-skinned black woman the same amber color as Andre crisscrossed the stage in dark leggings and a sparkly halter top, rapping about bringing down the system and some other crap Andre could care less about. The band was tight, but Andre wasn't feeling the rapper who began singing.

"She's just average," Andre said.

"Not her, *her*," Bethanny said, sweeping her ash blonde hair into a bun with one hand and pointing with the other. Andre looked again.

"Give it up for Chocolate Tye, y'all!" the female rapper hyped.

A dark-skinned force of nature stepped center stage, her mic held like a weapon in front of full lips painted a shimmery blue. Close-cropped hair dyed sunset red with a matching flame-colored corset and purple mini-skirt, the singer called Chocolate Tye ripped into the set. She led the band into a rousing Sly & the Family Stone mash-up with some hard-hitting original music, and then she erupted into a classical number where her voice soared above the crowd and then dove into the audience, holding them all hostage with aural pleasure.

"You like that?" Chocolate Tye asked the audience, and Andre found himself responding enthusiastically with the crowd. She was slaying her set.

"Goddammit, she's good," he said.

"I told you . . . oh yes! This is it! This is the song I wanted you to hear." Bethanny gripped Andre's arm, her mouth pressed close to his ear. "She's from Mali, just like your father, and this song is a Dogon lullaby that she has freaked. You'll love it!"

Andre moved closer to the stage so that he was directly in the center gazing up at Chocolate Tye. This girl could sing about a bag of Doritos and he would listen.

Inadvertently he found himself looking up her skirt, watching small rivulets of sweat course down her thighs and legs, then drip off her nose bleed red high heels. Her face shined and for a moment their eyes locked when she glanced down. Although he was half-black himself, Andre had never found black women that attractive, especially the darker ones. He liked to think he was a liberal fuck-around-the-rainbow type of guy, but the reality was, he fucked everything that wasn't the dark meat on the chicken. So he found it absurd and thrilling that he was getting a slight hard-on by looking at her skin, those hips, and an ass so fat he could see it from the front.

Bethanny stood next to him, running her fingers through his thick and cultivated out-of-control 'fro. He nudged her hand away. He wanted to focus on the music.

Chocolate Tye pulled out a two-inch metal tube and stuck it between her lips. She started making noises with her throat that flowed through the tube like breathy flute sounds. The tones shifted and the sounds turned into yelps. She played with the tonality in her throat for a minute, creating poly-phonic rhythms and then removed the tube. She sang soft words and Andre felt the hair on his arms stand at attention. He recognized it as the language of his father who spoke Jam Sai. For a moment Andre thought of his father and the way his father's soft tenor voice used to sound like magic when he spoke or sang in Jam Sai or even French.

Women around Andre began swaying, doing their corny

goddess dances that he used to mock Bethanny for. He saw that they were really mimicking Chocolate Tye's swaying hips. The song then became non-language, just sweet vocal inflections that her soprano voice enveloped with deepening emotion. No one in that audience had any idea what Chocolate Tye was saying. It didn't matter. They were caught up in the rapture of her gift.

Andre glanced down when he felt moisture on his wrist. The lullaby had moved him to tears. He had been crying and didn't even realize it. Many people were weepy-eyed in the audience when Andre scanned the other faces as he quickly wiped his cheeks. When he looked at the stage, Chocolate Tye was gone.

"You have to talk to her," Bethanny said. She was pink in the face from sobbing. "You must convince her to sing *Three Voices*, Andre. I think she's the only person who can pull it off for you."

Andre wasn't listening. He was searching for Chocolate Tye.

He found her posted up on the side wall outside of Lestat's, smoking a joint and talking to other musicians. Several people approached her, praising her performance, and she was thankful, telling them to check out her website and Twitter handle. Andre waited through four people fawning over her and taking pictures before he was able to get in a word.

"Hi, I'm Andre Irving, I'm teaching over at UCSD," he said, holding out his hand.

"Oh, the composer, Bethanny Allen's friend, right? She told me about you. I'm Tye Amma." She shook his hand. They were the same height, which made her six feet easy. Andre wasn't used to women looking him eye to eye. She was wearing flat sandals after her performance, so there was no cheating on her part. But her eyes made him feel so much shorter than her. She was called Chocolate Tye because of her rich skin color, but her eyes were a shade of subtle brown which made them seem to glow.

"Is Bethanny here?"

"She's getting coffee inside."

"She told me she was bringing you. I hear you're a bit of a recluse. Brilliant composer, but not a people person. Self-centered, self-absorbed, borderline megalomaniac—"

"She told you all that?"

"And a little bit more. You supposedly have this master-piece that you composed seven years ago that no one can sing, and you've been on a quest to find the perfect voice to bring your creation to life, and . . ." she blew marijuana smoke in his face, "you like to get high."

She handed him her spliff. He puffed on it. Passed it back. She took a long drag, stepped closer to him, and pressed her lips to his. He opened his lips slightly. She blew the smoke in. Stayed close to him.

"What did you think of my performance?" she asked.

"You are . . . amazing."

"Amazing enough to do *Three Voices*?"

"Yeah."

"Good. Call me when you're ready to lay it down."

Tye crossed the street before he became aware that she was leaving him.

"Wait! I don't have your number," he called after her.

"Bethanny has it," she yelled without looking back.

He watched her stroll through the dwindling crowd and link arms with the drummer in her band. They walked towards another bandstand that featured a banjo player. Bethanny brought him a coffee and he didn't notice she was next to him until she tapped his shoulder with the cup.

Tracking Tye with his eyes, Andre made a note to re-think his black female discriminatory practices. He could still taste her weed in his mouth.

Andre met Tye inside a theater in the Conrad Prebys Music Center. He brought a laptop and small speakers perched on a piano. He had a song book with heavily notated music sheets on a stand. He played a segment of *Three Voices* for her. Tye was attentive, listening with her eyes closed. The song had no words. No musical accompaniment. Just repetitive vocal sounds.

"There will be two speakers on stage with two separate pre-recorded tracks of you singing. You will sing along with those two other tracks. The song will last an hour and fifteen minutes non-stop," he said. Tye smiled.

"I have to have stamina," she said, looking over the song book. "Damn, Andre, if I sing this part, I wouldn't breathe for about ... seven minutes! No wonder you can't find a singer to do this. They die before they get to the end!"

"That's the fun part, as the singer you have to find where and when to breathe without sacrificing the rhythm—"

"What if my mouth gets dry? Can I swallow my own spit?"

"You better note it on the music sheet when to do it."

"I like a challenge. Who is singing this version?"

"Bethanny. She's only singing ten minutes of it. She couldn't sing it all the way through the way it's intended to be sung. I broke it into segments just to get the vocals down on tape. My mother told me that my father wrote this for me on my tenth birthday."

"So your mother is white?"

"Ukraine and Jewish mix," he said.

"What part of the song did you write? I see your name here under the credits."

Andre flipped the music sheets to the back. He pointed to a starred note on the side of one page.

"According to Moms, Dad finished the song, and then threw away the entire ending for some reason. He was a perfectionist. Typical artist, huh?"

"Songs change. Writers get new ideas, they tweak things," she said. Andre shook his head.

"No, this was different. My mother said the song was completed. My father said so himself. He actually recorded a version of himself singing it, and then he erased that. He was supposed to present it at an experimental music concert in L.A., but then he left us."

"Left you?"

"Moms went to pick him up at the Burbank airport, and he wasn't on the flight. Never showed up for the concert. Never heard from him again. There were rumors he ran off with a woman, and some speculation that his visa expired, but . . ." Andre shrugged.

Tye glanced down at the sheet music. Andre tapped his finger on the last page.

"It took me a long time to write an ending that I think kinda works. I used the incomplete original recording of my father, but I used Bethanny's voice to imagine how it would finish. I renamed it *Three Voices*."

"What did your father call it?"

"*Home*."

"I like *Three Voices* better," she said.

She touched his hand. A slight shiver went up his arm. She smelled like cloves and cinnamon.

"Shall we get started?" she asked. They were so close together. He could feel her warmth. "Yeah."

They worked together three times a week, five hours each time. Andre was impressed with Tye's vocal abilities, but her discipline was lacking. She felt three hours was enough time for practicing. She complained when he became demanding, sometimes yelled at him when he refused to allow her to change a note that she believed sounded better. He was bullish towards her when he explained that *Three Voices* had to be performed exactly as it was presented on the music sheet. This was not improvisation. No jazz scatting, no hip-hop free-style cypher, none of the vocal gymnastics she was used to doing on stage. No matter how strange and experimental it sounded, this was serious music. She had to submit to the precision of the work.

During rehearsal breaks, Tye would impress Andre and the sound engineer with various vocal riffs. She was born in Mali, but raised in Los Angeles among various musical styles. She once imitated one of her favorite singers, Yma Sumac, by making bird sounds and low guttural moans from one of Sumac's famous songs, *Five Bottles Mambo*. Another time she took two microphones and sang with one mic pressed against her throat, and the other near her mouth and blew them away with the music she could make beat-boxing, and harmonizing with her mouth closed, sounding like a Tuva folk singer doing overtone throat singing. She could separate the harmonics into two or three distinct pitches.

In those moments, Andre found her playful, sexy, giving into any sound that pleased her, not embarrassed to try things that didn't work and sounded dreadful. She was musically free. But when Andre cracked the whip, and they delved back into *Three Voices*, she lost that flair. In order to move through the song with any chance of finishing it from start to finish, she had to shelve the diva in herself. Any extra oomph she put into Andre's song only tripped her up. She would lose the tempo, forget to swallow, forget to breathe, expend needed energy to keep her lungs full and her diaphragm open.

By the third week of rehearsal, the differences in their work styles eroded into a passive aggressive boycott on her part.

Tye complained of headaches and rehearsals ended early. She was irritable when she missed a note, her mouth dry, and her eyes blazing from too much weed consumption. They had recorded a complete second track and were set to practice the entire song when she called in complaining of dehydration. She took off for a week.

He sent Bethanny over to check on her, and eventually Tye returned, but she was sullen. Andre found himself more concerned when she stopped joking with him or singing whatever she wanted during breaks.

"What's going on?" he asked her after a grueling and unproductive session in the theater.

"Nothing. Just tired."

"I've seen you tired, Tye. This is different. Talk to me." He sat in one of the orange theater seats facing the mic. Tye stood before him, hair dyed platinum, wearing ratty jeans and an even rattier T-shirt. She started crying. It startled him. He'd seen singers cry out of frustration before or after he'd ripped into them, but Tye was . . . Tye. Always taut and together. He stood and walked over to her.

"Hey, Tye." He embraced her and she melted into his arms. He felt solid with her, like they were meant to be fused this way. He wiped away her tears and held her face.

"Snot doesn't look good on you, girl. Doesn't match your hair color this week." She laughed and he smiled.

"This fucking song is getting on my nerves," she said.

"I told you it wouldn't be easy."

"I thought I could find my way into this bitch, but now

261

". . . it feels like I'm trying to climb up a mountain with roller skates on."

"Let's quit for the night," he said. She nodded. He didn't want to let her go, so he held her a little longer. Pressed her head onto his shoulder and rocked her.

"When we finish this thing, I'm going to compose a song just for you. Something light and easy—"

"And with words, for God's sake," she whispered. She sounded better. She pushed away from his arms and sauntered over to one of the theater seats. He sat next to her. She leaned in towards him.

"I spoke to Bethanny. I know why she could never finish *Three Voices*," she said.

Andre drew in a deep breath and let it out slow. Tye watched his face with intense scrutiny. When Andre didn't respond, her eyes narrowed.

"She told me she developed throat polyps after training with you. She never had throat problems ever until she started singing *Three Voices*. Even after throat surgery, she wasn't able to sing professionally again—"

"That had nothing to do with the song, Tye. Many singers develop throat nodules when they overuse their voice."

Tye reached into the back pocket of her jeans and pulled out her cell phone. She opened up an App page and Andre winced when he saw the picture of the woman on the screen.

"What about her? I remember this woman, Andre. I always wondered what happened to her."

Andre took the cell phone from Tye's hand. He stared at the picture and the text from a news article from three years prior. The woman, Nelia Cardoso, was a Brazilian singer from Pernambuco who had shot to stardom performing dance club hits, but had been classically trained in Portugal and New York. The article described her bout with throat cancer which ultimately led to having her vocal cords removed. She had been under Andre's tutelage to bring *Three Voices* to life in Manhattan prior to developing cancer.

"First Bethanny, and then Nelia. How many others before them, Andre?"

"Coincidences, that's all."

"No. There were others. Bethanny mentioned two. I'm sure there's more. I know how obsessed you are with this thing. Bethanny was smart enough to quit and break up with you."

Andre placed the phone on Tye's lap and walked over to the piano and sat on a bench. Tye stuck the phone in her back pocket. Andre started playing a few bars on the piano.

"Your father destroyed his recording for a reason. He probably knew something was wrong with it. Maybe when he sang it himself it damaged him. Maybe that's why he went away."

"Listen to how you sound. It's a difficult piece, I know. It strains the throat, but if I had the right singer for it—"

"Has the thought ever crossed your selfish mind that something could happen to me?"

Tye left her seat and walked to Andre. She rested her hands on the side of the piano and watched him.

"Well, has it?"

"You have gone the furthest than anyone else I've had—"

"But do you fucking care if anything happens to me? That's my question to you," she said. Sullen, he didn't say anything for a few minutes and continued playing the keys until she started gathering her things.

"I care," he said in a near whisper.

"Really?"

"Has anything . . . anything—"

"No," she said. The firmness in her voice made him look

up at her face. She tilted back her head, parted her lips and sang the last section of "O Mio Babbino Caro" without breaking a sweat.

"Take me home, it's late," she said.

When he dropped her off at her apartment, he handed her a flash drive with her complete tracks so she could practice at home if she wanted. On the drive over he waited for her to tell him that she was going to quit too, but she remained silent the whole way until she stepped out of his BMW. She thanked him for the ride, and for a second, he thought she would ask him to come in. He wanted to. She waved and walked away from his car.

That night, Andre stayed with Bethanny. They were not officially together again, but it was hard for him to be around Tye all day and go home alone. And Bethanny had started to act more protective of Tye. Sometimes Andre asked Bethanny to do vocal exercises with Tye to free him up to work on other things. She would do it, but he would see Bethanny and Tye fall into their easy banter, and sometimes they whispered together when they were all in the theater listening to playbacks. He knew then that their whispering was really Bethanny talking about her experiences with the song. A sisterly warning perhaps.

Tye didn't answer her cell phone for two days after she asked about Nelia Cardoso. On the morning of the third day, Andre called Bethanny and asked her to call Tye for him. By the afternoon all Andre saw was a short text message from Tye that read "Call U Soon." When the day turned into night, Andre drove to her apartment.

He walked up four flights of stairs and saw Tye's drummer/boyfriend Slim Charles smoking a cigar on a hallway balcony with another man. Loud music reverberated behind a closed door from the apartment closest to the balcony.

"What it do?" Slim said, extending a hand to Andre.

"Hunting Tye down," said Andre.

Slim chuckled. The other man smiled and blew cigar smoke out towards the street.

"She here, bruh, but be careful," Slim said, scratching his bearded chin, "nothin' but blunts and booty in there."

"Dangerous," the second man quipped. He took a sip from a plastic red cup. The man raised the cup towards Andre. "Blunts 'n booty for real, son."

Slim laughed, "Good luck."

Andre gave the men a puzzled stare, then turned to open Tye's front door. Heavy bass rattled the door knob as he twisted it. The door opened easily and Andre stepped into a sparsely furnished living room filled with about eight women. They were drinking, smoking, laughing, and watching Tye and another woman toke thick joints while bending over barstools shaking their behinds in loose rayon short-shorts. The air in the room was enveloped in a hazy beige cloud of kush. High grade by the smell of it. The woman competing with Tye in the shake-fest dropped into a Chinese split and Andre gave a silent prayer to her mother for the beauty of its execution. Each of her round cheeks bounced in time to the music, a mix of go-go beats and Andre guessed New Orleans bounce.

The music grew more frenetic and Tye left the barstool and stood over the woman on the floor, her backside facing Andre too, and she lowered herself so that her gyrating rump was barely touching the fatness already on the floor. Tye stuck her blunt in her mouth, laid her hands on her knees, and just when Andre thought he couldn't take much more syncopated ass-shaking, Slim and his male companion stepped into the room.

"Ah shit," Slim said, "she about to put it on Melody."

The music switched into a calculated trap beat, and as if on cue, Tye lifted both of her arms above her head, and looked over her left shoulder. She blew smoke from between her teeth. She saw Andre and moved her body slower. All the women screamed, and some fanned Tye's backside with paper plates pretending to cool her off.

Tye moved away from Melody and helped her up. Slim walked over and removed the joint from Tye's mouth, playfully slapping her backside before grabbing a beer from the bar table. Tye turned down the volume of the music and pulled Andre into a corner of the room near an open window.

"Needed another break, I see," he said.

"Yeah, a little one," she said.

"You could call and tell me that instead of leaving me hanging for two days."

Someone turned the music back up. Andre moved closer to hear Tye speak.

"Something's going on with me . . . with the song," she said.

Laughter in the room distracted Andre. Slim was trying to dance for the ladies and they were booing him. Tye grabbed Andre's hand and pulled him into her tiny kitchen.

"Slim caught me singing the song in my sleep," she said, coughing a bit.

"And?"

"It's not the same song. It sounds like it because it's wordless, but I had him record me. It's different . . ."

"Tye, it's like sleep-talking, a waking dream state. Things get jumbled when you're dreaming."

"Wait here," she said. She left the kitchen and he watched her walk across from the kitchen and step down into her open bedroom door which had a sunken floor. She returned with a digital recorder in her hand.

"Listen," she said.

They both heard Slim fumbling with the recorder, probably trying to move it towards her mouth in the dark. They listened to her voice and she was right. Although the cadence was similar to *Three Voices*, the sounds coming from her sleep state were indeed different. Slim walked into the kitchen.

"She got you listening to her snoring?" he teased. Slim pulled Tye next to him, bent his muscular frame down to kiss her neck. Andre felt crowded in the kitchen, and a bit annoyed that Slim was easing into their conversation. It agitated Andre even more to see the man rubbing on Tye's hip in front of him.

"Oscar and me about to jet. Don't have your neighbors calling the cops on you," Slim said. He kissed her cheek. "See ya, Maestro," he said, nodding at Andre.

Tye stopped the recorder. Andre rewound it, and listened again.

"I like how it sounds," he said.

"Hmmm," she mumbled. Her right hand lifted to her mouth suddenly, and she coughed several times. A small spurt of reddened saliva dribbled on her chin at the last spasm. She grabbed a paper towel from the roll above her sink and wiped up blood from her fingers and lips. Andre reached for her arm. She threw the paper towel away and ran water from the kitchen faucet into a coffee mug. She gulped down the water and looked at him with weary eyes.

"Take this home and listen to it all the way through," she said.

"Your throat?" he asked.

"Just sore. I think you can use some of the recording to help make a cleaner ending," she said. He stared at her neck and her lips. A sore throat was always the beginning of problems in the past. Then came the blood.

Next were the lumps of traitorous polyps or inflamed cysts. And finally the singers left him, physically damaged by the work. But maybe this time . . .

"Let me know if you can use any of it," she said.

He took the recorder from her hand.

"Will you be at practice on time?" he asked.

"Sure. Of course."

He left her place with plans to reschedule the performance two weeks earlier than planned. Before her voice gave out.

Tye struggled to put forth effort, even with the changes he incorporated from the digital recording. She had a hard time sustaining her concentration on the final sections of the song. The energy just wasn't there. When they reached a place where they agreed she was ready, they stopped rehearsals. She wanted to spend her pre-show free time with Slim Charles before he left for Europe to drum for a new band.

Enjoying his respite from the intensity of *Three Voices*, Andre slept with Bethanny. His sex with her was comfortable, easy, and familiar. She was sharp angular muscles, taut thighs, perky breasts, and an eager mouth. All the right weaponry that had hooked him from the beginning. An image of Tye drifted into his mind as he made love to Bethanny. Tye was . . . damn, Tye was curvy round thickness, tits that flowed over, and a derriere that bounced, bounced, bounced. He came so hard that he called out Tye's name.

Bethanny didn't say a word. Andre rolled off of her, uncomfortable as hell. The silence was voluminous between them. When his cell phone rang he sprang up to answer it, turning his back to Bethanny.

"Hello?"

"*Three Voices* . . ."

"Tye? What's wrong?" He left the bedroom. Bethanny jumped out of bed and slammed the door behind him.

"It's doing something to me, changing me. I feel myself changing."

He couldn't let her slip away from him. They were so close.

"Can you just tell me exactly what the problem is? We can fix it." He hoped he really could.

"I know why your father erased it."

"What?"

"You think you're singing the song, but the song is singing you."

She hung up.

Andre ran back into the cold bedroom, put on his clothes under Bethanny's heated gaze, and left.

It took a while for Tye to open her front door. For a moment he was afraid she had done something drastic, like swallowed pills or smoked herself into a coma. But the door opened and she was in front of him in an oversized Steelers football jersey and sweatpants. Fine worry-lines creased her forehead. Lines that had never been there when he first met her.

"Thank God, you scared me," he said while walking in. He took a seat on her couch. She sat next to him. Lit a joint.

"Maybe you should stop smoking so much. It's making you paranoid. Talk to me." He took the joint from her and smoked it himself.

"I know I was supposed to be resting, but I played one track and started singing the opening to it. I had it down, and then it was weird. I thought I was having a stroke. My face got numb and my hands had pressure on them. Swear to God, I felt like someone was squeezing me from the bottom like a tube of toothpaste."

He could see trembling in her hands.

"I thought maybe I was having a panic attack. I suffer from anxiety from time to time, that's why I smoke weed, so I can stay off meds. I've had bad reactions to some prescriptions before. But I'm not on anything. It's the song. The song is alive . . ."

"Don't talk crazy. Too much smoking is the problem," he said.

"The moment I stopped singing, the pain stopped."

"Try singing it again."

"Hell no."

Andre sat back on the couch. He closed his eyes. Let his head fall back into the sofa.

"People are coming to this show Friday. Publicity has gone out. I already taped the public radio spot for it. I can't cancel the performance. I won't be able to book the theater again until months from now."

She threw a small couch pillow at him. It hit him square in the face.

"You bitch ass! The song hurt me!"

"It's stress. Bad weed. Exhaustion."

"No, it's not! Look at my forehead. Look at this." She knelt in front of him. He looked at her. In the center of her forehead was a small lump. The size of a pencil eraser. It looked like a large pimple. He touched it and she flinched. It felt like it was filled with tiny granules of sand.

"How long have you had that?"

"Today. Right after I sang the opening of your song." She took her joint back and smoked it down to nothing.

"Could you sing it for me? I have to see. If it hurts again, just stop." She hesitated. Then moved to her desktop computer and played *Three Voices*. Her voices. She took a breath and joined in with the two tracks. There was a stutter in her voice. She sang for five minutes then stopped.

"Pain?" he asked.

"No. I just didn't feel anything. This was the part where

I started to feel the tingling in my face and hands." She sat down next to him.

"What are you thinking?" he asked.

"I was all over this thing in the beginning. Who wouldn't want to be the singer who sings the impossible? Things don't feel right to me, and it's not my throat. I'm scared to do it, and I'm scared not to do it. Does that make sense? Shit, I'm not making sense."

Tye shook her head. Andre took her hand. Pulled her closer so that they sat hip to hip.

"Tye, you ever wonder how it is, that of all the singers in the world who could've crossed my path, there was only you? Someone who shares the same blood as me? We aren't related but we have ties to the same obscure village. That is fate. We were meant to do this together. I promise you, if you can just push through this and do the song, you will be the most famous voice on the scene. No lie. Future singers will try to imitate your perfection. Your voice will be studied in music classes across the globe. Hell, I'll be famous."

He reached over and touched her forehead. The bump was less prominent. He lifted one of her fingers and helped her trace the spot.

"See? Almost gone. Just stress. A fear of failure. You will not fail. I won't let you."

He kissed her fingers, and then grew bold. Kissed her cheek. Then her neck. She accepted his affections, but stopped him when he tried to kiss her on the lips.

"That's not us," she said.

"Maybe I want to make it us," he said.

"You may think you do, but not really."

He pulled away from her. She held onto his hand.

"There's more, Andre."

Tye reached into the pocket of her sweatpants. Pulled out the digital recorder.

"I kept it on voice activated."

She pushed play. This time, there was no noise of fumbling fingers. Andre stared at the steel gray recorder. All he heard was the sound of Tye's steady breathing in her sleep. Her exhalations of air grew stronger, there was a whimpering sound on the recorder, like she was having a fitful sleep, and in that moment Andre wanted to turn it off, dreading the quivery noise of escalating whimpers and deepening inhalations. He found his fingers inching towards her hand to stop the machine, trying to keep the shaky flip flopping in his stomach from spreading to his legs. She said it before he heard it escaping from the tiny square speaker.

"That's not my voice."

He took the recorder from her hand and held it in front of his face. The dulcet sounds of Tye's soprano were replaced with a raspy, heavy depth that was masculine in tone.

"I know it's coming from my mouth, but that isn't me. It can't be. Not that deep." He turned off the recorder for her.

She lit another joint and they shared it together until she fell asleep on the couch next to him. He didn't want to go home and be alone. And he didn't want to go back to Bethanny's. He sat and watched Tye sleep, looking for signs of her lips moving, content to be in her space. He erased all the voice files on her recorder, and before he pocketed it, he saw that his own hands were trembling.

On the day of the performance, Andre was calm. Once he was in the theater and knew Tye was backstage getting ready, he made plans in his head to take the music to New York, and then overseas.

The theater held less than 200 seats, and tickets were hard to come by. Friends started calling for favors, and the guest list had to be rearranged several times to accommodate patrons of UCSD, some esteemed faculty, and of course an eager public. People who knew the back-story of *Three Voices* scrambled to hear it live and in one continuous performance. Andre was shocked to even see Nelia Cardoso in the audience, the scars from her throat surgery still prominent on her neck. The stakes were high. But Andre prayed that Tye would handle it.

A hesitant stage manager handed Andre a note slipped to her from Tye. She had a request. Andre read the note. Stared at the stage manager.

"Really? She wants to do that?"

"Yes she does."

"Okay, run off some warning note for the programs then," he said.

When the house lights dimmed and then came up again, Tye sauntered onstage. She was naked. Barefoot and clean shaven from head to toe. Her body was decorated with red, black and white body paint. She had drawn crude designs on her breasts and belly. A map of some sort. There were polite gasps from some audience members. Although they had been slipped a warning note in the program about the nudity, seeing Tye under the bright lights, expectant and silent, was a lot to take in. But she was beautiful. And Andre felt an intense, self-obsessed love for her.

He sat in the front row. Bethanny sat behind him. Despite their messy relationship, he was glad she still wanted to see the performance for the sake of the art.

Tye lifted up her head, and parted her lips. Her voice enveloped the theater, and when her two other voices joined her, creating the triad of harmony, Andre knew they had succeeded. The richness of the three voices in the theater was astounding. Andre could feel people moving forward in their seats. As expected, the first fifteen minutes lulled the listeners into a meditative trance. Tye had the tempo under control. She seemed to be pushing her two other voices up higher. She radiated confidence, like this song had been written for her and only her. Andre tried to concentrate on her singing, but he was mesmerized by her face, so serious and mask-like. No emotion.

And then a strange thing happened.

Andre did not recognize the song anymore. It was his song, the one they spent weeks practicing in sections, and now that it was put together as one seamless tapestry, nearing its conclusion, the notes shifted into something new and . . . *Jesus*—

An undulating liquid sound wave floated from Tye's mouth, like a mirage shimmering on a hot dry surface. It drifted up about thirty feet above her head. A second and third wave floated from the speakers, moved up and spread out, forming a triangle with the first.

The song, Andre, the song is alive . . . that's what she told him the night he wanted to make love to her.

Tye kept singing, but the color from her skin faded, the melanin draining away from her flesh. The top of her scalp slowly *unraveled*, the strands of her flesh spinning upwards in spiraling tendrils . . . but she kept singing, a crescendo building in her voices. Building, building, while she was coming apart. Soon, the top of her forehead was unthreading, particles of her floating up into the triangular sound wave of ebon space that pulsed. Andre could see actual darkness bulging outward and then open like lips drawing liquid up through a straw. She was being siphoned up into a vortex of space that her voices ripped open.

You think you're singing the song, but the song is singing you . . .

A new dimension seeped into the theater. The audience was paralyzed. The voices had them frozen. The beautiful and voiceless Nelia Cardosa stood up in the audience, her hand jammed near her mouth. Only Bethanny spoke.

"Andre, stop her, she has to stop singing! Make her stop!"

Andre stared at his beloved masterwork on stage. Tye's eyes were missing, but she still sang, even as her neck and shoulders stretched and unbraided themselves. They flew away as particles of light. How could she sing with no head? There were still three voices racing to the end of the song.

Andre looked over at the two speakers that helped her triangulate and open a doorway. He leapt to his feet and ran to the plugs, yanking them out to stop the pre-recorded tracks. But even unplugged, the two voices kept going with the third. He turned to watch all that was left of her still winding away into the vortex. He lunged and grabbed her legs. Her hips were coming undone. He saw her fading, nearly clear like a gelatinous jellyfish: skin, then muscle, then bone. There was a force pulling her up. He held onto her, feeling his weight lifted. He looked up into the triangular void, and saw a face he remembered. Andre screamed.

Her legs vanished in his arms and her voices stopped. He fell to the floor. Panting and a bit delirious. He looked out at the theater seats. Under the bright lights he could only make out a few blank, unblinking faces still lost in a trance. And he heard Bethanny sobbing.

Some in the audience that night suggested that they experienced something akin to group hypnosis. No one could remember what they saw or heard. But they felt as if they had witnessed a miracle of some sort. Still, there were others who thought it was performance art, a calculated stunt to turn *Three Voices* into an urban legend.

Andre locked himself away in his La Jolla digs, refusing

to see anyone, including Bethanny and a distraught Slim Charles. He knew what he had to do.

Clutching the music sheets with Tye's careful song notations, he set up two speakers inside his livingroom and opened his bay front windows to look out at the Pacific Ocean. He undressed himself and stood nude before his computer. He pushed play on the two pre-recorded tracks he made of himself. He now knew that the song was a map that his father left for him.

When Andre's two voices filled the room, he added the third voice. It was what his father meant for him to do. And hopefully Tye would be waiting for him there. Just like his father.

THE FOOD OF LOVE

VLADIMIR NABOKOV

MUSIC
(1932)

Translated by Vladimir Nabokov
and Dmitri Nabokov

THE ENTRANCE HALL overflowed with coats of both sexes; from the drawing room came a rapid succession of piano notes. Victor's reflection in the hall mirror straightened the knot of a reflected tie. Straining to reach up, the maid hung his overcoat, but it broke loose, taking down two others with it, and she had to begin all over again.

Already walking on tiptoe, Victor reached the drawing room, whereupon the music at once became louder and manlier. At the piano sat Wolf, a rare guest in that house. The rest – some thirty people in all – were listening in a variety of attitudes, some with chin propped on fist, others sending cigarette smoke up toward the ceiling, and the uncertain lighting lent a vaguely picturesque quality to their immobility. From afar, the lady of the house, with an eloquent smile, indicated to Victor an unoccupied seat, a pretzel-backed little armchair almost in the shadow of the grand piano. He responded with self-effacing gestures – it's all right, it's all right, I can stand; presently, however, he began moving in the suggested direction, cautiously sat down, and cautiously folded his arms. The performer's wife, her mouth half-open, her eyes blinking fast, was about to turn the page; now she has turned it. A black forest of ascending notes, a slope, a gap, then a separate group of little trapezists in flight. Wolf had long, fair eyelashes; his translucent ears were of a delicate crimson hue; he struck the keys with extraordinary velocity and vigor and, in the lacquered depths of the open keyboard lid, the doubles of his hands were engaged in a ghostly, intricate, even somewhat clownish mimicry.

To Victor any music he did not know – and all he knew was a dozen conventional tunes – could be likened to the patter of a conversation in a strange tongue: in vain you strive to define at least the limits of the words, but everything slips and merges, so that the laggard ear begins to feel boredom. Victor tried to concentrate on listening, but soon caught himself watching Wolf's hands and their spectral reflections. When the sounds grew into insistent thunder, the performer's neck would swell, his widespread fingers tensed, and he emitted a faint grunt. At one point his wife got ahead of him; he arrested the page with an instant slap of his open left palm, then with incredible speed himself flipped it over, and already both hands were fiercely kneading the compliant keyboard again. Victor made a detailed study of the man: sharp-tipped nose, jutting eyelids, scar left by a boil on his neck, hair resembling blond fluff, broad-shouldered cut of black jacket. For a moment Victor tried to attend to the music again, but scarcely had he focused on it when his attention dissolved. He slowly turned away, fishing out his cigarette case, and began to examine the other guests. Among the strange faces he discovered some familiar ones – nice, chubby Kocharovsky over there – should I nod to him? He did, but overshot his mark: it was another acquaintance, Shmakov, who acknowledged the nod: I heard he was leaving Berlin for Paris – must ask him about it. On a divan, flanked by two elderly ladies, corpulent, red-haired Anna Samoylovna, half-reclined with closed eyes, while her husband, a throat specialist, sat with his elbow propped on the arm of his chair. What is that glittering object he twirls in the fingers of his free hand? Ah yes, a pince-nez on a Chekhovian ribbon. Further, one shoulder in shadow, a hunchbacked, bearded man known to be a lover of music listened intently, an index finger stretched up against his temple. Victor could never remember his name and patronymic. Boris? No, that wasn't it. Borisovich? Not that either. More faces. Wonder if the Haruzins are here. Yes, there they are. Not looking my way. And in the next instant, immediately behind them, Victor saw his former wife.

At once he lowered his gaze, automatically tapping his cigarette to dislodge the ash that had not yet had time to form. From somewhere low down his heart rose like a fist to deliver an uppercut, drew back, struck again, then went into a fast, disorderly throb, contradicting the music and drowning it. Not knowing which way to look, he glanced askance at the pianist, but did not hear a sound: Wolf seemed to be pounding a silent keyboard. Victor's chest got so constricted that he had to straighten up and draw a deep breath; then, hastening back from a great distance, gasping for air, the music returned to life, and his heart resumed beating with a more regular rhythm.

They had separated two years before, in another town, where the sea boomed at night, and where they had lived since their marriage. With his eyes still cast down, he tried to ward off the thunder and rush of the past with trivial thoughts: for instance, that she must have observed him a few moments ago as, with long, noiseless, bobbing strides, he had tiptoed the whole length of the room to reach this chair. It was as if someone had caught him undressed or engaged in some idiotic occupation; and, while recalling how in his innocence he had glided and plunged under her gaze (hostile? derisive? curious?), he interrupted himself to consider if his hostess or anyone else in the room might be aware of the situation, and how had she got here, and whether she had come alone or with her new husband,

and what he, Victor, ought to do: stay as he was or look her way? No, looking was still impossible; first he had to get used to her presence in this large but confining room – for the music had fenced them in and had become for them a kind of prison, where they were both fated to remain captive until the pianist ceased constructing and keeping up his vaults of sound.

What had he had time to observe in that brief glance of recognition a moment ago? So little: her averted eyes, her pale cheek, a lock of black hair, and, as a vague secondary character, beads or something around her neck. So little! Yet that careless sketch, that half-finished image already *was* his wife, and its momentary blend of gleam and shade already formed the unique entity which bore her name.

How long ago it all seemed! He had fallen madly in love with her one sultry evening, under a swooning sky, on the terrace of the tennis-club pavilion, and, a month later, on their wedding night, it rained so hard you could not hear the sea. What bliss it had been. Bliss – what a moist, lapping, and plashing word, so alive, so tame, smiling and crying all by itself. And the morning after: those glistening leaves in the garden, that almost noiseless sea, that languid, milky, silvery sea.

Something had to be done about his cigarette butt. He turned his head, and again his heart missed a beat. Someone had stirred, blocking his view of her almost totally, and was taking out a handkerchief as white as death; but presently the stranger's elbow would go and she would reappear, yes, in a moment she would reappear. No, I can't bear to look. There's an ashtray on the piano.

The barrier of sounds remained just as high and impenetrable. The spectral hands in their lacquered depths continued to go through the same contortions. "We'll be happy forever" – what melody in that phrase, what shimmer! She was velvet-soft all over, one longed to gather her up the way one could gather up a foal and its folded legs. Embrace her and fold her. And then what? What could one do to possess her completely? I love your liver, your kidneys, your blood cells. To this she would reply, "Don't be disgusting." They lived neither in luxury nor in poverty, and went swimming in the sea almost all year round. The jellyfish, washed up onto the shingly beach, trembled in the wind. The Crimean cliffs glistened in the spray. Once they saw fishermen carrying away the body of a drowned man; his bare feet, protruding from under the blanket, looked surprised. In the evenings she used to make cocoa.

He looked again. She was now sitting with downcast eyes, legs crossed, chin propped upon knuckles: she was very musical, Wolf must be playing some famous, beautiful piece. I won't be able to sleep for several nights, thought Victor as he contemplated her white neck and the soft angle of her knee. She wore a flimsy black dress, unfamiliar to him, and her necklace kept catching the light. No, I won't be able to sleep, and I shall have to stop coming here. It has all been in vain: two years of straining and struggling, my peace of mind almost regained – now I must start all over again, trying to forget everything, everything that had already been almost forgotten, plus this evening on top of it. It suddenly seemed to him that she was looking at him furtively and he turned away.

The music must be drawing to a close. When they come, those stormy, gasping chords, it usually signifies that the end is near. Another intriguing word, *end* . . . Rend, impend . . . Thunder rending the sky, dust clouds of impending doom. With the coming of spring she became strangely unresponsive. She spoke almost without moving her lips.

285

He would ask "What is the matter with you?" "Nothing. Nothing in particular." Sometimes she would stare at him out of narrowed eyes, with an enigmatic expression. "What *is* the matter?" "Nothing." By nightfall she would be as good as dead. You could not do anything with her, for, despite her being a small, slender woman, she would grow heavy and unwieldy, and as if made of stone. "Won't you finally tell me what is the matter with you?" So it went for almost a month. Then, one morning – yes, it was the morning of her birthday – she said quite simply, as if she were talking about some trifle, "Let's separate for a while. We can't go on like this." The neighbors' little daughter burst into the room to show her kitten (the sole survivor of a litter that had been drowned). "Go away, go away, later." The little girl left. There was a long silence. After a while, slowly, silently, he began twisting her wrists – he longed to break all of her, to dislocate all her joints with loud cracks. She started to cry. Then he sat down at the table and pretended to read the newspaper. She went out into the garden, but soon returned. "I can't keep it back any longer. I have to tell you everything." And with an odd astonishment, as if discussing another woman, and being astonished at her, and inviting him to share her astonishment, she told it, told it all. The man in question was a burly, modest, and reserved fellow; he used to come for a game of whist, and liked to talk about artesian wells. The first time had been in the park, then at his place.

The rest is all very vague. I paced the beach till nightfall. Yes, the music does seem to be ending. When I slapped his face on the quay, he said, "You'll pay dearly for this," picked up his cap from the ground, and walked away. I did not say good-bye to her. How silly it would have been to think of killing her. Live on, live. Live as you are living now; as you are sitting now, sit like that forever. Come, look at me, I implore you, please, please look. I'll forgive you everything, because someday we must all die, and then we shall know everything, and everything will be forgiven – so why put it off? Look at me, look at me, turn your eyes, *my* eyes, my darling eyes. No. Finished.

The last many-clawed, ponderous chords – another, and just enough breath left for one more, and, after this concluding chord, with which the music seemed to have surrendered its soul entirely, the performer took aim and, with feline precision, struck one simple, quite separate little golden note. The musical barrier dissolved. Applause. Wolf said, "It's been a very long time since I last played this." Wolf's wife said, "It's been a long time, you know, since my husband last played this piece." Advancing upon him, crowding him, nudging him with his paunch, the throat specialist said to Wolf: "Marvelous! I have always maintained that's the best thing he ever wrote. I think that toward the end you modernize the color of sound just a bit too much. I don't know if I make myself clear, but, you see—"

Victor was looking in the direction of the door. There, a slightly built, black-haired lady with a helpless smile was taking leave of the hostess, who kept exclaiming in surprise, "I won't hear of it, we're all going to have tea now, and then we're going to hear a singer." But she kept on smiling helplessly and made her way to the door, and Victor realized that the music, which before had seemed a narrow dungeon where, shackled together by the resonant sounds, they had been compelled to sit face-to-face some twenty feet apart, had actually been incredible bliss, a magic glass dome that had embraced and imprisoned him and her, had made it possible for him to breathe the same air as she; and now everything had been broken and scattered, she was

287

disappearing through the door, Wolf had shut the piano, and the enchanting captivity could not be restored.

She left. Nobody seemed to have noticed anything. He was greeted by a man named Boke who said in a gentle voice, "I kept watching you. What a reaction to music! You know, you looked so bored I felt sorry for you. Is it possible that you are so completely indifferent to it?"

"Why, no. I wasn't bored," Victor answered awkwardly. "It's just that I have no ear for music, and that makes me a poor judge. By the way, what was it he played?"

"What you will," said Boke in the apprehensive whisper of a rank outsider. " 'A Maiden's Prayer,' or the 'Kreutzer Sonata.' Whatever you will."

IVAN TURGENEV

THE SONG OF
TRIUMPHANT LOVE
(1881)

Translated by Constance Garnett

This is what I read in an old Italian manuscript: –

I

ABOUT THE MIDDLE of the sixteenth century there were living in Ferrara (it was at that time flourishing under the sceptre of its magnificent archdukes, the patrons of the arts and poetry) two young men, named Fabio and Muzzio. They were of the same age, and of near kinship, and were scarcely ever apart; the warmest affection had united them from early childhood ... the similarity of their positions strengthened the bond. Both belonged to old families; both were rich, independent, and without family ties; tastes and inclinations were alike in both. Muzzio was devoted to music, Fabio to painting. They were looked upon with pride by the whole of Ferrara, as ornaments of the court, society, and town. In appearance, however, they were not alike, though both were distinguished by a graceful, youthful beauty. Fabio was taller, fair of face and flaxen of hair, and he had blue eyes. Muzzio, on the other hand, had a swarthy face and black hair, and in his dark brown eyes there was not the merry light, nor on his lips the genial smile of Fabio; his thick eyebrows overhung narrow eyelids, while Fabio's golden eyebrows formed delicate half-circles on his pure, smooth brow. In conversation, too, Muzzio was less animated. For all that, the two friends were both alike looked on with favour by ladies, as well they might be, being models of chivalrous courtliness and generosity.

At the same time there was living in Ferrara a girl named Valeria. She was considered one of the greatest beauties in the town, though it was very seldom possible to see her, as she led a retired life, and never went out except to church, and on great holidays for a walk. She lived with her mother, a widow of noble family, though of small fortune, who had no other children. In every one whom Valeria met she inspired a sensation of involuntary admiration, and an equally involuntary tenderness, and respect, so modest was her mien, so little, it seemed, was she aware of all the power of her own charms. Some, it is true, found her a little pale; her eyes, almost always downcast, expressed a certain shyness, even timidity; her lips rarely smiled, and then only faintly; her voice scarcely any one had heard. But the rumour went that it was most beautiful, and that, shut up in her own room, in the early morning when everything still slumbered in the town, she loved to sing old songs to the sound of the lute, on which she used to play herself. In spite of her pallor, Valeria was blooming with health; and even old people, as they gazed on her, could not but think, "Oh, how happy the youth for whom that pure maiden bud, still enfolded in its petals, will one day open into full flower!"

II

FABIO AND MUZZIO saw Valeria for the first time at a magnificent public festival, celebrated at the command of the Archduke of Ferrara, Ercol, son of the celebrated Lucrezia Borgia, in honour of some illustrious grandees who had come from Paris on the invitation of the Archduchess, daughter of the French king Louis XII. Valeria was sitting beside her mother on an elegant tribune, built after a design of Palladio, in the principal square of Ferrara, for the most honourable ladies in the town. Both Fabio and Muzzio fell passionately in love with her on that day; and, as they never had any secrets from each other, each of them soon knew what was passing in his friend's heart. They agreed together that both should try to get to know Valeria; and if she should deign to choose one of them, the other should submit without a murmur to her decision. A few weeks later, thanks to the excellent renown they deservedly enjoyed, they succeeded in penetrating into the widow's house, difficult though it was to obtain an entry to it; she permitted them to visit her. From that time forward they were able almost every day to see Valeria and to converse with her; and every day the passion kindled in the hearts of both young men grew stronger and stronger. Valeria, however, showed no preference for either of them, though their society was obviously agreeable to her. With Muzzio she occupied herself with music; but she talked more with Fabio, with him she was less timid. At last, they resolved to learn once for all their fate, and sent a letter to Valeria, in which they begged her to be open with them, and to say to which she would be ready to give her hand. Valeria showed this letter to her mother, and declared that she was willing to remain unmarried, but if her mother considered it time for her to enter upon matrimony, then she would marry whichever one her mother's choice should fix upon. The excellent widow shed a few tears at the thought of parting from her beloved child; there was, however, no good ground for refusing the suitors, she considered both of them equally worthy of her daughter's hand. But, as she secretly preferred Fabio, and suspected that

Valeria liked him the better, she fixed upon him. The next day Fabio heard of his happy fate, while all that was left for Muzzio was to keep his word, and submit.

And this he did; but to be the witness of the triumph of his friend and rival was more than he could do. He promptly sold the greater part of his property, and collecting some thousands of ducats, he set off on a far journey to the East. As he said farewell to Fabio, he told him that he should not return till he felt that the last traces of passion had vanished from his heart. It was painful to Fabio to part from the friend of his childhood and youth. . . . but the joyous anticipation of approaching bliss soon swallowed up all other sensations, and he gave himself up wholly to the transports of successful love.

Shortly after, he celebrated his nuptials with Valeria, and only then learnt the full worth of the treasure it had been his fortune to obtain. He had a charming villa shut in by a shady garden, a short distance from Ferrara; he moved thither with his wife and her mother. Then a time of happiness began for them. Married life brought out in a new and enchanting light all the perfections of Valeria. Fabio became an artist of distinction – no longer a mere amateur, but a real master. Valeria's mother rejoiced, and thanked God as she looked upon the happy pair. Four years flew by unperceived, like a delicious dream. One thing only was wanting to the young couple, one lack they mourned over as a sorrow: they had no children . . . but they had not given up all hope of them. At the end of the fourth year they were overtaken by a great, this time a real sorrow; Valeria's mother died after an illness of a few days.

Many tears were shed by Valeria; for a long time she could not accustom herself to her loss. But another year went by; life again asserted its rights and flowed along its old channel.

And behold, one fine summer evening, unexpected by every one, Muzzio returned to Ferrara.

III

DURING THE WHOLE space of five years that had elapsed since his departure no one had heard anything of him; all talk about him had died away, as though he had vanished from the face of the earth. When Fabio met his friend in one of the streets of Ferrara he almost cried out aloud, first in alarm and then in delight, and he at once invited him to his villa. There happened to be in his garden there a spacious pavilion, apart from the house; he proposed to his friend that he should establish himself in this pavilion. Muzzio readily agreed and moved thither the same day together with his servant, a dumb Malay – dumb but not deaf, and indeed, to judge by the alertness of his expression, a very intelligent man. ... His tongue had been cut out. Muzzio brought with him dozens of boxes, filled with treasures of all sorts collected by him in the course of his prolonged travels. Valeria was delighted at Muzzio's return; and he greeted her with cheerful friendliness, but composure; it could be seen in every action that he had kept the promise given to Fabio. During the day he completely arranged everything in order in his pavilion; aided by his Malay, he unpacked the curiosities he had brought; rugs, silken stuffs, velvet and brocaded garments, weapons, goblets, dishes and bowls, decorated with enamel, things made of gold and silver, and inlaid with pearl and turquoise, carved boxes of jasper and ivory, cut bottles, spices, incense, skins of wild beasts, and feathers of unknown birds, and a number of other things, the very use of which seemed mysterious and incomprehensible. Among all these precious things there was a rich pearl necklace, bestowed upon Muzzio by the king of Persia for some great and secret service; he asked permission of Valeria to put this necklace with his own hand about her neck; she was struck by its great weight and a sort of strange heat in it ... it seemed to burn to her skin. In the evening after dinner as they sat on the terrace of the villa in the shade of the oleanders and laurels, Muzzio began to relate his adventures. He told of the distant lands he had seen, of cloud-topped mountains and deserts, rivers like seas; he told of immense buildings and temples, of trees a thousand years old, of birds and flowers of the colours of the rainbow: he named the cities and the peoples he had visited ... their very names seemed like a fairy tale. The whole East was familiar to Muzzio; he had traversed Persia, Arabia, where the horses are nobler and more beautiful than any other living creatures; he had penetrated into the very heart of India, where the race of men grow like stately trees; he had reached the boundaries of China and Thibet, where the living god, called the Grand Llama, dwells on earth in the guise of a silent man with narrow eyes. Marvellous were his tales. Both Fabio and Valeria listened to him as if enchanted. Muzzio's features had really changed very little; his face, swarthy from childhood, had grown darker still, burnt under the rays of a hotter sun, his eyes seemed more deep-set than before – and that was all; but the expression of his face had become different: concentrated and dignified, it never showed more life when he recalled the dangers he had encountered by night in forests that resounded with the roar of tigers or by day on solitary ways where savage fanatics lay in wait for travellers, to slay them in honour of their iron goddess who demands human sacrifices. And Muzzio's voice had grown deeper and more even; his hands, his whole body had lost the freedom of gesture peculiar to the Italian race. With the aid of his servant, the obsequiously alert Malay, he showed his hosts a few of the feats he had learnt from the Indian Brahmins. Thus for instance, having first hidden himself behind a curtain, he suddenly appeared sitting in the air cross-legged, the tips of his fingers pressed lightly on a bamboo cane placed vertically, which astounded Fabio not a little and positively alarmed Valeria. . . . "Isn't he a sorcerer?" was her thought. When he proceeded, piping on a little flute, to call some tame snakes out of a covered basket, where their dark flat heads with quivering tongues appeared under a parti-coloured cloth, Valeria was terrified and begged Muzzio to put away these loathsome horrors as soon as possible. At supper Muzzio regaled his friends with wine of Shiraz from a round long-necked flagon; it was of extraordinary fragrance and thickness, of a golden colour with a shade of green in it, and it shone with a strange brightness as it was poured into the tiny jasper goblets. In taste it was unlike European wines: it was very sweet and spicy, and, drunk slowly in small draughts, produced a sensation of pleasant drowsiness in all the limbs. Muzzio made both Fabio and Valeria drink a goblet of it, and he drank one himself. Bending over her goblet he murmured something, moving his fingers as he did so. Valeria noticed this; but as in all Muzzio's doings, in his whole behaviour, there was something strange and out of the common, she only thought, "Can he have adopted some new faith in India, or is that the custom there?" Then after a short silence she asked him: "Had he persevered with music during his travels?" Muzzio, in reply, bade the Malay bring his Indian violin. It was like those of to-day, but instead of four strings it had only three, the upper part of it was covered with a bluish snake-skin, and the slender bow of reed was in the form of a half-moon, and on its extreme end glittered a pointed diamond.

Muzzio played first some mournful airs, national songs as he told them, strange and even barbarous to an Italian ear; the sound of the metallic strings was plaintive and feeble. But when Muzzio began the last song, it suddenly gained force and rang out tunefully and powerfully; the passionate melody flowed out under the wide sweeps of the bow, flowed out, exquisitely twisting and coiling like the snake that covered the violin-top; and such fire, such triumphant bliss glowed and burned in this melody that Fabio and Valeria felt wrung to the heart and tears came into their eyes; ... while Muzzio, his head bent, and pressed close to the violin, his cheeks pale, his eyebrows drawn together into a single straight line, seemed still more concentrated and solemn; and the diamond at the end of the bow flashed sparks of light as though it too were kindled by the fire of the divine song. When Muzzio had finished, and still keeping fast the violin between his chin and his shoulder, dropped the hand that held the bow, "What is that? What is that you have been playing to us?" cried Fabio. Valeria uttered not a word – but her whole being seemed echoing her husband's question. Muzzio laid the violin on the table – and slightly tossing back his hair, he said with a polite smile: "That – that melody ... that song I heard once in the island of Ceylon. That song is known there among the people as the song of happy, triumphant love." "Play it again," Fabio was murmuring. "No; it can't be played again," answered Muzzio. "Besides, it is now too late. Signora Valeria ought to be at rest; and it's time for me too ... I am weary." During the whole day Muzzio had treated Valeria with respectful simplicity, as a friend of former days, but as he went out he clasped her hand very tightly, squeezing his fingers on her palm, and looking so intently into her face that though she did not raise her eyelids, she yet felt the look on her suddenly flaming cheeks.

She said nothing to Muzzio, but jerked away her hand, and when he was gone, she gazed at the door through which he had passed out. She remembered how she had been a little afraid of him even in old days . . . and now she was overcome by perplexity. Muzzio went off to his pavilion: the husband and wife went to their bedroom.

IV

VALERIA DID NOT quickly fall asleep; there was a faint and languid fever in her blood and a slight ringing in her ears . . . from that strange wine, as she supposed, and perhaps too from Muzzio's stories, from his playing on the violin . . . towards morning she did at last fall asleep, and she had an extraordinary dream.

She dreamt that she was going into a large room with a low ceiling . . . Such a room she had never seen in her life. All the walls were covered with tiny blue tiles with gold lines on them; slender carved pillars of alabaster supported the marble ceiling; the ceiling itself and the pillars seemed half transparent . . . a pale rosy light penetrated from all sides into the room, throwing a mysterious and uniform light on all the objects in it; brocaded cushions lay on a narrow rug in the very middle of the floor, which was smooth as a mirror. In the corners almost unseen were smoking lofty censers, of the shape of monstrous beasts; there was no window anywhere; a door hung with a velvet curtain stood dark and silent in a recess in the wall. And suddenly this curtain slowly glided, moved aside . . . and in came Muzzio. He bowed, opened his arms, laughed . . . His fierce arms enfolded Valeria's waist; his parched lips burned her all over. . . . She fell backwards on the cushions.

Moaning with horror, after long struggles, Valeria awaked. Still not realising where she was and what was happening to her, she raised herself on her bed, looked round . . . A tremor ran over her whole body. . . . Fabio was lying beside her. He was asleep; but his face in the light of the brilliant full moon looking in at the window was pale as a corpse's . . . it was sadder than a dead face. Valeria waked her husband, and directly he looked at her. "What is the matter?" he cried. "I had – I had a fearful dream," she whispered, still shuddering all over.

But at that instant from the direction of the pavilion came floating powerful sounds, and both Fabio and Valeria recognised the melody Muzzio had played to them, calling it the song of blissful triumphant love. Fabio looked in perplexity at Valeria . . . she closed her eyes, turned away, and both holding their breath, heard the song out to the end. As the last note died away, the moon passed behind a cloud, it was suddenly dark in the room. . . . Both the young people let their heads sink on their pillows without exchanging a word, and neither of them noticed when the other fell asleep.

V

THE NEXT MORNING Muzzio came in to breakfast; he seemed happy and greeted Valeria cheerfully. She answered him in confusion – stole a glance at him – and felt frightened at the sight of that serene happy face, those piercing and inquisitive eyes. Muzzio was beginning again to tell some story . . . but Fabio interrupted him at the first word.

"You could not sleep, I see, in your new quarters. My wife and I heard you playing last night's song."

"Yes! Did you hear it?" said Muzzio. "I played it indeed; but I had been asleep before that, and I had a wonderful dream too."

Valeria was on the alert. "What sort of dream?" asked Fabio.

"I dreamed," answered Muzzio, not taking his eyes off Valeria, "I was entering a spacious apartment with a ceiling decorated in Oriental fashion, carved columns supported the roof, the walls were covered with tiles, and though there were neither windows nor lights, the whole room was filled with a rosy light, just as though it were all built of transparent stone. In the corners, Chinese censers were smoking, on the floor lay brocaded cushions along a narrow rug. I went in through a door covered with a curtain, and at another door just opposite appeared a woman whom I once loved. And so beautiful she seemed to me, that I was all aflame with my old love . . ."

Muzzio broke off significantly. Valeria sat motionless, and only gradually she turned white . . . and she drew her breath more slowly.

"Then," continued Muzzio, "I waked up and played that song."

"But who was that woman?" said Fabio.

"Who was she? The wife of an Indian – I met her in the town of Delhi . . . She is not alive now – she died."

"And her husband?" asked Fabio, not knowing why he asked the question.

"Her husband, too, they say is dead. I soon lost sight of them both."

"Strange!" observed Fabio. "My wife too had an extraordinary dream last night" – Muzzio gazed intently at Valeria – "which she did not tell me," added Fabio.

But at this point Valeria got up and went out of the

room. Immediately after breakfast, Muzzio too went away, explaining that he had to be in Ferrara on business, and that he would not be back before the evening.

VI

A FEW WEEKS before Muzzio's return, Fabio had begun a portrait of his wife, depicting her with the attributes of Saint Cecilia. He had made considerable advance in his art; the renowned Luini, a pupil of Leonardo da Vinci, used to come to him at Ferrara, and while aiding him with his own counsels, pass on also the precepts of his great master. The portrait was almost completely finished; all that was left was to add a few strokes to the face, and Fabio might well be proud of his creation. After seeing Muzzio off on his way to Ferrara, he turned into his studio, where Valeria was usually waiting for him; but he did not find her there: he called her, she did not respond. Fabio was overcome by a secret uneasiness; he began looking for her. She was nowhere in the house; Fabio ran into the garden, and there in one of the more secluded walks he caught sight of Valeria. She was sitting on a seat, her head drooping on to her bosom and her hands folded upon her knees; while behind her, peeping out of the dark green of a cypress, a marble satyr, with a distorted malignant grin on his face, was putting his pouting lips to a Pan's pipe. Valeria was visibly relieved at her husband's appearance, and to his agitated questions she replied that she had a slight headache, but that it was of no consequence, and she was ready to come to sit to him. Fabio led her to the studio, posed her, and took up his brush; but to his great vexation, he could not finish the face as he would have liked to. And not because it was somewhat pale and looked exhausted . . . no; but the pure, saintly expression, which he liked so much in it, and which had given him the idea of painting Valeria as Saint Cecilia, he could not find in it that day. He flung down the brush at last, told his wife he was not in the mood for work, and that he would not prevent her from lying down, as she did not look at all well, and put the canvas with its face to the wall. Valeria agreed with him that she ought to rest, and repeating her complaints of a headache, withdrew into her bedroom.

Fabio remained in the studio. He felt a strange confused sensation incomprehensible to himself. Muzzio's stay under his roof, to which he, Fabio, had himself urgently invited him, was irksome to him. And not that he was jealous – could any one have been jealous of Valeria! – but he did not recognise his former comrade in his friend. All that was strange, unknown and new that Muzzio had brought with him from those distant lands – and which seemed to have entered into his very flesh and blood – all these magical feats, songs, strange drinks, this dumb Malay, even the spicy fragrance diffused by Muzzio's garments, his hair, his breath – all this inspired in Fabio a sensation akin to distrust, possibly even to timidity. And why did that Malay waiting at table stare with such disagreeable intentness at him, Fabio? Really any one might suppose that he understood Italian. Muzzio had said of him that in losing his tongue, this Malay had made a great sacrifice, and in return he was now possessed of great power. What sort of power? and how could he have obtained it at the price of his tongue? All this was very strange! very incomprehensible! Fabio went into his wife's room; she was lying on the bed, dressed, but was not asleep. Hearing his steps, she started, then again seemed delighted to see him just as in the garden. Fabio sat down beside the bed, took Valeria by the hand, and after a short silence, asked her, "What was the extraordinary dream that had frightened her so the previous night? And was it the same sort at all as the dream Muzzio had described?" Valeria crimsoned and said hurriedly: "O! no! no! I saw . . . a sort of monster which was trying to tear me to pieces." "A monster? in the shape of a man?" asked Fabio. "No, a beast . . . a beast!" Valeria turned away and hid her burning face in the pillows. Fabio held his wife's hand some time longer; silently he raised it to his lips, and withdrew.

Both the young people passed that day with heavy hearts. Something dark seemed hanging over their heads . . . but what it was, they could not tell. They wanted to be together, as though some danger threatened them; but what to say to one another they did not know. Fabio made an effort to take up the portrait, and to read Ariosto, whose poem had appeared not long before in Ferrara, and was now making a noise all over Italy; but nothing was of any use. . . . Late in the evening, just at supper-time, Muzzio returned.

VII

HE SEEMED COMPOSED and cheerful – but he told them little; he devoted himself rather to questioning Fabio about their common acquaintances, about the German war, and the Emperor Charles: he spoke of his own desire to visit Rome, to see the new Pope. He again offered Valeria some Shiraz wine, and on her refusal, observed as though to himself, "Now it's not needed, to be sure." Going back with his wife to their room, Fabio soon fell asleep; and waking up an hour later, felt a conviction that no one was sharing his bed; Valeria was not beside him. He got up quickly and at the same instant saw his wife in her night attire coming out of the garden into the room. The moon was shining brightly, though not long before a light rain had been falling. With eyes closed, with an expression of mysterious horror on her immovable face, Valeria approached the bed, and feeling for it with her hands stretched out before her, lay down hurriedly and in silence. Fabio turned to her with a question, but she made no reply; she seemed to be asleep. He touched her, and felt on her dress and on her hair drops of rain, and on the soles of her bare feet, little grains of sand. Then he leapt up and ran into the garden through the half-open door. The crude brilliance of the moon wrapt every object in light. Fabio looked about him, and perceived on the sand of the path prints of two pairs of feet – one pair were bare; and these prints led to a bower of jasmine, on one side, between the pavilion and the house. He stood still in perplexity, and suddenly once more he heard the strains of the song he had listened to the night before. Fabio shuddered, ran into the pavilion . . . Muzzio was standing in the middle of the room playing on the violin. Fabio rushed up to him.

"You have been in the garden, your clothes are wet with rain."

"No . . . I don't know . . . I think . . . I have not been out . . ." Muzzio answered slowly, seeming amazed at Fabio's entrance and his excitement.

Fabio seized him by the hand. "And why are you playing that melody again? Have you had a dream again?"

Muzzio glanced at Fabio with the same look of amazement, and said nothing.

"Answer me!"

" 'The moon stood high like a round shield . . .
    Like a snake, the river shines . . .
    The friend's awake, the foe's asleep . . .
    The bird is in the falcon's clutches . . . Help!' "

muttered Muzzio, humming to himself as though in delirium.

Fabio stepped back two paces, stared at Muzzio, pondered a moment . . . and went back to the house, to his bedroom.

Valeria, her head sunk on her shoulder and her hands hanging lifelessly, was in a heavy sleep. He could not quickly awaken her . . . but directly she saw him, she flung herself on his neck, and embraced him convulsively; she was trembling all over. "What is the matter, my precious, what is it?" Fabio kept repeating, trying to soothe her. But she still lay lifeless on his breast. "Ah, what fearful dreams I have!" she whispered, hiding her face against him. Fabio would have questioned her . . . but she only shuddered. The window-panes were flushed with the early light of morning when at last she fell asleep in his arms.

VIII

THE NEXT DAY Muzzio disappeared from early morning, while Valeria informed her husband that she intended to go away to a neighbouring monastery, where lived her spiritual father, an old and austere monk, in whom she placed unbounded confidence. To Fabio's inquiries she replied, that she wanted by confession to relieve her soul, which was weighed down by the exceptional impressions of the last few days. As he looked upon Valeria's sunken face, and listened to her faint voice, Fabio approved of her plan; the worthy Father Lorenzo might give her valuable advice, and might disperse her doubts. . . . Under the escort of four attendants, Valeria set off to the monastery, while Fabio remained at home, and wandered about the garden till his wife's return, trying to comprehend what had happened to her, and a victim to constant fear and wrath, and the pain of undefined suspicions. . . . More than once he went up to the pavilion; but Muzzio had not returned, and the Malay gazed at Fabio like a statue, obsequiously bowing his head, with a well-dissembled – so at least it seemed to Fabio – smile on his bronzed face. Meanwhile, Valeria had in confession told everything to her priest, not so much with shame as with horror. The priest heard her attentively, gave her his blessing, absolved her from her involuntary sin, but to himself he thought: "Sorcery, the arts of the devil . . . the matter can't be left so," . . . and he returned with Valeria to her villa, as though with the aim of completely pacifying and reassuring her. At the sight of the priest Fabio was thrown into some agitation; but the experienced old man had thought out beforehand how he must treat him. When he was left alone with Fabio, he did not of course betray the secrets of the confessional, but he advised him if possible to get rid of the guest they had invited to their house, as by his stories, his songs, and his whole behaviour he was troubling the imagination of Valeria. Moreover, in the old man's opinion, Muzzio had not, he remembered, been very firm in the faith in former days, and having spent so long a time in lands unenlightened by the truths of Christianity, he might well have brought thence the contagion of false doctrine, might even have become conversant with secret magic arts; and, therefore, though long friendship had indeed its claims, still a wise prudence pointed to the necessity of separation. Fabio fully agreed with the excellent monk. Valeria was even joyful when her husband reported to her the priest's counsel; and sent on his way with the cordial good-will of both the young people, loaded with good gifts for the monastery and the poor, Father Lorenzo returned home.

Fabio intended to have an explanation with Muzzio immediately after supper; but his strange guest did not return to supper. Then Fabio decided to defer his conversation with Muzzio until the following day; and both the young people retired to rest.

IX

VALERIA SOON FELL asleep; but Fabio could not sleep. In the stillness of the night, everything he had seen, everything he had felt presented itself more vividly; he put to himself still more insistently questions to which as before he could find no answer. Had Muzzio really become a sorcerer, and had he not already poisoned Valeria? She was ill . . . but what was her disease? While he lay, his head in his hand, holding his feverish breath, and given up to painful reflection, the moon rose again upon a cloudless sky; and together with its beams, through the half-transparent window-panes, there began, from the direction of the pavilion – or was it Fabio's fancy? – to come a breath, like a light, fragrant current . . . then an urgent, passionate murmur was heard . . . and at that instant he observed that Valeria was beginning faintly to stir. He started, looked; she rose up, slid first one foot, then the other out of the bed, and like one bewitched of the moon, her sightless eyes fixed lifelessly before her, her hands stretched out, she began moving towards the garden! Fabio instantly ran out of the other door of the room, and running quickly round the corner of the house, bolted the door that led into the garden. . . . He had scarcely time to grasp at the bolt, when he felt some one trying to open the door from the inside, pressing against it . . . again and again . . . and then there was the sound of piteous passionate moans . . .

"But Muzzio has not come back from the town," flashed through Fabio's head, and he rushed to the pavilion . . .

What did he see?

Coming towards him, along the path dazzlingly lighted up by the moon's rays, was Muzzio, he too moving like one moonstruck, his hands held out before him, and his eyes open but unseeing. . . . Fabio ran up to him, but he, not heeding him, moved on, treading evenly, step by step, and his rigid face smiled in the moonlight like the Malay's. Fabio would have called him by his name . . . but at that instant he heard, behind him in the house, the creaking of a window. . . . He looked round. . . .

Yes, the window of the bedroom was open from top to bottom, and putting one foot over the sill, Valeria stood in the window . . . her hands seemed to be seeking Muzzio . . . she seemed striving all over towards him. . . .

Unutterable fury filled Fabio's breast with a sudden inrush. "Accursed sorcerer!" he shrieked furiously, and seizing Muzzio by the throat with one hand, with the other he felt for the dagger in his girdle, and plunged the blade into his side up to the hilt.

Muzzio uttered a shrill scream, and clapping his hand to the wound, ran staggering back to the pavilion. . . . But at the very same instant when Fabio stabbed him, Valeria screamed just as shrilly, and fell to the earth like grass before the scythe.

Fabio flew to her, raised her up, carried her to the bed, began to speak to her. . . .

She lay a long time motionless, but at last she opened her eyes, heaved a deep, broken, blissful sigh, like one just rescued from imminent death, saw her husband, and twining her arms about his neck, crept close to him. "You, you, it is you," she faltered. Gradually her hands loosened their hold, her head sank back, and murmuring with a blissful smile, "Thank God, it is all over. . . . But how weary I am!" she fell into a sound but not heavy sleep.

X

FABIO SANK DOWN beside her bed, and never taking his eyes off her pale and sunken, but already calmer, face, began reflecting on what had happened . . . and also on how he ought to act now. What steps was he to take? If he had killed Muzzio – and remembering how deeply the dagger had gone in, he could have no doubt of it – it could not be hidden. He would have to bring it to the knowledge of the archduke, of the judges . . . but how explain, how describe such an incomprehensible affair? He, Fabio, had killed in his own house his own kinsman, his dearest friend? They will inquire, What for? on what ground? . . . But if Muzzio were not dead? Fabio could not endure to remain longer in uncertainty, and satisfying himself that Valeria was asleep, he cautiously got up from his chair, went out of the house, and made his way to the pavilion. Everything was still in it; only in one window a light was visible. With a sinking heart he opened the outer door (there was still the print of blood-stained fingers on it, and there were black drops of gore on the sand of the path), passed through the first dark room . . . and stood still on the threshold, overwhelmed with amazement.

In the middle of the room, on a Persian rug, with a brocaded cushion under his head, and all his limbs stretched out straight, lay Muzzio, covered with a wide, red shawl with a black pattern on it. His face, yellow as wax, with closed eyes and bluish eyelids, was turned towards the ceiling, no breathing could be discerned: he seemed a corpse. At his feet knelt the Malay, also wrapt in a red shawl. He was holding in his left hand a branch of some unknown plant, like a fern, and bending slightly forward, was gazing fixedly at his master. A small torch fixed on the floor burnt with a greenish flame, and was the only light in the room. The flame did not flicker nor smoke. The Malay did not stir at Fabio's entry, he merely turned his eyes upon him, and again bent them upon Muzzio. From time to time he raised and lowered the branch, and waved it in the air, and his dumb lips slowly parted and moved as though uttering soundless words. On the floor between the Malay and Muzzio lay the dagger, with which Fabio had stabbed his friend; the Malay struck one blow with the branch on the blood-stained blade. A minute passed . . . another. Fabio approached the Malay, and stooping down to him, asked in an undertone, "Is he dead?" The Malay bent his head from above downwards, and disentangling his right hand from his shawl, he pointed imperiously to the door. Fabio would have repeated his question, but the gesture of the commanding hand was repeated, and Fabio went out, indignant and wondering, but obedient.

He found Valeria sleeping as before, with an even more tranquil expression on her face. He did not undress, but seated himself by the window, his head in his hand, and once more sank into thought. The rising sun found him still in the same place. Valeria had not waked up.

XI

FABIO INTENDED TO wait till she awakened, and then to set off to Ferrara, when suddenly some one tapped lightly at the bedroom door. Fabio went out, and saw his old steward,

Antonio. "Signor," began the old man, "the Malay has just informed me that Signor Muzzio has been taken ill, and wishes to be moved with all his belongings to the town; and that he begs you to let him have servants to assist in packing his things; and that at dinner-time you would send pack-horses, and saddle-horses, and a few attendants for the journey. Do you allow it?" "The Malay informed you of this?" asked Fabio. "In what manner? Why, he is dumb." "Here, signor, is the paper on which he wrote all this in our language, and very correctly." "And Muzzio, you say, is ill?" "Yes, he is very ill, and can see no one." "Have they sent for a doctor?" "No. The Malay forbade it." "And was it the Malay wrote you this?" "Yes, it was he." Fabio did not speak for a moment. "Well, then, arrange it all," he said at last. Antonio withdrew.

Fabio looked after his servant in bewilderment. "Then, he is not dead?" he thought . . . and he did not know whether to rejoice or to be sorry. "Ill?" But a few hours ago it was a corpse he had looked upon!

Fabio returned to Valeria. She waked up and raised her head. The husband and wife exchanged a long look full of significance. "He is gone?" Valeria said suddenly. Fabio shuddered. "How gone? Do you mean . . ." "Is he gone away?" she continued. A load fell from Fabio's heart. "Not yet; but he is going to-day." "And I shall never, never see him again?" "Never." "And these dreams will not come again?" "No." Valeria again heaved a sigh of relief; a blissful smile once more appeared on her lips. She held out both hands to her husband. "And we will never speak of him, never, do you hear, my dear one? And I will not leave my room till he is gone. And do you now send me my maids . . . but stay: take away that thing!" she pointed to the pearl necklace, lying on a little bedside table, the necklace given her by Muzzio, "and throw it at once into our deepest well. Embrace me. I am your Valeria; and do not come in to me till . . . he has gone." Fabio took the necklace – the pearls he fancied looked tarnished – and did as his wife had directed. Then he fell to wandering about the garden, looking from a distance at the pavilion, about which the bustle of preparations for departure was beginning. Servants were bringing out boxes, loading the horses . . . but the Malay was not among them. An irresistible impulse drew Fabio to look once more upon what was taking place in the pavilion. He recollected that there was at the back a secret door, by which he could reach the inner room where Muzzio had been lying in the morning. He stole round to this door, found it unlocked, and, parting the folds of a heavy curtain, turned a faltering glance upon the room within.

XII

MUZZIO WAS NOT now lying on the rug. Dressed as though for a journey, he sat in an arm-chair, but seemed a corpse, just as on Fabio's first visit. His torpid head fell back on the chair, and his outstretched hands hung lifeless, yellow, and rigid on his knees. His breast did not heave. Near the chair on the floor, which was strewn with dried herbs, stood some flat bowls of dark liquid, which exhaled a powerful, almost suffocating, odour, the odour of musk. Around each bowl was coiled a small snake of brazen hue with golden eyes that flashed from time to time; while directly facing Muzzio, two paces from him, rose the long figure of the Malay, wrapt in a mantle of many-coloured brocade, girt round the waist with a tiger's tail, with a high hat of the shape of a pointed tiara on his head. But he was not motionless: at one moment he bowed

313

down reverently, and seemed to be praying, at the next he drew himself up to his full height, even rose on tiptoe; then, with a rhythmic action, threw wide his arms, and moved them persistently in the direction of Muzzio, and seemed to threaten or command him, frowning and stamping with his foot. All these actions seemed to cost him great effort, even to cause him pain: he breathed heavily, the sweat streamed down his face. All at once he sank down to the ground, and drawing in a full breath, with knitted brow and immense effort, drew his clenched hands towards him, as though he were holding reins in them . . . and to the indescribable horror of Fabio, Muzzio's head slowly left the back of the chair, and moved forward, following the Malay's hands. . . . The Malay let them fall, and Muzzio's head fell heavily back again; the Malay repeated his movements, and obediently the head repeated them after him. The dark liquid in the bowls began boiling; the bowls themselves began to resound with a faint bell-like note, and the brazen snakes coiled freely about each of them. Then the Malay took a step forward, and raising his eyebrows and opening his eyes immensely wide, he bowed his head to Muzzio . . . and the eyelids of the dead man quivered, parted uncertainly, and under them could be seen the eyeballs, dull as lead. The Malay's face was radiant with triumphant pride and delight, a delight almost malignant; he opened his mouth wide, and from the depths of his chest there broke out with effort a prolonged howl. . . . Muzzio's lips parted too, and a faint moan quivered on them in response to that inhuman sound. . . .

But at this point Fabio could endure it no longer; he imagined he was present at some devilish incantation! He too uttered a shriek and rushed out, running home, home as quick as possible, without looking round, repeating prayers and crossing himself as he ran.

XIII

THREE HOURS LATER, Antonio came to him with the announcement that everything was ready, the things were packed, and Signor Muzzio was preparing to start. Without a word in answer to his servant, Fabio went out on to the terrace, whence the pavilion could be seen. A few pack-horses were grouped before it; a powerful raven horse, saddled for two riders, was led up to the steps, where servants were standing bare-headed, together with armed attendants. The door of the pavilion opened, and supported by the Malay, who wore once more his ordinary attire, appeared Muzzio. His face was death-like, and his hands hung like a dead man's – but he walked . . . yes, positively walked, and, seated on the charger, he sat upright and felt for and found the reins. The Malay put his feet in the stirrups, leaped up behind him on the saddle, put his arm round him, and the whole party started. The horses moved at a walking pace, and when they turned round before the house, Fabio fancied that in Muzzio's dark face there gleamed two spots of white. . . . Could it be he had turned his eyes upon him? Only the Malay bowed to him . . . ironically, as ever.

Did Valeria see all this? The blinds of her windows were drawn . . . but it may be she was standing behind them.

XIV

AT DINNER-TIME she came into the dining-room, and was very quiet and affectionate; she still complained, however, of weariness. But there was no agitation about her now, none of her former constant bewilderment and secret dread; and when, the day after Muzzio's departure, Fabio set to work again on her portrait, he found in her features the pure expression, the momentary eclipse of which had so troubled him . . . and his brush moved lightly and faithfully over the canvas.

The husband and wife took up their old life again. Muzzio vanished for them as though he had never existed. Fabio and Valeria were agreed, as it seemed, not to utter a syllable referring to him, not to learn anything of his later days; his fate remained, however, a mystery for all. Muzzio did actually disappear, as though he had sunk into the earth. Fabio one day thought it his duty to tell Valeria exactly what had taken place on that fatal night . . . but she probably divined his intention, and she held her breath, half-shutting her eyes, as though she were expecting a blow. . . . And Fabio understood her; he did not inflict that blow upon her.

One fine autumn day, Fabio was putting the last touches to his picture of his Cecilia; Valeria sat at the organ, her fingers straying at random over the keys. . . . Suddenly, without her knowing it, from under her hands came the first notes of that song of triumphant love which Muzzio had once played; and at the same instant, for the first time since her marriage, she felt within her the throb of a new palpitating life. . . . Valeria started, stopped. . . .

What did it mean? Could it be . . .

At this word the manuscript ended.

KAZUO ISHIGURO

MALVERN HILLS

From

NOCTURNES

(2009)

I'D SPENT THE spring in London, and all in all, even if I hadn't achieved everything I'd set out to, it had been an exciting interlude. But with the weeks slipping by and summer getting closer, the old restlessness had started to return. For one thing, I was getting vaguely paranoid about running into any more of my former university friends. Wandering around Camden Town, or going through CDs I couldn't afford in West End megastores, I'd already had too many of them come up to me, asking how I was getting on since leaving the course to "seek fame and fortune". It's not that I was embarrassed to tell them what I'd been up to. It was just that – with a very few exceptions – none of them was capable of grasping what was or wasn't, for me at this particular point, a "successful" few months.

As I've said, I hadn't achieved every goal I'd set my sights on, but then those goals had always been more like long-term targets. And all those auditions, even the really dreary ones, had been an invaluable experience. In almost every case, I'd taken something away with me, something I'd learned about the scene in London, or else about the music business in general.

Some of these auditions had been pretty professional affairs. You'd find yourself in a warehouse, or a converted garage block, and there'd be a manager, or maybe the girl-friend of a band member, taking your name, asking you to wait, offering you tea, while the sounds of the band, stopping and starting, thundered out from the adjoining space. But the majority of auditions happened at a much more shambolic level. In fact, when you saw the way most bands went about things, it was no mystery why the whole scene in London was dying on its feet. Time and again, I'd walk past rows of anonymous suburban terraces on the city outskirts, carry my acoustic guitar up a staircase, and enter a stale-smelling flat with mattresses and sleeping bags all over the floor, and band members who mumbled and barely looked you in the eye. I'd sing and play while they stared emptily at me, till one of them might bring it to an end by saying something like: "Yeah, well. Thanks anyway, but it's not quite our genre."

I soon worked out that most of these guys were shy or plain awkward about the audition process, and that if I chatted to them about other things, they'd become a lot more relaxed. That's when I'd pick up all kinds of useful info: where the interesting clubs were, or the names of other bands in need of a guitarist. Or sometimes it was just a tip about a new act to check out. As I say, I never came away empty-handed.

On the whole, people really liked my guitar-playing, and a lot of them said my vocals would come in handy for harmonies. But it quickly emerged there were two factors going against me. The first was that I didn't have equipment. A lot of bands were wanting someone with electric guitar, amps, speakers, preferably transport, ready to slot right into their gigging schedule. I was on foot with a fairly crappy acoustic. So no matter how much they liked my rhythm work or my voice, they'd no choice but to turn me away. This was fair enough.

Much harder to accept was the other main obstacle – and I have to say, I was completely surprised by this one. There was actually a problem about me writing my own songs.

I couldn't believe it. There I'd be, in some dingy apartment, playing to a circle of blank faces, then at the end, after a silence that could go on for fifteen, thirty seconds, one of them would ask suspiciously: "So whose number was that?" And when I said it was one of my own, you'd see the shutters coming down. There'd be little shrugs, shakes of the head, sly smiles exchanged, then they'd be giving me their rejection patter.

The umpteenth time this happened, I got so exasperated, I said: "Look, I don't get this. Are you wanting to be a covers band for ever? And even if that's what you want to be, where do you think those songs come from in the first place? Yeah, that's right. Someone writes them!"

But the guy I was talking to stared at me vacantly, then said: "No offence, mate. It's just that there are so many wankers going around writing songs."

The stupidity of this position, which seemed to extend right across the London scene, was key to persuading me there was something if not utterly rotten, then at least extremely shallow and inauthentic about what was going down here, right at the grass-roots level, and that this was undoubtedly a reflection of what was happening in the music industry all the way up the ladder.

It was this realisation, and the fact that as the summer came closer I was running out of floors to sleep on, that made me feel for all the fascination of London – my university days looked grey by comparison – it would be good to take a break from the city. So I called up my sister, Maggie, who runs a cafe with her husband up in the Malvern Hills, and that's how it came to be decided I'd spend the summer with them.

Maggie's four years older and is always worrying about me,

so I knew she'd be all for my coming up. In fact, I could tell she was glad to be getting the extra help. When I say her cafe is in the Malvern Hills, I don't mean it's in Great Malvern or down on the A road, but literally up there in the hills. It's an old Victorian house standing by itself facing the west side, so when the weather's nice, you can have your tea and cake out on the cafe terrace with a sweeping view over Herefordshire. Maggie and Geoff have to close the place in the winter, but in the summer it's always busy, mainly with the locals – who park their cars in the West of England car park a hundred yards below and come panting up the path in sandals and floral dresses – or else the walking brigade with their maps and serious gear.

Maggie said she and Geoff couldn't afford to pay me, which suited me just fine because it meant I couldn't be expected to work too hard for them. All the same, since I was getting bed and board, the understanding seemed to be that I'd be a third member of staff. It was all a bit unclear, and at the start, Geoff, in particular, seemed torn between giving me a kick up the arse for not doing enough, and apologising for asking me to do anything at all like I was a guest. But things soon settled down to a pattern. The work was easy enough – I was especially good at making sandwiches – and I sometimes had to keep reminding myself of my main objective in coming out to the country in the first place: that's to say, I was going to write a brand-new batch of songs ready for my return to London in the autumn.

I'm naturally an early riser, but I quickly discovered that breakfast at the cafe was a nightmare, with customers wanting eggs done this way, toast like that, everything getting overcooked. So I made a point of never appearing until around eleven. While all the clatter was going on downstairs, I'd open the big bay window in my room, sit on the broad window sill and play my guitar looking out over miles and miles of countryside. There was a run of really clear mornings just after I arrived, and it was a glorious feeling, like I could see forever, and when I strummed my chords, they were ringing out across the whole nation. Only when I turned and stuck my head right out of the window would I get an aerial view of the cafe terrace below, and become aware of the people coming and going with their dogs and pushchairs.

I wasn't a stranger to this area. Maggie and I had grown up only a few miles away in Pershore and our parents had often brought us for walks on the hills. But I'd never been much up for it in those days, and as soon as I was old enough, I'd refused to go with them. That summer though, I felt this was the most beautiful place in the world; that in many ways I'd come from and belonged to the hills. Maybe it was something to do with our parents having split up, the fact that for some time now, that little grey house opposite the hairdresser was no longer "our" house. Whatever it was, this time round, instead of the claustrophobia I remembered from my childhood, I felt affection, even nostalgia, about the area.

I found myself wandering in the hills practically every day, sometimes with my guitar if I was sure it wouldn't rain. I liked in particular Table Hill and End Hill, at the north end of the range, which tend to get neglected by day-trippers. There I'd sometimes be lost in my thoughts for hours at a time without seeing a soul. It was like I was discovering the hills for the first time, and I could almost taste the ideas for new songs welling up in my mind.

Working at the cafe, though, was another matter. I'd catch a voice, or see a face coming up to the counter while I was preparing a salad, that would jerk me back to an earlier part of my life. Old friends of my parents would come up and grill me about what I was up to, and I'd have to bluff until they decided to leave me in peace. Usually they'd sign off with something like: "Well at least you're keeping busy," nodding towards the sliced bread and tomatoes, before waddling back to their table with their cup and saucer. Or someone I'd known at school would come in and start talking to me in their new "university" voice, maybe dissecting the latest Batman film in clever-clever language, or else starting on about the real causes of world poverty.

I didn't really mind any of this. In fact, some of these people I was genuinely quite glad to see. But there was one person who came into the cafe that summer, the instant I saw her, I felt myself freezing up, and by the time it occurred to me to escape into the kitchen, she'd already seen me.

This was Mrs Fraser – or Hag Fraser, as we used to call her. I recognised her as soon as she came in with a muddy little bulldog. I felt like telling her she couldn't bring the dog inside, though people always did that when they came to get things. Hag Fraser had been one of my teachers at school in Pershore. Thankfully she retired before I went into the sixth form, but in my memory her shadow falls over my entire school career. Her aside, school hadn't been that bad, but she'd had it in for me from the start, and when you're just eleven years old, there's nothing you can do to defend yourself from someone like her. Her tricks were the usual ones twisted teachers have, like asking me in lessons exactly the questions she sensed I wouldn't be able to answer, then making me stand up and getting the class to laugh at me. Later, it got more subtle. I remember once, when I was four-teen, a new teacher, a Mr Travis, had exchanged jokes with me in class. Not jokes against me, but like we were equals, and the class had laughed, and I'd felt good about it. But a couple of days later, I was going down the corridor and Mr Travis was coming the other way, talking with *her*, and as I came by she stopped me and gave me a complete bollocking about late homework or something. The point is she'd done this just to let Mr Travis know I was a "troublemaker"; that if he'd thought for one moment I was one of the boys worthy of his respect, he was making a big mistake. Maybe it was because she was old, I don't know, but the other teachers never seemed to see through her. They all took whatever she said as gospel.

When Hag Fraser came in that day, it was obvious she remembered me, but she didn't smile or call me by name. She bought a cup of tea and a packet of Custard Creams, then took them outside to the terrace. I thought that was that. But then a while later, she came in again, put her empty cup and saucer down on the counter and said: "Since you won't clear the table, I've brought these in myself." She gave me a look that went on a second or two longer than was normal – her old if-only-I-could-swat-you look – then left.

All my hatred for the old dragon came back, and by the time Maggie came down a few minutes later, I was completely fuming. She saw it straight away and asked what was wrong. There were a few customers out on the terrace, but no one inside, so I started shouting, calling Hag Fraser every filthy name she deserved. Maggie got me to calm down, then said:

"Well, she's not anybody's teacher any more. She's just a sad old lady whose husband's gone and left her."

"Not surprised."

"But you have to feel a bit sorry for her. Just when she thought she could enjoy her retirement, she's left for a younger woman. And now she has to run that bed-and-breakfast by herself and people say the place is falling apart."

This all cheered me up no end. I forgot about Hag Fraser soon after that, because a group came in and I had to make a lot of tuna salads. But a few days later when I was chatting to Geoff in the kitchen, I got a few more details from him; like how her husband of forty-odd years had gone off with his secretary; and how their hotel had got off to a reasonable start, but now all the gossip was of guests demanding their money back, or checking out within hours of arrival. I saw the place myself once when I was helping Maggie with the cash-and-carry and we drove past. Hag Fraser's hotel was right there on the Elgar Route, a fairly substantial granite house with an outsize sign saying "Malvern Lodge".

But I don't want to go on about Hag Fraser too much. I'm not obsessed with her or with her hotel. I'm only putting this all here now because of what happened later, once Tilo and Sonja came in.

Geoff had gone into Great Malvern that day, so it was just me and Maggie holding the fort. The main lunch rush was over, but at the point when the Krauts came in, we still had plenty going on. I'd clocked them in my mind as "the Krauts" the moment I heard their accents. I wasn't being racist. If you have to stand behind a counter and remember who didn't want beetroot, who wanted extra bread, who gets what put on which bill, you've no choice but to turn all the customers into characters, give them names, pick out physical peculiarities. Donkey Face had a ploughman's and two coffees. Tuna mayo baguettes for Winston Churchill and his wife. That's how I was doing it. So Tilo and Sonja were "the Krauts".

It was very hot that afternoon, but most of the customers – being English – still wanted to sit outside on the terrace, some of them even avoiding the parasols so they could go bright red in the sun. But the Krauts decided to sit indoors in the shade. They had on loose, camel-coloured trousers, trainers and T-shirts, but somehow looked smart, the way people from the continent often do. I supposed they were in their forties, maybe early fifties – I didn't pay too much attention at that stage. They ate their lunch talking quietly to each other, and they seemed like any pleasant, middle-aged couple from Europe. Then after a while, the guy got up and starting wandering about the room, pausing to study an old faded photo Maggie has on the wall, of the house as it was in 1915. Then he stretched out his arms and said:

"Your countryside here is so wonderful! We have many fine mountains in Switzerland. But what you have here is different. They are hills. You call them hills. They have a charm all their own because they are gentle and friendly."

"Oh, you're from Switzerland," Maggie said in her polite voice. "I've always wanted to go there. It sounds so fantastic, the Alps, the cable-cars."

"Of course, our country has many beautiful features. But here, in this spot, you have a special charm. We have wanted to visit this part of England for so long. We always talked of it, and now finally we are here!" He gave a hearty laugh. "So happy to be here!"

"That's splendid," Maggie said. "I do hope you enjoy it. Are you here for long?"

"We have another three days before we must return to our work. We have looked forward to coming here ever since we observed a wonderful documentary film many years ago, concerning Elgar. Evidently Elgar loved these hills and explored them thoroughly on his bicycle. And now we are finally here!"

Maggie chatted with him for a few minutes about places they'd already visited in England, what they should see in the local area, the usual stuff you were supposed to say to tourists. I'd heard it loads of times before, and I could do it myself more or less on automatic, so I started to tune out. I just took in that the Krauts were actually Swiss and that they were travelling around by hired car. He kept saying what a great place England was and how kind everyone had been, and made big laughing noises whenever Maggie said anything halfway jokey. But as I say, I'd tuned out, thinking they were just this fairly boring couple. I only started paying attention again a few moments later, when I noticed the way the guy kept trying to bring his wife into the conversation, and how she kept silent, her eyes fixed on her guidebook and behaving like she wasn't aware of any conversation at all. That's when I took a closer look at them.

They both had even, natural suntans, quite unlike the sweaty lobster looks of the locals outside, and despite their age, they were both slim and fit-looking. His hair was grey, but luxuriant, and he'd had it carefully groomed, though in a vaguely seventies style, a bit like the guys in Abba. Her hair was blonde, almost snowy white, and her face was stern-looking, with little lines etched around the mouth that spoilt what would otherwise have been the beautiful older woman look. So there he was, as I say, trying to bring her into the conversation.

"Of course, my wife enjoys Elgar greatly and so would be most curious to visit the house in which he was born."

Silence.

Or: "I am not a great fan of Paris, I must confess. I much prefer London. But Sonja here, she loves Paris."

Nothing.

Each time he said something like this, he'd turn towards his wife in the corner, and Maggie would be obliged to look over to her, but the wife still wouldn't glance up from her book. The man didn't seem especially perturbed by this and went on talking cheerfully. Then he stretched out his arms again and said: "If you will excuse me, I think I may for a moment go and admire your splendid scenery!"

He went outside, and we could see him walking around the terrace. Then he disappeared out of our view. The wife was still there in the corner, reading her guidebook, and after a while Maggie went over to her table and began clearing up. The woman ignored her completely until my sister picked up a plate with a tiny bit of roll still left on it. Then suddenly she slammed down her book and said, far more loudly than necessary: "I have not finished yet!"

Maggie apologised and left her with her piece of roll – which I noticed the woman made no move to touch. Maggie looked at me as she came past and I gave her a shrug. Then a few moments later, my sister asked the woman, very nicely, if there was anything else she'd like.

"No. I want nothing else."

I could tell from her tone she should be left alone, but with Maggie it was a kind of reflex. She asked, like she really wanted to know: "Was everything all right?"

For at least five or six seconds, the woman went on reading, like she hadn't heard. Then she put down her book again and glared at my sister.

"Since you ask," she said, "I shall tell you. The food was perfectly okay. Better than in many of the awful places you have around here. However, we waited thirty-five minutes simply to be served a sandwich and a salad. Thirty-five minutes."

I now realised this woman was livid with anger. Not the sort that suddenly hits you, then drains away. No, this woman, I could tell, had been in a kind of white heat for some time. It's the sort of anger that arrives and stays put, at a constant level, like a bad headache, never quite peaking and refusing to find a proper outlet. Maggie's always so even-tempered she couldn't recognise the symptoms, and probably thought the woman was complaining in a more or less rational way. Because she apologised and started to say: "But you see, when there's a big rush like we had earlier . . ."

"Surely you get it every day, no? Is that not so? Every day, in the summer, when the weather is fine, there is just such a big rush? Well? So why can't you be ready? Something that happens every day and it surprises you. Is that what you are telling me?"

The woman had been glaring at my sister, but as I came out from behind the counter to stand beside Maggie, she transferred her gaze to me. And maybe it was to do with the expression I had on my face, I could see her anger go up a couple more notches. Maggie turned and looked at me, and began gently to push me away, but I resisted, and kept gazing at the woman. I wanted her to know it wasn't just her and Maggie in this. God knows where this would have got us, but at that moment the husband came back in.

"Such a marvellous view! A marvellous view, a marvellous lunch, a marvellous country!"

I waited for him to sense what he'd walked into, but if he noticed, he showed no sign of taking it into account. He smiled at his wife and said, presumably for our benefit in English: "Sonja, you really must go and have a look. Just walk to the end of the little path out there!"

She said something in German, then went back to her book. He came further into the room and said to us:

"We had considered driving on to Wales this afternoon. But your Malvern Hills are so wonderful, I really think we might stay here in this district for the remaining three days of our vacation. If Sonja agrees, I will be overjoyed!"

He looked at his wife, who shrugged and said something

else in German, to which he laughed his loud, open laugh.

"Good! She agrees! So it is settled. We will no longer drive to Wales. We will hang out here in your district for the next three days!"

He beamed at us, and Maggie said something encouraging. I was relieved to see the wife putting her book away and getting ready to leave. The man, too, went to the table, picked up a small rucksack and put it on his shoulder. Then he said to Maggie:

"I wonder. Is there by any chance a small hotel you can recommend for us nearby? Nothing too expensive, but comfortable and pleasant. And if possible, with something of the English flavour!"

Maggie was a bit stumped by this and delayed her answer by saying something meaningless like: "What sort of place did you want?" But I said quickly:

"The best place around here is Mrs Fraser's. It's just down along the road to Worcester. It's called Malvern Lodge."

"The Malvern Lodge! That sounds just the ticket!"

Maggie turned away disapprovingly and pretended to be clearing away more things while I gave them all the details on how to find Hag Fraser's hotel. Then the couple left, the guy thanking us with big smiles, the woman not giving a backward glance.

My sister gave me a weary look and shook her head. I just laughed and said:

"You've got to admit, that woman and Hag Fraser really deserve one another. It was just too good an opportunity to miss."

"It's all very well for you to amuse yourself like that," Maggie said, pushing past me to the kitchen. "I have to live here."

"So what? Look, you'll never see those Krauts again. And

if Hag Fraser finds out we've been recommending her place to passing tourists, she's hardly going to complain, is she?"

Maggie shook her head, but there was more of a smile about it this time.

The cafe got quieter after that, then Geoff came back, so I went off upstairs, feeling I'd done more than my share for the time being. Up in my room, I sat at the bay window with my guitar and for a while got engrossed in a song I was halfway through writing. But then – and it seemed like no time – I could hear the afternoon tea rush starting downstairs. If it got really mad, like it usually did, Maggie was bound to ask me to come down – which really wouldn't be fair, given how much I'd done already. So I decided the best thing would be for me to slip out to the hills and continue my work there.

I left the back way without encountering anyone, and immediately felt glad to be out in the open. It was pretty warm though, especially carrying a guitar case, and I was glad of the breeze.

I was heading for a particular spot I'd discovered the previous week. To get there you climbed a steep path behind the house, then walked a few minutes along a more gradual incline till you came to this bench. It's one I'd chosen carefully, not just because of the fantastic view, but because it wasn't at one of those junctions in the paths where people with exhausted children come staggering up and sit next to you. On the other hand it wasn't completely isolated, and every now and then, a walker would pass by, saying "Hi!" in the way they do, maybe adding some quip about my guitar, all without breaking stride. I didn't mind this at all. It was kind of like having an audience and not having one, and it gave my imagination just that little edge it needed.

I'd been there on my bench for maybe half an hour when I became aware that some walkers, who'd just gone past with the usual short greeting, had now stopped several yards away and were watching me. This did rather annoy me, and I said, a little sarcastically:

"It's okay. You don't have to toss me any money."

This was answered by a big hearty laugh which I recognised, and I looked up to see the Krauts coming back towards the bench.

The possibility flashed through my mind that they'd gone to Hag Fraser's, realised I'd pulled a fast one on them, and were now coming to get even with me. But then I saw that not only the guy, but the woman too, was smiling cheerfully. They retraced their steps till they were standing in front of me, and since by this time the sun was falling, they appeared for a moment as two silhouettes, the big afternoon sky behind them. Then they came closer and I could see they were both gazing at my guitar – which I'd continued to play – with a look of happy amazement, the way people gaze at a baby. Even more astonishing, the woman was tapping her foot to my beat. I got self-conscious and stopped.

"Hey, carry on!" the woman said. "It's really good what you play there."

"Yes," the husband said, "wonderful! We heard it from a distance." He pointed. "We were right up there, on that ridge, and I said to Sonja, I can hear music."

"Singing too," the woman said. "I said to Tilo, listen, there is singing somewhere. And I was right, yes? You were singing also a moment ago."

I couldn't quite accept that this smiling woman was the same one who'd given us such a hard time at lunch, and I looked at them again carefully, in case this was a different couple altogether. But they were in the same clothes, and though the man's Abba-style hair had come undone a bit in the wind, there was no mistaking it. In any case, the next moment, he said:

"I believe you are the gentleman who served us lunch in the delightful restaurant."

I agreed I was. Then the woman said:

"That melody you were singing a moment ago. We heard it up there, just in the wind at first. I loved the way it fell at the end of each line."

"Thanks," I said. "It's something I'm working on. Not finished yet."

"Your own composition? Then you must be very gifted! Please do sing your melody again, as you were before."

"You know," the guy said, "when you come to record your song, you must tell the producer *this* is how you want it to sound. Like this!" He gestured behind him at Herefordshire stretched out before us. "You must tell him this is the sound, the aural environment you require. Then the listener will hear your song as we heard it today, caught in the wind as we descend the slope of the hill . . ."

"But a little more clearly, of course," the woman said. "Or else the listener will not catch the words. But Tilo is correct. There must be a suggestion of outdoors. Of air, of echo."

They seemed on the verge of getting carried away, like they'd just come across another Elgar in the hills. Despite my initial suspicions, I couldn't help but warm to them.

"Well," I said, "since I wrote most of the song up here, it's no wonder there's something of this place in it."

"Yes, yes," they both said together, nodding. Then the woman said: "You must not be shy. Please share your music with us. It sounded wonderful."

"All right," I said, playing a little doodle. "All right, I'll sing you a song, if you really want me to. Not the one I haven't finished. Another one. But look, I can't do it with you two standing over me like this."

"Of course," Tilo said. "We are being so inconsiderate. Sonja and I have had to perform in so many strange and difficult conditions, we become insensitive to the needs of another musician."

He looked around and sat down on a patch of stubbly grass near the path, his back to me and facing the view. Sonja gave me an encouraging smile, then sat down beside him. Immediately, he put an arm around her shoulders, she leaned towards him, then it was almost like I wasn't there any more, and they were having an intimate lovey-dovey moment gazing over the late-afternoon countryside.

"Okay, here goes," I said, and went into the song I usually open with at auditions. I aimed my voice at the horizon but kept glancing at Tilo and Sonja. Though I couldn't see their faces, the whole way they remained snuggled up to each other with no hint of restlessness told me they were enjoying what they were hearing. When I finished, they turned to me with big smiles and applauded, sending echoes around the hills.

"Fantastic!" Sonja said. "So talented!"

"Splendid, splendid," Tilo was saying.

I felt a little embarrassed by this and pretended to be absorbed in some guitar work. When I eventually looked up again, they were still sitting on the ground, but had now shifted their positions so they could see me.

"So you're musicians?" I asked. "I mean, *professional* musicians?"

"Yes," said Tilo, "I suppose you could call us professionals. Sonja and I, we perform as a duo. In hotels, restaurants. At weddings, at parties. All over Europe, though we like best to

335

work in Switzerland and Austria. We make our living this way, so yes, we are professionals."

"But first and foremost," Sonja said, "we play because we believe in the music. I can see it is the same for you."

"If I stopped believing in my music," I said, "I'd stop, just like that." Then I added: "I'd really like to do it professionally. It must be a good life."

"Oh yes, it's a good life," said Tilo. "We're very lucky we are able to do what we do."

"Look," I said, maybe a little suddenly. "Did you go to that hotel I told you about?"

"How very rude of us!" Tilo exclaimed. "We were so taken by your music, we forgot completely to thank you. Yes, we went there and it is just the ticket. Fortunately there were still vacancies."

"It's just what we wanted," said Sonja. "Thank you."

I pretended again to become absorbed in my chords. Then I said as casually as I could: "Come to think of it, there's this other hotel I know. I think it's better than Malvern Lodge. I think you should change."

"Oh, but we're quite settled now," said Tilo. "We have unpacked our things, and besides, it's just what we need."

"Yeah, but . . . Well, the thing is, earlier on, when you asked me about a hotel, I didn't know you were musicians. I thought you were bankers or something."

They both burst out laughing, like I'd made a fantastic joke. Then Tilo said:

"No, no, we're not bankers. Though there have been many times we wished we were!"

"What I'm saying," I said, "is there are other hotels much more geared, you know, to artistic types. It's hard when strangers ask you to recommend a hotel, before you know what sort of people they are."

"It's kind of you to worry," said Tilo. "But please, don't do so any longer. What we have is perfect. Besides, people are not so different. Bankers, musicians, we all in the end want the same things from life."

"You know, I'm not sure that is so true," Sonja said. "Our young friend here, you see he doesn't look for a job in a bank. His dreams are different."

"Perhaps you are right, Sonja. All the same, the present hotel is fine for us."

I leaned over the strings and practised another little phrase to myself, and for a few seconds nobody spoke. Then I asked: "So what sort of music do you guys play?"

Tilo shrugged. "Sonja and I play a number of instruments between us. We both play keyboards. I am fond of the clarinet. Sonja is a very fine violinist, and also a splendid singer. I suppose what we like to do best is to perform our traditional Swiss folk music, but in a contemporary manner. Sometimes even what you might call a radical manner. We take inspiration from great composers who took a similar path. Janáček, for instance. Your own Vaughan Williams."

"But that kind of music", Sonja said, "we don't play so much now."

They exchanged glances with what I thought was just a hint of tension. Then Tilo's usual smile was back on his face.

"Yes, as Sonja points out, in this real world, much of the time, we must play what our audience is most likely to appreciate. So we perform many hits. Beatles, the Carpenters. Some more recent songs. This is perfectly satisfying."

"What about Abba?" I asked on an impulse, then immediately regretted it. But Tilo didn't seem to sense any mockery.

"Yes, indeed, we do some Abba. 'Dancing Queen'. That one always goes down well. In fact, it is on 'Dancing Queen' I actually do a little singing myself, a little harmony part.

Sonja will tell you I have the most terrible voice. So we must make sure to perform this song only when our customers are right in the middle of their meal, when there is for them no chance of escape!"

He did his big laugh, and Sonja laughed too, though not so loudly. A power-cyclist, kitted out in what looked like a black wetsuit, went speeding by us, and for the next few moments, we all watched his frantic, receding shape.

"I went to Switzerland once," I said eventually. "A couple of summers ago. Interlaken. I stayed at the youth hostel there."

"Ah yes, Interlaken. A beautiful place. Some Swiss people scoff at it. They say it is just for the tourists. But Sonja and I always love to perform there. In fact, to play in Interlaken on a summer evening, to happy people from all over the world, it is something very wonderful. I hope you enjoyed your visit there."

"Yeah, it was great."

"There is a restaurant in Interlaken where we play a few nights every summer. For our performance, we position ourselves under the restaurant's canopy, so we are facing the dining tables, which of course are outdoors on such an evening. And as we perform, we are able to see all the tourists, eating and talking together under the stars. And behind the tourists, we see the big field, where during the day the paragliders are landing, but which at night is lit up by the lamps along the Höheweg. And if your eye may travel further, there are the Alps overlooking the field. The outlines of the Eiger, the Mönch, the Jungfrau. And the air is pleasantly warm and filled with the music we are making. I always feel when we are there, this is a privilege. I think, yes, it is good to be doing this."

"That restaurant," Sonja said. "Last year, the manager

338

made us wear full costumes while we performed, even though it was so hot. It was very uncomfortable, and we said, what difference does it make, why must we have our bulky waist-coats and scarves and hats? In just our blouses, we look neat and still very Swiss. But the restaurant manager tells us, we put on the full costumes or we don't play. Our choice, he says, and walks away, just like that."

"But Sonja, that is the same in any job. There is always a uniform, something the employer insists you must wear. It is the same for bankers! And in our case, at least it is something we believe in. Swiss culture. Swiss tradition."

Once again something vaguely awkward hovered between them, but it was just for a second or two, and then they both smiled as they fixed their gazes back on my guitar. I thought I should say something, so I said:

"I think I'd enjoy that. Being able to play in different countries. It must keep you sharp, really aware of your audiences."

"Yes," Tilo said, "it is good that we perform to all kinds of people. And not only in Europe. All in all, we have got to know so many cities so well."

"Düsseldorf, for instance," said Sonja. There was some-thing different about her voice now – something harder – and I could see again the person I'd encountered back at the cafe. Tilo, though, didn't seem to notice anything and said to me, in a carefree sort of way:

"Düsseldorf is where our son is now living. He is your age. Perhaps a little older."

"Earlier this year," Sonja said, "we went to Düsseldorf. We have an engagement to play there. Not the usual thing, this is a chance to play our real music. So we call him, our son, our only child, we call to say we are coming to his city. He does not answer his phone, so we leave a message. We leave

339

many messages. No reply. We arrive in Düsseldorf, we leave more messages. We say, here we are, we are in your city. Still nothing. Tilo says don't worry, perhaps he will come on the night, to our concert. But he does not come. We play, then we go to another city, to our next engagement."

Tilo made a chuckling noise. "I think perhaps Peter heard enough of our music while he was growing up! The poor boy, you see, he had to listen to us rehearsing, day after day."

"I suppose it can be a bit tricky," I said. "Having children and being musicians."

"We only had the one child," Tilo said, "so it was not so bad. Of course we were fortunate. When we had to travel, and we couldn't take him with us, his grandparents were always delighted to help. And when Peter was older, we were able to send him to a good boarding school. Again, his grandparents came to the rescue. We could not afford such school fees otherwise. So we were very fortunate."

"Yes, we were fortunate," Sonja said. "Except Peter hated his school."

The earlier good atmosphere was definitely slipping away. In an effort to cheer things up, I said quickly: "Well, anyway, it looks like you both really enjoy your work."

"Oh yes, we enjoy our work," said Tilo. "It's everything to us. Even so, we very much appreciate a vacation. Do you know, this is our first proper vacation in three years."

This made me feel really bad all over again, and I thought about having another go at persuading them to change hotels, but I could see how ridiculous this would look. I just had to hope Hag Fraser pulled her finger out. Instead, I said:

"Look, if you like, I'll play you that song I was working on earlier. I haven't finished it, and I wouldn't usually do this. But since you heard some of it anyway, I don't mind playing you what I've got so far."

The smile returned to Sonja's face. "Yes," she said, "please do let us hear. It sounded so beautiful."

As I got ready to play, they shifted again, so they were facing the view like before, their backs to me. But this time, instead of cuddling, they sat there on the grass with surprisingly upright postures, each with a hand up to the brow to shield away the sun. They stayed like that all the time I played, peculiarly still, and what with the way each of them cast a long afternoon shadow, they looked like matching art exhibits. I brought my incomplete song to a meandering halt, and for a moment they didn't move. Then their postures relaxed, and they applauded, though perhaps not quite as enthusiastically as the last time. Tilo got to his feet, muttering compliments, then helped Sonja up. It was only when you saw how they did this that you remembered they were really quite middle-aged. Maybe they were just tired. For all I know, they might have done a fair bit of walking before they'd come across me. All the same, it seemed to me they found it quite a struggle to get up.

"You've entertained us so marvellously," Tilo was saying. "Now we are the tourists, and someone else plays for us! It makes a pleasant change."

"I would love to hear that song when it is finished," Sonja said, and she seemed really to mean it. "Maybe one day I will hear it on the radio. Who knows?"

"Yes," Tilo said, "and then Sonja and I will play our cover version to our customers!" His big laugh rang through the air. Then he did a polite little bow and said: "So today we are in your debt three times over. A splendid lunch. A splendid choice of hotel. And a splendid concert here in the hills!"

As we said our goodbyes, I had an urge to tell them the truth. To confess that I'd deliberately sent them to the worst hotel in the area, and warn them to move out while there was still time. But the affectionate way they shook my hand made it all the harder to come out with this. And then they were going down the hill and I was alone on the bench again.

The cafe had closed by the time I came down from the hills. Maggie and Geoff looked exhausted. Maggie said it had been their busiest day yet and seemed pleased about it. But when Geoff made the same point over supper – which we ate in the cafe from various left-overs – he put it like it was a negative thing, like it was awful they'd been made to work so hard and where had I been to help? Maggie asked how my afternoon had gone, and I didn't mention Tilo and Sonja – that seemed too complicated – but told her I'd gone up to the Sugarloaf to work on my song. And when she asked if I'd made any progress, and I said yes, I was making real headway now, Geoff got up and marched out moodily, even though there was still food on his plate. Maggie pretended not to notice, and fair enough, he came back a few minutes later with a can of beer, and sat there reading his newspaper and not saying much. I didn't want to be the cause of a rift between my sister and brother-in-law, so I excused myself soon after that and went upstairs to work some more on the song.

My room, which was such an inspiration in the daytime, wasn't nearly so appealing after dark. For a start, the curtains didn't pull all the way across, which meant if I opened a window in the stifling heat, insects from miles around would see my light and come charging in. And the light I had was just this one bare bulb hanging down from the ceiling rose, which cast gloomy shadows all round the room, making it look all the more obviously the spare room it was. That evening, I was wanting light to work by, to jot down lyrics as they occurred to me. But it got far too stuffy, and in the end I switched off the bulb, pulled back the curtains, and opened

342

the windows wide. Then I sat in the bay with my guitar, just the way I did in the day.

I'd been there like that for about an hour, playing through various ideas for the bridge passage, when there was a knock and Maggie stuck her head round the door. Of course everything was in darkness, but outside down on the terrace there was a security light, so I could just about make out her face. She had on this awkward smile, and I thought she was about to ask me to come and help with yet another chore. She came right in, closed the door behind her and said:

"I'm sorry, love. But Geoff's really tired tonight, he's been working so hard. And now he says he wants to watch his movie in peace?"

She said it like that, like it was a question, and it took me a moment to realise she was asking me to stop playing my music.

"But I'm working on something important here," I said.

"I know. But he's really tired tonight, and he says he can't relax because of your guitar."

"What Geoff needs to realise," I said, "is that just as he's got his work to do, I've got mine."

My sister seemed to think about this. Then she did a big sigh. "I don't think I ought to report that back to Geoff."

"Why not? Why don't you? It's time he got the message."

"Why not? Because I don't think he'd be very pleased, that's why not. And I don't really think he'd accept that his work and your work are quite on the same level."

I stared at Maggie, for a moment quite speechless. Then I said: "You're talking such rubbish. Why are you talking such rubbish?"

She shook her head wearily, but didn't say anything.

"I don't understand why you're talking such rubbish," I said. "And just when things are going so well for me."

"Things are going well for you, are they, love?" She kept looking at me in the half-light. "Well, all right," she said in the end. "I won't argue with you." She turned away to open the door. "Come down and join us, if you like," she said as she left.

Rigid with rage, I stared at the door that had closed behind her. I became aware of muffled sounds from the television downstairs, and even in the state I was in, some detached part of my brain was telling me my fury should be directed not at Maggie, but at Geoff, who'd been systematically trying to undermine me ever since I'd got here. Even so, it was my sister I was livid at. In all the time I'd been in her house, she hadn't once asked to hear a song, the way Tilo and Sonja had done. Surely it wasn't too much to ask of your own sister, and one who'd been, I happened to remember, a big music fan in her teens? And now here she was, interrupting me when I was trying to work and talking all this rubbish. Every time I thought of the way she'd said: "All right, I won't argue with you," I felt fresh fury coursing through me.

I came down off the window sill, put away the guitar, and threw myself down on my mattress. Then for the next little while I stared at the patterns on the ceiling. It seemed clear I'd been invited here on false pretences, that this had all been about getting cheap help for the busy season, a mug they didn't even have to pay. And my sister didn't understand what I was trying to achieve any better than did her moron of a husband. It would serve them both right if I left them here in the lurch and went back to London. I kept going round and round with this stuff, until maybe an hour or so later, I calmed down a bit and decided I'd just turn in for the night.

I didn't speak much to either of them when I came down

as usual just after the breakfast rush. I made some toast and coffee, helped myself to some left-over scrambled eggs, and settled down in the corner of the cafe. All through my breakfast the thought kept occurring to me I might run into Tilo and Sonja again up in the hills. And though this might mean having to face the music about Hag Fraser's place, even so, I realised I was hoping it would happen. Besides, even if Hag Fraser's was truly awful, they'd never suppose I'd recommended it out of malice. There'd be any number of ways for me to get out of it.

Maggie and Geoff were probably expecting me to help again with the lunch rush, but I decided they needed a lesson about taking people for granted. So after breakfast, I went upstairs, got my guitar and slipped out the back way.

It was really hot again and the sweat was running down my cheek as I climbed the path leading up to my bench. Even though I'd been thinking about Tilo and Sonja at breakfast, I'd forgotten them by this point, and so got a surprise when, coming up the final slope, I looked towards the bench and saw Sonja sitting there by herself. She spotted me immediately and waved.

I was still a bit wary of her, and especially without Tilo around, I wasn't so keen to sit down with her. But she gave me a big smile and did a shifting movement, like she was making room for me, so I didn't have much choice.

We said our hellos, then for a time we just sat there side by side, not speaking. This didn't seem so odd at first, partly because I was still getting my breath back, and partly because of the view. There was more haze and cloud than the previous day, but if you concentrated, you could still see beyond the Welsh borders to the Black Mountains. The breeze was quite strong, but not uncomfortable.

"So where's Tilo?" I asked in the end.

"Tilo? Oh . . ." She put her hand up to shield her eyes. Then she pointed. "There. You see? Over there. That is Tilo."

Some way in the distance, I could see a figure, in what might have been a green T-shirt and a white sun cap, moving along the rising path towards Worcestershire Beacon.

"Tilo wished to go for a walk," she said.

"You didn't want to go with him?"

"No. I decided to stay here."

While she wasn't by any means the irate customer from the cafe, neither was she quite the same person who'd been so warm and encouraging to me the day before. There was definitely something up, and I started preparing my defence about Hag Fraser's.

"By the way," I said, "I've been working a bit more on that song. You can hear it if you like."

She gave this consideration, then said: "If you do not mind, perhaps not just at this minute. You see, Tilo and I have just had a talk. You might call it a disagreement."

"Oh okay. Sorry to hear that."

"And now he has gone off for his walk."

Again, we sat there not talking. Then I sighed and said: "I think maybe this is all my fault."

She turned to look at me. "Your fault? Why do you say that?"

"The reason you've quarrelled, the reason your holiday's all messed up now. It's my fault. It's that hotel, isn't it? It wasn't very good, right?"

"The hotel?" She seemed puzzled. "That hotel. Well, it has some weak points. But it is a hotel, like many others."

"But you noticed, right? You noticed all the weak points. You must have done."

She seemed to think this over, then nodded. "It is true, I noticed the weak points. Tilo, however, did not. Tilo, of

346

course, thought the hotel was splendid. We are so lucky, he kept saying. So lucky to find such a hotel. Then this morning we have our breakfast. For Tilo, this is a fine breakfast, the best breakfast ever. I say, Tilo, don't be stupid. This is not a good breakfast. This is not a good hotel. He says, no, no, we are so very lucky. So I become angry. I tell the proprietress everything that is wrong. Tilo leads me away. Let's go for a walk, he says. You will feel better then. So we come out here. And he says, Sonja, look at these hills, aren't they so beautiful? Aren't we fortunate to come to such a place as this for our vacation? These hills, he says, are even more wonderful than he imagined them when we listen to Elgar. He asks me, isn't this so? Perhaps I become angry again. I tell him, these hills are not so wonderful. It is not how I imagine them when I hear Elgar's music. Elgar's hills are majestic and mysterious. Here, this is just like a park. This is what I say to him, and then it is his turn to be cross. He says in that case, he will walk by himself. He says we are finished, we never agree on anything now. Yes, he says, Sonja, you and me, we are finished. And off he goes! So there you are. That is why he is up there and I am down here." She shielded her eyes again and watched Tilo's progress.

"I'm really sorry," I said. "If only I hadn't sent you to that hotel in the first place . . ."

"Please. The hotel is not important." She leaned forward to get a better view of Tilo. Then she turned to me and smiled, and I thought maybe there were little tears in her eyes. "Tell me," she said. "Today, you mean to write more songs?"

"That's the plan. Or at least, I want to finish the one I've been working on. The one you heard yesterday."

"That was beautiful. And what will you do then, once you have finished writing your songs here? You have a plan?"

"I'll go back to London and form a band. These songs need just the right band or they won't work."

"How exciting. I do wish you luck."

After a moment, I said, quite quietly: "Then again, I may not bother. It's not so easy, you know."

She didn't reply, and it occurred to me she hadn't heard, because she'd turned away again, to look towards Tilo.

"You know," she said eventually, "when I was younger, nothing could make me angry. But now I get angry at many things. I don't know how I have become this way. It is not good. Well, I do not think Tilo is coming back here. I will return to the hotel and wait for him." She got to her feet, her gaze still fixed on his distant figure.

"It's a shame," I said, also getting up, "you having a row on your holiday. And yesterday, when I was playing to you, you seemed so happy together."

"Yes, that was a good moment. Thank you for that." Suddenly, she held out her hand to me, smiling warmly. "It has been so nice to meet you."

We shook hands, in the slightly limp way you do with women. She started to walk away, then stopped and looked at me.

"If Tilo were here," she said, "he would say to you never be discouraged. He would say, of course, you must go to London and try and form your band. Of course you will be successful. That is what Tilo would say to you. Because that is his way."

"And what would *you* say?"

"I would like to say the same. Because you are young and talented. But I am not so certain. As it is, life will bring enough disappointments. If on top, you have such dreams as this . . ." She smiled again and shrugged. "But I should not say these things. I am not a good example to you. Besides,

348

I can see you are much more like Tilo. If disappointments do come, you will carry on still. You will say, just as he does, I am so lucky." For a few seconds, she went on gazing at me, like she was memorising the way I looked. The breeze was blowing her hair about, making her seem older than she usually did. "I wish you much luck," she said finally.

"Good luck yourself," I said. "And I hope you two make it up okay."

She waved a last time, then went off down the path out of my view.

I took the guitar from its case and sat back on the bench. I didn't play anything for a while though, because I was looking into the distance, towards Worcestershire Beacon, and Tilo's tiny figure up on the incline. Maybe it was to do with the way the sun was hitting that part of the hill, but I could see him much more clearly now than before, even though he'd got further away. He'd paused for a moment on the path, and seemed to be looking about him at the surrounding hills, almost like he was trying to reappraise them. Then his figure started to move again.

I worked on my song for a few minutes, but kept losing concentration, mainly because I was thinking about the way Hag Fraser's face must have looked as Sonja laid into her that morning. Then I gazed at the clouds, and at the sweep of land below me, and I made myself think again about my song, and the bridge passage I still hadn't got right.

WILLA CATHER

THE GARDEN LODGE

From

THE TROLL GARDEN

(1905)

WHEN CAROLINE NOBLE'S friends learned that Raymond d'Esquerré was to spend a month at her place on the Sound before he sailed to fill his engagement for the London opera season, they considered it another striking instance of the perversity of things. That the month was May, and the most mild and florescent of all the blue-and-white Mays the middle coast had known in years, but added to their sense of wrong. D'Esquerré, they learned, was ensconced in the lodge in the apple orchard, just beyond Caroline's glorious garden, and report went that at almost any hour the sound of the tenor's voice and of Caroline's crashing accompaniment could be heard floating through the open windows, out among the snowy apple boughs. The Sound, steel-blue and dotted with white sails, was splendidly seen from the windows of the lodge. The garden to the left and the orchard to the right had never been so riotous with spring, and had burst into impassioned bloom, as if to accommodate Caroline, though she was certainly the last woman to whom the witchery of Freya could be attributed; the last woman, as her friends affirmed, to at all adequately appreciate and make the most of such a setting for the great tenor.

Of course, they admitted, Caroline was musical – well, she ought to be! – but in that as in everything she was para-mountly cool-headed, slow of impulse, and disgustingly practical; in that, as in everything else, she had herself so provokingly well in hand. Of course it would be she, always mistress of herself in any situation, she who would never be lifted one inch from the ground by it, and who would go on superintending her gardeners and workmen as usual, it would be she who got him. Perhaps some of them suspected that this was exactly why she did get him, and it but nettled them the more.

Caroline's coolness, her capableness, her general success, especially exasperated people because they felt that, for the most part, she had made herself what she was, that she had cold-bloodedly set about complying with the demands of life and making her position comfortable and masterful. That was why, every one said, she had married Howard Noble. Women who did not get through life so well as Caroline, who could not make such good terms either with fortune or their husbands, who did not find their health so unfailingly good, or hold their looks so well, or manage their children so easily, or give such distinction to all they did, were fond of stamping Caroline as a materialist and called her hard.

The impression of cold calculation, of having a definite policy, which Caroline gave, was far from a false one; but there was this to be said for her, that there were extenuating circumstances which her friends could not know.

If Caroline held determinedly to the middle course, if she was apt to regard with distrust everything which inclined toward extravagance, it was not because she was unacquainted with other standards than her own, or had never seen another side of life. She had grown up in Brooklyn, in a shabby little house under the vacillating administration of her father, a music teacher who usually neglected his duties to write orchestral compositions for which the world seemed to have no especial need. His spirit was warped by bitter vindictiveness and puerile self-commiseration, and he spent his days in scorn of the labour that brought him bread and in

pitiful devotion to the labour that brought him only disappointment, writing interminable scores which demanded of
the orchestra everything under heaven except melody.

It was not a cheerful home for a girl to grow up in. The
mother, who idolized her husband as the music lord of the
future, was left to a life-long battle with broom and dust-pan,
to never ending conciliatory overtures to the butcher and
grocer, to the making of her own gowns and of Caroline's,
and to the delicate task of mollifying Auguste's neglected
pupils.

The son, Heinrich, a painter, Caroline's only brother,
had inherited all his father's vindictive sensitiveness without his capacity for slavish application. His little studio on
the third floor had been much frequented by young men
as unsuccessful as himself, who met there to give themselves over to contemptuous derision of this or that artist
whose industry and stupidity had won him recognition.
Heinrich, when he worked at all, did newspaper sketches
at twenty-five dollars a week. He was too indolent and
vacillating to set himself seriously to his art, too irascible
and poignantly self-conscious to make a living, too much
addicted to lying late in bed, to the incontinent reading of
poetry and to the use of chloral, to be anything very positive
except painful. At twenty-six, he shot himself in a frenzy,
and the whole wretched affair had effectually shattered his
mother's health and brought on the decline of which she
died. Caroline had been fond of him, but she felt a certain
relief when he no longer wandered about the little house,
commenting ironically upon its shabbiness, a Turkish cap
on his head and a cigarette hanging from between his long,
tremulous fingers.

After her mother's death Caroline assumed the management of that bankrupt establishment. The funeral expenses

were unpaid, and Auguste's pupils had been frightened away by the shock of successive disasters and the general atmosphere of wretchedness that pervaded the house. Auguste himself was writing a symphonic poem, Icarus, dedicated to the memory of his son. Caroline was barely twenty when she was called upon to face this tangle of difficulties, but she reviewed the situation candidly. The house had served its time at the shrine of idealism; vague, distressing, unsatisfied yearnings had brought it low enough. Her mother, thirty years before, had eloped and left Germany with her music teacher, to give herself over to life-long, drudging bondage at the kitchen range. Ever since Caroline could remember, the law in the house had been a sort of mystic worship of things distant, intangible and unattainable. The family had lived in successive ebullitions of generous enthusiasm, in talk of masters and masterpieces, only to come down to the cold facts in the case; to boiled mutton and to the necessity of turning the dining-room carpet. All these emotional pyrotechnics had ended in petty jealousies, in neglected duties and in cowardly fear of the little grocer on the corner.

From her childhood she had hated it, that humiliating and uncertain existence, with its glib tongue and empty pockets, its poetic ideals and sordid realities, its indolence and poverty tricked out in paper roses. Even as a little girl, when vague dreams beset her, when she wanted to lie late in bed and commune with visions, or to leap and sing because the sooty little trees along the street were putting out their first pale leaves in the sunshine, she would clench her hands and go to help her mother sponge the spots from her father's waistcoat or press Heinrich's trousers. Her mother never permitted the slightest question concerning anything Auguste or Heinrich saw fit to do, but from the time Caroline could reason at all she could not help thinking that many things went wrong at home. She knew, for example, that her father's pupils ought not to be kept waiting half an hour while he discussed Schopenhauer with some bearded socialist over a dish of herrings and a spotted table cloth. She knew that Heinrich ought not to give a dinner on Heine's birthday, when the laundress had not been paid for a month and when he frequently had to ask his mother for car fare. Certainly Caroline had served her apprenticeship to idealism and to all the embarrassing inconsistencies which it sometimes entails, and she decided to deny herself this diffuse, ineffectual answer to the sharp questions of life.

When she came into the control of herself and the house, she refused to proceed any further with her musical education. Her father, who had intended to make a concert pianist of her, set this down as another item in his long list of disappointments and his grievances against the world. She was young and pretty, and she had worn turned gowns and soiled gloves and improvised hats all her life. She wanted the luxury of being like other people, of being honest from her hat to her boots, of having nothing to hide, not even in the matter of stockings, and she was willing to work for it. She rented a little studio away from that house of misfortune, and began to give lessons. She managed well and was the sort of girl people liked to help. The bills were paid and Auguste went on composing, growing indignant only when she refused to insist that her pupils should study his compositions for the piano. She began to get engagements in New York to play accompaniments at song recitals. She dressed well, made herself agreeable, and gave herself a chance. She never permitted herself to look further than a step ahead, and set herself with all the strength of her will to see things as they are and meet them squarely in the broad day. There were two things she feared even more than poverty; the part of one that sets up an idol and the part of one that bows down and worships it.

When Caroline was twenty-four she married Howard Noble, then a widower of forty, who had been for ten years a power in Wall Street. Then, for the first time, she had paused to take breath. It took a substantialness as unquestionable as his; his money, his position, his energy, the big vigour of his robust person, to satisfy her that she was entirely safe. Then she relaxed a little, feeling that there was a barrier to be counted upon between her and that world of visions and quagmires and failure.

Caroline had been married for six years when Raymond d'Esquerré came to stay with them. He came chiefly because Caroline was what she was; because he, too, felt occasionally the need of getting out of Klingsor's garden, or dropping down somewhere for a time near a quiet nature, a cool head, a strong hand. The hours he had spent in the garden lodge were hours of such concentrated study as, in his fevered life, he seldom got in anywhere. She had, as he told Noble, a fine appreciation of the seriousness of work.

One evening two weeks after d'Esquerré had sailed, Caroline was in the library giving her husband an account of the work she had laid out for the gardeners. She superintended the care of the grounds herself. Her garden, indeed, had become quite a part of her; a sort of beautiful adjunct, like gowns or jewels. It was a famous spot, and Noble was very proud of it.

"What do you think, Caroline, of having the garden lodge torn down and putting a new summer house there at the end of the arbour; a big rustic affair where you could have tea served in mid-summer?" he asked.

"The lodge?" repeated Caroline looking at him quickly.

"Why, that seems almost a shame, doesn't it, after d'Esquerré has used it?"

Noble put down his book with a smile of amusement.

"Are you going to be sentimental about it? Why, I'd sacrifice the whole place to see that come to pass. But I don't believe you could do it for an hour together."

"I don't believe so, either," said his wife, smiling.

Noble took up his book again and Caroline went into the music-room to practise. She was not ready to have the lodge torn down. She had gone there for a quiet hour every day during the two weeks since d'Esquerré had left them. It was the sheerest sentiment she had ever permitted herself. She was ashamed of it, but she was childishly unwilling to let it go.

Caroline went to bed soon after her husband, but she was not able to sleep. The night was close and warm, presaging storm. The wind had fallen and the water slept, fixed and motionless as the sand. She rose and thrust her feet into slippers and putting a dressing-gown over her shoulders opened the door of her husband's room; he was sleeping soundly. She went into the hall and down the stairs; then, leaving the house through a side door, stepped into the vine covered arbour that led to the garden lodge. The scent of the June roses was heavy in the still air, and the stones that paved the path felt pleasantly cool through the thin soles of her slippers. Heat-lightning flashed continuously from the bank of clouds that had gathered over the sea, but the shore was flooded with moonlight and, beyond, the rim of the Sound lay smooth and shining. Caroline had the key of the lodge, and the door creaked as she opened it. She stepped into the long, low room radiant with the moonlight which streamed through the bow window and lay in a silvery pool along the waxed floor. Even that part of the room which lay in the shadow was vaguely illuminated; the piano, the tall candlesticks, the picture frames and white casts standing out as clearly in the half-light as did the sycamores and black poplars of the garden against the still, expectant night sky. Caroline sat down to think it all over. She had come here to do just that every day of the two weeks since d'Esquerré's departure, but far from ever having reached a conclusion, she had succeeded only in losing her way in a maze of memories – sometimes bewilderingly confused, sometimes too acutely distinct – where there was neither path, nor clue, nor any hope of finality. She had, she realized, defeated a life-long regimen; completely confounded herself by falling unaware and incontinently into that luxury of revery which, even as a little girl, she had so determinedly denied herself; she had been developing with alarming celerity that part of one which sets up an idol and that part of one which bows down and worships it.

It was a mistake, she felt, ever to have asked d'Esquerré to come at all. She had an angry feeling that she had done it rather in self-defiance, to rid herself finally of that instinctive fear of him which had always troubled and perplexed her. She knew that she had reckoned with herself before he came; but she had been equal to so much that she had never really doubted she would be equal to this. She had come to believe, indeed, almost arrogantly in her own malleability and endurance; she had done so much with herself that she had come to think that there was nothing which she could not do; like swimmers, overbold, who reckon upon their strength and their power to hoard it, forgetting the ever changing moods of their adversary, the sea.

And d'Esquerré was a man to reckon with. Caroline did not deceive herself now upon that score. She admitted it humbly enough, and since she had said good-bye to him she had not been free for a moment from the sense of his formidable power. It formed the undercurrent of her consciousness; whatever she might be doing or thinking, it went on, involuntarily, like her breathing; sometimes welling up until suddenly she found herself suffocating. There was a moment of this to-night, and Caroline rose and stood shuddering, looking about her in the blue duskiness of the silent room. She had not been here at night before, and the spirit of the place seemed more troubled and insistent than ever it had been in the quiet of the afternoons. Caroline brushed her hair back from her damp forehead and went over to the bow window. After raising it she sat down upon the low seat. Leaning her head against the sill, and loosening her night-gown at the throat, she half closed her eyes and looked off into the troubled night, watching the play of the sheet-lightning upon the massing clouds between the pointed tops of the poplars.

Yes, she knew, she knew well enough, of what absurdities this spell was woven; she mocked, even while she winced. His power she knew, lay not so much in anything that he actually had – though he had so much – or in anything that he actually was; but in what he suggested, in what he seemed picturesque enough to have or be – and that was just anything that one chose to believe or to desire. His appeal was all the more persuasive and alluring that it was to the imagination alone, that it was as indefinite and impersonal as those cults of idealism which so have their way with women. What he had was that, in his mere personality, he quickened and in a measure gratified that something without which – to women – life is no better than sawdust, and to the desire for which most of their mistakes and tragedies and astonishingly poor bargains are due.

D'Esquerré had become the centre of a movement,

and the Metropolitan had become the temple of a cult. When he could be induced to cross the Atlantic, the opera season in New York was successful; when he could not, the management lost money; so much every one knew. It was understood, too, that his superb art had disproportionately little to do with his peculiar position. Women swayed the balance this way or that; the opera, the orchestra, even his own glorious art, achieved at such a cost, were but the accessories of himself; like the scenery and costumes and even the soprano, they all went to produce atmosphere, were the mere mechanics of the beautiful illusion.

Caroline understood all this; to-night was not the first time that she had put it to herself so. She had seen the same feeling in other people; watched for it in her friends, studied it in the house night after night when he sang, candidly putting herself among a thousand others.

D'Esquerré's arrival in the early winter was the signal for a feminine hegira toward New York. On the nights when he sang, women flocked to the Metropolitan from mansions and hotels, from typewriter desks, school-rooms, shops and fitting-rooms. They were of all conditions and complexions. Women of the world who accepted him knowingly, as they sometimes took champagne for its agreeable effect; sisters of charity and overworked shop-girls, who received him devoutly; withered women who had taken doctorate degrees and who worshipped furtively through prism spectacles; business women and women of affairs, the Amazons who dwelt afar from men in the stony fastnesses of apartment houses. They all entered into the same romance; dreamed, in terms as various as the hues of phantasy, the same dream; drew the same quick breath when he stepped upon the stage, and, at his exit, felt the same dull pain of shouldering the pack again.

There were the maimed, even; those who came on crutches, who were pitted by smallpox or grotesquely painted by cruel birth stains. These, too, entered with him into enchantment. Stout matrons became slender girls again; worn spinsters felt their cheeks flush with the tenderness of their lost youth. Young and old, however hideous, however fair, they yielded up their heat – whether quick or latent – sat hungering for the mystic bread wherewith he fed them at this eucharist of sentiment.

Sometimes when the house was crowded from the orchestra to the last row of the gallery, when the air was charged with this ecstasy of fancy, he himself was the victim of the burning reflection of his power. They acted upon him in turn; he felt their fervent and despairing appeal to him; it stirred him as the spring drives the sap up into an old tree; he, too, burst into bloom. For the moment he, too, believed again, desired again, he knew not what, but something.

But it was not in these exalted moments that Caroline had learned to fear him most. It was in the quiet, tired reserve, the dullness, even, that kept him company between these outbursts that she found that exhausting drain upon her sympathies which was the very pith and substance of their alliance. It was the tacit admission of disappointment under all this glamour of success – the helplessness of the enchanter to at all enchant himself – that awoke in her an illogical, womanish desire to in some way compensate, to make it up to him.

She had observed drastically herself that it was her eighteenth year he awoke in her – those hard years she had spent in turning gowns and placating tradesmen, and which she had never had time to live. After all, she reflected, it was better to allow one's self a little youth; to dance a little at the carnival and to live these things when they are natural and lovely, not to have them coming back on one and demanding arrears when they are humiliating and impossible. She went over to-night all the catalogue of her self-deprivations; recalled how, in the light of her father's example, she had even refused to humour her innocent taste for improvising at the piano; how, when she began to teach, after her mother's death, she had struck out one little indulgence after another, reducing her life to a relentless routine, unvarying as clockwork. It seemed to her that ever since d'Esquerré first came into the house she had been haunted by an imploring little girlish ghost that followed her about, wringing its hands and entreating for an hour of life.

The storm had held off unconscionably long; the air within the lodge was stifling, and without the garden waited, breathless. Everything seemed pervaded by a poignant distress; the hush of feverish, intolerable expectation. The still earth, the heavy flowers, even the growing darkness, breathed the exhaustion of protracted waiting. Caroline felt that she ought to go; that it was wrong to stay; that the hour and the place were as treacherous as her own reflections. She rose and began to pace the floor, stepping softly, as though in fear of awakening someone, her figure, in its thin drapery, diaphanously vague and white. Still unable to shake off the obsession of the intense stillness, she sat down at the piano and began to turn over the first act of the *Walküre*, the last of his rôles they had practised together; playing listlessly and absently at first, but with gradually increasing seriousness. Perhaps it was the still heat of the summer night, perhaps it was the heavy odours from the garden that came in through the open windows; but as she played there grew and grew the feeling that he was there, beside her, standing in his accustomed place. In the duet at the end of the first act she heard him clearly: "*Thou art the Spring for which I sighed in*

364

Winter's cold embraces." Once as he sang it, he had put his arm about her, his one hand under her heart, while with the other he took her right from the keyboard, holding her as he always held *Sieglinde* when he drew her toward the window. She had been wonderfully the mistress of herself at the time; neither repellant nor acquiescent. She remembered that she had rather exulted, then, in her self-control – which he had seemed to take for granted, though there was perhaps the whisper of a question from the hand under her heart. "*Thou art the Spring for which I sighed in Winter's cold embraces.*" Caroline lifted her hands quickly from the keyboard, and she bowed her head in them, sobbing.

The storm broke and the rain beat in, spattering her night-dress until she rose and lowered the windows. She dropped upon the couch and began fighting over again the battles of other days, while the ghosts of the slain rose as from a sowing of dragon's teeth. The shadows of things, always so scorned and flouted, bore down upon her merciless and triumphant. It was not enough; this happy, useful, well-ordered life was not enough. It did not satisfy, it was not even real. No, the other things, the shadows – they were the realities. Her father, poor Heinrich, even her mother, who had been able to sustain her poor romance and keep her little illusions amid the tasks of a scullion, were nearer happiness than she. Her sure foundation was but made ground, after all, and the people in Klingsor's garden were more fortunate, however barren the sands from which they conjured their paradise.

The lodge was still and silent; her fit of weeping over, Caroline made no sound, and within the room, as without in the garden, was the blackness of storm. Only now and then a flash of lightning showed a woman's slender figure rigid on the couch, her face buried in her hands.

Toward morning, when the occasional rumbling of

thunder was heard no more and the beat of the rain drops upon the orchard leaves was steadier, she fell asleep and did not waken until the first red streaks of dawn shone through the twisted boughs of the apple trees. There was a moment between world and world, when, neither asleep nor awake, she felt her dream grow thin, melting away from her, felt the warmth under her heart growing cold. Something seemed to slip from the clinging hold of her arms, and she groaned protestingly through her parted lips, following it a little way with fluttering hands. Then her eyes opened wide and she sprang up and sat holding dizzily to the cushions of the couch, staring down at her bare, cold feet, at her labouring breast, rising and falling under her open night-dress.

The dream was gone, but the feverish reality of it still pervaded her and she held it as the vibrating string holds a tone. In the last hour the shadows had had their way with Caroline. They had shown her the nothingness of time and space, of system and discipline, of closed doors and broad waters. Shuddering, she thought of the Arabian fairy tale in which the Genii brought the princess of China to the sleeping prince of Damascus, and carried her through the air back to her palace at dawn. Caroline closed her eyes and dropped her elbows weakly upon her knees, her shoulders sinking together. The horror was that it had not come from without, but from within. The dream was no blind chance; it was the expression of something she had kept so close a prisoner that she had never seen it herself; it was the wail from the donjon deeps when the watch slept. Only as the outcome of such a night of sorcery could the thing have been loosed to straighten its limbs and measure itself with her; so heavy were the chains upon it, so many a fathom deep it was crushed down into darkness. The fact that d'Esquerré happened to be on the other side of the world meant nothing;

had he been here, beside her, it could scarcely have hurt her self-respect so much. As it was, she was without even the extenuation of an outer impulse, and she could scarcely have despised herself more had she come to him here in the night three weeks ago and thrown herself down upon the stone slab at the door there.

Caroline rose unsteadily and crept guiltily from the lodge and along the path under the arbour, terrified lest the servants should be stirring, trembling with the chill air, while the wet shrubbery, brushing against her, drenched her night-dress until it clung about her limbs.

At breakfast her husband looked across the table at her with concern. "It seems to me that you are looking rather fagged, Caroline. It was a beastly night to sleep. Why don't you go up to the mountains until this hot weather is over? By the way, were you in earnest about letting the lodge stand?"

Caroline laughed quietly. "No, I find I was not very serious. I haven't sentiment enough to forgo a summer-house. Will you tell Baker to come to-morrow to talk it over with me? If we are to have a house party, I should like to put him to work on it at once."

Noble gave her a glance, half humorous, half vexed. "Do you know I am rather disappointed?" he said. "I had almost hoped that, just for once, you know, you would be a little bit foolish."

"Not now that I've slept over it," replied Caroline, and they both rose from the table, laughing.

IN CONCERT

IAIN BANKS

From

ESPEDAIR STREET
(1987)

CHAPTER 12

YES, IT IS like sex. Performance; the show, the live act.

We had never been bad at it, and by now we were very good. I always thought I was the weak link, standing there just playing non-virtuoso bass and occasionally tapping my foot, but according to some people I was the base, too; something the others could build on; a rock, a foundation. Well, so they say. I think too many things are over-analysed, and a lot of the effort's wasted, just unnecessary. We were popular; end of story and so what?

But it is like sex. Of course. Getting out there and doing it, under the bright darkness of the hiding lights, in the bowl or beneath the arch, after the build-up of tension and the slow engorging of the venue where the people sit and stand together, sharing that warmth and sweat and scent, sharing the same obsession, the same fixation and anticipation. Oh, you enter into it, you become part of it; secreted beneath, preparing nervously in some distant dressing room, you can usually hear, you can always sense; you can *taste* it.

And there, suddenly appearing, in the blaze and smoke and the crashing chords, or just drifting in, like we did once, pretending to be road crew, fiddling with the gear, then starting to play, one at a time, almost casually, so that people only realised slowly, and the roar grew slowly, swelling and filling the place around us . . . the initial nerves evaporating, the beat setting in, taking over, governing. And the great-er rhythm, the light and shade of slower songs and faster songs and the few spoken intervals, when either Davey or Christine could just stop, listening and gauging and feeling, and mumble or shout or scream or just talk reasonably, make a joke; whatever fitted the mood, whatever moved us on, whatever kept that unstated game-plan on course and sent us all forward again.

To the climax, to the big finish that was one of many, to the stamping, chanting, swaying recalls, the encores, and the anticipated fetishes of old favourites, the old textures everybody knew and could join in with and be part of. Finally, sweating, betowelled, the lights back on, a last, quieting, basically acoustic, two-person finale, to smooth the raw exhausted edges of that ecstatic energy away; a last scene of touch and tenderness, like a breathed post-coital stroking, like a hug, before the people go, drained, fulfilled, buzzing into the dark streets and home.

Sometimes you thought you could go on forever and never stop, sometimes you just wanted it all never to end; there were ten times like that for every one of the few when you just weren't in the mood and it was done – though professionally, and to the insensitive, just as excitingly – mechanically, by rote.

But when it did seem you could keep going forever, time went odd, and it was as though it had stopped, or vastly extended, stretching out . . . yet when it was all over, when it had all gone and you were thinking about it, back in normality, everything within that singularity, everything about that unutterably different period of time seemed to have taken up only one single instant. Sometimes, whole tours were like that, as though it had all happened to somebody else and you were another person entirely and had only heard about it, second hand, third hand, at any number of removes.

You played, and you were part of it as it was part of you;

you were no less you – in fact, you felt *more* alive, more alert and capable and . . . coherent – but, at the same time, though continually conscious of that differentiation, you were integrated too, a part not apart; a component in something that was the product, not the sum, of its constituents.

A sort of ecstasy, all right; a charging, pulsing sense of shared *joy*; a bodily delight felt as much in the brain as in the guts and skin and the beating heart.

Ah, to go on and on like that, you thought; to be at that level forever . . . Well, it was impossible, of course. It was light and shade again, the sheer contrast of the mundane and the fabulous; the dull grey weight of the endless workaday days, and the bright, startling burst of light in the darkness, as though the five or more of us on stage before those thousands, even tens of thousands, were a concentration of excitement, glamour, life; the very pinpoint place where all those ordinary lives somehow focused, and ignited.

I never did work out who took energy from whom, who was really exploited, who was, if you like, on top. Sure they paid, so that act might be called prostitution, but, like a lot of bands, we actually lost out on some tours. Playing live, we gave them their money's worth, sometimes more. The albums were where we coined it in, not the tours. You paid your pounds or your dollars or your yen for the particular wavy pattern of gouged, printed vinyl, for the hidden noise a diamond could bring out, or for a certain rearrangement of magnetic particles on a thin length of tape, and that was us making a living, thank you very much. Me especially, me more than the rest, even though we'd come to an agreement where the others got between five and ten per cent of the composition rights, as an arrangement fee (well, it was only fair).

But playing, touring, going up there and doing never

quite the same thing each night, or every second night; that was the buzz, those were the times that made you feel you were really doing something different from everybody else, something worthwhile. God knows it got to me, and I always did stay in the background. What it was like for Davey or Christine, the binary stars of that focal point, standing at the ground zero of our self-created storm, I can't even imagine.

And it was addictive. You always thought you could give it up, but you always found you wanted more, and it was worth a lot of time and effort and expense to make sure you did. The applause, the screams, the shouts and yells, the stamping feet, the crowds and the ingenious, mad or pathetic attempts to make it through our layers of defence to get to see us individually, one-to-one, just to look, or to hug, or to gibber, or to pass on a tape and entreat.

For Davey and Christine, at the epicentre of it all, it meant more than it did to me, and, because they were different people from me, because they felt almost like a different species sometimes, they lapped it up, they revelled in it, they drank it deep. I tried, even with just the pale version of the fame that was my share, but I couldn't take to it naturally, the way they did.

It frightened me. For a long time it wasn't too bad anyway, and then for a longer time after that it was new, different and interesting and exciting, but then, after the first few tours, it started to get to me . . .

The crowds, the sheer weight and press of them. The invisible, besieging hordes out there in the darkness, baying and bellowing and stamping their feet. The way it took so many of them so long to recognise a track . . .

Jesus, if I even half-know a band's work I can spot a song within a bar; the first few notes of the introduction and I know it; but we'd play an intro, just the way it was on the album, and it would take . . . seconds, bars and bars for our fans to spot which favourite it was, and start trying to drown us out . . . I thought maybe it was just the time delay, sound taking that long to get from them to us, but I worked it out, and it wasn't; it was just people being *slow*.

But I'm not a natural crowd person; I don't pretend to understand or to relate to any of that sort of behaviour. I've never felt like part of a mass of people, not even at a football match. In a crowd of any sort, at a game, a concert, in a cinema or wherever, I never get totally carried away with whatever's going on. Part of me is always detached, observing, watching the other people around me; reacting to how they react, not to what they're reacting to.

There was a lot more I found worrying; like the people who wanted to know what sort of toothpaste we used and what our lucky number was, and what we wore in bed; like the backwoods geeks that were convinced to the point of inanity and insanity that they were The One for Davey, or Christine, or – God help them – both.

Then there were the Christians. Oh, jumping Jesus, the fundamentalists, the people who made old Ambrose Wykes and his folly look positively sensible and sane, and necessary.

Largely my fault. I'd said the wrong things.

It had happened on our first big tour in the States. I'd always been happy for Davey and Christine to do all the talking; they were the beautiful ones, after all, whereas I looked like a henchman in a Bond movie; hardly ideal prime time or front cover material. But in New York a lovely, intelligent, serious girl had requested an interview specifically with me, for a college magazine. I'd said I'd do it, but I'd been determined to put on my dumb and stuttering act the instant she asked me what my favourite colour was or how did I feel about being a rich and famous rock star?

Instead she asked sensible, reasonable questions, several of which actually had me thinking about them – suddenly seeing things in a new light – before answering; usually we all just regurgitated the same old answers to the same old questions. She was sweet and witty and nobody's fool, and I even made a date with her, after the tour was over, after failing to convince her she should join us for the post-concert party. Jeez, I wasn't heavy, I wasn't pawing her, I didn't even flirt with her; I acted the gentleman and I just said I'd enjoyed talking to her and could we meet again?

Bitch sold the interview to the *National Enquirer*. About two per cent of that interview was about religion, another three per cent about politics, another five about sex; in the paper, that's all we talked about. *I* talked about.

According to that article I was a communist atheist who'd screw anything in skirts and was anyway bisexual (I'd admitted I'd slept with a guy once, just to see what it was like; it was nothing special and I kept having to think of women to keep a hard-on, and I made the point that I'd avoided sodomy from either end, so to speak and, while the whole experience wasn't totally unpleasant, I'd no intention of repeating it; *and, damn it, I'd said it was off the record*!). I was also trying to corrupt and pervert the minds of all decent, patriotic, mom- and dad-loving American children with my vicious, drug, Marx, anti-Christ and semen-sodden song lyrics.

Oh, did we have some albums burned south of the Mason–Dixon line.

Suddenly it was noticed that the instrumental on the first side of *Liquid Ice* was called "Route 666". The number of the beast! Oh God, oh Jesus, lock up your nuns! This was a joke, of course; I'd originally called the song "25/68", naming it according to the opus-numbering system I'd used when the only places my songs existed were in an old school exercise jotter, a low-fidelity, high-hiss C-60 cassette, and between my ears. "25/68" sounded too much like "25 or 6 to 4", by Chicago, so I renamed it after about ten seconds' thought, in the studio just after we'd recorded it.

Meant nothing. But suddenly it was a Sign that I was a Devil Worshipper. All the other lyrics were put under the microscope as well then; professors of colleges in the South where the level of learning was such they thought evolution was a blasphemy started writing learned articles proving that everything I wrote was directed at destroying the American Family, Flag and Way of Life.

Holy shit; *I* should have been so lucky!

Ah, what the hell; we didn't lose out. We must have sold another three or four extra albums for every one thrown onto flaming pyres, just because of all the publicity. And having maniacal fundamentalist Christians turn up shrieking and waving banners where we were playing eventually became part of the show; they were as much part of the entourage as the groupies.

But there were death threats. I started to get paranoid, worrying about car bombs, people breaking into my hotel room . . . worst of all – because you could always protect yourself from that sort of threat, with enough security, sufficient money – I worried about somebody with a rifle in the auditorium. It might have been crazy, because of course there were always police and security men outside and inside the venues, but maybe not that crazy. If somebody was determined, they could get in, they could smuggle a rifle in beforehand and then buy a ticket; they could even get a job in the place, long before we arrived – tours are set up long enough in advance – and take a gun and a telescopic sight in any time they wanted. A spotlight operator would be the ideal person; those were the people that scared me most, I don't know why . . . the man with the Super Trooper and the Winchester M/70 Magnum . . .

I know it's crazy, but I started wearing a bullet-proof vest on stage. It made me feel like a looney, but it was the only thing that let me play; the worry about being out there, naked and exposed under the lights, picked out with the others, a tall, broad, stationary target, was starting to affect my playing. Sticky fingers; almost stage fright, a couple of times.

The vest was embarrassing – I kept it a secret from the others for months – but it calmed me; it worked. I could face the unseen mob and play them their music, and afterwards, as the police shoved people back from our limo and we crawled past clutching hands and anguished faces mouthing God knows what, secure within our thick green glass windows and armoured steel, on our way to secure hotel suites and whole floors patrolled by large men with bulging armpits, I could look into the night-time craziness of the people who wanted to tear us apart because they loved us and the people who wanted to tear us apart because they hated us, and feel less crazy: a sensible madman in a world where only paranoia prepared you for reality.

The Great Contra-Flow Smoke Curtain, the idea conceived that day in the English countryside outside Winchester, when Inez and I made a cloud and I danced in the ashes, the total bastard of an idea it took several months and a hundred grand to get just right, was produced by using lots of dry ice, fans, heaters, smoke machines, and lights, both laser and ordinary.

It consisted of fan-driven dry-ice machines, positioned above the front of the stage, and smoke machines – also fitted with fans, plus powerful electric heating elements – which were set at the edge of the stage beneath, directly under the line of ice machines, but staggered, so that each two-metre-wide nozzle pointed at the space between the equally large ice-smoke outlets above, where giant intakes sucked the warm smoke away to outside vents; similar intakes between the smoke machines sucked the dry-ice fumes away as well, to avoid filling the whole auditorium with freezing fog.

There were lights positioned inside both smoke and ice machines, shining straight up and straight down respectively, as well as batteries of lasers and spots and strobes set up to illuminate the Curtain itself from various angles and directions. The Curtain was created by the opposing, interspersed streams of vapour, alternately boiling up and fuming down.

We had twenty-four of those units, though the number we actually used on any given night varied according to the size and shape of the venue's stage. It looked impressive as hell once it was all working, but getting the streams set just right, so that the currents didn't get all mixed up, and making sure the intakes didn't suck the ice fumes or smoke from the machines right alongside them, proved to be extremely tricky; we needed a Curtain check before the gig that was longer than the lighting and sound checks combined; and the Curtain had to be fine-tuned for each different auditorium. We were never entirely sure it was going to work.

We couldn't just leave it at that, of course, even with all the fabulous lights; we set up a massive battery of fans and what I guess were de-tuned concussion grenades or claymore mines or something, so that, instead of just switching the Curtain off, we could blast a gigantic hole out through it, revealing the band in one vast, backlit explosion of smoke and sound and light. And we had big booms and moving platforms built too, and wire harnesses set up, so that we could just suddenly appear through the Curtain, more or less anywhere.

We played a few gigs in Britain, without the Curtain, getting ourselves together, trading freshness for tightness, I guess, then we were ready to head across the pond for the American part of a world tour that was intended to take us through South America, Japan, Australia, and even – firsts for us – India and Nigeria before heading back through Europe (East and West) and Scandinavia, for a final set of British dates.

We'd just brought out *Nifedge*, the vastly complicated double album we'd been working on since '78. Symphonic, lyricless, frighteningly expensive (not to mention twice as long as it had been supposed to be), we'd recorded it in '78 and '79, and spent a year trying to mix the bastard. Recording and releasing *And So The Spell Is Ended* (not intended to be a prophetic title, but apt as it turned out) in late '79, was quick and simple by comparison, even though it was still the most musically complicated and studio-time-guzzling album we'd recorded, apart from *Nifedge*.

Even the songs on *Ended* were starting to sound too contrived to me; we'd taken twice as long to record single songs for that album as we had to lay down the whole of *Liquid Ice*. We were getting to be obsessive, losing sight of the music in the beguiling mathematical filigree of production and mixing possibilities. Wes, ever the perfectionist, was the instigator of all this, but we were all affected. We were becoming . . . I don't know; choked; decadent, even.

Looking back, I'm surprised we avoided it as long as we did, given that we were hardly bursting with street cred to start with.

And So The Spell Is Ended went platinum in what seemed

like about a nanosecond; it outsold anything else we'd done. It was a muscle-bound, over-developed, strangled album; a collection of fairly reasonable songs held together with tourniquets, but it sold. Topped the American charts for weeks; they were rationing it in some stores, selling it straight out the back of trucks in other places. I'd suggested a special flammable edition with some kind of compressed, flattened fireworks worked into the vinyl and the cover, for the mental fundamentalists to burn, but this sensitive and caring idea was cruelly rejected by ARC, by now, of course, headed by Mr Rick Tumber himself.

It was my turn to receive the platinum album; it was presented to me at a ceremony in New York where I got very drunk later on and slightly disgraced myself. I thought I'd lost the damn thing then, but a couple of years ago, unpacking some cases in the folly, I found it again. I prised it out of its glass case and tried playing it, just for a laugh.

It was a James Last record.

Jesus, we're not even on the same label.

You want it in a nutshell?

Phht. Dribble. Crack. Whee. Crash, Splash. Zzt. Beeeeep.

The "Beeeeep" was Davey dying, Davey dead. It happened like this.

We'd done Boston, New York, Philly, Washington, and Atlanta; everything was working, the tickets had sold out within hours, punters were going bananas for us, and even the fundamentalists seemed to have gotten tired and largely given up on us, partly, perhaps, because by that time Davey and Christine were back together again and talking about getting married and having a family. Mickey Watson's exemplary bourgeois and stable family life was also made the subject of several exclusive illustrated articles. Also, Big Sam had made sure I hadn't been allowed to do any more interviews, and had put out rumours that I'd just been kidding some poor gullible cub reporter when I'd said all those horrible things. So the moral majority mob and the people who thought the universe was six thousand years old had mostly drifted off.

We'd had fairly stiff security in Atlanta, all the same, but it hadn't been needed, not for axe-wielding Bible-thumpers, anyway. The Official Souvenir Programme wielders/thumpers were another matter, and probably no less lethal if they'd come within range. We arranged similarly tight minding for Miami too, even though we knew it probably wasn't necessary; Florida is Florida, not Dixie.

Our convoy of trucks was delayed getting to Miami; one of the Macks was involved in a crash on the freeway. Nothing too serious, but the driver and his load were held up by the local sheriff. We'd hired a 737 (painted gold, but of course) for the American part of the tour, so we got there in plenty of time, but setting up all the equipment in time for the show proved a frenetic and slightly chaotic experience for the road crew.

The auditorium we were playing was one of the smaller ones on the tour, though the stage was wide enough to use twenty of the smoke/ice units. We'd sold out, they told us. Could have filled the place twice over, easy. There'd been some confusion over the number of tickets for sale at the door, but otherwise everything was looking good.

It was a hot, sticky, muggy day, followed by a hot, sticky, muggy evening; the air conditioning in the dressing room was noisy and dripped water, the champagne was not vintage, the bread for our sandwiches was rye, not wholegrain, and Christine's Chablis hadn't been chilled properly . . . but you learn to live with these hardships when you're on the road.

I was learning to put up with something else; not having Inez around. Things had never been completely right between us after Naxos – though, looking back from far enough away, maybe they'd been going wrong since Wes' party at the house overlooking Watergate Bay . . . hard to tell. Ah hell, it's all a long story, and there's doubtless still a lot of it I don't know, but what happened in the end was Inez married Lord Bod. Remember him? Photographer and socialite and one-time ARC shareholder (not any more, or I'd have left the label). They'd been conducting a discreet on–off relationship ever since they'd met, ever since Inez and I'd met, at Manorfield Studios and Lord Bod's house, where the leaves blew and fell and I watched a juggler from up a tree.

Lady Bodenham. Hot damn; did she have her sights on that all along? Did that strategic, middle-class planning get me again? God knows; *I*'m not going to ask her.

So Inez had pulled out of the tour with two weeks' notice and we'd had to find a third backing singer in the middle of the usual last-minute organisational panic just before a major tour; could have sued her under the contract we had, but we didn't have the heart.

I tried not to think about her; I involved myself in the logistics of the tour and spent all my spare time writing new songs. And despite missing Inez, at first it felt good to be back on the road again.

Back on the road . . . with no idea we were about to crash, that night.

The set we were playing included a quarter – twenty minutes – of *Nifedge*. We had had plans to perform the whole thing, making it the second half of a three-hour-plus concert, but there were too many problems. The main problem was we didn't have the nerve to do it, but that's just a personal opinion. Big Sam and ARC both thought it was a potentially disastrous and fan-losing departure to perform a lyricless piece of music as long as a movie to entire stadia of people who'd probably come to hear us re-create our singles. Probably correct, but pretty gutless. If you did *nothing* but give people what they already like, there'd be no new sounds at all (a state it's possible to feel we are already fast approaching if you listen to some radio stations).

Anyway. We were doing the song "And So The Spell Is Ended" (itself a good twelve minutes long, just on the album), and the first side of *Nifedge*. Plus all the favourites, to keep the unadventurous happy.

We'd been delayed getting to the auditorium, held up while we waited for a helicopter to fly us in; the crowds and traffic outside the place were too dense to get a limo through. We started about half an hour late, in an atmosphere of sweat and heat. The air conditioning in the main hall had broken down and the place must have been sweltering even before they let twenty thousand excited, often dancing, mostly smoking humans inside it. Once they were in place it became like a sort of vast communal sauna.

We'd decided to start slow, so began with "Balance", where everything's black dark (saving the Curtain for later; people had already heard about it, so we didn't always start with it working), and first the drums, then one, then two guitars, then vocals and finally bass and synth together gradually join in and build up, each lit as they slot in, but (the clever bit) all at about half-volume. We played a different, quieter, more wistful version of the song for concerts anyway, using harmonising backing vocals where on the album version there's just the band playing raw and a purposeful, eventually driving,

386

beat, and the lulling effect on a keyed-up audience was always – assuming we played it with conviction – dramatic.

After the last line of "Balance" faded away ("... as the balance ... of your mind ... was disturbed ..."), Wise William, our mixing wizard, wound the volume up to near maximum, we fired all lights and slammed into "Oh Cimmaron".

Audience reaction: Wild.

We played another twenty, twenty-five minutes of well-known stuff, then let the stage go dark, and kept it that way while the Curtain was switched on. Lights, music; on into "And So The Spell Is Ended".

Our first on-the-night hitch with the Curtain; one of the dry-ice machines had packed up. The fan had fused, motor burned out. After a couple of minutes a few wisps of dry-ice vapour leaked over the unit, but otherwise there was nothing; just a vertical column of clear air where there should have been a soft waterfall of cold mist, just left of stage centre, about where Davey usually stood.

We carried on anyway, as we'd agreed if something like that went wrong. It would take too long to fix, and the effect was still impressive. Spots spotted, lasers lased, and the Burst (when the whole centre of the Curtain was blown out by small explosive charges), all worked fine.

We started side one of *Nifedge*.

I was sweating. I felt thirsty already, and the noise was intense; I didn't know whether we had the monitors turned up too high, the crowd were just exceptionally rowdy, or there was just some sort of weird resonance with the main speakers and the shape of the auditorium, but the noise sounded deafening to me; an internal feedback. I had pro-grammed myself well enough by that time (translation; I was professional enough) not to be unduly put off, so I still did my bit, played my part and my music, but I felt ... strange.

Perhaps, I remember thinking, we've hit that point in a tour when you've lost the initial impetus of enthusiasm, have yet to work up the momentum of routine, and cannot yet tap the energy of knowing it will all be over soon. Happens that way sometimes, I told myself.

We played. They listened. A few must have heard the album on import, or got their newly released copies very early (or been incredibly avid fans) because some of them seemed to recognise a few of the tunes, and even sang along with one or two of Christine's lyricless voice parts.

The Curtain had gone through its paces, firing all up, then all down, then sweeping through a whole slow staccato sequence of firings, flowing left-right, right-left across the stage. The still-misfiring unit near centre stage made the whole display less than perfect, but you could tell just from the noises the punters were making the overall effect still impressed.

We got to the end of our twenty-minute (nearer twenty-five minutes, on stage) excerpt of *Nifedge*. That side, that movement (if you like), ends with one vast sustaining chord, punched out by every voice and instrument on stage, plus a synth key-triggered echo and reverberation sequence looping the resulting noise through a pre-figured programme for a digital analyser/sequencer which, at the time, was state of the art.

A stunning, sublimely furious noise, with the sound system at a hundred per cent plus whatever reverberations the venue could provide.

In Miami, the noise sounded like the crack of doom, like the whiplash of a galactic arm snapping, like an earthquake wave riding a major power line; we hit our individual assemblage of notes all at once, in a single blasting moment of impacted noise.

And brought a small section of the house down.

Ho ho, ha ha.

And killed Davey.

Because the dry-ice unit above him had blown a fuse, and the fan didn't work. Because the unit had been put up wrong; in the rush to construct the set, they'd put some part on upside down, and excess vapour and liquid couldn't drain away. Because the air in the hall was very humid, and the moisture in the air, the natural heat of that steamy city, and the collected body-breath of all those worshipping people, had collected around the great unused lump of granulated dry ice sitting way above the stage there. Because a bolt had been tightened up with a monkey wrench, not a torque wrench. Because this was before the days of radio mikes and leadless guitars, so we were all connected up, linked to the machinery.

So the whole lot snapped and crashed and fell. Missed Davey by a good few feet, but spilled its load of collected water all over him and his guitar and, in seconds, while we were still trying to work out what the hell had happened, and the audience were still applauding the spectacular effect (that burgeoning bursting bow-wave of water had happened to be caught in an accidentally delightful pattern of lights and lasers), the water rushed and/or seeped into some errant wire, some badly connected part of an amplifier, and promptly electrocuted our Davey.

Lasted . . . maybe two seconds, maybe five. Seemed like about three hours, but you could probably find some ghoulish bastard with a bootleg tape who could give you it down to the nearest tenth of a second.

Before we ran for him, before he fell, before that ghastly,

jerking, stiff parody of a guitarist dropped from rigidity to slackness across the stage, before Wise William and his cohorts finally realised the circuit breakers – also too hastily installed, we found out later – weren't working, and cut the power manually.

And we gathered him up, and we took him to the stage exit. He was blue, silent, heart still beating weakly, but breathing only with the assistance of us all; taking turns at first until the paramedics in the ambulance took over. The medics and the ambulance were there according to the contract, but they only let Davey die slower. A chopper was ordered, but would take too long to get there.

We went with the ambulance, but it got us, effectively, nowhere.

The crowds were too great.

There were just too many people. We got him into the ambulance, we surrounded him with our own bodies, we did all we could, but none of it was enough, because there had been a mix-up with the tickets, especially with the number for sale at the door, and so there were even more people milling, ticketless and frustrated outside the auditorium than there were inside.

And we just couldn't get through the crowds.

I stood on the ambulance roof at one point. Stood there with its lights flashing round my ankles and its exhaust smoke rising around me, like some tiny image of our stage show, me the star at last, and howled at those people, looking down a crowded alley of them to a crowded street of them, and fists clenched, head back, I screamed with all my might, "Get oot the fuckin WAY!"

. . . but did nothing, accomplished nothing, communicated . . . nothing.

The swarming chanting tides close round the ambulance

and its quiet, unminding cargo, like antibodies round an infection.

We all thought that he would somehow live, that he of all people would find a way to pull through; another crazy death-defying stunt . . .
But, he didn't; a last practical joke.
DOA.
Davey Balfour. 1955–1980.
RIP

And that, folks, was very much the end of that.
end of (a) story
roll up that circuit diagram
finished with engines
shantih

E. M. FORSTER

From

HOWARDS END
(1910)

CHAPTER 5

IT WILL BE generally admitted that Beethoven's Fifth Symphony is the most sublime noise that has ever penetrated into the ear of man. All sorts and conditions are satisfied by it. Whether you are like Mrs Munt, and tap surreptitiously when the tunes come – of course, not so as to disturb the others; or like Helen, who can see heroes and shipwrecks in the music's flood; or like Margaret, who can only see the music; or like Tibby, who is profoundly versed in counterpoint, and holds the full score open on his knee; or like their cousin, Fräulein Mosebach, who remembers all the time that Beethoven is "echt Deutsch"; or like Fräulein Mosebach's young man, who can remember nothing but Fräulein Mosebach: in any case, the passion of your life becomes more vivid, and you are bound to admit that such a noise is cheap at two shillings. It is cheap, even if you hear it in the Queen's Hall, dreariest music-room in London, though not as dreary as the Free Trade Hall, Manchester; and even if you sit on the extreme left of that hall, so that the brass bumps at you before the rest of the orchestra arrives, it is still cheap.

"Who is Margaret talking to?" said Mrs Munt, at the conclusion of the first movement. She was again in London on a visit to Wickham Place.

Helen looked down the long line of their party, and said that she did not know.

"Would it be some young man or other whom she takes an interest in?"

"I expect so," Helen replied. Music enwrapped her, and she could not enter into the distinction that divides young men whom one takes an interest in from young men whom one knows.

"You girls are so wonderful in always having – oh dear! We mustn't talk."

For the Andante had begun – very beautiful, but bearing a family likeness to all the other beautiful Andantes that Beethoven has written, and, to Helen's mind, rather disconnecting the heroes and shipwrecks of the first movement from the heroes and goblins of the third. She heard the tune through once, and then her attention wandered, and she gazed at the audience, or the organ, or the architecture. Much did she censure the attenuated Cupids who encircle the ceiling of the Queen's Hall, inclining each to each with vapid gesture, and clad in sallow pantaloons, on which the October sunlight struck. "How awful to marry a man like those Cupids!" thought Helen. Here Beethoven started decorating his tune, so she heard him through once more, and then she smiled at her cousin Frieda. But Frieda, listening to Classical Music, could not respond. Herr Liesecke, too, looked as if wild horses could not make him inattentive; there were lines across his forehead, his lips were parted, his pince-nez at right angles to his nose, and he had laid a thick, white hand on either knee. And next to her was Aunt Juley, so British, and wanting to tap. How interesting that row of people was! What diverse influences had gone to their making! Here Beethoven, after humming and hawing with great sweetness, said "Heigho" and the Andante came to an end. Applause, and a round of wunderschöning and prachtvolleying from the German contingent. Margaret started talking to her new young man; Helen said to her aunt: "Now comes the wonderful movement: first of all the goblins, and then a trio of elephants dancing"; and Tibby implored the company generally to look out for the transitional passage on the drum.

"On the what, dear?"

"On the *drum*, Aunt Juley."

"No; look out for the part where you think you have done with the goblins and they come back," breathed Helen, as the music started with a goblin walking quietly over the universe, from end to end. Others followed him. They were not aggressive creatures; it was that that made them so terrible to Helen. They merely observed in passing that there was no such thing as splendour or heroism in the world. After the interlude of elephants dancing, they returned and made the observation for the second time. Helen could not contradict them, for, once at all events, she had felt the same, and had seen the reliable walls of youth collapse. Panic and emptiness! Panic and emptiness! The goblins were right.

Her brother raised his finger: it was the transitional passage on the drum.

For, as if things were going too far, Beethoven took hold of the goblins and made them do what he wanted. He appeared in person. He gave them a little push, and they began to walk in a major key instead of in a minor, and then – he blew with his mouth and they were scattered! Gusts of splendour, gods and demigods contending with vast swords, colour and fragrance broadcast on the field of battle, magnificent victory, magnificent death! Oh, it all burst before the girl, and she even stretched out her gloved hands as if it was tangible. Any fate was titanic; any contest desirable; conqueror and conquered would alike be applauded by the angels of the utmost stars.

And the goblins – they had not really been there at all? They were only the phantoms of cowardice and unbelief?

One healthy human impulse would dispel them? Men like the Wilcoxes, or President Roosevelt, would say yes. Beethoven knew better. The goblins really had been there. They might return – and they did. It was as if the splendour of life might boil over and waste to steam and froth. In its dissolution one heard the terrible, ominous note, and a goblin, with increased malignity, walked quietly over the universe from end to end. Panic and emptiness! Panic and emptiness! Even the flaming ramparts of the world might fall.

Beethoven chose to make all right in the end. He built the ramparts up. He blew with his mouth for the second time, and again the goblins were scattered. He brought back the gusts of splendour, the heroism, the youth, the magnificence of life and of death, and, amid vast roarings of a superhuman joy, he led his Fifth Symphony to its conclusion. But the goblins were there. They could return. He had said so bravely, and that is why one can trust Beethoven when he says other things.

Helen pushed her way out during the applause. She desired to be alone. The music had summed up to her all that had happened or could happen in her career. She read it as a tangible statement, which could never be superseded. The notes meant this and that to her, and they could have no other meaning, and life could have no other meaning. She pushed right out of the building, and walked slowly down the outside staircase, breathing the autumnal air, and then she strolled home.

"Margaret," called Mrs Munt, "is Helen all right?"

"Oh yes."

"She is always going away in the middle of a programme," said Tibby.

"The music has evidently moved her deeply," said Fräulein Mosebach.

"Excuse me," said Margaret's young man, who had for some time been preparing a sentence, "but that lady has, quite inadvertently, taken my umbrella."

"Oh, good gracious me! – I am so sorry. Tibby, run after Helen."

"I shall miss the Four Serious Songs if I do."

"Tibby love, you must go."

"It isn't of any consequence," said the young man, in truth a little uneasy about his umbrella.

"But of course it is. Tibby! Tibby!"

Tibby rose to his feet, and wilfully caught his person on the backs of the chairs. By the time he had tipped up the seat and had found his hat, and had deposited his full score in safety, it was "too late" to go after Helen. The Four Serious Songs had begun, and one could not move during their performance.

"My sister is so careless," whispered Margaret.

"Not at all," replied the young man; but his voice was dead and cold.

"If you would give me your address—"

"Oh, not at all, not at all"; and he wrapped his greatcoat over his knees.

Then the Four Serious Songs rang shallow in Margaret's ears. Brahms, for all his grumbling and grizzling, had never guessed what it felt like to be suspected of stealing an umbrella. For this fool of a young man thought that she and Helen and Tibby had been playing the confidence trick on him, and that if he gave his address they would break into his rooms some midnight or other and steal his walking-stick too. Most ladies would have laughed, but Margaret really minded, for it gave her a glimpse into squalor. To trust people is a luxury in which only the wealthy can indulge; the poor cannot afford it. As soon as Brahms had grunted himself out, she gave him her card and said: "That is where we live; if you preferred, you could call for the umbrella after the concert, but I didn't like to trouble you when it has all been our fault."

His face brightened a little when he saw that Wickham Place was W. It was sad to see him corroded with suspicion, and yet not daring to be impolite, in case these well-dressed people were honest after all. She took it as a good sign that he said to her, "It's a fine programme this afternoon, is it not?" for this was the remark with which he had originally opened, before the umbrella intervened.

"The Beethoven's fine," said Margaret, who was not a female of the encouraging type. "I don't like the Brahms, though, nor the Mendelssohn that came first – and ugh! I don't like this Elgar that's coming."

"What, what?" called Herr Liesecke, overhearing. "The 'Pomp and Circumstance' will not be fine?"

"Oh, Margaret, you tiresome girl!" cried her aunt. "Here have I been persuading Herr Liesecke to stop for 'Pomp and Circumstance', and you are undoing all my work. I am so anxious for him to hear what *we* are doing in music. Oh, you mustn't run down our English composers, Margaret."

"For my part, I have heard the composition at Stettin," said Fräulein Mosebach. "On two occasions. It is dramatic, a little."

"Frieda, you despise English music. You know you do. And English art. And English literature, except Shakespeare, and he's a German. Very well, Frieda, you may go."

The lovers laughed and glanced at each other. Moved by a common impulse, they rose to their feet and fled from "Pomp and Circumstance".

"We have this call to pay in Finsbury Circus, it is true,"

said Herr Liesecke, as he edged past her and reached the gangway just as the music started.

"Margaret—" loudly whispered by Aunt Juley. "Margaret, Margaret! Fräulein Mosebach has left her beautiful little bag behind her on the seat."

Sure enough, there was Frieda's reticule, containing her address-book, her pocket dictionary, her map of London and her money.

"Oh, what a bother – what a family we are! Fr – Frieda!"

"Hush!" said all those who thought the music fine.

"But it's the number they want in Finsbury Circus—"

"Might I – couldn't I—" said the suspicious young man, and got very red.

"Oh, I would be so grateful."

He took the bag – money clinking inside it – and slipped up the gangway with it. He was just in time to catch them at the swing-door, and he received a pretty smile from the German girl and a fine bow from her cavalier. He returned to his seat upsides with the world. The trust that they had reposed in him was trivial, but he felt that it cancelled his mistrust for them, and that probably he would not be had over his umbrella. This young man had been "had" in the past – badly, perhaps overwhelmingly – and now most of his energies went in defending himself against the unknown. But this afternoon – perhaps on account of music – he perceived that one must slack off occasionally, or what is the good of being alive? Wickham Place, W., though a risk, was as safe as most things, and he would risk it.

So when the concert was over and Margaret said, "We live quite near; I am going there now. Could you walk round with me, and we'll find your umbrella?" he said "Thank you" peaceably, and followed her out of the Queen's Hall. She wished that he was not so anxious to hand a lady downstairs, or to carry a lady's programme for her – his class was near enough her own for its manner to vex her. But she found him interesting on the whole – everyone interested the Schlegels on the whole at that time – and while her lips talked culture her heart was planning to invite him to tea.

"How tired one gets after music!" she began.

"Do you find the atmosphere of Queen's Hall oppressive?"

"Yes, horribly."

"But surely the atmosphere of Covent Garden is even more oppressive."

"Do you go there much?"

"When my work permits, I attend the gallery for the Royal Opera."

Helen would have exclaimed, "So do I. I love the gallery," and thus have endeared herself to the young man. Helen could do these things. But Margaret had an almost morbid horror of "drawing people out", of "making things go". She had been to the gallery at Covent Garden but she did not "attend" it, preferring the more expensive seats; still less did she love it. So she made no reply.

"This year I have been three times – to *Faust*, *Tosca*, and—" Was it "Tannhouser" or "Tannhoyser"? Better not risk the word.

Margaret disliked *Tosca* and *Faust*. And so, for one reason and another, they walked on in silence, chaperoned by the voice of Mrs Munt, who was getting into difficulties with her nephew.

"I do in a *way* remember the passage, Tibby, but when every instrument is so beautiful it is difficult to pick out one thing rather than another. I am sure that you and Helen take me to the very nicest concerts. Not a dull note from beginning to end. I only wish that our German friends would have stayed till it finished."

"But surely you haven't forgotten the drum steadily beating on the low C, Aunt Juley?" came Tibby's voice. "No one could. It's unmistakable."

"A specially loud part?" hazarded Mrs Munt. "Of course I do not go in for being musical," she added, the shot failing. "I only care for music – a very different thing. But still I will say this for myself – I do know when I like a thing and when I don't. Some people are the same about pictures. They can go into a picture gallery – Miss Conder can – and say straight off what they feel, all round the wall. I never could do that. But music is so different to pictures, to my mind. When it comes to music I am as safe as houses, and I assure you, Tibby, I am by no means pleased by everything. There was a thing – something about a faun in French – which Helen went into ecstasies over, but I thought it most tinkling and superficial, and said so, and I held to my opinion too."

"Do you agree?" asked Margaret. "Do you think music is so different to pictures?"

"I – I should have thought so, kind of," he said.

"So should I. Now my sister declares they're just the same. We have great arguments over it. She says I'm dense; I say she's sloppy." Getting under way, she cried: "Now, doesn't it seem absurd to you? What *is* the good of the arts if they're interchangeable? What *is* the good of the ear if it tells you the same as the eye? Helen's one aim is to translate tunes into the language of painting, and pictures into the language of music. It's very ingenious, and she says several pretty things in the process, but what's gained, I'd like to know? Oh, it's all rubbish, radically false. If Monet's really Debussy, and Debussy's really Monet, neither gentleman is worth his salt – that's my opinion."

Evidently these sisters quarrelled.

"Now, this very symphony that we've just been having

– she won't let it alone. She labels it with meanings from start to finish; turns it into literature. I wonder if the day will ever return when music will be treated as music. Yet I don't know. There's my brother – behind us. He treats music as music, and oh, my goodness! He makes me angrier than anyone, simply furious. With him I daren't even argue."

An unhappy family, if talented.

"But, of course, the real villain is Wagner. He has done more than any man in the nineteenth century towards the muddling of the arts. I do feel that music is in a very serious state just now, though extraordinarily interesting. Every now and then in history there do come these terrible geniuses, like Wagner, who stir up all the wells of thought at once. For a moment it's splendid. Such a splash as never was. But afterwards – such a lot of mud; and the wells – as it were, they communicate with each other too easily now, and not one of them will run quite clear. That's what Wagner's done."

Her speeches fluttered away from the young man like birds. If only he could talk like this, he would have caught the world. Oh, to acquire culture! Oh, to pronounce foreign names correctly! Oh, to be well-informed, discoursing at ease on every subject that a lady started! But it would take one years. With an hour at lunch and a few shattered hours in the evening, how was it possible to catch up with leisured women, who had been reading steadily from childhood? His brain might be full of names, he might even have heard of Monet and Debussy; the trouble was that he could not string them together into a sentence, he could not make them "tell", he could not quite forget about his stolen umbrella. Yes, the umbrella was the real trouble. Behind Monet and Debussy the umbrella persisted, with the steady beat of a drum. "I suppose my umbrella will be all right," he was thinking. "I don't really mind about it. I will think about music instead. I suppose my umbrella will be all right." Earlier in the afternoon he had worried about seats. Ought he to have paid as much as two shillings? Earlier still he had wondered, "Shall I try to do without a programme?" There had always been something to worry him ever since he could remember, always something that distracted him in the pursuit of beauty. For he did pursue beauty, and, therefore, Margaret's speeches did flutter away from him like birds.

Margaret talked ahead, occasionally saying, "Don't you think so? Don't you feel the same?" And once she stopped, and said, "Oh, do interrupt me!" which terrified him. She did not attract him, though she filled him with awe. Her figure was meagre, her face seemed all teeth and eyes, her references to her sister and her brother were uncharitable. For all her cleverness and culture, she was probably one of those soulless, atheistical women who have been so shown up by Miss Corelli. It was surprising (and alarming) that she should suddenly say: "I do hope that you'll come in and have some tea."

"I do hope that you'll come in and have some tea. We should be so glad. I have dragged you so far out of your way."

They had arrived at Wickham Place. The sun had set, and the backwater, in deep shadow, was filling with a gentle haze. To the right the fantastic skyline of the flats towered black against the hues of evening; to the left the older houses raised a square-cut, irregular parapet against the gray. Margaret fumbled for her latchkey. Of course she had forgotten it. So, grasping her umbrella by its ferrule, she leant over the area and tapped at the dining-room window.

"Helen! Let us in!"

"All right," said a voice.

"You've been taking this gentleman's umbrella."

"Taken a what?" said Helen, opening the door. "Oh, what's that? Do come in! How do you do?"

"Helen, you must not be so ramshackly. You took this gentleman's umbrella away from Queen's Hall, and he has had the trouble of coming round for it."

"Oh, I am so sorry!" cried Helen, all her hair flying. She had pulled off her hat as soon as she returned, and had flung herself into the big dining-room chair. "I do nothing but steal umbrellas. I am so very sorry! Do come in and choose one. Is yours a hooky or a nobbly? Mine's a nobbly – at least, I *think* it is."

The light was turned on, and they began to search the hall, Helen, who had abruptly parted with the Fifth Symphony, commenting with shrill little cries.

"Don't you talk, Meg! You stole an old gentleman's silk top-hat. Yes, she did, Aunt Juley. It is a positive fact. She thought it was a muff. Oh, heavens! I've knocked the In and Out card down. Where's Frieda? Tibby, why don't you ever – no, I can't remember what I was going to say. That wasn't it, but do tell the maids to hurry tea up. What about this umbrella?" She opened it. "No, it's all gone along the seams. It's an appalling umbrella. It must be mine."

But it was not.

He took it from her, murmured a few words of thanks, and then fled, with the lilting step of the clerk.

"But if you will stop—" cried Margaret. "Now, Helen, how stupid you've been!"

"What ever have I done?"

"Don't you see that you've frightened him away? I meant him to stop to tea. You oughtn't to talk about stealing or holes in an umbrella. I saw his nice eyes getting so miserable. No, it's not a bit of good now." For Helen had darted out into the street, shouting, "Oh, do stop!"

"I dare say it is all for the best," opined Mrs Munt. "We know nothing about the young man, Margaret, and your drawing-room is full of very tempting little things."

But Helen cried: "Aunt Juley, how can you! You make me more and more ashamed. I'd rather he *had* been a thief and taken all the apostle spoons than that I – well, I must shut the front door, I suppose. One more failure for Helen."

"Yes, I think the apostle spoons could have gone as rent," said Margaret. Seeing that her aunt did not understand, she added: "You remember 'rent'? It was one of father's words – rent to the ideal, to his own faith in human nature. You remember how he would trust strangers, and if they fooled him he would say, 'It's better to be fooled than to be suspicious' – that the confidence trick is the work of man, but the want-of-confidence trick is the work of the devil."

"I remember something of the sort now," said Mrs Munt, rather tartly, for she longed to add: "It was lucky that your father married a wife with money." But this was unkind, and she contented herself with "Why, he might have stolen the little Ricketts picture as well."

"Better that he had," said Helen stoutly.

"No, I agree with Aunt Juley," said Margaret. "I'd rather mistrust people than lose my little Ricketts. There are limits."

Their brother, finding the incident commonplace, had stolen upstairs to see whether there were scones for tea. He warmed the teapot – almost too deftly – rejected the Orange Pekoe that the parlour-maid had provided, poured in five spoonfuls of a superior blend, filled up with really boiling water, and now called the ladies to be quick or they would lose the aroma.

"All right, Auntie Tibby," called Helen, while Margaret, thoughtful again, said: "In a way, I wish we had a real boy in the house – the kind of boy who cares for men. It would make entertaining so much easier."

"So do I," said her sister. "Tibby only cares for cultured females singing Brahms." And when they joined him she said rather sharply: "Why didn't you make that young man welcome, Tibby? You must do the host a little, you know. You ought to have taken his hat and coaxed him into stopping, instead of letting him be swamped by screaming women."

Tibby sighed, and drew a long strand of hair over his forehead.

"Oh, it's no good looking superior. I mean what I say."

"Leave Tibby alone!" said Margaret, who could not bear her brother to be scolded.

"Here's the house a regular hen-coop!" grumbled Helen.

"Oh, my dear!" protested Mrs Munt. "How can you say such dreadful things? The number of men you get here has always astonished me. If there is any danger it's the other way round."

"Yes, but it's the wrong sort of men, Helen means."

"No, I don't," corrected Helen. "We get the right sort of man, but the wrong side of him, and I say that's Tibby's fault. There ought to be a something about the house – an – I don't know what."

"A touch of the W.s, perhaps?"

Helen put out her tongue.

"Who are the W.s?" asked Tibby.

"The W.s are things I and Meg and Aunt Juley know about and you don't, so there!"

"I suppose that ours is a female house," said Margaret, "and one must just accept it. No, Aunt Juley, I don't mean that this house is full of women. I am trying to say something much more clever. I mean that it was irrevocably feminine, even in father's time. Now I'm sure you understand! Well,

I'll give you another example. It'll shock you, but I don't care. Suppose Queen Victoria gave a dinner-party, and that the guests had been Leighton, Millais, Swinburne, Rossetti, Meredith, Fitzgerald, etc. Do you suppose that the atmosphere of that dinner would have been artistic? Heavens, no! The very chairs on which they sat would have seen to that. So with our house – it must be feminine, and all we can do is to see that it isn't effeminate. Just as another house that I can mention, but won't, sounded irrevocably masculine, and all its inmates can do is to see that it isn't brutal."

"That house being the W.s' house, I presume," said Tibby.

"You're not going to be told about the W.s, my child," Helen cried, "so don't you think it. And on the other hand I don't the least mind if you find out, so don't you think you've done anything clever, in either case. Give me a cigarette."

"You do what you can for the house," said Margaret. "The drawing-room reeks of smoke."

"If you smoked too, the house might suddenly turn masculine. Atmosphere is probably a question of touch and go. Even at Queen Victoria's dinner-party – if something had been just a little different – perhaps if she'd worn a clinging Liberty tea-gown instead of a magenta satin—"

"With an Indian shawl over her shoulders—"

"Fastened at the bosom with a Cairngorm pin—"

Bursts of disloyal laughter – you must remember that they are half German – greeted these suggestions, and Margaret said pensively: "How inconceivable it would be if the Royal Family cared about Art." And the conversation drifted away and away, and Helen's cigarette turned to a spot in the darkness, and the great flats opposite were sown with lighted windows, which vanished and were relit again, and vanished incessantly. Beyond them the throughfare roared gently – a tide that could never be quiet, while in the east, invisible behind the smokes of Wapping, the moon was rising.

"That reminds me, Margaret. We might have taken that young man into the dining-room, at all events. Only the majolica plate – and that is so firmly set in the wall. I am really distressed that he had no tea."

For that little incident had impressed the three women more than might be supposed. It remained as a goblin footfall, as a hint that all is not for the best in the best of all possible worlds, and that beneath these superstructures of wealth and art there wanders an ill-fed boy, who has recovered his umbrella indeed, but who has left no address behind him, and no name.

BERNARD MacLAVERTY

From

GRACE NOTES
(1997)

From PART TWO

CATHERINE KNEW THAT, given her luck, she would get her period on the first day of rehearsal. She had stood in front of the largely male orchestra, her knees trembling, her back aching. She'd wanted to run away and curl up somewhere, to be anywhere but there, doing anything but that. If Andy the Flute said he didn't like his part then she'd have agreed to scrap it. If Robert Percussion complained that it was all too much for him she'd have given in and rewritten the part for tambourine. I am a nobody, a pain in the ass. Who am I to be on this podium talking to these talented people? The conductor, Randal Kresner, had made a suggestion about the entry of the cellos. If he'd suggested that, then he must have hated the way it was before. Look Randal, she wanted to say, why don't we scrap the whole thing? It's nothing but a piece of pretentious crap with a pretentious bloody title. *Vernicle*. It's hard to believe. Why don't we jack it in and everybody can go home. I'll do better next time. But it's more likely, given the way I feel at the moment, that I'll never write another note. I just want to go to my bed. I want my hot-water bottle.

Now, on the evening of the concert, it was a different angst. Her confidence had come back in like a tide. The music was good – what was bad were her nerves. She sat on the toilet, her head held in her hands. She felt as if her stomach had fallen out of her and only wind remained. She was dying for a swig of Nurse Harvey's Gripe Mixture – stuff

413

she'd poured into Anna for the colic. Then she could have a good belch. She was on the verge of nausea. Earlier, before the concert, her mouth had flooded with saliva and she'd dashed to the toilet and hunkered down beside the bowl. But nothing had come. A dry boke. She'd swallowed again and again until the spasm passed. Now on this second visit she'd just had evidence that she was suffering from diarrhoea. She closed her eyes and covered them with her hands. What would happen if she threw up in the bloody concert hall? Or shat herself on the radio? She started to laugh. There was no need for this. The piece had been well rehearsed. She and the conductor had talked long and hard about it. Indeed Randal, in various subtle ways, had made it sound better than when she'd first imagined it.

Above the noise of cisterns refilling she could distantly hear instruments being tuned. Stuttering trumpets, violins being sawed, flutes tootling, a tuba pomping. Above all she could hear someone working with a Lambeg drum. She had watched the drums being tuned before rehearsal – the Ulster men called it "pulling them". One held the drum firm while the other used his knee as a brace to pull each linen rope in turn.

"The long journey," said the big man as he worked his way round. He wore gloves and pulled hard until the skin of the drum was the right tension.

The four Orangemen from Portadown had arrived mid-week in a mini-bus. They had been offered an hotel but had preferred to stay with friends in Bridgeton. One of the things that had enticed them over had been the thought of seeing Rangers playing at Ibrox on Saturday. They had driven straight from Stranraer to the first rehearsal. Catherine shook hands with the man who seemed to be the leader.

"The name's Sandy Foster. And this is Billy McIlwham.

Norman Hutchinson. And last but definitely least, Cameron Lawlor." They seemed sheepish. And a bit nervous. Without thinking, Cameron Lawlor rubbed his hand on the backside of his jeans after shaking Catherine's hand. He said, "Where's the composer?"

"That's me."

"You . . ." his voice almost screeched. "You're too young to be anything." The leader said, "Pay no attention to Cammy – he's always like this."

"Any danger of a cuppa tea?" said Cammy.

"I'll put the kettle on," Catherine said. The echo of the hard skin of Cammy's hand was still with her. Scar tissue. She heard her father.

They bleed their wrists. Against the rim. Sheer bloody bigotry.

The handshakes had taken place at the back of the hall. While Catherine went off to the kitchen all four men began to look around them. At the stained-glass windows, the pulpit, the water font. When she came back Sandy said, "What kind of a church is it?"

"It's not a church any longer."

"But what was it – in its day?"

"Church of Scotland, I think," said Catherine. Cammy wiped imaginary sweat off his brow.

"Whew!"

The first time all four Lambegs had come on in rehearsal Catherine watched the faces of the players in the orchestra. They were genuinely astonished. They looked at one another in disbelief. The building resonated to the enormous blattering. The air vibrated.

"We very rarely bate a trevally on the drums indoors," Cammy said. "Because the buildings fall down afterwards."

At break-time the members of the orchestra, mostly the men, gathered round to poke and finger the drums and ask questions.

"The shell's of oak," said Sandy, "and the drum heads are goat skin. I've seen brass shells as well."

"How long have you been playing?"

"Since his arsehole wasn't the size of a shirt button," said Cammy.

"Mind your tongue," hissed Sandy, "there's ladies about."

"You mean me?" Catherine said, coming into the circle. "What about the sticks?"

"Sticks?" Cammy's voice went up. "Malucca canes, if you don't mind."

"They say you play tunes," said Robert Percussion.

"Not so's you'd notice. In the beginning it was always the fife and drum. The fife played the tune, the drum bate a trevally along with it. Then over the years the fifing fell away. But the drumming went on. It'll go on for ever, if you ask me."

"You're accompanying a tune which doesn't exist any more," said Catherine.

"You might be right."

She looked down at his wrists. "Any scars?"

"Nonsense – a good drummer's wrists never touch the rim." Cammy looked at her. "That's Roman Catholic propaganda – to make us look like fanatics."

The concert was sponsored by the European Broadcasting Union and was being transmitted live to about twenty European countries. Earlier, she could hardly get in by the dressing-room door for BBC vans and strewn cables. And there was an audience of people out there buzzing with talk and expectation. Her anonymity would disappear. She knew, however well- or ill-received it was, she would have to go up to the rostrum and take the applause. Bad and all as that was, it wasn't the worst thing – the worst thing was that her notes were going to be played to people who might hate them, might ridicule them. They might say, *who does she think she is?* She shuddered. This was the unknown. It was like the blind man diving. What if everyone had conspired to lie? And her piece *Vernicle* was awful? Pain for fuck all, as Marge had said. An act of no creation. Alasdair Kirkpatrick at the Royal Scottish Academy of Music and Drama had said, "Composers seek praise in exact proportion to how unsure they are of themselves. An artist who is sure doesn't need any praise, he knows. Whereas someone who's unsure, hearing the applause, says to himself – maybe it's better than I thought."

What if the audience reacted to her the way she had reacted to Schoenberg or Stockhausen? She had heard a performance of Stockhausen's *Gruppen*, for three orchestras under three conductors, and had thought it a complete waste of time and space – so much musical talent thrown away. This was what happened when everyone had conspired to lie. Something ugly got no better when viewed in three mirrors, something ineffectual got no better when tripled, like Olga blessing herself. Stockhausen's was music written without regard for the ear – a totally abstract concept. Because one theme was a retrograde inversion of another didn't automatically make it good. It was theoretical music. But in some circles it was so highly regarded. How different to Messiaen and Stravinsky.

The buzzer for the end of the interval sounded. A harsh jagged electric sound. But still she sat on the toilet. The first half of the concert had been two works, Lyell Creswell's *Dragspil*, which was really a concerto for accordion (the

417

programme note pointed out that *dragspil* was Icelandic for accordion) and Eddie McGuire's *Calgacus*, which climaxed with the entrance of a piper in full Highland regalia, walking up the middle aisle of the church giving it everything he'd got, vying with the orchestra. When the European Broadcasting Union had invited submissions, it had said it would look favourably on works which included an instrument more associated with music of ethnic origins. The Lambeg drum was not normally associated with Irish folk music but it was undoubtedly ethnic.

Her piece had played in rehearsal at twenty-eight minutes and formed the whole second half of the programme. The first half of the concert had all gone over her head. She'd sat as still as she could but found it impossible to concentrate. Her mind was on her own piece. Its shortcomings, how it could have been improved.

The sound the men from Portadown made at rehearsal was exactly what Catherine had hoped for. Now she was ridiculously worried about how they would look on the night of the performance. She had always hated evening dress on the platform. They were the only profession whose working clothes were ball-gowns. The men, she said, should have black-leather elbows fitted – to make their duds last longer. Randal had talked to the guest musicians of the three pieces about what they would wear. Lyell Creswell's accordionist matched the orchestra in black tie and evening suit. His accordion was an unobtrusive gun-metal grey. In Eddie McGuire's *Calgacus* the piper had looked great in Highland regalia. But there was no equivalent for Northern Ireland. To dress the Lambeg drummers in black tie and tails for their entrance would have been ludicrous. Randal insisted that he didn't want them coming on in jeans and shirt-sleeves. It was Cammy who said they were members of the same band so why didn't they wear band uniforms. His friends in Bridgeton were members of a flute band and they could borrow four uniforms. No bother.

"Thank God it's radio," said Catherine. Cammy winked at her. She considered her music to be of high seriousness – why did something always come up at the last minute to trivialise the whole thing. The argument about the title of *Trumpetists and Tromboners*, now this – who cared how it would *look*? She cared. It would probably be acceptable to everyone else in the hall except herself. All she would see was a Kick the Pope band. So she resolved to keep her eyes down. She heard the outer door of the LADIES open and someone come in.

"Kate?" It was Liz. "Kate, are you there?"

"I'm in here."

"Are you all right?"

"I'm OK." She stood and flushed the toilet.

"We didn't know where you were."

Catherine unsnibbed the door and came out. She smiled bravely and went to wash her hands.

"They're beginning to move in for the second half. Your half."

"Don't," said Catherine. She looked at herself in the mirror, tilting her head a little. Even here in the toilets it was obvious that the place was a converted church – pointed archways, columns, a rose window high on the wall.

"Do I look OK? Am I too pale?"

"All that matters is you're late."

She reached her hand beneath the soap dispenser and pressed. It deposited a white splurge in her palm. She showed it to Liz and laughed.

"Don't say a word."

"You're awful," said Liz. The final buzzer was giving a long dithering screech. Catherine washed her hands thoroughly, as if she were going to an operating theatre rather than a concert hall.

"Come on, Kate."

"Don't panic."

She shook the drops from her hands and went to the towel machine and tugged a new area of white cloth into position. The buzzer ceased. Catherine dried her hands slowly. Liz took her by the elbow and half dragged, half hurried her out of the door, past the Christmas tree in the foyer and into the hall.

"Face the music," she said.

Liz's husband Peter was looking round for them. He grinned as they excuse me'd their way to where he sat in the middle of the row. They were among the last to be seated. Liz still held on to Catherine's arm. She squeezed it as the audience went quiet. Catherine covered Liz's hand and squeezed back in thanks. There were two microphone booms, like huge fishing rods dangling over the orchestra. And one hung over the audience for recording applause.

She found it hard to believe that *Vernicle* was about to have its first performance. She picked up the printed sheets being used as a handout. She was shaking. The paper fluttering in her hand. She steadied her hand against her thigh. There was a brief biographical note and an interview with each of the composers in the programme. She'd avoided reading her contribution during the first half.

Catherine Anne McKenna *was born in Co. Derry, and studied composition at Queen's University, Belfast and later at the Royal Scottish Academy of Music and Drama in Glasgow. Winner of the Moncrieff-Hewitt Travel Award she studied composition briefly with Anatoli Melnichuck in Kiev. She has* now left teaching to devote herself to full-time composition. She lives in Glasgow.

Principal Compositions: *A Suite for Trumpetists and Tromboners* for orchestral brass; *The Goat Paths* – a song cycle for high voice and piano – text of poems by James Stephens; Three Piano Trios; Preludes and Fugues for piano.

How can I say what I go through writing an instrumental composition? The same as a poet except that he uses words. It is a kind of musical confession. Told from the head, full of musical ideas. Except that music is far richer, much more subtle than words. It can scourge the heart. Music comes from pre-hearing. You sit down to your desk and listen to what's inside your head. Things appear suddenly and unexpectedly. I don't mean it's like inspiration or anything like that but, put it this way, you are there with a 3B pencil in your hand should you hear anything good. If you are in a notion of working, the idea takes root and won't let you go. It puts out twigs and branches. These twigs get leaves and thorns and maybe, if you are lucky, blossoms. And fruit. Occasionally you get fruit to sustain you. And then grey lichens grow on the branches and so on and so on. Maybe a ladybird comes. Maybe a woodcutter comes if it's a fairy-tale. The problem is that the seed must appear at the right time – you can only carry so much in your head until the next time you come across pencil and paper. The baby must be in bed. And asleep. The washing must be done. And the dishes and God knows what else. When it's going well there's a kind of joy to it – even if you are writing something which is sombre, something really dark. You sort of lose touch with the world around you, your body ceases to be of any importance. One musical idea comes hard on the heels of another. Sometimes I shake when it's going well. But that's rare. The worst thing that can happen at a time like this is an interruption. The baby starts crying. The phone rings. I get so mad when that happens. It's like interrupted sex. When the interruption is over it's very hard to get the same momentum going again.

Catherine's eye slid over the page. Jesus, did she really say that? She had laughed a lot during the interview – but that hadn't come out. Where was the irony, the self-deprecation? Only some of what she had said was true. The studying composition with Melnichuck was a bit of an exaggeration – although he was a good name to have on her CV. But she didn't dare mention the worst thing of all. To write something really dark, despairing even, is so much better than being silent. If you're depressed your mind says there's no point in writing anything. You just want to sit with your mouth hanging open – your mind full of scorpions. There was no formula for getting around that.

Liz was reading her copy of the programme. She broke off and leaned over. "Kate, what's this about interrupted sex?"

Catherine laughed and shrugged. "My sex life has been interrupted."

"You're shaking," said Liz, her eyes widening.

"You think I haven't noticed? It's all the orgasms I've missed."

Liz grinned and squeezed her arm. She continued to stare all around her. "What's that?" Liz nodded at the wall. Multi-faceted boxes were set at intervals all over its surface.

"It's baffling."

"I know – that's why I'm asking." Liz squealed too loudly at her own joke and covered her mouth with her hand. Catherine rolled her eyes at her then looked away again. Where the altar used to be was the orchestral platform. Above it soared two stained-glass windows, elongated and black. During rehearsals the sun had made the Victorian windows vivid. Flecks of colour shone on the walls and floor, on the cloth of the practising musicians' shoulders. The windows depicted Victorian religious sentiments. Apostles. Old Testament types. Wycliffe. Erasmus. Catherine said she would like to have seen one devoted to the Twelve Apostates. Written words appeared here and there. TRUTH & TOLERANCE. FERVOUR & FAITH. And above all TO THE GLORY OF GOD. But now the windows were featureless and dead, facing out into the night. To see them properly you would have to be outside the church.

Suddenly there was a hand-clap and then everyone was applauding, including herself. The players of the orchestra were coming on from both sides of the transept. The applause stopped and the audience noise died down. It was a kind of embarrassing silence because nothing seemed to be happening. Someone was talking somewhere. An indistinct but loud single voice. Catherine panicked – was something wrong? Was the conductor refusing at the last moment? Was there an argument with one of the Orangemen? Then she remembered the same thing had happened in the first half and that what she was hearing was the voice of the announcer. Then she noticed the red light was on. Like a BBC sacristy lamp. Out of the listening silence she heard her own name. The voice said *Catherine Anne McKenna* but she could make out little else. In embarrassment she put her hand to her face and smelled the strange liquid soap she had just used.

She thought of the radio at home in her parents' kitchen. It sat to one side of the cooker and was almost always tuned to Radio Eireann. After mass her mother listened to *Sunday Miscellany* and the house would be filled with the rich talking voice of Benedict Kiely. It was a tape-cassette and radio combined – the tape part of it had ceased to function long ago. When new it had a matt aluminium finish with two round speakers of dark mesh on the front. Over the years the mesh had become clogged with flour dust and fat japped from the pan. It was operated by levers, more trendy than knobs at the time. The air in the kitchen left an atomic layer of grease on anything which didn't move. And the radio hadn't been moved in years. Its satin aluminium finish had dulled and the levers were sticky to the touch so her parents just switched it on and off at the plug. But it gave them the news and *Sunday Miscellany* and any important Gaelic football matches.

She should have told them. Even a polite card to say she was having a piece performed on radio. But she'd delayed too long. And there had been last-minute revisions suggested by Randal. She hadn't done it, and that was that. A girl who doesn't tell her parents of her success is more estranged than one who conceals her mistakes. Would there have been any chance that someone in the know would have told them? Maybe Miss Bingham – she used to go through the *Radio Times* with a red pen circling the programmes. And seeing Catherine's name maybe she would have phoned and they would be listening? Both of them, sitting now in the kitchen, nervous as she was? Nervous *for* her. Anyway they would hate what she had written. John McCormack and "I Hear You Calling Me" it was not.

It was unheard of. For an only child to walk out like that. An only girl.

It sounded now like the announcer was rhyming off the names of all the places where the broadcast was being received. She made out the words Germany, Greece, Hungary, Iceland, Italy, Poland, Portugal. Liz leaned across and said, "This is the only bit a geographer like me understands."

She wondered if Huang Xaio Gang could be performing or teaching in any of these places. Would he hear *Vernicle*?

Not that he would know in a million years who it was by. She hoped he would be intrigued and listen, keeping time with his greying head.

It was the last concert in the *Cutting Edge* series given by the BBC Scottish Symphony Orchestra from the Henry Wood Hall, Glasgow. Before the beginning a nice BBC man had asked them to make sure that their watch alarms were not set to go off in the midst of the broadcast.

"They don't want them to drown out your Lambeg drums, Kate," said Liz.

The announcement after the interval finished and again the hush came. Everything seemed to take an interminable amount of time. Catherine stared at the backs of people's heads. The intricacy of hair – the way it curls and grows and disappears. Different kinds and stages of baldness. One man had the track of his hat band still on his hair. It was odd to be sitting like this, row upon row in the light. In the cinema it was dark. The only equivalent, she thought, was sitting in church. But this *was* church. One of the few Scottish poems they'd done in school was "To a Louse". Applause as Randal strode on to the platform. He went straight to the podium, faced the orchestra with his baton upraised and waited for absolute silence.

It began with a wisp of music, barely there – a whispered five-note phrase on the violins and she was right back on that beach with her baby. If the audience thought themselves mistaken she would be well pleased. Did I hear that correctly? Like the artist's hand which moves to begin a drawing but makes no mark. Preliminary footering – throat clearing. Then the phrase repeated an eyelash louder. I did hear something. The listeners feel that they must pay absolute attention to hear anything more. But the pause is longer, seems interminable before the music begins again. Is it over?

they should be saying. Or, have they not started yet? The phrase repeats a third time on the violas. They sound like violins with a cold. Yes, it has started, that there is something there is undeniable. But it is so very ordinary. Everyday stuff. Nevertheless starting friction has been overcome and now the phrase unravels and strengthens, becomes louder – becomes a fugue-like figure and is joined by the cellos, then the basses. Darkening and growing, rising and falling by the narrowest of intervals. Plaiting bread. Her mother's hands, three pallid strands, pale fingers over and under, in and out. Weaving. Like ornament in the Book of Kells. Under and over, out and in. Like pale fingers interlocked in prayer. Grace notes with a vaguely Celtic flavour. More and more threads slowly and imperceptibly surround what the violins are saying, repeating over and over again to themselves. This is the ascent. This is the climbing of steps.

The music is simple. A simple idea, the way life is simple – a woman produces an egg and receives a man's seed into her womb and grows a baby and brings another person into the world. Utterly simple. Or so amazingly complex that it cannot be understood. So far beyond us that it is a mystery. And yet it happens every minute of every day. How can something be utterly simple and amazingly complex at the same time? Things are simple or complex according to how much attention is paid to them. She has reached down into the tabernacle of herself for this music and feels something sacred in its performance.

Gradually the great arch of the movement begins to take shape. She is absorbed in her own music – its drama. Her shaking has stopped. How can a thing have drama if you know what is going to happen? Like football on television. Dave always knew the result but the drama of how it was achieved was never diminished. He knew the score. Ha-ha.

She was absorbed in what would be next even though she *knew* what would be next. She was paying attention with her whole body. She was now utterly still. Reacting to the mystery. Filling herself with her own grace. And yet she was walking again the firm sand in bare feet. Step by step. One foot after the other. She closed her eyes. Testing her bravery, her faith. Trusting that the wind would not turn to rock.

Randal was perfect – in his phrasing, in his tempi and textures. All her self-criticism had been put aside. It was as if her nervousness had evaporated the moment the music began. And she was into it – working at listening. Eavesdropping on her own life.

The strings begin to converge and insist on the one note, F sharp, until everyone is pulled into the wake of this note. The ascent is complete, the climactic point is reached. But there is no vista from the top. Suddenly everything is cut short by the entrance of the Lambegs. It is almost like machine-gun fire. A short burst – enough to kill and maim. Silence. It's the kind of silence induced by a slap in the face or the roarings of a drunk. Catherine keeps her eyes closed. She cannot bear to look and see the four men in band uniform emerging from both sides of the transept. It could be, would be ludicrous. The strings try again but darken. The sections of the orchestra begin to ask who or what is this – what is going on? What right have they to elbow their way in here? She feels a remembered angst and is momentarily afraid the music will induce it again for real. Oh Jesus. Even a memory of the blackness of her depression startles her. It was that bad. It was *worse* than that bad. For a second time the Lambegs open fire. This time it is a sustained burst. The subsequent silence is longer. The vault throbbing with the echoes of the huge drums. The orchestra begins again, stating and restating an inversion of the five-note motif of the opening.

427

Annoyance has crept in. The orchestra is angry and shrill now as it has a post-mortem on the intervention and what can be done if it happens again. Clarinets and flutes squeal, the trombones rasp. Then, almost with nonchalance, with a swagger one drum begins, then the second, then the third and fourth. Insistent, cacophonous rhythm. Disintegration. The tormented orchestra tries to keep its head above the din of these strangers. The black blood of hatred stains every ear. The brass, like hatchets, chopping into the noise. Eventually, after an intense struggle, the orchestra falls away section by section until only the drums are left pulsing. It reminds her of the candle flames snuffing out beneath the invisible tide of suffocating gas. Step after step. Dark after dark. Four toads ballooning out their throats, blattering the air above them and leaving it throbbing. She was amazed at how well the drums sounded as the four men gave it everything, raw – improvised almost, exactly as she'd imagined. Their aggression, their swagger put her in mind of Fascism. She was not trying to copy the vulgarity of Shostakovitch Seven – the march of the Nazis on Leningrad – but that was the effect. A brutalising of the body, the spirit, humanity. Thundering and thundering and thundering and thundering. When the drums stopped on a signal from Randal the only thing that remained was a feeling of depression and darkness. Utter despair.

The audience remained petrified for some moments. Intimidated. Stunned. Then the throat clearing began. The shuffling. Catherine tried to interpret the agitation. Were they annoyed? Did they hate it? Was it naïvely simple? She looked up at Liz who made a face, like the Man in the Moon, her mouth an open O. What did that mean? Was she impressed by the racket the musicians had made? Beyond Liz, Peter nodded and winked at her. At the end of the row a man sat, his knuckles to his forehead. He was frowning. He was definitely frowning. Catherine turned her eyes to the floor and kept them fixed there. She felt a trickle of sweat run from her armpit down past her bra, down the folds of skin of her left side. She held her elbows tight to her body to trap any further perspiration and keep it in its place. Randal raised his baton again and all the fidgeting stopped.

The second movement is the other side of the arch – she hoped it would have the bilateral symmetry of a scallop shell – again starting quietly, the strings meandering almost. The music still quiet enough for the flutes to be breathy. There is a feeling that the music is messing around. Where to? It is as if the orchestra has not forgotten what happened on the first side of the arch and are playing, looking over their shoulders, waiting for the reappearance of the Lambegs. The first real textural difference is the introduction of the bells. Small sharp raps of the wooden hammer playing a clarion call of seven notes. A bright hard sound, as if heard at some distance over ice. A statement sounded out, remembered from the bell tower in Kiev. The bitter cold of her fingers as she wrote it down. The tower reverberating in the soles of her shoes. Tintinnabulation. Hearing with her sternum – listening with the bones of her head, paying attention with her heart. Visceral music. Sound shaking the blood from the walls of her womb. The rhythm of a woman's life is synchronised with the moon and the moon is synchronised with the sea, ergo – a woman is synchronised with the tides. She had made the raid and come away with something significant. The organism was a spore – conditions had come right. It was flowering in front of her ears. She had been to the hard shell at her centre. The iron room – the safe place, the tabernacle. And come away with gold.

Now the listeners know they are going somewhere. They

cannot see their destination but they know they are on a journey. Through snow. Then the bell figure is inverted and repeated on the strings, but distorted. Sizzled, in descending leaps, swoops. Back to the child in the playground who preferred climbing the steps to sliding down the shute. Next a slalom. Bowed near the bridge to produce a glassy, metallic effect. The bell theme is taken up by everyone. It grows in confidence and in volume. Gradually the horror of the first movement falls away, is forgotten. There is a new feeling in the air. It is urgent and hopeful and the tempo quickens. Things are possible. Work can be done – good work, at that. Love is not lost or wasted. The music builds, laying down substantial foundations, the strength of which signal to the listener the size of the crescendo to come. It sweeps everyone along, draws the reluctant into its slipstream.

What happens next is difficult to explain. It is in sound terms like counterpoint – the ability unique to music to say two or more things at once. But it is not like counterpoint – more like an optical illusion in sound. The drawing was in psychology books – either an old woman or a girl. The eye could not accommodate both images at once. Either one or the other. The mind flicked. Grandmother? Girl? Girl. Grandmother. Another one was a chalice or was it two profiles staring at each other? The same thing could be two things. Transubstantiation. How could the drum battering of the first movement be the same as the drum battering of the second movement – how could the same drumming in a different context produce a totally opposite effect? The sound has transformed itself. Homophones. Linseed oil. Lynn C. Doyle. Bar talk. Bartók – the same sound but with a different meaning. Catherine heard it inside her head and knew that it was possible to achieve it, once the idea was conceived. At the moment when the music comes to its climax, a carillon of bells and brass, the Lambegs make another entry at maximum volume. The effect this time is not one of terror or depression but the opposite. Like scalloped curtains being raised, like a cascade of suffocation being drawn back to the point it came from and lights reappearing. The great drone bell sets the beat and the treble bells yell the melody. The whole church reverberates. The Lambegs have been stripped of their bigotry and have become pure sound. The black sea withdraws. So too the trappings of the church – they have nothing to do with belief and exist as colour and form. It is infectious. On this accumulating wave the drumming has a fierce joy about it. Exhilaration comes from nowhere. The bell-beat, the slabs of brass, the whooping of the horns, the battering of the drums. Sheer fucking unadulterated joy. Passion and pattern. An orchestra at full tilt – going fortissimo – the bows, up and down, jigging and sawing in parallel – the cellos and basses sideways. The brass shining and shouting at the back. The orchestra has become a machine, a stitching machine. The purpose of training an army is to dehumanise, to make a machine of people yet here all this discipline, all this conformity was to express the individuality and uniqueness of one human being. Catherine Anne's vision. A joy that celebrates being human. A joy that celebrates its own reflection, its own ability to make joy. To reproduce.

The orchestra soars in conjunction with the Lambegs, and the Lambegs roar in response to the orchestra and the effect is as she had hoped for. Her baby. *Deo Gratias.* Anna's song.

Her face is wet. Catherine is weeping. Her eyes are streaming yet again. But this time the tears are different. Just as the drum sound could be two things – so too could the tears. Anna. Vernicle. Music, her faith.

One final lurch and the orchestra stops. The Orangemen

continue drumming but now they are walking away. Diminuendo. The Lambegs continue to sound in the sacristy, distantly. On a signal from Randal they stop.

There was a moment's silence which was broken by a man's voice shouting. Then the hall was full of applause. Bravo. Catherine stared at her knees. Her nerves returned. She wondered if she would shake visibly if she stood up. Would her legs bear her weight? Still the applause went on. Some people whistled. Others shouted and cheered. Liz leaned over and squeezed Catherine's arm.

"Good for you," Liz said looking around. "There's no booing. They really liked it. I've no idea why, but they really liked it. Hey – you've been crying. It wasn't that bad." Both of them were laughing. A male voice shouted bravo again. Catherine shouted, "Did *you* like it?"

"Yes, yes." Liz nodded her head. And Catherine knew that it didn't matter whether her friend liked it or not. As long as she liked *her*. Liz said, "Linguists would insist on that man shouting *brava*."

Randal came back and pointed to the various sections of the orchestra and they stood. He looked down into the audience and beckoned Catherine with a high wave to the podium. *Bravo*.

She rose.

ENCORE

PHILIP K. DICK

THE PRESERVING MACHINE

MACHINE

(1953)

DOC LABYRINTH LEANED back in his lawn chair, closing his eyes gloomily. He pulled his blanket up around his knees.

"Well?" I said. I was standing by the barbecue pit, warming my hands. It was a clear cold day. The sunny Los Angeles sky was almost cloud-free. Beyond Labyrinth's modest house a gently undulating expanse of green stretched off until it reached the mountains – a small forest that gave the illusion of wilderness within the very limits of the city. "Well?" I said. "Then the Machine did work the way you expected?"

Labyrinth did not answer. I turned around. The old man was staring moodily ahead, watching an enormous dun-colored beetle that was slowly climbing the side of his blanket. The beetle rose methodically, its face blank with dignity. It passed over the top and disappeared down the far side. We were alone again.

Labyrinth sighed and looked up at me. "Oh, it worked well enough."

I looked after the beetle, but it was nowhere to be seen. A faint breeze eddied around me, chill and thin in the fading afternoon twilight. I moved nearer the barbecue pit.

"Tell me about it," I said.

Doctor Labyrinth, like most people who read a great deal and who have too much time on their hands, had become convinced that our civilization was going the way of Rome. He saw, I think, the same cracks forming that had sundered the ancient world, the world of Greece and Rome; and it was his conviction that presently our world, our society, would pass away as theirs did, and a period of darkness would follow.

Now Labyrinth, having thought this, began to brood over all the fine and lovely things that would be lost in the reshuffling of societies. He thought of the art, the literature, the manners, the music, everything that would be lost. And it seemed to him that of all these grand and noble things, music would probably be the most lost, the quickest forgotten.

Music is the most perishable of things, fragile and delicate, easily destroyed.

Labyrinth worried about this, because he loved music, because he hated the idea that some day there would be no more Brahms and Mozart, no more gentle chamber music that he could dreamily associate with powdered wigs and resined bows, with long, slender candles, melting away in the gloom.

What a dry and unfortunate world it would be, without music! How dusty and unbearable.

This is how he came to think of the Preserving Machine. One evening as he sat in his living room in his deep chair, the gramophone on low, a vision came to him. He perceived in his mind a strange sight, the last score of a Schubert trio, the last copy, dog-eared, well-thumbed, lying on the floor of some gutted place, probably a museum.

A bomber moved overhead. Bombs fell, bursting the museum to fragments, bringing the walls down in a roar of rubble and plaster. In the debris the last score disappeared, lost in the rubbish, to rot and mold.

And then, in Doc Labyrinth's vision, he saw the score come burrowing out, like some buried mole. Quick like a mole, in fact, with claws and sharp teeth and a furious energy.

If music had that faculty, the ordinary, everyday instinct of survival which every worm and mole has, how different it would be! If music could be transformed into living creatures, animals with claws and teeth, then music might survive. If only a Machine could be built, a Machine to process musical scores into living forms.

But Doc Labyrinth was no mechanic. He made a few tentative sketches and sent them hopefully around to the research laboratories. Most of them were much too busy with war contracts, of course. But at last he found the people he wanted. A small midwestern university was delighted with his plans, and they were happy to start work on the Machine at once.

Weeks passed. At last Labyrinth received a postcard from the university. The Machine was coming along fine; in fact, it was almost finished. They had given it a trial run, feeding a couple of popular songs into it. The results? Two small mouse-like animals had come scampering out, rushing around the laboratory until the cat caught and ate them. But the Machine was a success.

It came to him shortly after, packed carefully in a wood crate, wired together and fully insured. He was quite excited as he set to work, taking the slats from it. Many fleeting notions must have coursed through his mind as he adjusted the controls and made ready for the first transformation. He had selected a priceless score to begin with, the score of the Mozart G Minor Quintet. For a time he turned the pages, lost in thought, his mind far away. At last he carried it to the Machine and dropped it in.

Time passed. Labyrinth stood before it, waiting nervously, apprehensive and not really certain what would greet him when he opened the compartment. He was doing a fine and tragic work, it seemed to him, preserving the music of the great composers for all eternity. What would his thanks be? What would he find? What form would this all take, before it was over?

There were many questions unanswered. The red light of the Machine was glinting, even as he meditated. The process was over, the transformation had already taken place. He opened the door.

"Good Lord!" he said. "This is very odd."

A bird, not an animal, stepped out. The mozart bird was pretty, small and slender, with the flowing plumage of a peacock. It ran a little way across the room and then walked back to him, curious and friendly. Trembling, Doc Labyrinth bent down, his hand out. The mozart bird came near. Then, all at once, it swooped up into the air.

"Amazing," he murmured. He coaxed the bird gently, patiently, and at last it fluttered down to him. Labyrinth stroked it for a long time, thinking. What would the rest of them be like? He could not guess. He carefully gathered up the mozart bird and put it into a box.

He was even more surprised the next day when the beethoven beetle came out, stern and dignified. That was the beetle I saw myself, climbing along his red blanket, intent and withdrawn, on some business of its own.

After that came the schubert animal. The schubert animal was silly, an adolescent sheep-creature that ran this way and that, foolish and wanting to play. Labyrinth sat down right then and there and did some heavy thinking.

Just what *were* survival factors? Was a flowing plume better than claws, better than sharp teeth? Labyrinth was stumped. He had expected an army of stout badger creatures, equipped with claws and scales, digging, fighting, ready to gnaw and kick. Was he getting the right thing? Yet who could say what was good for survival? – the dinosaurs had been well armed, but there were none of them left. In any case the Machine was built; it was too late to turn back, now.

Labyrinth went ahead, feeding the music of many composers into the Preserving Machine, one after another, until the woods behind his house were filled with creeping, bleating things that screamed and crashed in the night. There were many oddities that came out, creations that startled and astonished him. The brahms insect had many legs sticking in all directions, a vast, platter-shaped centipede. It was low and flat, with a coating of uniform fur. The brahms insect liked to be by itself, and it went off promptly, taking great pains to avoid the wagner animal who had come just before.

The wagner animal was large and splashed with deep colors. It seemed to have quite a temper, and Doc Labyrinth was a little afraid of it, as were the bach bugs, the round ball-like creatures, a whole flock of them, some large, some small, that had been obtained for the Forty-Eight Preludes and Fugues. And there was the stravinsky bird, made up of curious fragments and bits, and many others besides.

So he let them go, off into the woods, and away they went, hopping and rolling and jumping as best they could. But already a sense of failure hung over him. Each time a creature came out he was astonished; he did not seem to have control over the results at all. It was out of his hands, subject to some strong, invisible law that had subtly taken over, and this worried him greatly. The creatures were bending, changing before a deep, impersonal force, a force that Labyrinth could neither see nor understand. And it made him afraid.

Labyrinth stopped talking. I waited for a while but he did not seem to be going on. I looked around at him. The old man was staring at me in a strange, plaintive way.

"I don't really know much more," he said. "I haven't been

441

back there for a long time, back in the woods. I'm afraid to. I know something is going on, but—"

"Why don't we both go and take a look?"

He smiled with relief. "You wouldn't mind, would you? I was hoping you might suggest that. This business is beginning to get me down." He pushed his blanket aside and stood up, brushing himself off. "Let's go then."

We walked around the side of the house and along a narrow path, into the woods. Everything was wild and chaotic, overgrown and matted, an unkempt, unattended sea of green. Doc Labyrinth went first, pushing the branches off the path, stooping and wriggling to get through.

"Quite a place," I observed. We made our way for a time. The woods were dark and damp; it was almost sunset now, and a light mist was descending on us, drifting down through the leaves above.

"No one comes here." Then Doc stopped suddenly, looking around. "Maybe we'd better go and find my gun. I don't want anything to happen."

"You seem certain that things have got out of hand." I came up beside him and we stood together. "Maybe it's not as bad as you think."

Labyrinth looked around. He pushed some shrubbery back with his foot. "They're all around us, everywhere, watching us. Can't you feel it?"

I nodded absently. "What's this?" I lifted up a heavy, moldering branch, particles of fungus breaking from it. I pushed it out of the way. A mound lay outstretched, shapeless and indistinct, half buried in the soft ground.

"What is it?" I said again. Labyrinth stared down, his face tight and forlorn. He began to kick at the mound aimlessly. I felt uncomfortable. "What is it, for heaven's sake?" I said. "Do you know?"

Labyrinth looked slowly up at me. "It's the schubert animal," he murmured. "Or it was, once. There isn't much left of it, any more."

The schubert animal – that was the one that had run and leaped like a puppy, silly and wanting to play. I bent down, staring at the mound, pushing a few leaves and twigs from it. It was dead all right. Its mouth was open, its body had been ripped wide. Ants and vermin were already working on it, toiling endlessly away. It had begun to stink.

"But what happened?" Labyrinth said. He shook his head. "What could have done it?"

There was a sound. We turned quickly.

For a moment we saw nothing. Then a bush moved, and for the first time we made out its form. It must have been standing there watching us all the time. The creature was immense, thin and extended, with bright, intense eyes. To me, it looked something like a coyote, but much heavier. Its coat was matted and thick, its muzzle hung partly open as it gazed at us silently, studying us as if astonished to find us there.

"The wagner animal," Labyrinth said thickly. "But it's changed. It's changed. I hardly recognize it."

The creature sniffed the air, its hackles up. Suddenly it moved back, into the shadows, and a moment later it was gone.

We stood for a while, not saying anything. At last Labyrinth stirred. "So, that's what it was," he said. "I can hardly believe it. But why? What—"

"Adaptation," I said. "When you toss an ordinary house cat out it becomes wild. Or a dog."

"Yes." He nodded. "A dog becomes a wolf again, to stay alive. The law of the forest. I should have expected it. It happens to everything."

I looked down at the corpse on the ground, and then around at the silent bushes. Adaptation – or maybe something worse. An idea was forming in my mind, but I said nothing, not right away.

"I'd like to see some more of them," I said. "Some of the others. Let's look around some more."

He agreed. We began to poke slowly through the grass and weeds, pushing branches and foliage out of the way. I found a stick, but Labyrinth got down on his hands and knees, reaching and feeling, staring near-sightedly down.

"Even children turn into beasts," I said. "You remember the wolf children of India? No one could believe they had been ordinary children."

Labyrinth nodded. He was unhappy, and it was not hard to understand why. He had been wrong, mistaken in his original idea, and the consequences of it were just now beginning to become apparent to him. Music would survive as living creatures, but he had forgotten the lesson of the Garden of Eden: that once a thing has been fashioned it begins to exist on its own, and thus ceases to be the property of its creator to mold and direct as he wishes. God, watching man's development, must have felt the same sadness – and the same humiliation – as Labyrinth, to see His creatures alter and change to meet the needs of survival.

That his musical creatures should survive could mean nothing to him any more, for the very thing he had created them to prevent, the brutalization of beautiful things, was happening in *them*, before his own eyes. Doc Labyrinth looked up at me suddenly, his face full of misery. He had ensured their survival, all right, but in so doing he had erased any meaning, any value in it. I tried to smile a little at him, but he promptly looked away again.

"Don't worry so much about it," I said. "It wasn't much

of a change for the wagner animal. Wasn't it pretty much that way anyhow, rough and temperamental? Didn't it have a proclivity towards violence—"

I broke off. Doc Labyrinth had leaped back, jerking his hand out of the grass. He clutched his wrist, shuddering with pain.

"What is it?" I hurried over. Trembling, he held his little old hand out to me. "What is it? What happened?"

I turned the hand over. All across the back of it were marks, red cuts that swelled even as I watched. He had been stung, stung or bitten by something in the grass. I looked down, kicking the grass with my foot.

There was a stir. A little golden ball rolled quickly away, back toward the bushes. It was covered with spines like a nettle.

"Catch it!" Labyrinth cried. "Quick!"

I went after it, holding out my handkerchief, trying to avoid the spines. The sphere rolled frantically, trying to get away, but finally I got it into the handkerchief.

Labyrinth stared at the struggling handkerchief as I stood up. "I can hardly believe it," he said. "We'd better go back to the house."

"What is it?'

"One of the bach bugs. But it's changed . . ."

We made our way back along the path, toward the house, feeling our way through the darkness. I went first, pushing the branches aside, and Labyrinth followed behind, moody and withdrawn, rubbing his hand from time to time.

We entered the yard and went up to the back steps of the house, onto the porch. Labyrinth unlocked the door and we went into the kitchen. He snapped on the light and hurried to the sink to bathe his hand.

I took an empty fruit jar from the cupboard and carefully

dropped the bach bug into it. The golden ball rolled testily around as I clamped the lid on. I sat down at the table. Neither of us spoke, Labyrinth at the sink, running cold water over his stung hand, I at the table, uncomfortably watching the golden ball in the fruit jar trying to find some way to escape.

"Well?" I said at last.

"There's no doubt." Labyrinth came over and sat down opposite me. "It's undergone some metamorphosis. It certainly didn't have poisoned spines to start with. You know, it's a good thing that I played my Noah role carefully."

"What do you mean?"

"I made them all neuter. They can't reproduce. There will be no second generation. When these die, that will be the end of it."

"I must say I'm glad you thought of that."

"I wonder," Labyrinth murmured. "I wonder how it would sound, now, this way."

"What?"

"The sphere, the bach bug. That's the real test, isn't it? I could put it back through the Machine. We could see. Do you want to find out?"

"Whatever you say, Doc," I said. "It's up to you. But don't get your hopes up too far."

He picked up the fruit jar carefully and we walked downstairs, down the steep flights of steps to the cellar. I made out an immense column of dull metal rising up in the corner, by the laundry tubs. A strange feeling went through me. It was the Preserving Machine.

"So this is it," I said.

"Yes, this is it." Labyrinth turned the controls on and worked with them for a time. At last he took the jar and held it over the hopper. He removed the lid carefully, and the bach bug dropped reluctantly from the jar, into the Machine. Labyrinth closed the hopper after it.

"Here we go," he said. He threw the control and the Machine began to operate. Labyrinth folded his arms and we waited. Outside the night came on, shutting out the light, squeezing it out of existence. At last an indicator on the face of the Machine blinked red. The Doc turned the control to OFF and we stood in silence, neither of us wanting to be the one who opened it.

"Well?" I said finally. "Which one of us is going to look?"

Labyrinth stirred. He pushed the slot-piece aside and reached into the Machine. His fingers came out grasping a slim sheet, a score of music. He handed it to me. "This is the result," he said. "We can go upstairs and play it."

We went back up to the music room. Labyrinth sat down before the grand piano and I passed him back the score. He opened it and studied it for a moment, his face blank, without expression. Then he began to play.

I listened to the music. It was hideous. I have never heard anything like it. It was distorted, diabolical, without sense or meaning, except, perhaps, an alien, disconcerting meaning that should never have been there. I could believe only with the greatest effort that it had once been a Bach Fugue, part of a most orderly and respected work.

"That settles it," Labyrinth said. He stood up, took the score in his hands, and tore it to shreds.

As we made our way down the path to my car I said, "I guess the struggle for survival is a force bigger than any human ethos. It makes our precious morals and manners look a little thin."

Labyrinth agreed. "Perhaps nothing can be done, then, to save those manners and morals."

"Only time will tell," I said. "Even though this method

failed, some other may work; something that we can't foresee or predict now may come along, some day."

I said good night and got into my car. It was pitch dark; night had fallen completely. I switched on my headlights and moved off down the road, driving into the utter darkness. There were no other cars in sight anywhere. I was alone, and very cold.

At the corner I stopped, slowing down to change gears. Something moved suddenly at the curb, something by the base of a huge sycamore tree, in the darkness. I peered out, trying to see what it was.

At the base of the sycamore tree a huge dun-colored beetle was building something, putting a bit of mud into place on a strange, awkward structure. I watched the beetle for a time, puzzled and curious, until at last it noticed me and stopped. The beetle turned abruptly and entered its building, snapping the door firmly shut behind it.

I drove away.

ACKNOWLEDGMENTS

MAYA ANGELOU: "The Reunion" by Maya Angelou. Used with permission of Caged Bird Legacy, LLC.

IAIN BANKS: Chapter 12 from *Espedair Street*. Copyright © 1987 Iain Banks. Pan Macmillan.

DONALD BARTHELME: "The King of Jazz" by Donald Barthelme. Copyright © 1981, 1982 by Donald Barthelme. Used by permission of The Wylie Agency (UK) Limited. First published in *The New Yorker*, February 1977.

LISA BOLEKAJA: "Three Voices" from *Uncanny Magazine*, issue 4, 2015.

JONATHAN COE: "9th and 13th" from *Loggerheads and Other Stories* © Jonathan Coe, 2014. Reproduced by permission of Jonathan Coe and the Felicity Bryan Literary Agency. First published in *The Time Out Book of New York Short Stories*, 1997.

PHILIP K. DICK: "The Preserving Machine" from *The Collected Stories of Philip K. Dick* (Vol 1. – *The King of the Elves* [1947–1952]). Published by Subterranean Press. Copyright © The Estate of Philip K. Dick. The Wylie Agency (UK) Limited. First published in *The Magazine of Fantasy and Science Fiction*, June 1953.

E. M. FORSTER: Excerpt (Chapter 5) from *Howards End*. Copyright © 1910, 1973 by The Provost and Scholars of King's College, Cambridge. Hodder and Stoughton.

GUSTAVE FLAUBERT: Excerpt(s) from *Madame Bovary* by Gustave Flaubert, translated by Francis Steegmuller,

Titles in Everyman's Library
Pocket Classics

Golf Stories
Selected by Charles McGrath

Horse Stories
Selected by Diana Secker Tesdell

London Stories
Selected by Jerry White

Love Stories
Selected by Diana Secker Tesdell

Music Stories
Selected by Wesley Stace

New York Stories
Selected by Diana Secker Tesdell

Paris Stories
Selected by Shaun Whiteside

Prague Stories
Selected by Richard Bassett

Rome Stories
Selected by Jonathan Keates

Scottish Stories
Selected by Gerard Carruthers

Shaken and Stirred: Intoxicating Stories
Selected by Diana Secker Tesdell

Stories of Art and Artists
Selected by Diana Secker Tesdell

Stories of Books and Libraries
Selected by Jane Holloway

Stories of Fatherhood
Selected by Diana Secker Tesdell

Stories from the Kitchen
Selected by Diana Secker Tesdell

Stories of Motherhood
Selected by Diana Secker Tesdell

Stories of the Sea
Selected by Diana Secker Tesdell

Stories of Southern Italy
Selected by Ella Carr

Stories of Trees, Woods, and the Forest
Selected by Fiona Stafford

Venice Stories
Selected by Jonathan Keates

Wedding Stories
Selected by Diana Secker Tesdell

Saki: Stories
Selected by Diana Secker Tesdell

John Updike:
The Maples Stories
Olinger Stories